Surviving Lies

The Blue Ridge University Series: Book Two

By Krista Swanson

MoDaMa Publishing 2023

First published in 2023 by MoDaMa Publishing

All names and characters portrayed in this title are fictitious and any resemblance to real persons, living or dead, is coincidental.

The moral rights of the author have been asserted.

ISBN: 979-8-9876062-3-0 (Paperback)
       979-8-9876062-2-3 (eBook)

Cover designed by: Niki Ellis Design
Edited by: Chloe Cran

To those who enjoy a roller coaster ride of second chances playing with their emotions...buckle up, here we go again

Trigger Warnings

This book references some off page violence that has happened to a side character. Her story was told in the first book of the series, but the references are present in this book. If references to sexual assault bother you, this book may not be for you.

CHAPTER 1
Becca

I was done taking his shit, so we broke up. Let me rephrase that: *I* broke up with *him.* Saying "we" broke up makes it sound consensual, like we both wanted it or that we decided it was the right thing to do. It was neither of those things. I was just sick of his shit, so it had to end.

But with school starting up, I faced having to see him again.

For the first time.

And I decided I was going to make an impression.

"Oh darlin', this is going to look gorgeous. All your friends are going to be so jealous! Now you send them all my way when they are, sweetie, ya hear?"

What I really needed her to do was shut up and finish the dye job so I could get the hell out of here. I was second-guessing doing this more the longer I sat in this godforsaken chair. I loved my long, dark hair, and so did Ty. But wasn't that why I was doing it?

"These reddish highlights really make your green eyes pop, and with that tan you have, my God, you are one hot potato! Lula, come look at her!"

Oh, Jesus Christ, I was never getting out of there!

"Thanks so much, Ellen Jean, but I really need to get going. Big party to get to, and so many people will have time to see the new me! Thanks so much!" Turning around, I looked in the mirror, and immediately tears sprung to my eyes. Ellen Jean came right to my side, her bony arms going around my shoulders.

"Oh, honey, what's wrong? Don'tcha like it?"

That wasn't the problem. I actually loved it. What I didn't like was the feeling that I needed to change myself to get Ty's attention. And why did I want his attention, anyway? I broke up with him.

"I actually love it, Ellen Jean. Thank you so much!" I turned and hugged her. She hugged me back with a fierceness I didn't expect from those stick arms. "I'm sure all my friends will line up by next week."

"Now, remember," she said as she held me by my arms, "you'll need some maintenance on those roots in about five weeks or so, so I'll see you soon, sweetie." The bills barely made it in her hands before I ran out the door.

I raced to my car so I could make it back to our townhouse before Lanie, my roommate, got there. We were living together again this year, and I was hopeful our second year here at college would go better than our first. Xander and she were driving down from NOVA together. She stayed with him all summer, since her parents moved overseas last spring. Lanie and Xander went through so much last semester because of her sick ex-boyfriend back in Texas, who was now thankfully in jail. His family was mob related, and he was such a douchebag. He abused Lanie, like, really badly, sexually, mentally, in ways I didn't even like to think about. It took most of last year for her to open up to us about it. And thank God she found Xander. He was her saving grace. He saved her, literally and figuratively, I guess. But I played a big role, too. I stuck by her all year. I'm good like that. A good friend. That's me.

So I was racing to our new home together to be a good friend.

But I felt like a terrible friend.

The worst.

It would be the first time I was seeing her since last semester.

And that made me a terrible friend.

I raced into the apartment but came to a screeching halt when there were two other bodies inside I didn't recognize.

"Hey, you must be Becca," the one with long, brown hair and almost the same color skin said. "I'm Macie, and this is Ava." She pointed at the one with a black pixie cut and a few piercings. Christ, they were both beautiful. And since they were also my roommates, I would probably need to be friends with them. Well, of course I would be friends with them. I *wanted* to be friends with them. But they would meet Ty as well. Fuckity fuck! Why has he made me so fucking insecure?

"Hey guys, yeah, I'm Becca. Lanie should be here any minute, so you'll get to meet her, too. It's nice to put a face to all the texts we've been exchanging."

Ava turned to me, and I was stunned by her eyes. It was as if emeralds were popped into her head, literally. I mean, I had green eyes, but hers were outrageous. They had to be contacts. Combined with her hair, she was fucking hot.

"Sorry, Becca, that sucks. We'll have to wait to meet her later. We were just heading out." And she had a freaking deep, sultry voice to go along with it all, too. Shit.

"We're heading to a party right down the block if you guys want to head over when you get back. You won't be able to miss it," I told them both, hoping they could make it.

Macie was the one to chime in next. She was quite a bit taller than Ava, and me, for that matter. "Maybe we will," she said, her voice smooth, but more high-pitched than Ava's. "But we don't know exactly when we'll be back. If not, we'll catch up tomorrow, OK?" Her smile was bright as she waved and they walked out the door.

And they were gone. And I was alone. Nothing good came of me being alone lately. Me alone with my thoughts usually meant scrolling through social media or old pictures and getting myself more and more upset with each passing day. But the odd thing was that Ty had no new posts on any of his accounts this entire summer, not a single one. I mean, he was a guy, so he didn't post much, but he posted. But nothing. Nada. Nilch.

While I was upstairs putting some clothes in my closet, I heard the front door and I went running.

"Lanie, is that you?!" I called from the top of the stairs. As I turned the corner, I saw her and her oh-so-hot boyfriend standing in the hallway. Running full speed across the room, I wrapped her in a bear hug and squeezed tight.

"Oh my God, girl, I missed you so much. We can't go that long not seeing each other. Like, never again. I thought we made a promise last Christmas break to never do that, and this time it was even longer!" I said into her hair. She pulled away from me to look at me, I knew to look at one thing.

"Becca, oh my God, you look amazing! When did you do this?" Her face filled with amazement as she took my appearance in, holding my shoulders and keeping me in place. "And yes, I missed you too!" She hugged me again, and it felt so good. I didn't think Lanie really understood how much I relied on her. Last year, she needed me so much, but I needed her too and she didn't even know it.

"The hair? Oh, it's no biggie, I actually just did it today. Just felt like I needed a change, ya know? Start sophomore year off with a bang." Pulling away, I looked away quickly, not wanting her to see the lie in my eyes. Unfortunately, that put me in the direct gaze of Xander. And that one, he wasn't like most guys, in a lot of ways.

"And look at you. I think you've gotten hotter! Lanie, hold on to him. I'm going to steal him this year for sure if you don't." Her eyes were rolling, and she knew full well I was joking. But Xander knew better, and he knew something was up with me; he kept staring at me with a look in his eye that said, "Get your act together, Becca."

I went straight to him and gave him a hug next, just to make him even more uncomfortable. My arms went around his body, and I ran my hands up and down his back. I felt his body stiffen.

"Oh, Xander, lighten up. I'm allowed to appreciate a fine specimen of a man."

He pulled back and looked me straight in the eye, almost sad for me, and that made me feel pathetic. What was I doing, hitting on my best friend's boyfriend right in front of her the moment they got there? Shit, I was a real mess.

"OK, you two, break it up. I know we all haven't seen each other in a while, but come on now." Lanie was fine with me being a bitch, thank God. I needed to pull myself together. Xander was right. I pulled back and looked over at Xander, trying to convey my apology with my eyes.

"I missed you, too, Becca." He chuckled, and it lightened the mood. "Hey, birdie, I'm going to head over to my place." I loved the nickname he had for Lanie, though neither of them would tell me what it really meant. "Why don't you girls join us once you've caught up and unpacked? The guys are hanging out, I'm sure drinking already. I'm sure Ty told you to stop by, right, Becca?"

He looked at me, waiting for my answer, but I couldn't give him one. At least not right away. I knew there was a party, but not from Ty. Had he not told anyone that we broke up? Ty was rushing Xander's frat, and they would spend a lot of time together now that we were back at school, but I guess he hadn't seen him yet either. And I did my share of secret keeping this summer as well.

My gaze shifted to Lanie. Hers was more knowing. She could read me and knew there was something going on, but she couldn't quite figure out exactly what.

The two of them stood there, waiting.

"Uhm, we kind of . . . broke up."

If either of them was surprised, they held it in. Xander stood stoic, being the serious type, and looked ready to go beat him up if I needed him to. Lanie walked to me and wrapped me in a hug, knowing that was exactly what I needed.

"Oh Bec, are you OK? When did it happen?" Being around the two of them made me feel safe enough to drop the shields and *feel.* I hadn't let myself feel anything about it all summer long, not a tear dropped. Not until that very moment, with Lanie's arms around me.

"Oh fuck, Lanie, now you've got me crying!" With my safety net with me, I let it out, and she held me as I did. Xander wandered away to give us some time alone. Her arms didn't leave me until she felt the shakes and sobs subside. But then I knew the dreaded questions would be starting.

Lanie, of all people, was well aware of the problems Ty and I had. Freshman year, I confided how Ty treated me when I would go home with him. How the couple times we made the visit to his house, he acted like we were nothing more than friends. He wouldn't kiss me, hug me, not even hold my hand. It was as if he was embarrassed of me in front of his parents. Utterly and completely embarrassed. It was heart wrenching to realize the man I had fallen in love with was ashamed of me.

I was enjoying the comfort of Lanie's arms still around me when we were interrupted by a soft throat clearing from across the room as Xander's long strides brought him closer to us.

"I'm gonna leave you girls to it," Xander said to us both. "But Bec, if you need me to take care of anything, just let me know. I'll be at the house. You guys head over when you're ready." He kissed Lanie and walked out the back door.

Lanie and I went to sit on the pleather couch that came with the apartment, which was full of furniture safe enough for college parties, our legs squeaking against the material as we tried to get comfortable.

"Oh my God, we will need to put some blankets on this thing." Lanie's eyebrows shot up; she knew I was trying to change the subject. "OK, fine, what do you want to know? But, FYI, there isn't much to tell." I fell back against the couch in defeat, wiping the remaining tears from my cheeks.

"Well, I guess I'd like to know who broke it off? And why?"

Well, those were easy.

"Me, and it was just the same ol' shit. The summer started, and he said I couldn't come to his house. I was done. Don't need that shit. So I ended it." More tears welled up in my eyes. "The worst part is that he didn't really fight me on it, and we haven't spoken all summer." And now those tears spilled over again, and the lump in my throat was growing as the emotions were getting harder to keep tamped down.

"Bec, why didn't you tell me? Why didn't you call or text over the summer to talk about this? I could've made my way to you somehow if you needed me." There was a reason, but it wasn't a good one. There's never a good reason for a girl to not reach out to her bestie in a time of need.

"I didn't want to make it real. If I told you, it would have made it so . . . real, like I actually did it. I just wanted to go about my summer in blissful ignorance as if nothing was wrong. But here we are, and now I have to see him for the first time since I told him I was done with his shit."

She didn't offer any magic bullet fixes, only sat there with me, letting me know she would always be there.

"Ugh, why do I even care? Why don't I just let him go?"

"Well, a little birdie once told me we put up with their shit because they are good in bed. I'm sure that has something to do with it." Her small laugh told me she knew there was more to Ty and me than just sex.

But was there?

We both laid our heads back against the couch and stared up at the ceiling. "So listen," she started, her voice serious. "First, before you see him, you need to decide if what you really want is to still be broken up with him. Seeing him for the first time will most likely make you feel things, things that could confuse you."

I knew she was talking from experience. Lanie's ex forced her and Xander to spend time apart last semester, and it did things to her. And when she first saw him, let's just say she didn't handle it well.

"What's the second thing?" I asked her. She stared at me for a moment, her face unreadable, before answering.

"Well." And then another pause.

"Lanie, what is it?" My voice almost screaming, I sat up straight on the couch, getting nervous. She finally conceded.

"You look amazing, Becca. If you want to fade into the woodwork when we head over there, it ain't happening. But something tells me that wasn't the plan." Her eyebrows tilted in a knowing way. "I think you want to get his attention, and maybe the attention of others? But be careful if your plan is to get him jealous. I'm afraid that could backfire."

Shit, was I that transparent? I plopped against the back of the couch in defeat again.

"I'll be there with you. We can make it through today together. I can finally be there for you the way you were there for me." She grabbed both my hands in hers and squeezed them tight. We shared a knowing nod. We had been through a lot together last year.

We both stood up, and she headed toward the front door. "I'm going to get changed so we can head over there," I told her. I strode toward the stairs, knowing I would have to change the outfit I had picked out, maybe multiple times. "Come up and get ready with me!"

"No, I'm good. You know I don't really care what I'm wearing, Bec. I have a few more things in the car to bring in, and I'll be right back."

I went straight to my bed to look at the sexy green halter top I had picked out to wear—braless, of course. It would have played off my new hair color so damn well. But it also barely kept my tits contained, so I was wearing it with an agenda.

Lanie was right.

A whole new outfit was in order, and that could take hours. Plus, I still had to do my makeup. This day was not going the way I had envisioned.

"Becca, you almost ready?"

"No, I need a bit more time. But go ahead, you can head on over. I'll meet you there. You know which one it is, right? Go out the back door, look to the right, and you'll probably see some guys setting up in the yard."

"OK, I'll see you there. Hurry!"

I plopped on my bed in frustration and looked around the room. It was an amazing room. Pretty big for a sophomore in college, with a walk-in closet. So I had most of my clothes with me, which was part of the problem: I had too many choices. Lanie saw right through my intentions, which made me think I needed to switch things up. I needed a new plan.

I pulled out my best push-up bra; I would never forego using my best asset. But instead of the typical outfit, I reached for my prettiest little white sundress. It had eyelets and tiny spaghetti straps on the shoulders but was kind of low cut in the front, allowing my bra to do its job. It was short, but not too short, and the color really showed off my tan and my new hair color.

I threw on a pair of flip-flops, some mascara, and lip gloss.

The complete opposite of the Becca Reynolds everyone knew from last year.

I looked in the mirror and wasn't completely unhappy with what the reflection showed me. The tan definitely helped, but my winter look would have to be reconsidered. Before I changed my mind, I grabbed my phone and ran down the stairs.

As I walked over, my resolve weakened the closer I got. I realized that all the sexy clothes and makeup I wore were my security.

But in this, I felt naked.

Nothing to rely on to help with the facade.

I wanted to see Ty; I was desperate to see him. But what would I do if his response to seeing me wasn't what I wanted it to be? I mean, even though I broke up with him, I still wanted him to look at me like he wanted to take me upstairs and do the nasty. The closer I got to the house, the more nervous I was getting, close to hyperventilating.

Yeah, of course it bothered me he didn't even try to contact me over the summer once I broke it off. But I broke it off. It might have destroyed him for all I knew. I never gave him the chance to talk it over; I just ended it.

"Hey, Becca! How was your summer?"

"Hi, Becca! You look fucking hot! Are you still seeing Ty? Let me know if you're not."

"Hi, Becca, where's Lanie? Are you guys living together?"

"Hey, Becca, where's Ty?"

I was bombarded by people as I approached the party. Friends, other fraternity brothers, even people I didn't recognize. It was overwhelming. It would've been a nice welcome if I'd been in a better headspace, but all I could think about was seeing Ty. I nodded at everyone, smiled, but they must have thought I was a total bitch. I didn't stop to talk to anyone, just kept walking. My eyes scanned everyone as I did, and there was no sign of him.

He must have been inside.

I pushed the slider open and was met with a wall of heat, the A/C not keeping up because of the number of people. I stood there for a minute, my eyes trying to adjust to the darker room once inside.

The kitchen was immediately to my left, with tons of booze bottles on the island. Behind that was a living room, and that was where they had a keg set up. It looked like that was where most of the pledges were, tapping and pouring from the keg by a bar.

That's where I found him. He was by the keg. He'd been watching me since I'd come in. I couldn't read his look at all, which scared me a bit. Our eyes locked on each other, neither breaking the stare.

He looked mostly the same since the few months I'd seen him last. His golden locks were a bit more golden, the tips lightened by the summer sun, it appeared. His tanned skin made his light whiskey eyes pop even more from across the room. He looked like he'd been hitting the gym more than usual. Still not the total gym rat body, which I was happy about. But his muscles looked a bit thicker.

He looked more like a man. Less like a boy.

As he looked at me, refusing to take his eyes off of me, he leaned down and started talking into someone's ear. Only then did I realize he was talking to Xander, who immediately found me in the crowd. He nodded at whatever Ty said, then said something back. Ty nodded to Xander, never taking his eyes off mine.

I still hadn't moved.

I stood even more frozen as Ty walked toward me, guiding himself through the crowd effortlessly.

I stood, almost in fear of what this meant as he approached, afraid of what could and would happen once we talked.

What did this mean?

CHAPTER 2

"Christ, Ty, move your ass, dude." I couldn't remember the name of the frat brother yelling at me, which was a problem. Rushing required me to know all of them and how they wiped their asses, too. But there were so many of them and I didn't spend enough time this summer learning them like I needed to.

This summer.

This summer sucked. For so many reasons, but mostly because of Becca. I didn't blame her for breaking up with me. I was an asshole. Still was. But there were some things that needed to be the way they were, and I didn't have a choice.

I wasn't supposed to meet someone like Becca, someone who would make me want to fall in love. But she was right there, almost from the first day of freshman year. And it was super easy while we were at school to pretend that everything was OK.

But it wasn't OK. It never was, but she didn't know that. She only got an inkling there was a problem when we would go to my hometown for the weekend, to my house. But I was too much of a chickenshit to fess up and tell her what was going on in my life back at home. The real reason my parents treated her the way they did. Like she wasn't my girlfriend.

Because they had no idea she was.

"Hey, man, how ya doing?" I felt his hand on my back, and it startled me out of my dazed thoughts. I turned to see Xander, his hand held out.

"Hey," I greeted him with equal enthusiasm, grabbing his hand firmly. "Dude, how was your summer?" Xander was one of the future guys in the frat I was most looking forward to calling "brother." I stood by and watched how he handled everything he and Lanie went through last year. It made me feel like a bigger piece of shit for how I handled things with Becca. But I could only hope I could learn a thing or two from him over time.

"Well, from the sounds of it, my summer was better than yours." He motioned his head toward the back of the house, which only meant one thing.

He had already seen Becca.

"Um, yeah, so I'm guessing Becca got here?" I asked.

His eyebrows lifted high and his eyes widened before a tilt to his head told me that things did not go well in the other apartment. "You could say that," Xander replied, his tone holding a warning. "Man, I don't know what fuckin' happened between you two, and I don't want to know, but she's in a bad way. Can't say I've ever seen Becca Reynolds quite like that." And then he started walking away, working on getting some cases of beer for the party.

"Xander, dude, wait!" I whisper yelled. "You can't leave me hanging like that."

I ran to him behind the makeshift bar. We, the pledges, pushed the dining-room table close to the wall and put side tables next to it to protect the booze. The place was already filling up, students more than ready to party after a long summer away from their friends. Soon enough, it would be standing room only and the newcomers would have to move it to the yard. It was the responsibility of us pledges to keep an eye on the booze during the party, serving the guests but making sure it didn't go missing as well.

And then, when the party was over, it was our responsibility to clean the entire house. This pledging shit kinda sucked.

Xander was already with some frat brothers by the time I caught up to him, so I couldn't fucking talk to him. I made eye contact with him before I walked away, hoping he would know I needed to talk.

Seeing Xander made me realize how much I was missing my best friend. He was supposed to be here, by my side, doing all this stupid shit with me. We were supposed to have each other's backs. But he didn't return to school this fall.

Last year was rough for him. He brought some problems with him from home that resulted in him drinking too much. Most kids at college drink too much, but most kids when they drank didn't get overly handsy with the girl they claimed to be in love with. That was Logan—with Lanie. Unfortunately, it happened before any of us knew the extent of Lanie's abusive past, so it really hit her hard. But they worked it out, were even friends again by the end of freshman year. He turned it around a bit after that. Spring semester, he stayed dry and made it through. But apparently this summer did a lot of us in, him included. So, he's taking this semester off.

"Hey, Ty," Xander said as he appeared behind me. "Listen, don't worry too much about what I said about Becca. You know her. She can be, um . . ." He stumbled over his words, not wanting to offend me.

"Dramatic," I offered.

Our joint laugh lightened the mood.

"Yeah, dramatic," Xander concurred. "I'm sure Lanie is calming her down as we speak." As he said those words, his head snapped up as if attached to an invisible tether. His eyes widened as they zoned in on something across the room, and his mouth turned up in a small smile. I watched him drop everything he was doing and move effortlessly toward Lanie, reaching her before she even closed the back door. They weren't one of those couples that disgusted me; he didn't start making out with her right there in the middle of the room. No, they were more subtle than that.

But everyone knew Xander loved Lanie.

And I wish everyone knew I loved Becca. Because I did. But timing was everything in life.

"Ty!" Lanie called out as she approached us, almost jumping into my arms giving me her hug.

"Hey, Lane, how are you?" I asked into her hair since she was refusing to give up on the hug.

Her mouth found my ear, and her words were soft. "I think I'm doing better than you are. You OK?" She pulled back, making eye contact. The sadness in her eyes, combined with a hint of accusation, told me everything I needed to know. As happy as I was to see her, I wasn't ready for the inquisition. I started pulling back, but she held on. "Ty, I won't pry. But you've been a significant support for me. Last year, I couldn't have gotten through without all of you being there." I looked away, my eyes trying to find something else to focus on, knowing where this was going and wanting no part of it. "I'm here for you, Ty. I mean, with Logan not here, and now this with Becca, this is a lot for you. Talk to me if it will help. OK?"

I nodded, my eyes still nowhere near hers, and pulled out of her grasp. "Yeah, I'm fine, really."

Xander graciously interrupted a tense moment of silence. "Ty, can you work the bar? It's getting crowded and we need a few guys over there manning the keg."

I nodded—seemed it was all I could do at the moment—and started in that direction. But then I felt a small hand on my arm, holding me back.

"She's excited to see you."

I didn't look at Lanie but didn't walk away either, waiting to see if she had more to say.

She noticed my piqued interest and continued. "She's back there still, trying to pick the best outfit to wear, knowing she'll be seeing you."

I turned to her. Her wide eyes held concern and told me I needed to be ready, ready for the tornado known as Becca Reynolds when she fucking came through that door.

"That bad?" I asked.

"Well, I've seen her worse, let's put it that way. She's not mad, if that's what you're wondering. She's—" Lanie paused as she thought about what Becca was, making me even more concerned. "Becca is nervous."

Shit, that was worse than mad. That meant today could involve tears and talking. And I didn't have time for either. And she was going to read that completely the wrong way.

I would have to figure out some way to make some time to talk to her.

"Thanks, Lanie," I offered with a small smile. She nodded and headed to the bar to get a drink. I followed to the keg as Xander asked, the crowd already getting rowdy.

Today was setting up to be a full-on rager. Someone had said there were possibly over two hundred people already, and it was only three in the afternoon. If we weren't careful, it could easily get shut down by the cops. First weekend back, though, the cops were usually pretty chill about parties, as long as we kept it under control.

"Hey, man, you good?" Jake asked. He was one of my roommates this year, and a great guy. I met him last year when Logan and I went to the rush event for the fraternity. Once I knew Logan wouldn't be here, he and I hooked up with a few other guys we knew would be interested in rushing the frat.

"Yeah, I'm good." My voice didn't match my words.

"Ya sure, dude? You look like fucking shit. What's up? Today'll be fun. Look around at all the fine ass we have to pick from." His arms spread wide as his gaze scanned the girls he felt were at his disposal. He was a good-looking guy, and he usually had girls lining up to hook up with him at every party we were at. "I know we have to work a shit ton today, but there is no way I'm not getting my dick sucked by one of these hotties. I mean, look at them. Each one is hotter than the next." He sidled up to a gorgeous blonde with huge tits as he was talking, his arm hooking around her neck as she walked by. Her wide smile as she looked up at him told us both he was right; they would be upstairs in a matter of minutes.

"Where the fuck does Jake think he's going?" Xander's voice boomed in my ear. I turned his way and shrugged my shoulders. "Maybe later tonight you guys might have some time to hang out, but today is all about getting shit done as a team."

"You don't have to tell me." We both moved toward the keg, hearing one guy having trouble with it. As we were working on it, bent over, I felt the oddest sensation run up my spine. It was as if tiny explosions of electricity blasted each vertebra, making me bolt upright. It ran to my neck, spreading across my chest, constricting my breathing.

I froze. But only for a moment before I felt compelled to look up.

And that was when I saw her.

Standing by the back door, looking around the room, I think for me. She hadn't found me yet. The first thing I noticed about her was what she wore. The white dress was not as innocent as it first appeared. It was tight and low cut, pushing up her ample chest, making it about to spill out of the damn top. Up against her tanned skin, the dress looked damn sexy. And her hair. Fuck, it had some, like, reddish color to it that made her eyes pop even in the dim light of the room. Already some heads were turning, and that was pissing me off.

And then she found me. Our eyes connected. I had been standing still for what felt like hours but had to be only seconds. And Xander noticed.

"Hey man, I guess you're going to want to talk to her, huh?" he asked. I turned to him and bent low to ask him my question.

"Is there somewhere upstairs I can have a few minutes alone with her? I won't be long, I promise. But I need a few minutes, man." I looked up and knew he got me.

"Yeah, second room on the left should be open, but don't be too long. I'll get some shit for letting you off." I nodded before turning toward Becca.

And I started making my way toward her. I wasn't exactly sure what I was going to say or do once I got her upstairs. All I knew was that I needed to be close to her. And get her away from these guys who were staring at her. At least if they saw me take her upstairs, they might think she was still mine, even if she wasn't. There was no way of knowing if she was going to kiss me or punch me.

But that was a chance I would take.

CHAPTER 3
Becca

*H*e grabbed my hand when he finally reached me and I tried to pull it out of his, but he wouldn't let me, his grip fierce. His determination took me by surprise, I won't lie. But I liked him taking control and guiding me through the crowd.

How was he able to move us through the people so easily? I was stuck by the door, shoulder to shoulder, yet he was parting the seas. We made our way to the staircase, where there were far fewer people, and I thought we would stop there, but we didn't.

His grip tightened as he pulled me up the stairs. I tried to determine his mood, but I couldn't see his face as I trailed behind him. He appeared to be looking for a specific room at the top. Once inside, he slammed the door, locked it, and spun me around against the back of it.

Looking up, I still couldn't read him. The look in his eyes was one I'd never seen before. My heart was beating out of my chest. It felt like it was pounding against the door behind me, my hands flat against its wood, searching for something to grab hold of to help me stay upright. I felt a rivulet of sweat drip down my back.

I was about to start my usual blabbering, yelling at him again for what a terrible summer we had. Thank God I couldn't find my voice.

His hands caressed my face.

His eyes stared into mine, into my soul.

I couldn't breathe.

I wanted time to stop.

I never wanted this feeling to end.

This feeling, like I was the one, the only one.

And then he crushed his mouth to mine, as if he needed my breath to survive. His tongue seeking entrance, tasting me, devouring me. His hands entwined in my hair. My hands finally let go of the door behind me and landed on his chest, gripping his shirt, pulling him closer. I had been craving this. My body shook from its need for this, its desire.

Suddenly, he pulled his mouth from mine, his face still close, his breathing ragged next to my ear. His arms caged my head up against the door. His voice, a cracked whisper.

"Bec, I missed you." My heart swelled at his words. "I want to keep going, but . . ."

And then my heart sank. Because I had to agree.

"But we shouldn't," I agreed. His eyes popped open to stare at me in surprise. "We're not together anymore. And as good as this feels, it doesn't solve any of our issues." He placed a finger softly on my mouth to stop me from talking.

"That's not why." There was a tiny shake of his head before he continued. "I'm not supposed to be up here, away from the guys, the party. I'm gonna get in trouble, the other pledges will have my ass, but when I saw you walk in, shit, I couldn't think straight." He pulled back and was looking at me again, that same look in his eyes, like I was his only one. "I don't know if it's that we haven't seen each other in a while, or the new hair color, or this sexy dress, but I needed to touch you, to smell you, to be close to you. I begged Xander to let me have a few minutes up here with you."

Just then, there was a soft knock on the door.

"Hey guys, it's Lanie. Xander sent me up. Ty, he needs you to get back downstairs ASAP. I'm sorry, guys. I know it sucks. I'm heading back down, but don't be long."

"Jesus Christ, this pledging shit is ridiculous. Do they really have this much control over you?" I couldn't believe they could do this to him.

"Unfortunately, yeah, but these guys aren't as bad as some, so I'll take it."

His hands were still caging my head against the wall, showing no sign of letting me go. Lanie was right: seeing him again was making all the old emotions come bubbling right back to the top, making me forget the reason I cut him off to begin with. I scooted under his arm, knowing my resolve was close to coming to its end if I didn't get out of this room with him.

But Ty took that opportunity to grab a hold of my face and pull it up toward his, cradling it in both hands. His mouth came to my ear, his breath making the bumps rise on my skin.

"You look fucking amazing, Becca," he whispered. "What I really want to do is slide these tiny straps off of your shoulders and push everything down, letting your tits come out for me. I miss your tits, baby." His words were melting me and my willpower. His one finger dragged along my jaw, down my neck and stopping on my collarbone. It was his silent question as he stared into my eyes, asking for consent.

The answer should have been no; it needed to be no.

Instead, the answer came from me crashing my mouth into his. And he made quick work of pushing the dress under my breasts, them popping free. They were pushed up like an offering waiting for him, their peaks taut with pleasure and anticipation.

This was not a time for lingering movements or delayed gratification. He was on a mission with limited time. His lips moved from mine and captured a nipple in a grip so deep it felt as if it hit the roof of his mouth. Using his hands, he recklessly kneaded my breasts together, a man hungry for what he'd missed. His thumb teased the other nub, grazing it, forcing it to grow even larger with his touch. He then rolled it between two fingers, twisting and pulling, eliciting a moan from deep within me. The heat pooling between my legs begged for attention but would have to be allayed with a thigh rub.

But then I froze and pulled back slightly, making Ty's mouth slide from my nipple. His hooded eyes looked up at mine, filled with questions. I could tell he was about to ask them when I stopped him with my words.

"We can't do this." It came out like a whine. Because I wanted to be doing this. It felt good, better than good. And he looked at me that way again. "We're not together, Ty. We have to stop." He was about to argue, but I went on. "Nothing's changed, has it? No change in anything we've discussed or fought about? If not, then there's no reason for this to continue, Ty. I can't do this."

As he pushed farther away, his eyebrows drew together in frustration.

"Bec, I know we need to talk, and I don't have time to do that right now. I just wanted to steal this time with you. When you walked in, I . . ."

I pushed at his chest, forcing more space between us. Anger filtered through my veins, replacing the desire that was there moments ago. I put myself back inside my bra and pulled the dress up as I pivoted away from his hands, which reached out to help me.

"I'm good, Ty. I've got it."

He looked dejected as I walked away from him. "But this wasn't talking, was it, Ty? No, you saw me and you wanted to take up where we left off." My sudden coldness had both our heads spinning, but it really shouldn't have been a surprise.

"Bec," he whispered, almost a plea.

The pounding on the door had us both jumping.

"Jesus Christ, Ty, get the fuck downstairs! They'll have my ass for letting you up here in the first place." Xander yelled his words through the door. He was pissed.

"Go," I encouraged. "It's fine. I get it. I don't want you or Xander to get in trouble." I moved to the window, my arms wrapped around my middle as I stared into the yard filled with frat brothers and their cronies looking to hook up.

I knew he'd opened the door because of the onslaught of voices that bombarded our cocoon of safety. The hallway had filled up. I turned to look at him as he slipped out of the room and found his eyes on me, expectant.

"I won't say anything you want to hear, Ty. If you can't give me what I want, we're not getting back together. Hell, I might even look for a hookup today. I look too damn good to let it go to waste." We both knew I was full of shit, that

I talked a good game. But if saying it was enough to make him think he could lose me for good, then maybe it would get him thinking.

His mouth opened as if to rebut what I said, but he changed his mind. Instead, he left the room, closing the door with a quiet click.

And then I was alone. Like I had been all summer. And I missed his mouth on mine already. It would have been easy to fall back into our routine, step back into what we had, and forget about the issues. Our problems weren't the worst out there. Some couples dealt with issues much more complex than their boyfriend refusing to tell his parents about you.

But I wasn't willing to. I was worth knowing about. I was worth shouting from the rooftops about. And until he would do that, we would not be getting back together.

As I was alone with my thoughts, the door flew open and a couple tearing off each other's clothes came barreling through. I hurried toward the door as they moved to the bed, completely unaware of my presence.

"I'll just be going. Don't mind me." They paused for a moment, but it didn't seem to stop their progress, more clothes coming off before I could close the door behind me. By the time I turned around, the hallway was full of more people than I realized. It was shoulder to shoulder up here, making it near impossible to even find the stairs. A panic set in, but I tried to swallow it down as I scanned the unfamiliar faces.

"Hi." A calm voice was a little too close to my ear. I turned, hoping it was a familiar face, but it wasn't. However, I was looking into the darkest, sultriest eyes I'd ever seen, surrounded by a face that smiled and was all chiseled and shit. "You look a little shell-shocked. First party here?"

His equally chiseled upper body was now pushed up against me, not of his own doing, more because of the crowd behind him growing. He put his hand up on the wall next to my head to keep himself from crushing against me any further, but my chest was heaving against him already, my breasts firmly pushed against his chest.

For the first time in, well, maybe my life, I was speechless.

"What's wrong? Cat got your tongue?" His sly smile when he spoke told me he knew the effect he was having on me. But he wasn't cocky, just confident. I finally started breathing again, able to find my voice.

"No cats in this mouth. The only pussy I have is farther down." Why the fuck did I say that? Oh my God, not only did it seem the hottest guy in the place was up in my space, but I came on to him.

And my recently "ex-boyfriend" was downstairs.

And we just had the hottest make-out session of the past few months.

I was so stupid.

His grin turned into a full-blown smile, then laughter as his breaths blew in my ear, he was that close to my face. "I like your confidence, beautiful. What's your name?"

Where did this guy come from? I didn't think he was a frat brother. I would've seen him last year with Xander. His confidence made me think he may not even be in college anymore. The way he held himself, the tenacity that showed in his eyes, his shoulders, his entire presence, didn't happen to a beaten-down student.

I was looking up at him, his frame tall and lean, yet muscles very defined where visible. His bicep, close to touching my cheek, was bulging as he kept his arm bent over my head, almost in protection. His dark hair, longer on top, shorter on the sides, was cut in a professional manner, as if he could already be in the work world.

My lips separated, trying to answer him, when I felt a small hand on my elbow.

"There you are, Becca. I've been looking for you. All good up here?" Lanie had a tinge of concern in her voice, understandably, considering what she walked up on. My dark stranger pulled away slightly, but the surrounding crowd limited his movement.

"Becca, that fits you. Is it short for Rebecca?" He was studying me, blatantly ignoring Lanie.

"Um, yeah, I guess, but I've only ever gone by Becca. I hate Rebecca." I turned toward Lanie, giving her my best "I'm fine, isn't he hot" face, hoping she wouldn't make more of it than it was.

"That fits you too, not Rebecca. I'll keep that in mind. For next time. I'm Gage, by the way. Ladies." As he pulled himself away from us, he discreetly rubbed his hand along my arm from elbow to wrist, lingering on my extended fingers at my side, tugging on them as he disappeared into the mass of people. Lanie even noticed the shiver that it sent through my body.

"What the hell was that about? Who was that? And, just . . . why?" Lanie was just as speechless as I was as she tried to follow his form as he made his way down the stairs.

"That was . . . Gage."

That was all I could say. That was all I had.

"Yeah, and who is Gage? Do you know him? Did you know him before today? You guys looked mighty close when I got up here, like, 'have a history together' close." Lanie's interrogation got interrupted by a group of guys, who appeared to be fighting over a girl, accidentally pushing us into a wall. "Let's get out of here. I came up looking for you since Ty came down a while ago. He was looking for you, too." Her warning was clear in her eyes. "Just so you know." But I didn't seem to care as much right now. Actually, the thought of making Ty jealous exhilarated me.

And I think that was my new plan, with the help of my new friend Gage.

"So, Xander told me that Gage is a frat brother, but he graduated two years ago. He's back to go to grad school, so I think he's actually living in this complex. Becca, I think you need to be careful with him. He looks like he'll be dangerous for you." Again, her eyes conveyed a warning, one which I would not be heeding.

"Oh, he's dangerous all right, in all the right ways. And I'll be fine. A little flirting hurt no one, especially when one's 'ex-boyfriend' needs a kick in the ass. Am I right?"

We were in the dining room area, by the tap, filling our cups with the disgusting warm beer provided by the frat. The bar they had set up had long ago run out of cans on ice. Ty was still back there, responsible for "guarding" it, I guess. Most of the afternoon I would catch him looking at me, smiling, trying to remind me of our fleeting moment upstairs in his own way. I would occasionally steal glances at him, too, still smitten with those wavy golden locks and whiskey-colored eyes. I loved his long, lean muscles, which used to grab a hold of me and pull me closer, locking me in his grasp whether in bed or up against a wall in a hall.

When Ty had me up against that door upstairs, my face in his hands, his mouth on mine, it felt so right. It reminded me of what we had last year, the feelings when things were perfect. But things were no longer perfect. I guess they never were.

A sultry set of eyes found me from across the room, trying to lure my attention from my own thoughts. He had been trying to catch my eye all afternoon, but from afar, keeping his distance. It allowed me to admire him, discreetly of course, while he'd been mingling with everyone else.

"Would you quit checking out the new guy?!" Lanie stood in front of me, trying to block my view of Gage, who was across the room.

"Why? I'm allowed to move on with my life, Lanie. Ty and me are not together." I turned my attention toward Gage after saying this but kept talking. "Besides, I can be discreet. Ty doesn't need to see me looking."

"There is nothing subtle about you, Becca, never has been and never will be," Lanie scoffed.

I looked at her when she said this, ready to be mad, but her smile showed she meant it with love. I turned my attention back to the new hottie I had just met.

"And not only are you staring at him, but he is gawking at you, and I'm not the only one who sees it," she warned.

At that, I immediately peeked at her with a questioning look, trying to decipher who exactly she was referring to.

"Don't worry, I'm talking about Xander. I think Ty's too busy to notice, but give him a sec and he will, don't worry. I understand you guys aren't together, but I think it's kind of soon, don't you?" She looked around the room, looking for Ty. "I mean, it's the first day back, the first day you guys are seeing each other since you broke it off. Don't ya think it would rub it in his face to flirt with someone right in front of him?" She pulled me by the arm toward the slider to outside. "Come on, let's go outside for a while. Lots of the guys are playing games out there. It looks fun." She dragged me reluctantly while I stole glances to find those milk-chocolate eyes in the crowd.

But she was right. And she didn't even know that me and Ty had already hooked up before I then destroyed his world again. I would have to limit the flirting. Friends only.

Once outside, Lanie sidled up to Xander.

"You just wanted to come out here to get near your piece of ass, not that I blame you, Lanes. His ass is worth it. But you kind of tricked me." I looked around and saw little going on out here, just a few couples sitting on chairs and drinking, listening to music. There wasn't even a chair for me to sit in.

"Relax, the guys are bringing the table and other game things around from the cars. Be patient." And then I lost her, Xander stealing her away to a dark, shadowy corner. I was walking away, alone with my thoughts and my warm beer, when a familiar voice came from behind me.

"Why the sad face, Not Rebecca? You're at a party, a college party. No reason to be so glum." I stilled at his voice near my neck, stunned at the shiver it sent down my spine. He reached out and touched my shoulder, fingers toying with the strap of my dress, and I was positive that he saw his effect on me. "So, I either scared you or you're cold. And considering it's at least eighty degrees out here, I'll have to go with the first."

I turned to look at him, stunned again by his beauty, determined to not allow him to continue affecting me this way.

"Neither, actually." Finding his eyes, I fought for the courage to continue with my intended comeback. I swallowed, my throat suddenly dry. "I'm just very happy to see you again."

There, I did it.

And he liked it. His smile warmed his face, and his eyes crinkled with approval as the grin took over.

But I quickly regretted it. I decided to not flirt in front of Ty, and I was already doing it.

"Ugh, listen, Gage, I am glad to see you again, but I shouldn't be. I recently broke up with my boyfriend, and he's here. It's kind of awkward today. We talked, and it didn't go well. And I just don't think it's a good idea for us to, you know, I don't know, um . . . I'm not really in a position to move on or do anything with anyone else right now, so I don't want to lead you on." I turned my face away from looking at him, too embarrassed to see his response. I was moving away, thinking he would not want to talk to me anymore, when I felt his hand reach out for my arm, touching me gently.

"Hey, it's OK. There is such a thing as being friends, ya know. And I appreciate you being honest with me. That's not always the case with girls I meet here." He looked around and gestured to the crowd as if I would know what he meant. "I could use a friend. I just moved back to the area. Haven't been here for a couple years since graduating, so I don't know too many people anymore. I'm living one street over. Do you live in this complex?"

I stared at him, rendered speechless by him once again, not a minor feat.

I nodded, finally.

"Yeah, me and Lanie, the girl who stole me from you earlier, we actually just moved in today, right over there." I gestured to the unit down the way. But Gage wasn't looking where I pointed; rather, his gaze remained on me instead.

"I can't lie, I'm disappointed to hear about the ex, but at least it's not a boyfriend. Is he a frat brother? Maybe I know him."

But I didn't want that. I wanted to keep Gage, even if friends only, all to myself.

"He is, but he's a pledge, so he's not really allowed to hang out. I guess you know all about that. I hear you're a frat brother." His brow ticked up at that information, and he seemed curious why, but the moment passed.

"So, you've already done some digging on me, Becca, Not Rebecca?" His wide smile made my belly do weird things. I needed to look away to calm the emotions bubbling up in me uncontrollably.

"I didn't, but Lanie already doesn't trust you, and her boyfriend is Xander, so she got the inside scoop." His smile lingered as he guided me farther out in the yard by the elbow, seeing the pledges setting up the pong table and other games. I quickly looked around, wondering if Ty was out here, if he could see us. Gage caught on. He leaned in close.

"Is he out here? Did we get caught, Becca?" His eyes were full of mischief as we continued toward a keg they moved outside. "I know Xander, so Lanie is his girlfriend, huh? I heard a bit about all the shit that went down with them last year. Crazy stuff."

I turned toward him with a crazed enthusiasm at the fact that he was aware of their story. "Oh my God, you're telling me! Lanie was my roommate last year, too, so I lived it with her, and let me tell you, that guy was one crazy motherfu—"

"Hey, Bec."

Ty's voice was full of a lot of things, but mostly hurt.

I turned in time to catch him staring at Gage before his eyes moved to mine, looking for confirmation of his fears. He looked like he wanted to come closer, possibly kiss me, to stake a claim on me he no longer had.

"Hi, Ty! They released you from prison?" The extra zeal in my voice may have come across as forced when I spoke. But I stood my ground, not moving closer to him when my feet wanted me to.

"Nope, just grabbed a quick sec to say hi," he said as he was already heading away from us.

"This is Gage. He's a brother of yours." I tried to make it seem so much more innocent than it was.

"I know who he is. We need to know who all the alumni are." And that was it; he didn't even say hello to him. It made me wonder if that would get him in trouble or something. "Have fun, Bec. Don't get too drunk, OK?"

There was a silence now between Gage and me. It wasn't necessarily awkward, but it was longer than it should have been. He finally broke it.

"So that's the ex-boyfriend." He looked at me, trying to read me as he stood with the lip of his cup perched against his lower lip, ready to take a drink. I nodded, not really sure what else there was to say. "Well, OK then. Definitely appears he doesn't want to be your ex, but I guess that's a discussion for another day. He said have fun and not to get too drunk, so those are my orders, I guess." He grabbed my cup, filled it at the tap, and turned me around to face the yard. "Which game do you want to play first? There's pong or flip cup. Personally, I like flip cup, but I will let you choose since you're the lady of the hour."

I didn't think Gage would ever truly know how grateful I was to him in that moment, and for the rest of that night. He was a gentleman and so much fun to hang out with. I could truly forget my worries about Ty and me and enjoy the rest of the party.

But it definitely felt like something bigger was yet to come.

CHAPTER 4
Becca

"Lanie, why did you let me drink that much last night?" I was still in bed, and it had to be close to dinnertime. It had not been a good day dealing with the consequences of yesterday's overindulging.

"I didn't *let* you drink anything. I tried to get you to stop, but you refused to leave the game tables with your new bestie, so that's all on you." She actually sounded a little upset with me, and I guess I didn't blame her. I flirted with Gage all night. Plus, my "new bestie," as she called him, was supposed to make sure I didn't get drunk.

And he failed.

I never saw Ty again the whole night, at least not up close. We exchanged looks from afar. Mine were smiles and giggles and his were glares, mostly intended for Gage. The night didn't go in the direction I'd intended, especially with the way it started with me and Ty.

Gage was a perfect gentleman, despite what I felt may have been some effort on my part to encourage him otherwise. I wasn't proud of it and was thankful for him being the type of person he was. Mixed with the drinking, I turned into the type of person I shouldn't have been.

"I'm heading over to Xander's. You going to be OK?" Lanie was halfway out my bedroom door while asking this question. She was not dressed for a night on the town; that was not what the two of them ever did. I was sure they already had the movie picked out—the one they wouldn't be watching because they'd be knee-deep in each other's business before it even got started.

"Yeah, I'm good. I'll probably just put on *The Walking Dead* to match my mood." I rolled over but quickly decided a shower was in order as I could literally smell myself.

The hot spray did wonders, washing away the grime still on me from the day of drinking as well as clearing my head of all my negative thoughts. Because when I looked at my phone, the only messages I had were from my little brothers and my newest friend, Gage. Not a single text from Ty. Not that I should have any; I ended things with him. But I'd think he'd want to talk about stuff.

At least I would want to.

Gage had texted asking if I wanted to go shopping with him today to help with his new apartment. Considering how late it already was, I probably missed out on that. It would have worked, too, since I needed some things as well. I shot him a note, in case he was still interested, and continued to get dressed.

He responded immediately.

And I wasn't used to that recently.

Gage:
Hey Becca no I haven't gone out yet,
I'd love for you to join me I'll be by in 10
What's your apt number?

My mind was racing. Why was I doing this? Should I be doing this? I mean, I had done *nothing* with him, but he was definitely attractive.

Going shopping with someone was not relationship stuff. I was not going on a date with him. This was friend stuff. Plus, even though Ty showed interest in me at the start of yesterday, it didn't seem to carry over to today. As I debated what to do, I realized it made me feel immature, like a high schooler. I was a grown-ass woman, and I could do what I wanted. I wasn't doing anything wrong by going shopping for things for our apartments. Ty had friends who were girls.

Well, he had Lanie as a friend. She's a girl.

The argument going on in my head had spilled out of my mouth. I realized I was talking to myself, arguing aloud, as I was getting ready.

Thank God Lanie was gone, and neither of the other roommates were home, either. But I shot Lanie a message telling her where I was going, just in case I was dead in a ditch by the end of the night.

I ran down the stairs when I heard the beep, my heart beating out of my chest. I chalked that up to me needing more exercise. Upon opening the door, my stunned eyes took in a sight I never thought I'd see in person. It was the shade of a dark blue sky right before a storm was due to hit. The metallic shimmer sparkled as the waning sun hit it just the right way. As I walked closer, I took notice of the impeccable condition it was in.

"Holy shit, you have a Shelby convertible Mustang? This is one fine-ass car, Gage. I don't even feel worthy to get inside." He smiled his thousand-watt smile as I slid into the perfectly oiled leather seat next to him. The car was in pristine, restored condition.

"It's no big deal. I worked a bit before coming back to school." He tried to be nonchalant about it, but this was not some regular old car. "How do you know so much about cars?"

"Um, first, I call bullshit. No one can work for one year and afford this, and then quit, go back to school, and be able to live here. My parents are working their asses off to pay this rent for me." I rubbed my hand along the dash, completely in love with it already. "And second, my dad is a car fanatic. He likes to work on cars in the garage all the time. Gets him out of the house with all the crazy kids."

Gage laughed at my last comment.

"I never said I only worked for one year. And who told you I quit?" He looked over, and his expression was unreadable.

"I guess no one; I think I assumed that. How old are you?" I asked. Maybe I forgot what Lanie told me. "I thought someone said you graduated from here recently."

"Well, I did, not too long ago. I've been out for three years. I work in the family business but decided I needed the master's to keep moving up, so here I am." That made him about twenty-five years old. Older than I originally thought he was. He turned his head and continued driving, not making a big deal about any of this. I followed his lead and dropped it as well. "My job is still there for me when I'm done."

It piqued my interest why he would need another degree if he works for the family business. I guessed it was a cutthroat business.

"You mentioned 'all the kids' when talking about your dad and back home. How many siblings do you have?" he asked as he started driving away from my place.

"Oh, gosh, it's like a petting zoo back at my house," I told him. "I have four younger brothers and two parents that are basically workaholics. I couldn't wait to come to college."

His conspiratorial smile made me think he knew exactly what I was talking about.

"You have a big family too?" I asked.

He shook his head back and forth, which wasn't the answer I was expecting. "Nah, just me and my older brother." And then he said nothing more.

"So, where are we headed?" I wanted to break the sudden awkward silence and return the conversation to what we were doing. Looking out the window, I noticed we'd made it onto the highway out of town. "What do you need? Are we talking essentials and food, or do you need the big-ticket items?" I leaned back against the soft leather as I rattled off my questions and tried not to moan.

"Considering I slept on an air mattress last night and only had Starbucks today, I need it all."

"Oh wow, you really do. OK, this is going to be fun, but we won't be able to do it all tonight. It's already kind of late."

"Well, I did text you quite a few hours ago, and it is almost dinner time." He snuck a look at me, which told me he most likely knew why I hadn't responded. "I don't think I did my job very well last night, did I? Sorry, I think you probably had a rough morning, but we had fun yesterday. And we were the king and queen of flip cup!"

I didn't know how to respond. The more he said, the guiltier I felt. I smiled but turned my head and found the trees speeding by on the side of the road a welcome distraction. He remained quiet for a few moments, and I felt bad, worried I'd made it uncomfortable between us already.

"So, I was thinking furniture is the priority since it will most likely need to be ordered. I should focus on that, then maybe some food. What do ya think?" He kept his eyes on the road, his tone casual. I stole a peek as he drove, his large hand on the gearshift, the muscles in his forearm pulsing as he changed gears.

"Sounds like a plan. There are a couple decent furniture stores in Haven." It appeared that was where we were headed. "Maybe some of them have some floor models that you can buy, get it quicker."

"Yeah, maybe." His tone changed a bit when I said that, but I couldn't decipher in what way.

Gage knew where he was going, pulling into a store I'd never been to, never even seen.

"Wow, this is a bit too bougie for me, that's for sure. What type of budget are you on again?" Definitely not the typical college kid budget, but I should've guessed that by now. I felt he was keeping something from our conversation, that was for sure. But we didn't know each other, so I had no right to any information about his financial situation at all.

But I was damn curious. And impressed.

Then I took notice of what he was wearing: silky black dress pants that seemed to be tailored for his body, his thick thighs pushing the bounds of the material. His crisp white button-down pulled equally tight across his chest. He wasn't wearing a tie and had the sleeves rolled to his elbows, which I thought was why I didn't recognize the quality of his clothes at first.

I had on sweatpants, a tank top, and flip-flops. I felt very underdressed.

"Um, you're dressed pretty nice to go shopping, Gage. I am not. Is that going to be a problem with this place? I've never been here; it looks pretty fancy for a furniture store." I smoothed out my pants with my sweaty palms, as if that would make them more appropriate. My sudden nervousness took me by surprise.

"Becca, you look beautiful. You would look beautiful in anything you wore." I didn't catch the look on his face as he said this since he was already out of the car and coming around to my side. By the time I opened my door, his hand was reaching inside to help me out, and I took it. It was cool to the touch of my hot and sweaty fingers as he gripped me.

"Let's go find me some furniture." As he said this, he pulled me up and toward him, and I still held his hand as we stood by the car. I pulled it away, my breaths choppy as I did.

We headed through the doors of the store and looked around. I didn't know what he was looking for, and was about to ask when a saleswoman approached us.

"Hello, my name is Amanda. May I help you?" Her long blonde hair cascaded down her back, almost touching her waist. Her skirt was so short it barely contained her sky-high legs. The makeup she wore made her look like one of those TikTok girls who does makeup for her followers; it was gorgeous. She was gorgeous.

I felt totally, completely, one hundred percent inadequate.

And not that I cared, but she only had eyes for Gage.

"Yeah, my fiancée and I have just moved into the area and need a full apartment of furniture." His face was dead serious as he spoke, and her face twisted in disgust as she looked my way. I was pretty sure she didn't even see me until Gage mentioned me.

"Of course, let's get you both set up. How exciting that must be." She was not the least bit casual about looking at my hand for a ring and had not one ounce of excitement in her voice. And I wondered how Gage intended to keep the lie going. But we fell into step with her as he grabbed my hand, and his wide smile made me giggle.

Gage handed her his credit card. "Can you set me up with an account? And here's my card for the delivery."

She took his information and hurried away, I think realizing she probably hit the jackpot of all commissions with this sale.

"What are you doing? How the hell do you plan on pulling this one off?" I scoffed in his direction as I started walking around the showroom.

"Don't worry, I know her type. If I hadn't said it, she was going to ignore you the entire time. At least now you'll get some respect, the respect you deserve."

He was right; she treated me better thinking I was his fiancée, but not great. If he hadn't done that, she would have treated me differently. The first pieces he wanted to pick out were couches. Gage walked around the back room—quite picky for a guy, if you ask me—looking for the perfect couch. With what I knew of him already, I expected him to gravitate to the sleek black leather set I saw as soon as we walked in, but he passed it and moved on. No, instead, we stood in front of a white slipcovered sectional, complete with cushions that looked as though you would sink into them upon sitting.

"Go ahead," he said matter-of-factly, gesturing toward the sofa.

"What? Me? It's going to be your couch. You sit on it." At that, he pulled me close, one arm going around my waist while the other held my hand. His mouth was close to my ear, but he said nothing. He just breathed.

And it was intoxicating. To feel his breath against me, the reaction my skin was having to the warmth. Our chests were touching, a position we'd been in before. But this time, it was of our own volition. I didn't know if my thin lace bra was enough to contain my peaked nipples, or if he could feel them pushing against him. But they were rock hard.

"Becca, you smell amazing." He took another deep breath in, his jaw rubbing along my temple, its light stubble breaking through my hair and grazing my skin. He moved his mouth back to my ear to speak again. "I want to see how you'll look on the couch, since I have plans for you to be on it in the future."

Well, fuck. What was I supposed to say to that? I had nothing, literally no comeback. All I could do was pull back and look up at him. The question was in my eyes, he could see it, but neither of us said anything. He only nodded with his chin toward the couch, encouraging me to sit. I broke from his hold and turned to look at it, this beautiful four-thousand-dollar couch he was envisioning me on.

And I thought I could see it, too.

I chose the deep corner where the two sides met. It provided enough room to pull my legs up and still have room to spare. I curled up as if I were getting ready to watch tv or read a good book, digging into the cushions and loving the feel. It was the most comfortable couch I'd ever been on; I may have even moaned.

I bounced off the couch from the weight of him plopping next to me. My head snapped in his direction to figure out what he was doing. His head leaned in toward mine, and he motioned with his finger for me to move even closer, our heads now almost touching against the back cushion of the couch.

"Um," he whispered, "I'm not sure having you sit on the couch was such a great idea after all." I was surprised and a little annoyed by his sudden change in behavior. He could sense it and leaned in closer yet. "Becca, not Rebecca, I don't think you realize what you do to me. That little sound that came from the back of your throat, well, it did things to me, baby." He casually looked at the bulge in his pants before scanning the rest of the showroom, making sure we were alone. I daresay he was blushing. His hands went low and were trying to adjust himself, the attempt futile.

I had visions of him taking my hand and placing it on his lap, his pants stretched tight over his fully engorged erection. It would take all my restraint to not wrap my fingers around him right there in the middle of the store. I was trembling just thinking about it.

"Becca?" His voice rocked me from my fantasy. But it was only that, a fantasy, right? This was not a thing between him and I. We were just friends. Gage knew I was just getting out of my relationship with Ty, who was a fellow frat brother of his, for crying out loud. "Becca?"

"Yeah?" My voice was more breathy than I wanted it to be. I turned toward him and found him staring at me. His dark eyes bore the same message his dick did.

He wanted me.

"You're not going to make this easy on me, are you?" he laughed.

"Well, that's a loaded question, isn't it? What exactly are you referring to?" He didn't have time to answer me before my favorite salesperson interrupted us.

"So, any progress, Mr. Parker?" Amanda still refused to pay me much attention, but Gage continued to put her in her place.

"I don't know, you'll have to ask the boss. Babe, is this the one? Is this the couch you see us on every night?" His hand was casually on my knee, and my heart was pounding in my chest. I didn't have time to miss a beat, though.

"Yeah, babe, this is it. This one will do. It seems . . . firm enough, don't ya think?" I said this as I started bouncing up and down on the cushion.

"Amanda, we'll take this one. Could you give us a minute?" His tone was gruff as she turned on her heels, happy with the sale but not amused by me. I turned toward him, wondering why he would be mad. I thought I put on a pretty outstanding performance. His eyes followed Amanda out of the back room we were in. Once she was gone, he stood, pulling me up with him, flush against his chest again.

I could get used to this.

"Becca, I need you to stop doing that, please."

I was confused. I played along with his charade, followed his lead. And now he was angry and wanted me to stop? He buried his nose in my hair, once again inhaling my scent. All of this was such a contradiction. But I pushed away from him, not enjoying his games.

"Gage, I don't understand. I thought you wanted me to play along?" What I didn't need was another man messing with my head. "I don't need more bullshit in my life, Gage."

"Fuck, Becca, you're even turning me on when you're mad. Come here." I hesitated as he reached his hand out to me, but I relented. "I love how your eyebrows pinch together when you want to yell but are trying not to." He chuckled. "I needed you to stop bouncing on the couch, because your tank top is not leaving much to the imagination." Looking down at my shirt, I realized I wasn't wearing a very supportive bra, so I could only imagine how that looked. I was kind of spilling out of the shirt. "I can't have any other guys in this place seeing you do that. Hell, I think one more bounce and you could have Amanda coming home with you."

That made me bark out a laugh, and the tension between us thankfully subsided.

"Yeah, I doubt that. If she's coming home with us, she's putting me in the trunk." Gage gave me a weird look.

"I like how that sounds."

"What? Putting me in the trunk?"

"No." And that was all he said. But it was the way he said it. I wasn't sure what he meant by it, but I let it slide because the night had taken a turn I hadn't expected. "Come on, I need to pick out a mattress, but I will not be having you test those out with me. That would be the most dangerous thing I could do right now." He grabbed my hand, and we walked to the front of the store.

Usually, I would have a witty Becca Reynolds comeback. The words were in my head, ready to come out of my mouth. *What's wrong, Gage? Some time in bed with me scares you?* Or *Oh, Gage, I don't think you could handle me in bed.* But he was very good at taking away my words. And that made me uncomfortable. Really uncomfortable.

But here was the thing. I didn't think I could handle him in bed. Getting in bed with *him* scared *me.* So yeah, I kept my mouth shut.

The furniture was on order and would hopefully be in by next week. As we made our way to the car, Gage held my hand. I wasn't sure if it was to continue with the charade or not, but I didn't mind. Either way, I liked it. I knew I shouldn't, but I did. I liked a lot about him. His face, his body, his personality, the attention he gave me. But sadly, what I liked most was that he communicated with me. He actually returned my texts.

"I'd love to take you out for a bite to eat or a drink. Is that something we can do, or is it too soon?" His question jostled me from my thoughts. And it suddenly reminded me of something Lanie had said to me: I think the word she used to describe him was "dangerous." Gage was dangerous for me. And my thoughts about him were even more dangerous.

"No, probably not the best idea. Plus, I'm not even legal to get in a bar yet, so there's that, too." The rumble of the engine starting was the only sound, both of us quiet after that.

Once he pulled up to my place, he turned off the car and turned in his seat to face me, obviously ready to say something at that point.

"I don't want to make this hard for you. I know you're just getting out of a relationship, and it's unfair of me to be putting you in these situations." His dark eyes seemed to twinkle when he said this, as if full of mischief. He was full of shit, I thought.

But then he kept talking.

"I'm in no position to get involved with someone on a relationship level, either. I'd like to say we can be friends, but I think you and I both know that wouldn't work with us."

Wait, what?

"What was tonight? Why did you ask me to do this with you tonight if you didn't want to be friends with me, Gage?" I questioned. This was pissing me off. Where did he get off playing with my emotions like this? "You knew the situation. I'm really confused. I mean, I know we flirt with each other and shit, but I thought that seemed to be our thing, ya know?"

He sat silent, the sparkle in his eyes now dimmed. He wouldn't look at me. Instead, his eyes bounced between looking out the front window or at his console. Anywhere but at me. The tension ratcheted up a bit as we sat there in continued silence. Rather, his demeanor was more solemn, serious. He picked at a small bit of dirt stuck to the gear-shift, as if removing it would reveal the secret to life.

"Gage."

"Becca." He wanted to say more but hesitated for a moment. "So, here's the thing. I like you. A lot. But I know Ty is not over you." He paused, and a small sigh of air left his lips. "Let me rephrase that." He angled his body and looked me straight in the eyes before continuing. "Ty is still in love with you; it's obvious to everyone. Are you still in love with him?"

Well, shit.

My words were stuck behind an enormous lump in my throat. He laid it all out there in front of us. I'd gotten more honesty out of Gage in one day than I'd gotten from Ty in seven months.

"Hey, I'm sorry, Becca. I shouldn't put you on the spot like that. It's not fair. And, of course, you still have feelings for him. I get that. But here's the thing. I don't want to start something with you if you're not ready, but you need to understand, I'm not looking for a relationship. I'm only going to be here for about a year, and you have more years than that ahead of you here at school. If you're good with something casual, that's what this would be." He reached out for my hand, rubbing tiny circles on the back of it.

All I could do was stare at his thumb as it swirled on my skin. My thoughts were bouncing around like ping-pong balls in my head.

Of course, I still had feelings for Ty. Those don't end immediately. But I was the one to end it with Ty, and wasn't I looking to move on? Or was I really hoping ending it with Ty would get him to open up about why he hadn't told his family about us? I really had enjoyed the limited time I'd spent with Gage. He was gorgeous. And to have a casual fling with a guy who's as mature as he was would be kind of fun. Gage gave more in these two days than Ty had in months. *But Becca, you broke up with Ty!* Well, yeah, but he obviously wants to still be with me, considering how he acted at the day party, so why didn't he contact me all summer?

"Fuck." Oh my God, I think I said that out loud. I looked at Gage, and his smirk told me that yes, I did indeed say that out loud. "My head is not letting me really think for myself right now. It's full of thoughts I feel like I don't have control over. That's what that was about. I'm sorry. I didn't mean it in a way that I'm mad about anything you just said to me. It's just that it's got my emotions going . . ."

"Becca," he said with a voice that immediately calmed me down, "it's OK." His hand was now moving up to my face, cradling it. I was getting those squishy feelings in my belly, and lower down, too, as his thumb rubbed my cheek down to my lips. "Would it be OK if I kissed you goodnight? Those lips look like they need my lips on them."

"Yes, you can. I mean, yes, they do. I mean . . ."

He stopped my blabbering by placing his thumb over my mouth, pushing down on my lower lip just hard enough to encourage my lips to separate. His thumb grazed my tongue before he pulled it back and ran it along my bottom lip. The wetness left behind enticed me to lick my lips. When I did, he moaned and his hand wound around my neck with an intensity that startled me. He pulled me closer, and our mouths were about to touch when he stopped.

"After I kiss you, I want you to go inside and think about this kiss. Think about how it made you feel and think about if you would like more, on other parts of your body."

Jesus fuckin' Christ on a cracker. This guy couldn't be real. Because this stuff didn't happen to me. It only happened in those books Lanie read.

But Gage still stared at me while holding on to the back of my head, his mouth a breath away from mine. He was most definitely real.

"Promise me, Becca. Promise me you'll think about this kiss tonight."

My eyes were on his lips as he spoke, his warm words almost vibrating against me. "I promise." My whisper barely came out, but it was enough for him. He closed the small gap between us, our mouths connecting. He was gentle, his lips soft, as if he coated them with Vaseline nightly. The slight stubble above his lip rubbed against me, but not in a bad way. It contradicted the softness of his skin.

His hand knotted around my hair as the kiss escalated. His tongue forged a path inside, seeking mine, dancing with it. But then his tongue was gone, though his lips remained attached to me.

"Becca," he said against my lips, "open your eyes, baby. I want you to look at me when I'm kissing you."

I think I stopped breathing, but I opened my eyes. I was looking into his as our mouths hovered near one another, both of us frozen in place. His eyes were a unique shade of caramel brown with gold-and-green specks strewn throughout. They almost seemed to shimmer.

He opened his mouth a bit, his tongue coming out to wet his lips, wetting mine at the same time.

And that was hot. As. Fuck.

"I'm sure plenty of people have told you how gorgeous your green eyes are." His other hand came up to push back the hair threatening to cover my face. "But has anyone pointed out the gold band around your iris? It looks like the sun has exploded in your eyes. It's truly remarkable." I had to look away when he was saying these things, not used to the compliments. "Uh-uh, keep looking at me. Eyes on me." His hand brought my face back as his mouth came closer again, our eyes still connected.

It's not a simple thing to keep eye contact while kissing. The innate reaction is to close your eyes, revel in the feel. This slowed things down and brought it to a whole new level.

His mouth returned to mine, slightly open, his tongue licking my top lip. His hand behind my head held me tighter, our mouths crushing against one another with force. Our eyes remained connected as our tongues danced; his seemed to be telling me something I couldn't quite read.

When he pulled away, I felt an intense need to reach out for him. I wanted him close to me. And I thought he knew that as a smug grin spread across his face.

"I hope I gave you something worth thinking about." His smile wasn't as smug anymore. Rather, he looked like he was missing me already, too.

"Yeah, something to think about, and something to act on," I responded, my eyes rolling as he laughed. His hand moved toward his lap, adjusting his pants.

"I think I know what you mean."

And then silence.

But it wasn't awkward as we sat there together. We both knew I should get out of the car. The goodnight kiss had happened. But neither of us was ready for the night to end.

"So—"

"Can I—"

From silence to talking over one another. Our nervous laughs were a sign that we were both on edge.

"Ball's in your court, Becca. You think about it, us, that kiss. Let me know if you want to do this with me. You have my number." I nodded and reached for the door. He leaned over and helped push it open, both of us knowing if he got out of the car, the night wouldn't end.

"Good night, Gage."

"Night, Becca."

My pace was steady as I walked to my door, forcing myself not to turn around. The click of the door closing coincided with the rumble of his engine as he drove off, and my small smile grew wide.

CHAPTER 5

Ty

"Dude, c'mon, let's fuckin' go!" Jake was pushing me out the door because we were running late to get the buffalo wings delivered to a frat brother. Another one of our duties as pledges, to be at their beck and call to bring them food at any hour of the night. I guess it beat being forced to drink into oblivion; the last frat that did that to their pledges on campus got disbanded.

"Hey man, I've been meaning to ask you," Jake started as we hopped in my car. Shit, I knew what was coming. Actually surprised no one had confronted me about it already. "Where were you after the party on Saturday? You weren't around for any of the shit we did on Sunday or that night. But none of the frat brothers seemed to notice you were gone." My car peeled around a corner a bit too fast, the tires screeching on the pavement. My nervous response to his questions, combined with us being late, had me driving reckless. "None of us wanted to say anything."

His voice got quiet, and I glanced his way. "We, um . . ." He hesitated.

I didn't want to be having this conversation, but I had to give him something. I left my brothers, and we weren't supposed to do that. He deserved some kind of answer. But what?

"Yeah, man, I had some shit come up at home. Emergency. I talked to Sam; he told me it was OK to head home for the day." My eyes shifted back and forth from the road to him, trying to gauge if he bought it. It wasn't a complete lie, just not the whole fucking truth.

If I wasn't telling Becca, I wasn't telling him. But I felt like shit, because here I was telling him even more than I told her. Running home the morning after the party the first weekend at school kept me from being with my pledge class and our duties together. It kept me from trying to see more of Becca. Hell, I didn't even text her this weekend. My situation was less than ideal.

But it was my life. The part of my life I wasn't willing to share with anyone.

Yet.

"Oh, shit, Ty," Jake exclaimed as he sat up straighter in his seat. "Sorry, man. Hope everything's alright." He went back to fiddling with his phone to find a better song to blast through the speakers, us both enjoying a few moments of normalcy while we drove. The pledging shit had its good moments and its bad. Making better friends with guys like Jake was a good one. And that was what I liked best about Jake. He knew when to shut up.

"I don't mean to pry," Jake continued.

Fuck, maybe I was wrong about him. He wasn't giving up.

"Anything to do with Logan?" Jake continued, looking at his phone, the silence between songs allowing us a moment to talk. "He's a cool guy, and when I heard he wasn't coming back this year, well, that sucks." Jake finally looked my way just as I was pulling into a spot in front of the apartment we needed to be at. He reached behind the seat to grab the food as I responded.

"No, he's actually doing pretty good. Hoping he might make it back here for spring semester. He's bummed he couldn't pledge, though." And Logan was. He was the one who dragged me to all the pledging events freshman year. I'd had no intention of joining a fraternity. But here I was. And Logan was home, dealing with his own shit.

"That's cool. Be right back." He jumped out of the car to deliver the food. Smelling that food in the car had made me hungry. They didn't give us a lot of time to even eat during these weeks of hell.

The car bounced as Jake jumped back in, slamming his door.

"I'm fuckin' starving now!" he yelled. I laughed as I put the car in drive.

"Put that music on and text the guys. We should have enough time to pick something up." I headed downtown, giving us a choice of fast food drive-ups to go to. "What's next on our schedule tonight?"

Thankfully, we only had one more day of pledging left. Getting to school early in August to do most of this before the semester started was super smart. This last night was known as Big/Little night. It was the night each pledge got inducted into the fraternity and assigned their "Big Brother" family in the frat. I was psyched to be in Sam's family; having him as my Big was awesome. Not only had he helped me throughout the past month, allowing me to head home when I needed to, but he was a cool guy.

"Ty, man, welcome to the family!" Sam hugged me as the others poured a bottle of booze over our heads. Each pledge, when called up, got showered with liquor and took the bottle on their way down from the temporary stage in the main hall of the fraternity house. It was then ours to enjoy for the night. After the ceremony, a night of partying with two local sororities would start.

"Dude!" Nate grabbed me into a bear hug and pulled me off the floor. He was Sam's Big, which made him my "Grand-Big." "Welcome to the family. Now let's get you drunk!"

He grabbed the bottle from my hand, taking a long chug. Drinking was not an expectation with these guys, which was one of the main reasons Logan and I chose this frat. But I liked my share of drunken nights, and after the past few weeks, I knew this would be one of them. Nate handed the bottle back and I took a long swig, feeling the burn all the way to my stomach.

"Hey, Ty." I turned to find Xander with his arms extended, ready for a hug. We were not in the same family, but we were still brothers. "Welcome, man. Glad to have you," he said. As he slapped my back, I could feel the beer sloshing from his cup behind me.

"Thanks, man. Feels good to be on this end of it all, ya know?" I smiled as I raised the bottle in his direction. He raised the red cup in his hand in salute, and we both drank.

"I'm sure you wish Logan was here. Sorry he's not. For you, and for him." Xander had every reason to hate Logan for what he did to Lanie last year, but he didn't. I nodded, hoping he understood how much I respected him for the person he was. "So . . ." he started, but then stopped. His eyes searched the room rather than looking at me. His hesitation and the look on his face took my buzz away immediately; I could tell it had to be about Becca.

"What is it, Xander? Just spit it out. I haven't seen or talked to her. What the fuck is going on?" My heart was in my throat because I didn't think I really wanted to know. I thought giving her space was the right thing do to, but maybe I'd been wrong. With pledging and having to go home, I couldn't really spare the time to see her. Texting, I felt, was too impersonal. So I left it alone.

"Listen, man. I don't want to be involved. But I know you've been stuck here and dealing with whatever shit you have going on at home. Even more of a reason I really don't want to tell you, but if it were me, I'd want to know." He paused again, looking around the room, uncomfortable with the conversation.

"C'mon, man. You're driving me more crazy by not telling me." I fell back against the wall I was close to, exasperated by this point.

"She went out with someone the other night," he said. "Pretty sure it was Gage." His eyes were on mine as his measured words left his mouth. I tried to read his expression, to make sure his words were true. But they had to be; it was Xander. "Listen, it's not fair of me to do this to you tonight of all nights. I know that. But it's also the first night that you'll be able to see her in a while. I thought you might do that. And I thought you should know, before you got too drunk."

A pair of sympathetic eyes stared me down. My free hand flexed in and out of a fist as I raised the bottle to my lips. I tilted the half-empty container, draining it of the amber liquid, a trail of fire burning down my throat. It spilled from my mouth, dribbling down my chin, too much for me to take as a garbled yell expelled from my gut.

"Fuck!" I dropped the bottle to the ground, the hollow echo of the glass haunting me as it rolled along the floor and hit the wall. It sounded as empty as I felt. The back of my head hit the wall as I stared up at the ceiling, hoping Xander would just go away. But when I peered over, he was still there. "Did you see her go, or did Lanie tell you?"

He shook his head. "Nah, neither of us saw them leave, but Lanie heard her come home the other night, and saw his car driving away."

I didn't know what my next move should be, and Xander could see that.

"Just have fun tonight, Ty. But I know you'll head over to her place later. I get it. I would, too." He put his hand on my shoulder, supporting me with his grip and in his tone. "But be smart. You two aren't together. If you still want her, don't make things worse between the two of you than they already are."

I nodded.

It was sound advice; I only hoped I could follow it.

I was drunk. And there were a lot of hot girls at the house. A lot.

But none of them compared to Becca.

The night started feeling like a chore. I was going through the motions. Because all I could think about was her—nothing else but her.

Her with him.

I was sitting on the couch, alone, with an empty bottle of beer in my hand, when a girl plopped down next to me. She wove her fingers through my hair as a leg came across my lap. Her skirt hiked up, exposing the bottom of her panties, if you could call them that. There wasn't much material there.

"I heard there's a room open upstairs. Want to grab it, Ty?" a soft but intoxicated voice said next to me. I slowly turned my head, my eyes catching up with the motion a moment later. I was more wasted than I thought.

"Uhhh, hey, Kayla. What's up?"

I knew her. We had some classes together freshman year. "I take it you got into your sorority tonight?" She was wearing a skimpy tube top with her Greek letters across it, but it barely covered her tits. And she was definitely not wearing a bra.

"I did, and I thought the two of us could go upstairs and celebrate." She nuzzled her nose into my neck as her chest rubbed against my arm, causing the strip of cloth across her tits to push farther down. My eyes locked on to the sight. "Like what you see? I'll show you plenty more if we go upstairs."

To her surprise, I pushed her gently off of me and pulled her shirt up, covering her chest. "Kayla, you're a beautiful, sweet girl. You're too drunk to be doing this right now. Why don't you head home?" Her mouth fell open like she was a bit offended I wouldn't take her up on her offer. "I'm going to go find Becca."

I stood up and walked out the front door.

CHAPTER 6
Becca

My sleep had been restless for a couple nights. My dreams bounced between two different guys. And of course, that kiss from the other night in Gage's car took center stage in most of my fantasies.

He told me to think about it.

And I thought about it.

A lot.

Maybe too much. The way he grabbed my hair just a little too hard. And the way he told me to keep my eyes open. No, *ordered* me to keep my eyes open.

It was fucking hot.

I stirred in my bed, my thoughts waking me, and I needed to move. Those thoughts were making my body tingle in places that had not had much attention lately.

But as I stretched, I felt confined by arms wrapped around my body. His soft breath on the back of my head and the familiar smell of his clothes told me exactly who my sleep partner was.

"Hey, baby doll." His words slurred. I wasn't sure if from exhaustion, alcohol, or both. But once I turned my head, the unmistakable smell hit my nose and I had my answer.

"Ty, when did you get here? *Why* are you here?" My whisper was meant to not wake up the rest of the house. I hadn't heard from him since the party last weekend, and suddenly he was in my bed.

"Baby, I'm in. It's finally over. Tonight was Big/Little night, and I'm in the frat. Rushing is over, and I got my life back. You were my first stop." He snuggled up against me even more when he said that, his arms pulling me closer. "If I wasn't so tired, I'd be peeling these little shorts off of you. I miss you; other parts of my body miss you, too. But I'm exhausted. In the morning . . ." His voice trailed off as he fell back asleep. His hands had made their way under my shirt before he passed out again, his one hand firmly on my breast, the other across my belly. The same position we used to sleep in.

What. The. Hell.

Was he so drunk that he totally forgot we're not together? I elbowed him hard in his gut, trying to get him out of my bed. He wasn't a muscle head, but he was big and inebriated enough that I had trouble moving him.

"Ty!" It was a whisper yell; I didn't need the other roommates I barely knew to meet him this way, in the middle of the night with us fighting. "Ty, get up! What made you think coming here was a good idea? And how did you even get in here?" I wormed my way out of his grip and was crawling over the top of him to get to the floor. While I did that, he grabbed me by the waist and pulled me onto his lap, his tired face looking up at me.

He was literally shirtless, in his boxers.

"What are you doing?" I was exasperated at that point.

"Lanie picked me and Xander up from the party; she agreed to bring me here after a lot of begging." His slurred words forced me to listen closely. "The last time we saw each other, we said we were going to talk." His tired face looked like talking was the last thing on his mind, and his eyes could barely stay open. "Well, let's talk."

I sat still for a moment on his lap, admiring his handsome face as he struggled to stay alert.

"Ty, that's not exactly how I remember it. I think it was more like we started hooking up so you would try to get me to forget about everything we need to talk about."

That elicited a sly grin from him, under hooded eyes, as his fingers dug into my waist.

"Then, when I wanted to talk, you had no answers for my questions, as usual." And he was at it again, his hands rubbing along my thighs, working their way under my night-shirt. "It won't work again. I won't let it." I peeled myself off of him, and he let go easier than I expected. I could feel the defeat in his weakened grip. My departure from his lap was waking him; he suddenly seemed more alert.

"Becca, I don't want to lose you over something as silly as my parents not knowing about us. Why can't we just go with it for a while? I'll know the right time to tell them. Trust me."

My eyes grew wide at his words, but it was dark in the room, so I didn't think he could see me. I walked away from the bed, needing the distance. It gave me strength.

"Trust you? Do you hear yourself? Ty, the time for trusting you and believing you would do the right thing has passed. We were together for seven months. Seven months!" My voice rose. We would probably have an audience soon, but I was beyond caring. He sat on the edge of the bed, my words sobering him up with each syllable. "I visited your house on multiple occasions, and they had no idea I was the girl you were fucking and saying 'I love you' to each night."

"Bec." The pain in his voice was almost enough to break me. I felt like I was about to go against my better judgment, which was not known to be the best with him, and give in. He stood and tentatively stepped toward me. I wasn't sure if he was afraid I would yell or if he was trying to stay upright, but he eventually made it across the room to me. I stood my ground, standing tall with all of my five feet and five inches. My neck craned to look at him as he wrapped his arms around my waist. I put my hands on his chest, pushing him away as best I could. "I'm not giving up on us. Not yet, Bec. Are you?"

Well, fuckity fuck. Ty didn't know he had competition. Not yet, anyway. And I couldn't believe I allowed someone else into my head to be his competition.

"Ty, I kissed someone else."

I blurted it out before I even thought it through. I didn't know if it was to be completely transparent or to make him jealous. Could it have been both? His hands fell from me as he stumbled back in the room. But the look on his face made me think he already knew and this was only confirmation.

"I knew you went out with him, but you kissed him?" he whispered, the pained disbelief palpable in his voice. The light from the street-lamps hitting his face through the window gave me a clear view. Tears welled up in his eyes as he backpedaled to the bed. "Becca, what are you talking about? For fuck's sake, it was that asshole from the party, wasn't it? Fuck, Becca, what are you doing? Why? Why, baby?" His words weren't tinged with anger. It was all sadness. He knew he had done this.

It was hitting him. It was finally hitting him what was happening to us.

His legs hit the edge of the bed, but he didn't sit. Instead, his body seemed to bend in half, as if in pain, his hands on his knees to support his weight. The sudden urge to go to him, to comfort him, was strong. To fight it, I looked away, not wanting to see the pain I'd caused him.

But I needed to remember the pain he caused me most of last year. I needed those memories to bolster my strength to forge ahead through this. I didn't want to hurt him, but we couldn't remain the way we were, either.

"Ty, we aren't together. I broke up with you almost three months ago." I stared out the window as I spoke, knowing I couldn't look his way. "You didn't even try to change my mind over the summer. Yet we get here to school, and like always, it's as if everything is perfect." But I couldn't keep my eyes away from him. And as soon as I looked his way, he peeked up, his eyes searching for a possibility, a chance for us. He fell onto the bed, his hands falling between his knees. "Ty, why didn't you call me for months?"

And then I saw it happen right before my eyes. It was as if a mask covered his face. A different Ty was in front of me after I asked that question. The Ty who was always present with me while we were with his parents stood in front of me.

"You're still not going to answer that question, are you? Don't you see, Ty? Until you can be completely honest with me, until there are no more secrets between us, no more lies, I can't do this!" Tears were threatening to spill from my eyes, and my voice cracked as I tried not to yell, but failed. I slid down the wall I was against and buried my face in my knees. If he wouldn't tell any truths, I was done talking.

The squeak of the bed told me Ty stood up. The muffled drag of his feet across the carpet let me know he was coming toward me. But his slow, tentative steps also told me he was unsure and nervous. I didn't look up. I couldn't. I knew my resolve would crack if I saw a single tear on his face.

I felt his presence above me. Then he slid against the wall, taking a seat next to me. He didn't talk, just sat there. I chanced a peek as I turned my head slightly, my eye glancing under the arm surrounding my head. The despair lining his face as he stared ahead, at nothing, was exactly what I didn't want to see. He must have sensed my movement, because he turned and our eyes connected.

And he broke.

The sobs that came were quiet at first; I knew he was trying to keep it all inside. But once he looked at me, all bets were off. And it shattered me. My hand had a mind of its own, making its way to his head, pulling him to me. I cradled him in my lap, trying to console him. Why? I guess because I still loved him. A love like ours didn't disappear simply because someone had made a mistake.

"Becca"—his voice cracked through the crying—"I'm so sorry. You're right, one hundred percent right. I'll fix this, I promise. I'll figure out a way to fix this, us. I will not lose you." He turned his face up, making sure I heard what he was saying. "I can't lose you, Bec. You're the best thing that's ever happened to me." And he broke, his face contorted. Inconsolable.

I moved his head off my lap, trying to motion for him to sit up. I needed to hold him, needed to get my arms around him to calm him down. We enveloped one another, arms and legs a puzzle. His head settled on my chest and we laid our bodies on the floor, our grip only tightening. His one hand was under my head, supporting me, while the other was across my belly. Soon enough, Ty's breathing returned to normal, and I wondered if he had fallen asleep. But when his hand on my belly made its way under my shirt, I had my answer. His fingers were rubbing circles on my stomach, my skin betraying me as the bumps rose to meet his touch. My back's small arch seemed to happen of its own accord as well. And these did not go unnoticed by Ty as he lifted his head, eyes now on mine.

"I miss you so much, baby. I miss touching this satin skin. I miss this perfect body." He dipped his head down, his lips now dotting my stomach with tiny kisses. His warm breath in between each made me want to squeeze my thighs together, the heat already building between my legs. "Please tell me we can work on us as I figure out a way to fix this. I won't let you down." His hooded eyes found mine as he peered up from my navel, his tongue dipping in and licking between his words. "It's been too long since we've touched each other. We need this, Becca, so bad."

I was not a stick-thin girl. I had curves. My thighs touched when I walked, and my stomach had a bit of a roundness to it. I didn't hate my body. I actually loved it. I just wasn't that typical skinny girl at college. But what Ty always did well was make me feel sexy. He said he loved the little extra I offered because it gave him something to hold on to. And I missed him doing that. Making me feel sexy. And holding on to the sexy parts.

My intention this year was for us to get back together. I knew I wasn't going to turn him down, even though the little voice in my head was telling me I should. Hooking up wouldn't solve anything.

But it would make me *feel* good.

His fingers moved to my panty line, about to move lower.

It was clear we shouldn't do what he wanted to do, but I was so close to giving in.

I missed him; I missed us.

I also knew he was waiting for me to give him the green light. He would never assume it was OK for us to move on without me saying so.

If I spent too much time thinking about my decision, I knew I would change my mind. So I let him know I was on board by wiggling out of my shirt and thong.

He pushed up onto his knees and stared down at me once I was naked.

"You are a fucking masterpiece."

His words took my breath away.

His hand started at my temple, the backs of his fingers trailing down the side of my face, my neck. His featherlight touches sparked little fires deep inside. My eyes closed, and I was swept away by the attention he was giving me. I hadn't noticed he was changing position until I felt him straddle me, his hard length pushing through his boxers against my pubic bone. This allowed him to use both hands to gather my breasts, his mouth lowering at the same time. His tongue darted out to wet the tip, my nipple growing as if reaching to him, desperate for more attention.

"Oh my God, Ty, I've missed you. I've missed your hands on me." My growled words became muffled when his one hand held my jaw, a finger slipping into my mouth.

"Get my finger wet, baby girl. Nice and wet." I loved when he talked like this to me. No one would think he was like this behind closed doors. Sweet and innocent Tyler Brennan had the dirtiest mouth I'd ever heard.

He took that wet finger and rubbed it along my nipple, then blew cool air over it, causing it to harden like a rock. My hand flew up to my breast, needing to grab and squeeze it. But he pushed my hand away.

"No, baby girl, not yet." One of his hands held both of mine above my head while his other started a slow torture between my legs. My body was on autopilot, my back arching, a silent plea for more as I spread my legs wider, hoping he would take the hint.

"Someone is really wet. You are dripping, Becca, fucking dripping all over my hand right now." As he said that, two fingers delved inside, deep, as his mouth attached to my nipple, his teeth grazing before sucking hard. He released my hands, thank God, and I grabbed my breasts, squeezing them together. My hands rested on his head, pushing him to suck on me harder yet. His other hand was relentless while inside me.

"Fuck, Ty, you're going to get me. I'm gonna come."

"That's a good girl, Becca. Come for me, baby. Come all over my hand." He reached up with his thumb while his fingers were still deep inside of me and rubbed my clit. My body tensed and stilled as the orgasm neared. He didn't stop, though, his hand moving constantly, pushing me closer to the edge. My entire body felt as though it lifted from the bed, the waves hitting hard and fast as I went soaring over that cliff.

I became frantic, reaching for his boxers, trying to push them down.

"Ty, I need you inside me, now." I wanted to feel the smooth, taut skin of his hard length. To stroke it and lick it before he pushed inside of me and made me lose all sense of reality. I was past caring about all of our problems; the need raging through me took over.

But he stilled my hands. He pushed my hands away from him, stopping me.

"What are you doing, Ty? C'mon, we can't stop now." I sounded desperate. And I was. My hands still tried to pull his underwear down as he was pushing to a sitting position.

"Becca, it's OK. We should stop."

"No, Ty, what are you talking about? Ty, it's been months since we've been together, months since I've felt you inside me. Don't make me beg." But I already was.

"Bec . . ." The hesitation in his voice told me I wouldn't like how he finished that sentence. "Babe, I don't have a condom."

I froze.

This had always been one of our biggest problems. Regardless of how long we were together and that I was on the pill and protected, he always wanted to wear a condom. I talked to him about it, asked him if it meant he was seeing other people. He insisted that wasn't the case. But every time he reached for that square foil packet when we were still together, I couldn't deny a small part of me always broke inside as I continued to think that maybe there was a part of him I didn't know.

This time, however, I had no right to be angry.

We weren't together and hadn't been for a few months.

Did I really know what he'd been doing?

I broke up with him. I brought this on myself. My breaths stayed even and calm, and I thought I was doing an

OK job keeping myself under control. I looked up, finding his eyes focused on me, studying me. My nod was slight, but I knew he saw it.

That was when I heard the soft knock on the door.

"Hey guys, just an FYI, the walls in this place are paper thin. We can hear *everything.*" Lanie's voice was quiet but held a level of concern. Sadness came through in her words as she waited by the door. The emphasis on that last word made me cringe, though. Not only had she heard us arguing around, but she heard us fooling around.

Ty cleared his throat as he moved into my closet to take cover, since he was still in his underwear.

"Sorry, Lanes. Ty was just leaving anyway," I said.

The disbelief on his face quickly transformed.

"Bec, I can't drive. I drank too much. How am I gonna get home? It's over a mile away and it's . . ." He looked at his watch. "It's three in the morning. Shit, Lanie, I'm sorry we woke you."

Lanie saw the look on my face and knew I needed my distance from him. "Hey, Ty, I can drive you home. That's not a problem," she told him.

I then climbed back into my bed and faced the wall. My defenses were up to avoid making this get any worse between us. I knew myself and didn't want to overreact. Their conversation continued as whispered hushes while I tried to avoid it all in my little corner.

Then I heard Lanie close the door, but Ty remained.

He didn't say anything for a moment, but I could hear him shuffling his feet closer to the bed. It eventually gave under his weight as he sat next to me. My eyes remained focused on a crack in the paint on the wall that my nose was almost touching.

"Bec," he whispered, his voice hoarse with emotion. "I know I've fucked us up. I obviously did us more damage than I even realized." He released a large breath that turned into a sigh before continuing. "I'm going to give you the break you obviously want from me." His voice cracked as he spoke, trying hard to keep from crying. "I won't be far. I'll be here, for you, if you need me. But..." He paused. "In the distance."

I felt the shift of his body behind me, though I wasn't sure what he was doing. Then I felt him over me, his lips on the side of my head, the kiss on my temple.

"I love you, Becca."

And then he was gone.

And I was free to cry in peace.

Chapter 7
Becca

*I*t took me hours to fall asleep once Ty left. And the sleep I got was fitful. Waking up late made the day already a bad one, considering classes started the next day. I had a ton to do and not a lot of time to do it. I threw on shorts and a tank and found Lanie; she would know how to make the day better.

Thankfully, she was in the kitchen with a full pot of coffee in hand.

"You're a lifesaver. Has anyone told you that lately?" I walked up behind her and wrapped her in a hug. "And I don't just mean for the coffee. I mean, yeah, the coffee is perfect, thank you." I plucked the cup out of her hand, since I knew she meant it for me. "But taking Ty home last night was the best thing you've ever done for me." After taking my first sip, I looked up at her again. "But you are the one who let him into my room, so maybe you owed me that anyway?"

Lanie walked to the cabinet and took out a mug, a guilty look consuming her face.

"OK, maybe I didn't think that one through," she said. "I'm sorry, but you weren't in the car with those two last night. Xander and him were so drunk, and all the two of them could talk about was how Ty spent the entire night talking about you and fending off girls just because he wanted to come see you." Lanie looked sheepishly my way, not sure if I truly was mad at her.

"It's OK; I probably would have done the same thing if you and Xander were in this spot. They are so good at convincing us to do shit like that."

The apologies out of the way, it was apparent Lanie had other topics she was waiting to talk about. She turned around and leaned against the counter, seeming to think about what to say as she stared at me.

"Just say it, Lanes. It can't be worse than what I'm already thinking."

She blew on her beverage before speaking. "Bec, I just don't understand. It seems so out of character for Ty to be like that. But here's the thing. Last year, we lived in the dorms, and you and I, we were never really in the same room with our boyfriends often, and it's been a while since I've seen the two of you interact." She came toward me and took the stool next to me at the island, her hand resting on mine. "I would have never guessed it was as bad as that with the two of you. I'm sorry, that's all." She squeezed my hand, and that was all it took. The tears I was holding back spilled down my cheeks.

I was sad. I think that was to be expected. It felt like I was mourning our relationship. I had no idea if we would ever get back to what we had, though what we had was a lie.

My intention when coming back to school this year was to get us back together. Instead, we were worse off than ever.

"Yeah, he was always great to me when we were at school, you saw it. So, it really wasn't this bad last year. But that he couldn't tell his family about me, that I was a 'secret' that had to be hidden. That makes a person feel like shit, a worthless piece of shit, after a while. Especially when you point it out and he still does nothing about it." I wiped my face dry, the tears already stopping. I thought I'd cried them all out the night before.

"That's the part I don't get. I mean, OK, his parents don't want him in a relationship so that his grades don't go down. But his grades were great his freshman year. Couldn't he use that argument to prove to them it would be fine?" Lanie had a good point.

I nodded in agreement. "I mean, isn't it normal to want to be the priority in your boyfriend's life? How about he just stands up to his parents' unreasonable demands?" I countered.

Shit. I knew I shouldn't have said it. Lanie looked away, letting it slide. But she had a fucked-up year last year with her ex, which was brought on by her parents forcing her into a terrible situation. So she knew what it was like to deal with parents and their unreasonable demands.

"Lanie, I'm sorry. Me and my big mouth."

"It's OK, Bec, but maybe he feels, like I did, that he *has* to do what he's doing. I don't know. I just wish he would tell you more. But I'm the queen of secrets, so I can't talk. He's giving you more space. That's what you want now, right?"

Her look was conspiratorial. I knew she was referring to Gage. Coming back to school this year, my only intention was to win Ty back. That wasn't going as planned.

"I don't know if that's what I want. When I'm with him, I feel like I want us to get back together, to try and work things out, until he starts with his 'untruths.' Then I can't take it anymore." I had calmed down but felt the tears threatening their return. "I just want to feel

important to him, though. Ya know? As important to him as I know you are to Xander." She nodded, understanding that anyone would want that. I wiped my face with the back of my arm. "Well, anyway, I have a lot to do today. What about you?" I smiled her way, hoping she would take the hint that I wanted to be done talking about Ty.

"Yeah, a trip to the bookstore seems in order. Want to head there soon?"

"Sure, I'll be down after I get dressed. Are Macie and Ava around?"

"I haven't seen them; I think it's just us today."

We spent the rest of the day together, getting ourselves ready for our sophomore year of college. Lanie did a fantastic job of keeping my mind off of Ty as we picked up books for class and shopped to fill our refrigerator with food.

"How have things been with your parents lately?" I asked Lanie as we exited the store.

A small smile appeared on her lips, something I wasn't expecting.

"Actually, we've been talking a lot more lately. My mom has been doing better, too. I think she's finally healing a bit from everything."

Lanie's mom kinda went off the deep end when the shit hit the fan last year and Max, her ex, came to try to take Lanie away from school. Her dad had kept a lot of what was going on in their lives a secret from both Lanie and her mom, thinking it would keep them safer. I think keeping them in the dark about the real nature of Max's family and their mafia connections hurt them rather than helped. But hindsight doesn't do much good.

"That's great, Lanie. Any plans for them to come back to the states?"

They moved to Italy to escape the craziness of the Marcello family. But that meant they also abandoned their daughter at the same time. Lanie never really expressed her true feelings about that, but I knew it had to hurt.

"We haven't gotten that far in our discussions." Her voice trailed off as if she had gotten lost in her own thoughts. She rebounded quickly, though. "What about you? How's your family life been lately? How was your summer at home?"

I never knew how to answer that. My family was unique. I loved them. But didn't always love spending time with them. It was a chaotic place to be with four younger brothers and two parents who worked nonstop. Plus, I never felt like my *space* was respected. My personal space and my physical space.

"The summer was long, especially not having Ty as a buffer to break up my time with all my brothers. They are a lot to be around all the time." Lanie was an only child, so she may not have completely understood where I was coming from with my complaints. "When they are all home from school, but my parents are still working, a lot falls on me." Right on cue, my phone came through with a message. I shook my head as I read it in disbelief, but wasn't really surprised. "Like this. It's one of my twin brothers texting me asking where his Legos are." I lifted my phone to show Lanie.

"But your parents are home?" she asked.

"Somewhere, yeah, but they're working." I loved my parents, and my brothers, but it was a lot being in my family. Being the oldest of five kids with the jobs my mom and dad held made me a third parent to them all the time. "And they're still too young to get that I'm too far away to come running to help them."

"How old are they again?" she asked as we were walking out of the store, arms full of groceries.

"The twins just started first grade."

She nodded in understanding, but I was doubtful she ever could truly get it.

"I have another question for you I've been meaning to ask, but I didn't want to pry with everything that happened with Ty last night." Lanie looked at me as we put the bags in the trunk of my car, her eyes seeking for permission for her to go on.

"What?" I asked, curious. But as soon as I said it, I knew exactly what she was going to say. Her raised eyebrows gave it away.

"The other night, where were you? You weren't home when I got back from Xander's. I heard a car but couldn't quite see who dropped you off." Her words said one thing while her face said another. She knew exactly who I was with.

I continued to load the bags, my silence speaking volumes. I smiled as I looked her way, and she poked me in the ribs.

"No! You didn't! You were out with him, weren't you?" Lanie's interrogation continued, but I kept my silence.

"I mean, I knew it was him; his car is hard not to recognize," she continued.

And my smile grew. I didn't expect thinking about him to make me feel so happy, so relaxed. And Lanie noticed.

"You like him." It was a statement, not a question. "Is that maybe part of the reason you're not giving Ty as much of a chance? Do you think your feelings for Gage are getting in the way of that?"

My head snapped toward her.

"Holy shit, do you really think that's what I could be doing? Fuck, Lanie, what if that is what I'm doing? I never even thought of it that way. Oh my God. It's all happening so quickly, I never even put it together." We made our way to the front seat of my car, not going anywhere yet, though. "But Ty had all summer. It's not like I haven't given him time to get his act together. I mean, he needs to figure this out. If I don't put my foot down, he'll go on like this forever, I know it."

"Bec . . ."

"No, I've given him enough time. It's not my responsibility to make this work anymore. It's on him now. He has . . ."

"Becca!" Lanie yelled.

I froze, stopped and stared at her.

"I was doing it again, wasn't I? Sorry, sometimes I just don't know when to stop." Lanie was good at keeping me from getting out of hand with my ramblings.

"Becca, I didn't mean to make you feel bad for seeing him. You and Ty aren't together. You're free to do what you want, sweetie. I only want what's best for you. If he makes you happy, then by all means, spend time with Gage."

I looked her way to determine if she was sincere. She seemed to be, but I didn't know how that made me feel. Having someone give me their blessing to move forward with Gage, someone other than me, made it feel . . . OK. Not wrong. Last year, we had this perfect little group at the beginning of the year. Me, Lanie, Ty, Xander, and Logan.

Well, things spiraled out of control since then. The only constants since then were that Lanie and Xander were still a couple, and Lanie and I were still best friends. And Logan? Well, he wasn't even back at school yet. His story was a sad one filled with too much drinking that swayed his decision-making skills. So hearing Lanie tell me she thought it was acceptable for me to move on with someone new was big. Another monumental change to our group.

"Yeah, he makes me happy. When I'm with him, I don't feel like I need to think about anything else other than what we're doing at that moment. He, um . . ." I stammered my next words, afraid it might change her mind. She waited patiently in her seat, allowing me the time to find my words. She never pushed me; it was one of her best qualities.

"He doesn't want a relationship. He wants to keep it casual. I guess he's looking for a fuck buddy?" I waited for her opinion to change, for her to gasp in disgust at the idea of it. But she continued to sit, content and waiting for me to continue. "That doesn't bother you? That he only wants to hang out, have sex, and nothing serious?"

"Well, it only bothers me if it bothers you. Does it? He was honest, upfront, right from the start. Seems like that's what you've been wanting. I don't know why that would be a problem." She raised her eyebrows a bit before continuing. "How many relationships in college are really more than short-term things or hookups? I mean, at least you know going in. And let me guess, he's heading back home when he's done with school, is that why?"

I think Lanie and I were the only girls on our floor last year in long-term relationships. Everyone else was doing exactly that: hooking up. Very casual sex or short-term things that didn't last. Lanie was right. I'd been desperate for honesty, and Gage was giving me that. Plus, he was offering me time with him with no strings attached. When I thought of it that way, it seemed like an easy decision.

"Plus," Lanie went on, "who wouldn't want sex with that god? He's . . ." She stammered a bit as her face turned a pale shade of pink.

"He's fucking hot is what he is. It's OK to say it. Doesn't mean you're cheating on Xander. Gage is *Xander* hot." She laughed out loud at that—we both did. "But here's the thing. I don't know if I'm ready to be rid of Ty forever. I told him I need him to change, to figure it out. What if he tries to do that and I've started this thing with Gage?"

Once I said that, Lanie got very serious, turning in her seat to face me head on. "Here is where I turn your advice to me right back on you. I'm not saying you should use Gage, but he's already said he wants casual. As long as you're honest with him about Ty, you never know. It might give Ty the kick in the ass he needs." The twinkle in her bright blue eyes brought me back to the conversation we had last year. I gave good advice, but she never took it. Things either worked out for her and Xander or she decided it wasn't the right path for her; I don't quite remember.

But it feels like the right path for me.

"OK, so I have a plan. I'll talk to Gage, tell him where I'm at with Ty, and see if he's still interested in us having our 'thing.'" My air quotes made us both giggle. I never expected to find myself in a hook-up situation.

"Your 'thing' will probably ruin you for every guy after him." Lanie chuckled. She turned herself around and pulled the belt in place. "We should get going. Classes start in the morning, and we have a lot of groceries to unpack. Plus, I still want to cook dinner for Xander."

But I was stuck on something she said.

"How will he ruin me?" I was genuinely confused.

She looked at me, stunned. "You don't get that feeling? He seems like he's going to be, well, pretty good at, ya know, this 'thing' you plan on doing with each other." She looked embarrassed. And then I understood, because Lanie was never comfortable talking about sex. "He looks like he will be amazing in bed, Becca. There, I said it. He looks like he will know his way around a woman's body. More than any guy here at college would, anyway."

Lanie's past with her ex and the trauma he put her through has made talking about sex a somewhat taboo thing for her. So the fact that she was in a relationship at all was a miracle. More amazing was that she was having sex with Xander. She didn't talk to me about it. I was graced with hearing it through our paper-thin walls. But I heard it, loud and clear. And it appeared Xander was pretty good at it.

"Well, you might be right. He's older, probably more experienced." I put my foot on the brake, ready to start the car, but turned to her instead. "I like us talking about sex, Lanie. Can we do this more when you feel comfortable? I need to confide some shit in you sometimes, ya know. If you're OK with it."

Her sideways look told me she was shying away from talking about it again. But she smiled and nodded, and that was good enough. Her sessions with her therapist were definitely helping her. Lanie seemed to show us a new side to her each day, evidence she was getting better.

"OK, time to go. I'm sure our ice cream is liquid by now." I put the car in gear and got us home.

Chapter 8

The drive to my hometown was only a few hours. It wasn't ideal that I needed to go home so many weekends as a college student; weekends were the time for parties and having fun. But I didn't have a choice. I had responsibilities at home I needed to tend to.

And my responsibilities were also my secret.

It was what I couldn't tell Becca, at least not yet. I wasn't ready.

But this time, I was running home the day before classes started.

The night before, in Becca's room, destroyed me. I needed to get away. And the only person I thought of seeing was Logan. So I drove home. Logan knew I was coming, and thankfully this was a day he had free. He was in a voluntary treatment program for his drinking and mental health, while doing online school as well. Some days he was at his facility all day, but not today.

I pulled into his driveway but didn't get out. Being back in my hometown, but not going to my house, gave me an odd feeling inside. It felt wrong to not go home, to not let them know I was in the area. But I needed this break, this time for me to see my friend without that added responsibility. I shot Logan a text.

My phone buzzed.

Logan:
Hey dude, you can walk right in, I'm in
my room

As I opened the front door, the house was still and quiet on the upper floors. I took a step inside, not sure if his parents were home, but quickly determined they weren't. The rooms were neat and orderly as I looked around: blankets folded on the backs of couches, shoes lined up along the front hall. Although, peering into the kitchen, I could see the remnants of a possible rushed breakfast still on the counter.

I was thankful they appeared to be at work. I liked Logan's parents, but I wasn't in the mood for questions. As I went down the stairs to the basement, which he converted to a mini apartment, I found Logan on his couch playing video games.

Perfect. It was just what I needed.

"Hey, man, how ya doin'?" Logan didn't get up, too busy with the level he was on to bother. But it didn't upset me; we were good that way. "You sounded like shit on the phone."

I found another controller and joined the game, helping shoot up the zombies attacking us. "Pledging ended last night. I was pretty hungover when I called." I saw him look over for a split second, I was sure pissed at himself for not being at school to have done that with me.

"Yeah," he responded, "that's cool. But it doesn't sound like you're too happy about it. Fuck! Watch that one—get him! No! Shoot that one in the corner! Shit, I'm dead." He threw his controller on the couch next to him and looked my way.

"No, it's cool," I told him. "The guys are great. My Big is Sam. Remember him from last year?" I looked his way to see him nod, a hint of a smile on his face. "He's a great guy. He's been great the whole pledge season about letting me, ya know, come home on the weekends." I played around with the controller in my hands, trying to find another game to play. But Logan took it out of my hands and put it on the table in front of me.

"So you drove three hours to tell me things are great." He leaned back on the couch, a hint of frustration coming through as he let out a sigh. "Ty, your life is fucked up right now. I mean, OK, you have the frat. And I'm glad you got in and all." He shook his head after saying that, hesitating. "But dude, you got some major shit you're dealing with. And what about Becca? Any changes with her?"

He cut right to the chase.

And as I sat there, knowing I came here to talk about exactly that, my words failed me. I flung myself against the cushion as my eyes tried to find answers in the cobwebs in the corners of the ceiling. Letting out a deep sigh, my lungs emptied, feeling just like my heart. Logan gave me the time I needed as he sat there, waiting patiently for me to say something.

"So, things are not going well with Becca, at all," I said.

He nodded in acknowledgment but remained quiet, giving me time to continue. But I didn't know what else

I wanted to tell him. If I put the words out there, into the universe, for him to hear, it made it *real.*

"Apparently she was really serious about this break-up," I said. As I leaned forward, my hands nervously twisted themselves together between my knees. "She, um, she went out with another guy already."

There was no reaction that I could see from Logan. Rather, he seemed to be studying me for my response to my own words. Once he realized he wasn't getting anything else out of me, he shook his head.

"And that surprises you?" he asked. "Listen, man. I really don't know what you're going through. It must be hard. But I have to say, I don't get not telling Becca. I mean, all last year? And still now? Dude, you're fuckin' up a good thing." He shook his head as he spoke, completely dumbfounded at my decisions. "It doesn't surprise me that she's moving on. Why would she wait around for you, Ty? You're not being honest with her."

"Christ, I know, Logan. I fucked up. But I don't know how to fix it now. How do I tell her this late in the game? I don't know what I was thinking. Like, why didn't I just tell her?" I pulled at my hair in anger and frustration at myself. "I told her last night I'd give her space, and I think if I don't, I'll push her away forever." Looking at him, hoping he had answers for me, I continued. "What if I already have? What if I've already lost her?"

"Nah, that's where you're not thinking clearly. It's Becca Reynolds we're talking about. She's probably fuckin' around with this guy to do exactly this." His hand pointed my way as an indication of the emotional toll this had on me. "She's no dummy, but ya know what she can be? She can be a manipulator, that one. And she doesn't lie about it;

she comes right out and tells you she's gonna go home with someone else to piss you off, Ty." He leaned forward, his hands folded on his knees, contemplating his next words. "You know she doesn't like lies. And that's all you've fed her, man."

"Would the truth have kept her around?" I said while still staring up at nothing. "I mean, once she knows, I don't think there's a chance in hell she'll stick around." My throat closed up again as I fought succumbing to tears in front of my best friend.

"How do you know that, though? You haven't given her the chance. The worst that could happen is you'd be right, and you'd be in the exact same spot you're in now. But what if you're wrong?" His voice held a hint of promise that he knew something I didn't.

"You really think she'd be in for what I've got going on? I don't think many would be, Logan." All I could do was shake my head.

"Ty, you might have gotten yourself into a tight spot, but you're handling it better than most. She would see that and respect it." He got up and walked to the pool table, racking up the balls for a game. With two sticks in his hand, he came back to me and tossed me one. "C'mon, let's play a few games. It'll take your mind off things. Maybe then we can talk about a plan to get her back."

We played a few games of pool and then went back to some video games. The creaking of floorboards above told me someone had gotten home. Logan lived with his mom and stepdad, who he had a decent relationship with; they were both instrumental in getting him into the outpatient program he was in.

His own dad wasn't around anymore. But the time they spent together was the source of Logan's issues. They didn't have the best relationship, and it had stuck with him in ways no one would have anticipated.

"How's the counseling sessions going?" I asked, not wanting to pry too much.

"Pretty good. They've got me opening up about shit I haven't talked to anyone about. Ever," he said. "So that's a good thing, I guess." He shrugged his shoulders, and I took that as my cue that he was done talking.

We continued playing our game in silence until we heard footsteps on the stairs to the basement. Both our heads swiveled to the door as it opened.

"Hey, Ty, nice to see you." Matt, his stepdad, came into the room as we both stood. He reached us and held his hand out, me gripping it tight with a shake. "What brings you back up north so quick? Doesn't the semester start soon?" Logan and I both shared a secretive glance before I responded. They didn't know what I was dealing with, either.

"Yeah, actually, classes start tomorrow. Just wanted a quick visit with Logan before I got too busy with school. See how he's doing." It wasn't a lie, just not the whole truth.

"Knew there was a reason I always liked you, Ty." Matt smiled widely as he slapped me on the back. "Logan's been doing great. We've been keeping up with his group meetings with the counselors, and they say if he keeps it up, they recommend he head back to school in the spring." His gaze shifted toward Logan, eyes wary as he waited for the reaction to his words. Logan kept his face neutral as the three of us stood quietly for an awkward moment. Needing to break the tension, I was the one to talk next.

"That's great to hear, Matt. It'll be great if Logan can be back there with me." And I meant it; I needed him there.

"Well, I'll leave you guys to it. Maeve should be home soon. Make sure to see her before you head out, Ty. Good to see you."

Once we were back on the couch, Logan finally seemed to relax. I gave him a minute before the inquisition.

"What was that about? I'd've thought you'd be looking to get back next semester." I picked up the controller, trying to be as nonchalant as I could. Starting up a new game, we both settled in to playing. It took a few minutes for him to say something.

"I am," he said, "but just because I want to get back there doesn't mean it's the right thing for me."

I wasn't exactly sure what he meant by that, but again, I decided to let it go. And a few minutes of silence passed between us as we continued with our game.

"I thought about a few things I've learned in my sessions," Logan suddenly blurted out, "that might help you with Becca. If you want to hear them." He seemed nervous to be talking about his program, his hands fidgeting with the controller but not really playing the game.

"Yeah, Logan, sure. I'd be interested in hearing about it even if it doesn't help me." He smiled warily at me, his nerves not yet settled. Pausing the game, we both put the controllers down. I turned myself toward him, giving my undivided attention.

"I mean, of course there's shit that's just about being sober. But there's other stuff that makes you think," he said.

There was a spark to his voice when he spoke, as if the information he was learning was sinking in and motivating him. I was happy to see this Logan in front of me. "One they make us say a lot is *'I am right where I am supposed to be.'* That just seems to work for you. This has happened for some reason, man. I don't know what it is, but there's a reason."

What the hell could the reason for the spot I got myself in be?

"There are so many that could help, but the other I think you need to hear is *'I am in control of my own life.'*" He stopped speaking for a moment, letting the words sink in. "That one's really hit home with me. I needed to be told that in order to take that control away from my dad. I still feel like he has control over me, even though . . ." An audible swallow and sharp exhale of breath told the story of where he was with his journey and his real father. "It's your life, Ty. You need to take some control of how it's going to look moving forward. Don't leave all the decisions to other people."

Logan had trouble making eye contact when he finished talking. I couldn't tell if he was embarrassed by the situations he put himself in or if he was uncomfortable being the one giving me advice.

But it was good advice. And they were words I needed to hear; he was right.

"Hey, it sounds like you *are* doing better. I'm happy for you, man." Reaching out, my arm wrapped around his wide shoulder and we did a hug thing. "I appreciate it, Logan, and you're right. It *is* my life. Deciding for myself, you're right on that one. I need to step up and do more of that. But other lives are affected by my actions as well."

He immediately nodded in agreement. "Of course, and I get it. But don't let other people control the destiny of your life."

"I will take those words under advisement." Logan didn't seem to want to say much more after that, and we both remained quiet, sitting on the couch together. Eventually the silence became deafening.

"So—" Logan started.

I talked over him and said, "I'm really happy for you, Logan. You definitely sound like you're on the right track. I hope that means you'll make it back to Blue Ridge next semester." I stood once I realized how late it was. I still had an over two-hour drive back to campus and an early class in the morning. Logan joined me as I started up the stairs and moved toward the front door. "I miss ya, man. I really would like you back there."

"We didn't even have time to talk about anyone else. You sure you have to leave already?" The desperation in his voice made me sad enough to stop heading toward the door. Once at the top of the stairs, I turned his way. There was a deep sadness in his downturned eyes, almost anguish. Looking away, he tried to hide that he was lonely and missing all of us. "How's Lanie? And Xander?"

Feeling the need to give him more of my time, I stopped in the foyer before heading out the front door. Seeing him, I knew he had more questions about Lanie than just how she was doing. I was pretty sure he still had feelings for her, but that didn't end well for him last year. Not when his drunken-ass hands manhandled her and it sent her into a full-blown panic attack. No one had been aware yet of the extent of "damage" her ex from home had done to her. Not that it excused his behavior, but her past made it worse. And his drinking resulted from his own issues.

"They're good. Better than me and Becca, let's put it that way. She and I are the ones providing the drama this year." He laughed at that, appreciating the picture it provided in his head. We continued out the door together and walked on the front path that led to my car in the street. I fiddled with my keys as my hands rested on the hood of my car, Logan on the sidewalk. "They've got two new roommates, Ava and Macie, that they're becoming good friends with. You would like them." His eyebrows rose when he mentioned the other girls, and I knew exactly where his mind went. "I won't be a stranger, alright? I'll be by. Keep up the good work with your counselors. I need ya there." I slapped my hand on the hood, alerting him I was heading out.

"Thanks, man, for the visit and all," he said.

"Hey, it was me who needed you today, not the other way around. Friends, right, man?"

His smile grew a bit as I opened the door to my car and slid in. Driving away, I saw Logan in the rearview mirror.

I thought about the words he said to me and how they might help me in my life.

I *was* in control of my own life. And I had made some terrible decisions, but now was the time to rectify some of those poor decisions and make good on them.

Giving Becca space was going to be one of the hardest things in my life. But I knew I needed to in order to win her back in the long run.

I only hoped I had the willpower to stay away from her.

CHAPTER 9

Becca

etting to class when not living on campus was a whole other ball of wax. Christ, I waited for three buses to come through, and all were full. I didn't get a parking permit because this damn school raved about how great their bus system was. But I only had twenty minutes to get to my first class of the semester with no more buses coming. My panic set in as I started the walk—rather, the slow jog—back to my apartment. Maybe I could find a spot on campus somewhere for the day and not get towed or a ticket.

Fat chance. What was I even thinking? The school preyed upon people like that. I think they made enough in those charges to run the entire athletic department. Tears threatened to spill from my eyes as I approached my apartment. I didn't have a plan. All of my roommates had earlier classes and were already gone. My mood hadn't been helped by the message I listened to this morning from Ty. When he called last night, I chose not to answer, letting it go to voicemail. I couldn't talk to him. My resolve hadn't done well for me with him this past week, and I needed to keep my distance for a bit.

My foot had hit the first step of my porch when I heard my name. I turned around and saw my knight in shining armor riding in his 'Stang.

"Gage!" I ran to his car, out of breath from my trek from the bus stop. "Oh my God, I'm so glad to see you. I couldn't get a bus to campus. Where are you headed? I'm going to miss my first class; no one is here to give me a ride. Do you have time?" I was rambling again, but it was rumored the professor of my first class was a hard-ass, so I needed to get there.

"Becca, take a breath, babe. Take a breath and hop in. That's where I'm headed. I can drop you off right at your building." Gage reached across his console and pushed the passenger door open as I rounded the car. I was excited because he had the top down today, too. I plopped myself in the seat and let out an enormous sigh. Immediately thankful for the hair tie on my wrist, I wrangled my hair into a messy bun to avoid wind-induced knots.

"Thank you, Gage. Thank you so much." Before I could start on another of my ramblings, his hand came over the top of mine, which was latched on to the strap of my backpack sitting on my lap. It was warm and comforting. It calmed me.

"Hey, no worries. I can probably get you to campus most days. We should compare our schedules. And even if I don't have class, chances are I'll need to be on campus, anyway. This grad program is not for the faint of heart." He worked my hand out of the strap and pulled it over the console between us, intertwining our fingers. It felt natural for him to be holding my hand, like everything else with him.

"Classes seem like they'll be tough this semester?" I asked while trying to act as normal as he was. Though my heart raced like it would beat out of my chest. Him holding my hand was part of it, but not all. I needed to take advantage of this impromptu meeting and just talk to him. He could probably tell. I think my pulse was throbbing in my wrist against his arm. And my palm became sweaty; he had to feel that.

"Yeah, and with the added responsibility of having to be a grad assistant in a lower-level class, my time will be tight," he responded.

As I nodded, I realized how little time I had. The ride was only six or seven minutes, but I had to ask him. I knew I needed to just blurt it out and get it over with.

"So, do you have any time to meet up on campus today? I thought we could talk." My voice was unusually choppy, and I didn't ramble. Two signs I was a nervous wreck. I stole a glance in his direction, and although his eyes remained on the road, his mouth turned up into a small grin.

"Yeah, I think I can find some time for you. What are you doing after this class? Want to meet up at the coffee shop?" His thumb started rubbing those circles on my hand while he spoke. How could such a simple movement have such a profound effect on me? Shit, my stomach dropped and felt like it had an insect trying to crawl out of it. And then my breaths were scarce, making me thankful the top was down for the extra air.

But I had to rein myself in. I remembered having these feelings with Ty as well. This was how it always felt when things were shiny and new. The excitement of the hunt and being the hunted was what I was experiencing, nothing more. This would fade.

"Sure, that sounds good." He had pulled up to my building and I started opening the door, but he stopped me. I turned toward him, and now his face held more than a grin. The sultry look took me by surprise, even more as he leaned over the console.

"I'm going to kiss you, Becca, not Rebecca." After he shifted the car to park, his hand reached out for the back of my head and pulled me close, our mouths about to touch. But then he stopped. "I want you to think of me while you're in class." And he didn't just kiss me—he devoured me. Our lips became one, our tongues lashed together as if in a fight. His grip on the back of my head tightened as he pulled at my hair, the pain heightening the sensation of our kiss. My hands reciprocated the action, running through his dark waves, trying to prolong what I knew was ending. His mouth started its retreat, his lips peppering mine with tiny pecks. But he remained close, our mouths touching, our breaths mingling. "I hope that was memorable enough for you."

And then a loud whistle sounded from someone walking by. Shit, I forgot the top was down and we were in the wide open for everyone to see.

But Gage didn't care; he laughed. He knew damn well what he'd done to me, my legs shifting in the seat, trying to stifle the need I was feeling.

"Don't worry; I could use a cold shower right about now as well." He needed to readjust his jeans with his other hand, but he still hadn't pulled away from my face. "Good thing I have some time before I need to meet with my advisor. I can let this thing settle down."

"I have to go," I whispered against his mouth. I couldn't be late to class simply because Gage was an amazing kisser. I pulled back and grabbed my bag while opening the door.

"See ya in a bit," he called to me over the top of the car, and I started up the path. As he pulled away, I waved and started walking toward my building. Being in a rush, I wasn't watching where I was going, and crashed right into a hard body exiting the building.

A body that I recognized the scent of.

Fuck.

Had he seen us in the car? And I didn't have time for this; I needed to get to class, which started in less than five minutes.

Ty's hands reached out to steady me, and that familiar buzz ran through my body. The feeling that was the entire reason I spent every waking moment with him last year. My body was immediately aching for him, every cell betraying my brain and my heart. I chanced a look up at him, hoping my resolve to continue this "break" wouldn't *break*. We might have been broken up. And he even knew about the kiss from the other night. But that didn't mean I wanted him to witness me making out with someone else already. That would just be cruel. Seeing him do that with someone else would destroy me.

But I realized he hadn't seen Gage and me. I could tell the moment I looked at him and he was smiling down at me.

"Hi, Bec." His voice was full of unsaid apologies, as were his eyes. Our chance meeting had made him happy. And his hands lingered on my arms.

But, I didn't have time.

"Hey, Ty, sorry, but I'm running so late for my first class. I've gotta go. I'll see ya later, OK?" I pulled myself from his hold just as his eyes caught sight of Gage's car pulling away. I took off through the doors and up the stairs. I made it to a seat with only seconds to spare before the lights went off and the projector started with the first slide of the lesson. Unsure if the feeling in my stomach was from the new emotions I was having for Gage or the run-in with Ty, I tried to forget them both and focus on the professor's voice.

Fat chance.

It felt good getting the first class out of the way, and the professor was nowhere near as bad as the rumors made him out to be. I started my walk to the commons area to meet up with Gage, enjoying the view along the way. BRU was one of the prettiest campuses in the country. As I looked around, I knew why. The mountains surrounding us were a distant landscape that was breathtaking, especially in the fall when the leaves were changing. We weren't there yet, but it would be here before we knew it. And the architecture of the buildings on site was amazing, all of them made from a gray stone quarried from local sources. It made the buildings look old even if they weren't, almost as if they were in a *Harry Potter* movie.

There was a third thing I always watched for as I walked the campus: the good-looking guys. There was a plethora of them here, no shortage in that department. Most likely because of the draw of the major sports teams we had to choose from. But today I kept my eyes forward and didn't let them stray.

Two was enough for me to handle.

I made my way to the coffee line, which was always long. I texted Gage, asking him for his order since I didn't see him anywhere. It took him a few minutes to get back to me.

Gage:

Hey Becca, running late, I'll meet you outside the commons door by the bench

Once I got to the bench, I remembered it was the same one I found Lanie sitting on at the beginning of last year. We didn't know each other well at that point, and she was still so quiet and reserved. I often thought she and I would never become friends, but I was glad I never gave up on her. She needed me then, and still did. And I needed her; I just didn't let on how much that often.

"Penny for your thoughts," Gage said as he sat next to me.

"Oh, hi. I didn't see you coming." My nerves kicked in. I was torn between thinking they were from the newness of everything or the talk I wanted to have. "Here's your coffee. Very boring, by the way."

He took the cup and let out one of his signature deep laughs I was becoming accustomed to hearing.

"Boring? Just because I don't order one of those drinks laden with syrups and sugar doesn't make me boring. It makes me traditional. There's nothing wrong with being traditional." He took a loud, exaggerated slurp of his "traditional" coffee. "Ahh, delicious. Simple and delicious." He looked over at my hands, the cup I was holding, gesturing with a nod of his chin. "Let me guess—that is some form of a spiced pumpkin latte with foam."

"Uhm, yes, it is. And it's fabulous." I then took my own exaggerated sip.

We both laughed, enjoying the simplicity of the moment.

"Want to take a walk?" he asked. "There's a spot on this campus I love, and I haven't seen it since I've been back. I thought we could have our talk there. That is, if you have enough time." He stood, and I grabbed his outstretched hand to stand with him.

"Yeah, sure. I don't have anything until two." We started walking, close to each other but not touching. As much as I enjoyed the feel of whatever this was, I couldn't deny the hint of nerves wrapped around my heart. *What if we ran into Ty? How would I handle that? How will I handle that?* It was bound to happen eventually, but I didn't look forward to hurting him.

We walked toward the pond. Safe to say it was not only his favorite spot, but the favorite of most students. It was a beautiful location, the water surrounded by a running path with large oak trees hanging overhead. Some might argue it was the size of a small lake, but its nickname on campus was "the pond."

We were on the path, but he kept walking, passing by several benches we could have sat on. I wasn't sure where he was taking us, and he sensed my hesitancy; he reached for my hand as we continued walking.

"It's right up here." He pulled me off the path, my feet sinking into the grass between the gravel and the water's edge. It was a warm day, and I was tempted to take my shoes off to enjoy the feel of those blades between my toes. We rounded a massive tree whose branches hung well over the body of the pond, making it look like we would step in water on its other side. But a hidden platform that jutted out surprised me. The tree kept it well covered in shade.

"Not many people know this is here. Unless you veer off the path, you can't really see it. I found it my sophomore year, and I've only told a handful of people about it." Gage took his shoes off once we arrived at its end, and then started rolling his pants up. "Go ahead, take your shoes off. At least you don't have long pants on, too."

Chucking my sandals behind us, I sat at the edge, but I was hesitant to put my feet in. "What's in this water? Are there fish or turtles, anything that can bite me? I really don't feel like losing a toe today." I dipped my big toe in, and the water felt amazing. The day was warming, the sun almost directly above us already. The leaves filtered the rays of the sun, but it was still going to be a hot day. Once my toe hit the water, I forgot about all critters and relished in the coolness it provided. Both my legs went in, the water almost up to mid-shin, as I leaned back on my hands, looking out.

We remained quiet for a while, soaking in our surroundings. The view from this vantage point was that of the distant mountain range. I made a mental note to come back when the leaves started changing.

"This was my spot to come to when I needed to escape or to think. It's calm here, don't ya think?" Gage asked.

My head slanted in his direction before I answered. "I could use some calm in my life." I knew I needed to tell him what we came here to discuss, but how does one say yes to a repeated booty call? Plus, I wasn't so sure he was going to like my terms.

"So, I have something I want to talk to you about." Looking out over the pond, I was suddenly short on words. "I, uh, want to talk about your, um, proposal from the other night." The heat of my embarrassment raced up my chest to my cheeks. A sheen of light sweat formed on my forehead as I tried to continue but couldn't.

"Becca, I'm not asking you to be my slut. You look really uncomfortable right now. When I said what I said, it was simply to make sure you had no expectations for the future. We would hang out, have fun. There's nothing wrong with that; we're adults."

I took a cleansing breath after he finished.

"I'm that transparent, huh?" I chuckled. "I've just never been in a non-relationship relationship before. It's new for me. And there's something else I want to talk about as well." My eyes fell away from his, focusing on a lily pad floating near my foot. I flicked my toes at it, watching the ripples make it bounce up and down in the mini waves I created. "You already know that I recently broke it off with Ty. He's not real happy that I saw you the other night, and he's still working on getting us back together." I struggled with my next words, wanting to make sure they came out right. "I don't want to be in *this*"—I gestured between us with my fingers—"without being completely upfront and honest, since that's not what I was getting from him. I'm attracted to you. I do want to do this, but I can't believe that there won't be drama, you know, when he finds out we're *more*. And I don't know if you're up for that." I snuck a peek at him once I finished my ramble. He was looking at me, a small grin warming his face.

"You're adorable when you're nervous." He pulled his legs out of the water and leaned his back against the tree next to the dock. He widened his legs and patted the spot between them, an invitation to join him. I settled against his chest, and his arms went around my waist, both of us looking at the water. His chin rested on the top of my head before he spoke again. "Becca, I'm a big boy. I think I can handle whatever comes our way. And if things get too complicated and you want out, well, that's why we're keeping it simple."

I moved, trying to get comfortable on the wooden platform, pushing myself closer to him between his legs.

And that was when I felt it.

His hardness against my lower back. And yes, he was a big boy.

His hands rubbed along my stomach as we sat there, those same fluttery feelings from before erupting in my belly again. Thankfully, he was behind me and didn't see the hardening of my nipples. I maneuvered a bit, trying to rub my thighs together, attempting to relieve some of the coiled tension building between my legs.

Then his fingers dipped under the lower edge of my tank, slowly working up my torso. Even though we were hidden, the chance of getting caught heightened my senses. My eyes scanned the area, checking for people, eyes on us, but I came up empty.

Bumps broke out all over my skin, and I knew he felt them. His low moan of approval told me so.

"Did you think about me in class, Becca?" he whispered in my ear. His sultry voice only intensified the burning that was building inside me.

"Yes," I said breathlessly.

"Good, because now I'd like to give you something else to remember. Just lean back and close your eyes." His words sounded like a command with no true bite to them, but I listened.

As soon as my head hit his chest, one hand pushed my shirt and bra up and out of the way, both breasts fully exposed. My hands instinctively covered myself as I opened my eyes in sudden fear.

"Relax, I'm looking out. I won't let anyone see you. I don't *want* anyone else to see you, so they won't. Sit back and let me do this." His hands came over mine and peeled them off my body. His fingers returned and went straight to my nipples, which were already hard from the fresh air. He rolled and pinched them, which sent shock waves to the nub between my legs. As soon as I closed my legs to aid in the intense need, a hand stopped me. "Uh-uh, no relief down there yet. It needs to build up. Let it build; then I'll take care of you." Gage was literally holding my thighs apart. Fuck! I needed to rub them together, and it was taking everything in me to not reach down and touch myself. But something told me he wouldn't let me do that, either.

As his left hand continued its assault on my nipple, the right kneaded the other breast, pushing them together. "Becca, I've been dreaming of touching you, touching your tits, ever since you were bouncing on that couch. They're amazing, perfect." His mouth was at my ear, kissing my lobe, his tongue dipping in, causing my body to shiver in his arms. "Your skin is like silk, from your ears," he whispered as his tongue moved farther down, "to your neck." His fingertips brushed the side of my breast, the sensation causing me to moan. "Shh, that will definitely attract some fans. I want you all to myself." He glided his hand along my side. "This skin right here"—he continued caressing my breast as he spoke—"on the side of your tit, that might be the softest skin I've felt in my life. I can't wait to taste it."

Then his hand moved to my thigh, grazing it lightly. I bit my lower lip to keep from making any noises as his hand migrated up, his fingers dipping under the hem of my shorts. As his fingers moved higher, his grip on my nipple increased, the pinch turning to a pull. The sensation intensified as his hand reached under my panties. But then, just as quickly, his hand retreated, landing on my inner thigh, giving me a squeeze.

I couldn't take any more. I started scrambling out of his arms, wanting him to do . . . more!

But he gripped me in place against his chest, one arm across my breasts, the other turning my head toward his mouth.

"I love that I do this to you, but you need to learn to take things slow. It's not a sprint. Allow this to spread through you, to take its time and grow. I'll take you to the edge and back many times, if you'll let me."

I squirmed in his arms. "I want to go *over* the edge, Gage."

"We'll take the plunge, don't worry, but you have to trust me." After he said that, he waited, not moving, as if needing my answer. I gave it to him by closing my eyes as I leaned my head back. I pushed his hands to my breasts and he kneaded them before starting the slow torture of my nipples once again. Thankfully, a hand started its journey down my body. My running shorts were stretchy enough for him to slide over, my core fully exposed and awaiting his touch. But the shorts wouldn't stay open for him, so he needed to use both of his hands, and they came around my hips and over my thighs.

"Becca, we should not leave those tits of yours unattended. I think you should take over for me." As his left hand pulled my shorts all the way open, my hands went to my chest, attacking my own breasts in anticipation of Gage's hand finally touching me.

"Please, Gage, I need you to touch me. I want you inside me."

But he still took his time. His finger found the edges of me, running up and down, teasing me. His finger touched every inch of me while being able to avoid the important parts; I was borderline frantic. Finally, he stopped at my entrance. His now wet finger traced a circle around my opening, teasing. My back arched, trying to force more from him, wanting more. But he held me against him, his hands pushing my thighs.

"Relax." That was his only word in my ear.

My fingers started an assault on my nipples, hoping to take the edge off. I pinched, I pulled, all the things I watched him do to me moments before.

His finger moved closer to my opening, almost pushing inside me, and I froze. I wanted to feel the moment he entered me. He pushed in, then pulled out, rubbing his finger all over my pussy.

"You are so wet, so fucking wet. You're dripping all over me. I look forward to the day when it's my tongue down there." His words brought me even closer to an orgasm than his hands did. As soon as he finished talking, his finger thrust deep inside me. While his other hand held me down, my hips tried to thrust up with the intensity. I turned my face into his chest, muffling my moans against his shirt. But then his other hand worked its way to the apex of my sex. He opened me up, exposing it, and grabbed a hold of my clit.

"Someone is really turned on, huh? Your clit is so swollen and big in my fingers. Do you want me to rub it or pinch it? What feels better?"

"Fuck!" I whisper screamed into his chest. "Gage, I'm going to come!"

"Tell me what to do to your clit, Becca. Rub or pinch?"

I didn't care at that moment; I just wanted him to keep touching me. I was so close. But then his hands stopped all movement.

My eyes shot up to him in disapproval, anger.

"Becca, tell me what you want. Gentle or rough?"

It had been so long, I really didn't care; I just knew I needed his hands on me, in me, doing anything he could to release these built-up sensations inside of me dying to get out.

"Rough! Fucking pinch me!" I yelled, needing him to get back to work.

And he did. He pulled my clit out of its hood, in between his two fingers, and squeezed it to the point where I almost had to tell him to stop. The combination of pleasure and pain was new to me, but I quickly determined that I fucking loved it as my body writhed in his grip. Then two fingers plunged inside me, pumping in and out, hard. I was at that cliff, ready to go over. The orgasm was at its peak when he somehow shifted us and I fell to the side of him. His lips landed on my nipple as he sucked it deep into his mouth. One hand now did the work of two, driving hard inside me as his thumb found my clit.

My hands reached for his head, pulling him against my chest as he furiously devoured my breast. As his hand worked his magic between my legs, he quickly learned the attention he gave my clit was what earned him the moans in his ear. That hard bundle of nerves became his entire focus as his fingers swirled it between them, pulling on it just the right amount.

That kicked me over the edge.

And I fell.

Hard.

My body shook uncontrollably as the orgasm soared through me, continuous, as if it would never end. My legs contorted in my ecstasy, their own attempt to move his hand, the feeling so intense. But Gage held tight, his fingers still swirling around my clit as his tongue laved my nipple. The movements slowed gradually; his mouth started peppering my breast with kisses as his hand rubbed along the inside of my thighs, the orgasm nearing its end.

And when it was over, my eyes found him smiling down on me. He used his one arm to hold me while the other put my shorts back in place. I pulled my bra and tank down, but he didn't let go, keeping me in his arms.

My immediate response was to reach for the button of his jeans. I felt the hard bulge beneath the zipper of his pants as I did. His hands came over the top of mine, holding them still. Eventually, he moved my hands away while keeping them in his grip. I looked up, the question in my eyes.

"Not now," he said. "This was just about you."

All I could offer him was a small smile and a nod.

We sat quietly for a few moments, me looking up at him while he stared out at the water. It was quiet around us since no one had come walking by on the path, which stressed the silence between us. I wouldn't say it had become awkward, but it was on its way. To prevent that from happening, I started sitting up, making my move to get going.

But he stilled me and pulled me to face him. Our eyes connected right before his lips consumed mine. A kiss was not what I was expecting. As contradictory as it may seem, a kiss felt too intimate. And I knew we'd kissed already, but this was supposed to be simple, a hookup. Kisses were more than that.

But kiss me he did.

"I think this has become my new favorite spot, too," I chuckled as he pulled his mouth from mine.

"Yeah, definitely a newfound love for this spot," he said.

Using my hands to push up, I sat next to him, further adjusting my clothes along the way.

"I've always loved coming here," he continued. "But I can honestly say it was never quite this exciting."

I looked over at him as my face flushed a deep crimson, suddenly embarrassed by what I allowed him to do. We barely knew each other, and that was, well, that was intense.

And Lanie was right; he knew his way around a woman's body, which made him very dangerous for me. But I wouldn't be thinking about that. Not now, anyway.

"Oh, shit! What time is it?" I screeched as I scrambled to my feet. Finding my sandals in the grass, I shoved my feet in them and hooked my backpack on my shoulder.

"Almost two. Have another class?" he asked, looking up at me casually from his seat against the tree.

"No, but I have a meeting for my business fraternity and I'm running late!"

The thousand-watt smile he gave me, coupled with the five o'clock shadow he had by midday, was almost enough to make me want to miss it; he looked fuckin' hot.

"Well, I'm sorry, Becca. I don't want you to be late."

"There are worse reasons to be late for something," I said as I stared down at him, wondering if he was going to get up or not. But I knew it would be better if he didn't; I wouldn't be able to leave anytime soon. I started taking a few steps down the pier, toward the path. "You're making a habit of sending me off with something to think of you by."

He laughed out loud. "I guess I am. How am I doing?" He leaned against his knees, watching me walk away.

"Not bad," I said, walking backward. "This last one, definitely your best effort. It might be hard to concentrate in this meeting."

"Well, that's better than 'not bad' then. That sounds like I did pretty damn good, if you ask me." He gave a small wave as I started walking faster.

"See ya later, Gage."

"See ya later, not Rebecca."

Chapter 10

Almost the entire week of classes passed and I hadn't seen Becca. Not since the first day, anyway. It saddened me. Last year we spent every spare moment together. At the same time, it also meant I hadn't seen her with Gage, either. I didn't know how I'd have handled it if I had.

I had nothing personal against Gage; apparently all the guys in the frat really liked him. And maybe I would have, too, if he wasn't moving in on Becca. He offered a lot of things to her I couldn't: mainly the ability to be completely honest with her.

Logan's words had been swimming around in my head since I saw him last week. I wasn't entirely sure *I'm where I'm supposed to be* in my life. But I could get on board with taking control of my own life. I needed to do more of that. Withholding my truth from her, I thought, had been the right decision; it wasn't something I felt she'd want to deal with. But I knew it was a mistake and I needed to fix it before I lost her for good.

If I hadn't already.

Now I needed to move on and figure out a new normal without her in my life, at least for now. Giving her the space I promised her was turning out to be a lot harder than I anticipated, considering our friends were mutual.

But I wasn't going to stop being friends with my friends.

Me:

Want to meet for lunch

Lanie:

Sure meet me around 1 usual spot

Me:

Will Becca be with you

Lanie:

She'll be coming at 1:30

OK, so I would have a quick lunch with Lanie and hightail it out of there before Becca showed up. Grabbing my backpack, I took off for the bus stop.

The cafeteria was crowded. It always was in the beginning of the semester until everyone got used to their schedules, and then it settled in. Scanning the crowded room for our usual spot, I didn't see Lanie there yet, but I was a few minutes early. I did see Jake, though, so I maneuvered through the masses of people.

"Hey, man, what's up?" Jake asked.

"Waiting for someone. Did you have class yet?"

He was already eating a full tray of food. There was a mix of some Asian food, plus a salad and even a sandwich in front of him. Nodding, he tried to answer me, but his mouth was unable to form words around the food spilling from it.

"Woah, dude, take it easy," I told him, clapping him on his back. He shrugged away from me, laughing.

"I'm fine," he said finally. "Yeah, already had a class, have another in about an hour. What about you?"

Pulling out the chair across from him, I took a seat while keeping my eyes on the crowd and making sure to not miss Lanie. "I've got a class in an hour as well. Came here to meet Lanie for lunch."

His head snapped up when I said that. "Lanie?" His tone said it all.

My eyes narrowed at him immediately. "Dude, she's one of my best friends. What the fuck? And so is Xander." Shaking my head, I continued looking around the room.

"Just checking. Wasn't sure why you weren't meeting Becca," he questioned.

But as he finished his words, I saw Lanie walk in the door. I waved, and I knew she saw me as her eyes lit up and she smiled wide. She made her way to the table, and I found a chair for her.

"Lanie, you remember Jake, my roommate, right?"

"Hi, Jake. Yeah, we saw each other at the party on the first day back. How are you?"

At least Jake was brought up well. He stood up, wiped his hands on a napkin, and held one out to Lanie. "Hey, Lanie, good to see you again. I'm fine, how are you?"

They continued with some pleasantries while I went to get some food for the two of us. I knew exactly what Lanie wanted, a green salad with grilled chicken, a most boring meal. But it was what she liked. When I returned, she had Jake laughing out loud.

"Holy shit, he did that?" Jake cackled. Somehow, I knew they were exchanging stories about me. But I was fine with it because I appreciated that they were connecting, even if it was at my expense.

"Yep," Lanie said, her side eye catching mine conspiratorially as her laugh settled. "But more about that later," she whispered. "Thanks, Ty." She took the tray of food from me and started making her salad the way she liked while I sat down with my huge sandwich and soda.

As I was about to take my first huge bite, I felt the chair next to me pull out, the metal legs scraping along the floor. Lanie's eyes went wide as a familiar body fell on the chair next to mine.

"Hey, Ty."

The sultry voice belonged to none other than Kayla.

"Hi, Kayla."

So many things were supposed to happen with those two words. They were supposed to be a nice enough greeting for her; I didn't want to be mean. But they also needed to let her know I wasn't interested. Plus, I needed them to show Lanie I had no interest in Kayla as well. I had no idea if any of that came through in my tone.

Kayla's hand went immediately to my arm.

I guessed I failed.

"You're Lanie, right?" Kayla said, thankfully not in a mean or rude way. She wasn't being her typical self at the moment. She was being . . . nicer.

"Hi, yes, I am. I remember you from some of the parties last year, but we never met. It's nice to meet you."

Lanie was probably only at one party, if that, last year where she could have met Kayla. But Lanie was always going to be this polite. Lanie's freshman year didn't leave her that many opportunities to have *fun* with all the shit she put up with from her ex. But with Xander in her corner, she got through it and has become a completely new person this year.

"Nice to meet you, too. You're still with Xander, aren't you? You guys make a really cute couple."

That made me turn my head in disbelief. She sounded, well, she sounded like a nice person for the second time already. Even Jake took notice.

"Better watch it, Kayla. The devils down below will be turning in their graves with all this niceness from you," Jake said. He laughed, but Kayla looked a bit hurt. Jake went right back to eating and hadn't noticed, but Lanie and I did.

Lanie caught my eye, and I knew what she was going to do.

"Do you want to join us for lunch, Kayla?"

I closed my eyes in despair. I knew it was the right thing to do. It was what she wanted; she was alone with no one to eat with.

But I didn't need her getting any wrong messages from me. At. All.

"Oh my God, I would love to, Lanie, thank you! I'm just gonna go grab something—I'll be right back." She jumped from her seat, securing it first with her bag, and literally ran to the food line.

Lanie caught my look immediately.

"What? She seemed so sad, Ty. So lonely. I had to ask her," she explained.

Nodding, I responded, "I know, I get it. But I need to be out of here before Becca gets here. That will be the worst thing that can happen right now for us. If she even thinks I'm talking to someone else..."

"Why don't we rearrange the seats? She can sit by me or Jake. Then, if Becca comes, it won't be such a big deal." But as we stood to rearrange the seats, Kayla returned and sat right next to me.

"Where are you guys going?" she asked.

Lanie and I slowly sat back down as if we were only fixing our chairs.

"Just trying to make more room; I think Xander is coming soon," Lanie offered.

I looked her way to see if it was true, and she nodded to let me know it was. That was good; I hadn't seen him since he gave me the bad news about Becca; I wanted to thank him for being honest with me.

Everyone fell into a normal conversation at the table while eating, including Jake. He was on the other side of Kayla and had taken up a chat with her, taking her attention from me, which was just fine. It was only then I had realized how quickly the time had passed.

It was already past one thirty.

Becca should have been here. And I should have been long gone. To keep my word to her.

Gathering up my half-eaten sandwich and wrapping it up for later, it was obvious I was starting to get ready to leave. Packing my belongings into my bag, I started to stand from my chair, but Kayla stopped me, her hand on my arm again.

"Ty, where are you going? You didn't finish eating?"

"Yeah, Ty, where are you going in such a rush?"

Everyone froze.

Lanie looked behind me, her blue eyes as big as saucers and a huge tell. I didn't need to turn around. I could feel her, sense her.

Defeated, I put my bag on my chair.

"Don't leave on my account, Ty," Becca said as she stomped around to the other side of the table toward Lanie.

Lanie's troubled eyes caught mine as I tried to decide what to do. I fiddled with the handle of my backpack and watched Becca pull out a chair, careful not to look at me once.

"I'll be back; I'm getting something to eat," Becca said in Lanie's direction.

"OK, Bec," Lanie said softly, her tone indicating she was almost as nervous as I was.

"Hey, everybody," a loud booming voice said from behind me. I jumped a little, not prepared for Xander's entrance. When I turned his way, he took stock of my face and looked toward Lanie next. "Everything OK? Something I should know about?" Xander's first concern was always Lanie, especially after what they went through last year.

But her warm smile set him at ease, his shoulders relaxing immediately. His hand went to my shoulder as he spoke again. "Ah, I'm guessing there's trouble in paradise?"

I left his question unanswered since I could see Becca making her way back to the table. Searching our setup, I realized we didn't have room for all of us anyway, which was the perfect reason for me to get up and go. As she approached her chair next to Lanie, I pulled away from mine. "Here, Xander, take my seat. I was just going."

Xander looked a bit confused, but then followed my sight line, seeing the same tight-lipped fake smile on Becca as she found her seat. If her eyes could bore a hole of fire through my skull, they would have at that moment. She turned to Lanie and said something quiet between the two of them, refusing to look my way.

I was in limbo. I had no idea if I should say anything to her or not. She was obviously mad at me, had obviously walked up on Kayla touching me. But she also hadn't seen that in the past ten minutes, Kayla's attention had been on Jake. The two of them had been talking nonstop.

"Hey, man, want me to go sit somewhere else with you?" Xander asked, I thought quiet enough the girls wouldn't hear. But they did hear.

Becca Reynolds was a firecracker. Everyone knew that. She always had a comeback for anyone's wiseass comment. She always got the last word in after a fight. But that was what people loved about her; that was what I loved about her. So I was fully expecting some snarky words from her, considering how she felt about me and our current state of affairs.

But when she lifted her head, I saw unshed tears in her eyes and the hard swallow in her throat that she needed to take in order to not let the tears fall.

And that nearly broke me.

"No," she said, so quiet we almost didn't hear her. "Xander, stay." She looked around the room, still avoiding me. But then her eyes connected with mine, the glistening wetness challenging her full lashes in an attempt to spill over them. "Ty, you should stay, too," she whispered, then looked away. The attempt to hide the tear that slid down her cheek failed.

I had to do something; I couldn't make her stay here like this.

"Hey, guys, you mind if I steal Becca for a minute?"

Lanie's eyes went to Becca, as did mine, as Becca's head pivoted to me after I said that.

"Ty," Becca said with more force this time, "we have nothing to say to one another." She paused, but then the assault came. "Besides"—her hand gestured down the table to where Jake and Kayla sat—"I don't want to keep you from your other *friends*. You seemed busy when I came in."

Huh, she *was* jealous.

I walked over to where Becca was sitting and placed my hand on her arm, encouraging her to stand with me. She didn't resist, rather giving in much easier than I'd anticipated. Keeping her head down, she wrapped her arms around her in a protective way, pulling out of my hold.

I leaned down, close to her ear, in an attempt to calm her down. "Bec, let's head somewhere to talk for a minute, OK? I don't like seeing you like this, and I don't want to leave with you crying."

She nodded as she moved against me in a move to leave with me, somewhere.

I looked around the cafeteria in a panic, realizing there wasn't anywhere to talk privately. But then Lanie came to my rescue.

"There's a bench out that door. It's not that secluded, but I don't think many people will pay attention to you outside." I nodded as she pointed to a door on the other side of the cafeteria. Becca started walking first, and I followed closely behind. We found it exactly where Lanie said it would be, and it even had the shade of a tree over it. Becca sat on one end, me on the other.

And then there was silence.

I leaned forward against my thighs, my hands between my knees, and looked her way. She was watching the people walk by, her gaze lofty as it focused in the distance.

Then I realized I needed to be the one to start this. "Bec, what you saw when you walked in was nothing. Kayla means nothing. She's already moved on to talking to Jake, if you haven't noticed," I said, motioning with my hands back toward the cafeteria. "She didn't even realize we left the table."

She turned her head a little toward me, though her eyes were on the ground. She pulled her legs up and wrapped her arms around them. As she rested her chin atop her knees, she let out a small sigh, almost like a small swoosh of air, from her mouth. Eventually, she turned her head to look at me, her cheek now resting on her knees. I could see the remnants of tears in her eyes as they sparkled from the wetness in the sunshine.

She was beautiful even when she was sad.

"Ty," she started, "I have no right to be mad at you for what I saw."

And even though I knew that, for some reason hearing those words, again, made them harder to swallow. Maybe it was because of the new development in her life. The new "person" in her life. I rubbed my hands up and down along my face and then through my hair to force myself not to respond to her words. Nothing I would say would make any of this any better. She looked over at me, full on, expecting me to talk, though.

"Can I ask you something?"

She nodded.

"Is there still an *us*, Becca? I need to know if there's anything worth me fighting for." I slid down the bench, closer to her, but not knowing if she was ready for me to touch her. "I'm willing to do whatever it takes. I'll give you the space you need, anything. I'm not ready to give up fighting for you, but I need to know how you feel. Do I still have a chance? With *him* in the picture?"

Then she looked away.

She wouldn't look at me or answer me for a few very long minutes. Eventually, her head turned in my direction. "Ty, until I walked into the cafeteria today, I think I would've said no, you don't have a chance." And then her eyes filled with tears again. "When I saw you sitting at that table with Kayla, fuck. I saw red." She looked away from me, wiping her cheeks as the tears fell. "And I have no right, not with what I'm doing. And you and me, we're not together. You can be with anyone you wanna be with."

"But I wouldn't, Bec . . ." But she interrupted me.

"Yeah, *I know*," she said. She was hiccupping through her tears. It took everything in me to not take her in my arms, but it felt like she needed to keep talking. "And that makes me feel even shittier that I've already moved on."

Those words.

She said she moved on.

Fuck. I couldn't breathe.

I needed to do something, say something. I abruptly stood up to move closer to her, and her head snapped toward me when I did.

"Becca," I started.

But then I froze. The truthful words were on the tip of my tongue—and yet I still couldn't say them. Instead, more lies came out.

"When I was in high school, I had a long-term girl-friend for, like, a long time."

Becca's eyes went big at my declaration, and she thought that I was finally giving her what she wanted. I felt like a complete asshole.

But I kept going.

"We were together for four years. Her name is Kelly." Not a lie, but I knew I wasn't setting myself up to tell her what I needed to. "My parents liked her at first, but, um, then our relationship became complicated. And it interfered with my grades." Becca's gaze hadn't left mine as I spoke. Her attention clung to every syllable, like she was hoping she would get all the answers she was looking for. "I started failing some classes, and I needed tutors, a lot of tutors. It cost my parents a ton of money. If they didn't do that, I probably wouldn't be in college."

I stopped talking. I couldn't believe how easily the lies were coming from my mouth. But the saddest part, as I looked at Becca, was she was believing every word I said.

"They told me I had to end things with her. I told them I did"—I paused—"but we were still seeing each other. And then they found out. She and I ended it before we left for college, but by then their trust in me was gone. My relationship with my parents was not in a good place." Becca was with me, her eyes still on mine. "They told me that if I was heading off to college and wanted them to pay for it, I couldn't be in a relationship."

My heart was beating a mile a minute, and I hoped she couldn't tell.

I was such a coward.

She sat there for a while, her gaze moving from me to the grassy oval adjacent to the cafeteria. It was full of students going to and from class or back to their dorms; they were all completely unaware that I tilted our world on its axis in this corner.

"Why couldn't you tell me that until now, Ty?" Becca sneered. Her glare pinned me in place. How did I answer that? "I know why. You finally told me because you're jealous," she snarled.

But as she said that, she covered her face with her hands and started crying again. I rushed to her side, falling to my knees in front of her. She stopped me, though, pushing me away with a hand. "But I get it!" she screamed. "I get it! Shit, Ty, when I saw you with Kayla before, it affected me in a way I wasn't expecting. I can only imagine what seeing me with Gage has felt like." She jumped up, almost knocking me back on my ass, and started pacing. She stood behind the bench with her back to me. Her arms wrapped around her middle as if she were in pain. "I never wanted to hurt you, Ty. I know I probably did, or am. It wasn't my intention. It came out of nowhere with Gage, and he makes me forget everything." She turned to look at me. "He helps me forget you." Tears streamed down her face steadily. "But I haven't forgotten. Not yet."

My heart opened wide as her green eyes, still wet with tears, looked at me and gave me hope. But I had no right to be feeling I had any hope; with the lies I told her, I had no right having anything with her ever again.

"And I appreciate you finally telling me about your issues from home. And I get it, parents can be assholes. Them not paying for your education because you have a girlfriend? That sucks."

She started moving back toward me, but I was unsure how close I could get to her. I still couldn't read the situation well. I didn't know where I stood yet.

"Well, I put them through hell, so I'm trying to respect them." The lies were just rolling off my tongue now. And the nausea was getting worse.

But she nodded in understanding, then came to stand right next to me. She had calmed, yet her face was still blotchy. I reached out to push her hair behind her ear, my finger grazing her cheek, hoping touching her would calm my nerves. Her eyes closed as I did. I kept my palm cradling her cheek until she opened her eyes. I then pulled her close to me, wrapping my arms around her.

"You feel like home, Ty," she said into my chest.

Her words melted my heart. I hated that this moment was created from my cowardice, my inability to tell her what I needed to tell her. But I still felt she wasn't ready to hear it.

I rested my chin on the top of her head, wishing this would never end, but knowing it had to. "Bec, I'm not sure where this puts us, but I'm still not going to push. I need you to let me know what *you* want, *when* you want it." I felt her nod under my chin.

"Ty, I have no idea what I want right now. I'm so confused. Give me time to let all of this sink in, ya know? I mean, I don't know. We've been broken up for months. You didn't call, you didn't text. And now that I'm seeing someone else, you decide to come clean. I just wish you had done it on your own." She let her head drop against my chest again but then let out a chuckle. "I guess I took my own advice," she said.

"Huh?" I asked, completely confused.

"Nothin'," she replied. "Never mind. Let's let this sit, OK?" She pulled away again and looked up with a smile. "But this is good, Ty. Thank you."

I pulled her close to me again, my arm around her shoulders.

The urge to kiss her, to reach down and kiss her, was so unbelievably strong I had to ball my hands into fists. My hands were clenched so tight that my short nails were digging into my palms. Giving in to these urges would jeopardize her trust, though, and I couldn't do that.

It was bad enough I convinced her to talk to me.

Worse I fed her a line of bullshit lies.

But you better believe I was going to revel in the feeling of her being in my arms, the feel of her against my body. I was sure she could feel the rapid rate of my heart about to jump out of my chest, her ear firmly against me there. But I didn't care.

CHAPTER 11
Becca

ive days. Five long days since I'd been with Gage by that pond. Well, let me dial that back. He drove me to campus a few times. And we met for coffee again once, but only coffee. But other than that, our schedules were not cooperating. And I'd been thinking about the time we spent together by the pond more times than I was willing to admit. Maybe doing a bit more than just thinking.

But then I saw Ty.

And Ty and I talked.

To say it confused me was an understatement. It shook me to the core, and I didn't know which way was up.

Ty finally opened up to me. After all this time, he gave me what I'd been wanting. Of course, it took me being with someone else for him to do it, but that was beside the point.

"Wasn't that *the* point?" Lanie asked, breaking my concentration, though my thoughts were all muddled. We were lying on her bed together. "If I remember correctly, and they may not be your exact words, but you once told me, '*If you want him back even sooner, start talking to some other guys. Make him jealous.*' I mean, you took your own advice, and it seemed to have worked." Her smug smile wasn't making me feel any better about the situation.

"Yeah, I don't think I thought that through so well."

Lanie's head snapped toward me in surprise. "What do you mean?"

"Well," I started as I sat up against the headboard, "it didn't feel so good when I saw him with Kayla yesterday. I mean, shit, they were only sitting next to each other. If Ty only knew what Gage and I have done. Lanie, do you think I need to tell him?" The horror I was feeling came through in my voice.

"I don't know; that's up to you," Lanie responded, her face still smooshed on her pillow. "You need to decide if that would help or not. You guys aren't together, he said he's giving you *space,* and he knows you're kind of seeing Gage. Don't you think he can put two and two together without knowing the gory details?"

"Yes!" I screamed in agreement, jumping off the bed. "Yes, so we agree that not telling him what Gage and I have done is the way to go, right?"

Lanie jerked her body up and leaned against a pillow, her curiosity truly piqued. "OK, maybe you don't have to tell him, but what about me? Does the best friend get to know? It sounds like I may have been right about Gage." Her knowing smile spread across her face.

The heat that spread from my chest to my face was a dead giveaway. And I suddenly had no words to even explain to Lanie what had happened between us.

"Becca Reynolds, are you blushing?" she asked.

All I could do was roll my eyes at her with my hands on my hips.

"Oh my God, have we found a guy who makes you speechless?" Lanie shrieked.

"Enough, woman! I have words. I have a voice!" I yelled back. Little did she know how many times he did indeed render me speechless. "But let's just say, yes, you were right. He knows his way around a woman's body." I smirked. "Very well."

And then we both laughed out loud.

Lanie suddenly got quiet, but surprised me when she said her next words. "Well, are you going to tell me anything?"

"OMG, do you want the gory details?" I asked.

Her head plopped back on the pillow, but a small smile landed on her lips.

I gave her an abridged version of our pond-side escapades, making sure to highlight what a selfless guy he was in the sex department.

"I knew it!" she exclaimed. "I knew he was going to be good at what he did!"

"He was more than good," I told her as I paced the room, full of energy from telling my story. "But now I've got Ty back in the picture," I said as I came back to the bed next to her. "Kind of," I corrected.

Lanie looked at me curiously. "So what did he say to you yesterday?" she asked.

"Well, apparently, there was a long-term relationship in high school that went south, and so did his grades. He needed a ton of tutors, and his parents hated her, Kallie or Kacie something. They told him to break up with her or else, but he didn't. They were pissed at him. Ty and her decided to end it before leaving for college, but his parents still told him no relationships while here or they weren't paying for school. So, yeah, that's it in a nutshell."

We went back to facing each other on her bed, a position we liked to be in when we counseled each other about our lives.

"Okaaay," was all Lanie said.

And she took the thought straight from my head, but I didn't want to say it myself. I slowly closed my eyes and turned my face into the pillow.

"Hey," she said, "it's better than nothing." I knew she was trying to make me feel better, and I would do the same for her.

"Is it? Is it though?" I asked, looking back at her. "I mean, yeah, I'm happy he felt the need to open up. But it took me being with someone else for him to feel as though he had to." I threw myself onto my back, my arms flailing above my head in frustration. "Why was I, alone, just me, not enough?"

Lanie didn't answer; she knew I wasn't looking for one. We both continued to lie there quietly, but I knew we were thinking the same thing.

"If he had told me this last year, or even over the summer, does he really think I would have left him?" I turned toward Lanie. "Do you think I would have left him? I mean, yeah, I understand now why he couldn't, or wouldn't, tell his parents. But if he had told me, do you think this is so bad I would have left him?" I stared at her, hoping she would be completely honest with me.

It took her a moment of thought before she answered.

"No, I don't think you would have. But we don't get to be inside his head." She shrugged her shoulders. "Maybe Ty was that scared of losing you."

"But he did lose me!" I yelled. "And he still never told me!"

Ugh, this just wasn't making sense to me. I was more confused than ever now that Ty had finally done what I wanted him to do.

"Listen, I will never judge what a person is dealing with at home. Never." My head snapped in her direction, and I listened to her words. "You might have met them, but I'm sure they didn't show their true selves with guests in the house. You may not have the real picture of what Ty is going through with his parents."

That made me take pause.

Lanie was right. And she knew from experience.

Maybe his parents were brutal assholes and made his life a living hell. I had no idea.

"So," she continued, "when you took up with Gage, Ty got scared. Really scared. And he told a *version* of what's going on. Trust me, I've lived that life." She got up from the bed and started toward her closet but popped her head back out. "Xander's coming for me soon; I need to get changed." She kept talking from inside the walk-in. "I'm not telling you what to do, but he has put the ball in your court. He's done all he can, I think." She came out, it appeared dressed the same, maybe with a different color shirt on. "You need to decide if it's enough."

I needed to decide if it was enough.

Yeah, that was the big question of the day.

"Are you going to tell Gage you and Ty talked?" she asked before she popped back into her closet.

Hmm. Good question. "I guess I have to. It's what I would want, so yeah," I told her. "Where are you and Xander going? I thought we were making our shirts for the game with Ava and Macie?" My confusion came through in my words as I got up from the bed. We had finally made plans for a girls' night with all four of us and she was already heading downstairs. It had been near impossible to get all of us together so far with our schedules.

"We're just going for pizza. It's still early." She looked at her phone. "We told Ava for them to be back at eight. I'll be back, no worries." She turned around once at the bottom, near the front door, to look at me. "Do ya wanna come?"

Living off campus meant we didn't eat our meals in the cafeteria as much as last year. So much had changed since the year before. I always liked the routine of the four or five of us eating almost every lunch or dinner together. This year, Logan wasn't here, Ty and I were barely talking, and most meals we cooked or brought in. I realized I didn't like change.

"I'm good. I'm not hungry."

Right then, my phone pinged with a message from my one of my younger brothers.

She stared at me with concern in her eyes that spread to her mouth as it pressed her lips into a thin line. "Well, if the roles haven't reversed from last year." A soft chuckle left her mouth, but she wasn't happy. Lanie went through a time last year, when she and Xander were having their struggles, that she barely ate. I guessed it was my turn. "Want me to bring anything back for you for later?"

"No, I'm good. Besides, my brothers want to FaceTime me, and that usually takes a while," I said with a bit of a whine in my voice. As soon as I said that, my phone started that familiar ring with the screen lighting up. "Want to say hi to them?"

"Yes! I love seeing their adorable faces," she shrieked. Lanie came home with me for Thanksgiving last year and therefore had the opportunity to meet my entire clan. I had four brothers. The older of the four were closer to me in age: Mason was sixteen, almost seventeen, and Nate was fourteen. But the other two. Well, let's just say that my parents definitely had an oops that resulted in twins. Jonah and Sam were both only six years old, just starting first grade.

The twins became attached to Lanie immediately when we were home together.

I picked up and Jonah had the phone facing out toward the driveway, showing me Sam about to do a jump on his bike over three bags of mulch lined up together.

"Hey guys, I don't know if that's the best idea! Why don't you set that up on the grass instead of the driveway in case that doesn't work out?" But they didn't listen. Sam's little legs worked as hard and fast as they could toward the ramp. I wanted to close my eyes but knew if I didn't watch, I'd have hell to pay from them for missing it.

"Shit, Becca, is he gonna make it?" Lanie asked in my ear.

"We'll know soon enough."

But just as Sam was heading off the ramp, Jonah dropped the phone, I assumed to watch it better himself, so we couldn't see a thing but the ground. We heard mumbled voices, what sounded like a tire skidding on the ground, and I waited to hear the telltale sound of crying.

But it didn't happen.

Then the phone was retrieved and two muddy faces filled the screen, both missing at least one front tooth, though thankfully that was from nature and their age and not their current antics.

"Did you see that, Becca?"

"I did it, Bec. It was great. I'm the best ramp jumper in the world!"

"Hey, I'm good, too!"

The little voices argued between themselves for another minute while Lanie and I looked on. Lanie's smile grew with each of their proclamations.

"They really are adorable," she said.

I nodded. "They are. From four hours away, they're even cuter."

We laughed.

"Guys!" I yelled into the phone. "Say hi to Lanie before she has to leave."

"Hi, Lanie," they said in unison.

Lanie waved to the screen, then waved to me before heading out the door to meet Xander.

And I caught up with two of my brothers, wondering where our parents were during their little stunt.

"I can't believe we're cutting these brand-new shirts that we spent like thirty dollars on into strips!" Ava complained.

"Oh, come on. This is the time in our lives to flaunt what we've got, right?" I countered. Ava had big boobs like I did, though. Maybe that was why she was complaining. I wasn't sure, either, if these strips of cloth we were making into bandeaus would hold in our girls. "Ava, maybe you should make yours into a halter. Ya know, for more support? I've seen some really cute pics online of them done like that." I grabbed my phone to pull them up.

The four of us, Lanie, Macie, Ava, and I, were busy making shirts to wear to the first home football game tomorrow. It was a tradition to dress covering as little of your body as possible. Well, for the girls, anyway. The tailgate was a huge party on Mid Street, an area where all the frats had houses that backed up to one another. It was a spot where thousands of college kids were within walking distance of the stadium, so the cops were pretty good about it.

"Ooh, Becca, that looks perfect! And it's still cute. Thank you," Ava said. I looked at the design and thought it might be best for my body as well.

"It is pretty cute. I'm going to make mine like that, too," I told her. Ava and I commenced following the YouTube directions for ours. Meanwhile, Lanie and Macie made theirs on the other table.

"Lanie, are you excited to be going to your first football game?" I asked her.

She turned to look at me, as did Ava and Macie. Now concerned I had opened up a conversation she may not want to have in mixed company, my wide eyes hopefully conveying my apology to her. But her smile that followed calmed my fast beating heart as she walked over and wrapped her arms around me.

"Yes, Becca, I am excited." She then faced the girls, knowing they were curious. "I resisted going out a lot last year, much to Becca's dismay. She tried. Oh, did she try. But I was stubborn."

"Yeah, but she had good reasons, it turned out," I told them. "And then we took her to the BRU Blackout and she had a blast, so it all worked out."

"Oh my God, that was so much fun!" Macie chimed in.

We all settled back into making our shirts, a comfortable silence taking over the room.

Right in the middle of an important cut, my phone buzzed. It was across the room, next to where Ava was working.

"Ava, could you see who that is?"

She looked down at the screen with scissors still in her hands.

"Who's Gage?" Ava asked. "I thought you were talking to Ty?"

My eyes flew to Lanie in confusion.

"Who told you that? Ty and I actually broke up over the summer. I mean, we still *talk*, like, we're not *not talking*, but we're not together at the moment."

Shit, if people didn't know Ty and I weren't together, they must have thought I was sleeping around. But I couldn't bother myself with those thoughts.

Gage texted me. And that made me smile. At first. But things were very complicated now. I finished the cut and took the phone from Ava.

Gage:

I'm outside, want to do something

Shit, it was the first time he'd reached out since our time at the pond. But we decided this was a girls' night. Not only that, but it was the first time all four of us girls, us roommates, were really doing something together.

Me:

Ugh girls' night we're making shirts for
tomorrow's game and drinking sorry

He didn't respond, and I didn't know what that meant. I stared at my phone for a few more seconds, my throat a bit clogged, then tossed it on the table, getting back to my shirt. I couldn't let this bother me; Gage and I were not serious. We weren't anything. We were "fuck buddies" in my mind.

And then there was a knock on our door. My head snapped up, searching for Lanie, our eyes connecting immediately. We both knew who would be behind that door.

Macie sped to it before any of us could say a word. Once she had it open, I heard the distant rumble of his deep tenor.

"Hey, I'm here to see Becca. Can I come in?" Gage's voice reverberated throughout the apartment, and everyone stopping what they were doing. Ava looked over my shoulder, trying to get a look at the person attached to the voice. They granted her wish as Macie came walking down the hall with him.

Standing in front of us was one of the most gorgeous men I thought I'd ever see in my life.

His shoulders seemed broader than usual as he stood in the narrow hallway. His normally perfect hair was a bit mussed tonight, making him seem boyish and super sexy. He had a shadow of a beard on his face, that perfect amount that wasn't quite full but just enough to be there. His jeans were tight around his thick thighs and hung low on his hips. The dark T-shirt was fitted just enough to stretch across his chest perfectly, as if it was made for him.

His eyes. Those caramel-brown eyes that stared only at me. My knees felt like they were going to buckle.

"Hey, Becca," he said in that sultry, porn star voice. I realized all I—along with all of my roommates—was doing was staring at him.

"Oh, hi, Gage." I quickly recovered and ran over to him, but then didn't know how to greet him. Did we kiss? We weren't a *couple*, per se. It was awkward, so I grabbed his hand and turned around to do the introductions. "You know Lanie," I started. Lanie gave a small wave. "And this is Macie, and that's Ava. All of us are making our next-to-nothing shirts for tomorrow's festivities."

He looked around at the mess on the tables. The scraps of the cloth spread across the floor, scissors scattered here and there. Plus the bottles of wine and half-filled glasses we were enjoying. "I remember those. Yeah, you girls are pretty creative with what you come up with, that's for sure." I had almost forgotten that he had gone through four years of this already; four years of girls throwing themselves at him, I was sure. There had to be so many girls who got their hearts broken by Gage Parker at Blue Ridge University. "So, making shirts to cover an important part of your body, under the influence. I think I see now why all the girls come dressed the way they do at the tailgates," he said, letting out a laugh afterward.

"Yeah, probably not the best combination. But haven't had a mishap yet." I looked up at him to find his eyes staring into mine.

"Let's hope tomorrow isn't the first," he offered quietly for only me to hear. He turned toward the girls and said, "Can I borrow Becca, just for a few minutes?"

Macie and Ava nodded as if on autopilot; they hadn't recovered from their initial viewing of Gage yet.

Lanie had a concerned look on her face. Her eyes were trying to bore a hole through my head without Gage noticing. At first, I didn't understand her unsaid words. But then . . .

Fuck!

"Why don't we head up to my room?" I offered. Suddenly nervous, I needed to be away from the prying eyes and ears. I had forgotten I was going to have to tell him about talking to Ty.

I pulled him toward the stairs by his hand. Letting go as I started heading up, I heard Gage rumble a low growl behind me.

"Seeing your ass at eye level, knowing I won't be able to keep you upstairs, is unfair, Becca." He reached out and rubbed his hand along my backside, a finger trailing between my legs as I reached the top step.

There was a landing at the top of the stairs, a small hall that branched off toward some bedrooms, mine being one of them. He was one step behind me, hand still on my ass, when I turned around to guide him to the correct door.

So quickly, he had me pinned against the wall, one hand behind my neck, the other still on my ass. His mouth nestled against my ear, his warm breath making bumps rise on my skin when he spoke.

"I've fuckin' missed you, Becca. These days we haven't seen each other have been torture." His tongue dipped in my ear, and he definitely felt the shivers that went through my body as he pushed his hips against mine. A tiny gasp escaped my mouth as my lips parted. He took advantage of that and slipped his tongue inside. Our tongues battled each other, a fight neither of us cared who won.

But then I withdrew. My tongue slowed first; then my hands pulled from his hair as I created a space between our bodies. He tilted my head to look up at him, the question in his eyes.

"Let's go in my room." But he could tell by my voice it was not an invitation into my bed.

He followed me, and I closed the door. I wasn't the cleanest of girls my age, and I became embarrassed by the pile of clothes outside my closet.

"Sorry, I'm still unpacking," I offered as I gestured to the mess on the floor. Not completely untrue. He wasn't looking around the room, though. He was only looking at me.

"I was busy this week, getting my schedule set up with my professors," he said. His voice held a note of seriousness; he'd picked up on the mood, I guess. "I wanted to reach out, to see you." He hesitated, but then went on. "I didn't know if I should text you or call. This is kinda new for me, too. I wanted to see you, make sure we were OK."

A nervous smile came across his face. He thought he fucked this up by not reaching out this week. To be honest, it bothered me a little. But I let it go because of what we were. I didn't want to be "clingy."

"After the way we left things on Monday," he continued, "after . . ."

And he was then at a loss for words.

"You mean after you made me come with your hands pond-side, in public. An earth-shattering orgasm that made my knees weak as I walked to class. An experience I haven't stopped thinking about since. *That* way we left things on Monday?"

We were staring at one another when his nervous smile morphed into a wide grin. He stood by the door, hands in the pockets of the jeans that appeared to have been made for him. It caused the waist to hang low on his hips, the band of his boxer briefs peeking out the top as he stalked toward me like a lion coming for its prey.

"I talked to Ty."

I had to blurt it out. If I hadn't, I would have made the mistake of letting him make it all the way over to me. I wouldn't have been able to control myself if he had.

And he stopped his advance, almost mid-step. But he kept his cool as I watched his face.

"OK," he said. "And how did that go?" He made his way over to my dresser and leaned back against it, crossing his feet at the ankles, his arms across his chest.

Shocked that he was as calm as he was, I didn't answer right away. Instead, I plopped on my bed, dreading having to move on with this conversation. But honesty was what I was missing with Ty; I wouldn't be guilty of not being honest myself.

But it sucked.

"Becca?" he coaxed. "Are you guys back together?"

"No!" I almost screamed at him. "No," I said more calmly. "But we ran into each other, and he finally gave me an explanation for what had been going on with him." I couldn't look at Gage. I even knew how this sounded.

"And do you believe him?" Gage asked.

Again, I didn't answer him right away.

"Or do you think he's saying whatever he's saying simply because he's jealous you're seeing me?" Gage suggested. "Becca, look at me." He walked toward the bed.

My body fell back on the bed and I looked up at the ceiling, not wanting to look at him. I knew I was being immature, not being able to talk to him. But I was confused. He was confusing me; him simply looking the way he did was confusing enough. Then I felt the bed dip as he sat on its edge. He lay his body next to mine, both of us staring at the ceiling as he reached for my hand, entwining our fingers. I turned my head in his direction as he turned to me.

"I'm not dumb, Gage. I'm sure that's why he came clean." Letting out a cleansing breath, I looked away again. I couldn't concentrate with his whiskey eyes looking at me. "And I'm not jumping into anything. I'm just trying to be completely honest with you because that's what I promised I'd do. And that's what I would want." I looked his way again, and he was still looking at me. "I know he, uh, wants us to get back together. I know that's his end game." I held his gaze to see his reaction when I told him.

A small nod was all I got. Then he grabbed my shoulder and pulled me to face him, our bodies belly to belly.

"Becca, this"—he gestured between us with his hand—"between us, whatever we want to call it, is supposed to be easy, fun. Not stressful. I'm not here to make your life hard or miserable. I knew what I was getting into when we started this. I knew he was still in love with you." A gentle hand came to rest on my cheek, then pushed the hair behind my ear. "Just make sure he's doing this for the right reasons. Make sure he's not backed against a wall because of *us* and feeding you shit you just want to hear."

Trying to juggle two guys just became very difficult. I'd suddenly realized that anything each of them said to me made sense. When Ty explained the situation with his parents and his senior year of high school, I could feel the tension in his voice. I felt he was telling me a truth he was living. As much as I'd been telling myself he'd been lying to me, what he was truly doing was withholding information. Although not great, there was a difference. And when he finally divulged what had come between us, I felt like we might work toward something. Maybe, in the future.

But then Gage threw a comment like that at me, and it made complete sense. Ty *was* backed against a wall, at least in his head. He felt threatened by me being with another guy, and he felt the need to do something, to tell me something.

And when Gage referred to us as *us*, it did something to me on the inside. I needed to make sure to keep this casual with him, to keep our emotions out of it.

This was all so confusing. I had no idea which way was up anymore.

"I can see the wheels turning in your head," Gage said.

I lifted my eyes to his. He was looking at me with compassion, almost a sadness on his face.

"It's all so confusing," I said. "I'm not confused about how I feel when I'm with you. Only about how that affects everything else in my life." I put my hands under my cheek. If I didn't, I knew they'd be touching parts of his body that would lead to us staying in this bed longer than I could, or should.

"That's fair, and I understand being confused, Becca." Reaching out, his thumb grazed my lower lip, playfully pulling on it. "I didn't mean to confuse you. Maybe we need to slow things down a bit." But as he said this, he dipped his thumb in my mouth, rubbing it along my bottom teeth.

And I didn't know if I wanted to slow things down with him. Ty was giving me *space*. Did I want Gage to be changing up what we had going on as well?

But he took my mind off of my own thoughts as his finger pushed further in, hitting my tongue, and I reflexively began sucking on it. A moan escaped my mouth, between my parted lips, as his hips pushed against mine. He eventually pulled his finger out and rubbed the wetness along my lips.

"Is this how you take things slower, Gage?" I said breathlessly.

"No," he responded, "I didn't quite get there yet." A soft chuckle came from deep in his chest.

My eyes opened slowly to find him staring at me. I returned his stare, trying to read him.

"Are you OK with slowing this down?" I asked, actually nervous about his answer. "That wasn't what we agreed on."

He kept his head on the pillow but turned to look at the ceiling. Not a good sign. My hand instinctively reached out to his chest, rubbing the hard muscle through the cotton. His large hand came over mine, covering it. I could feel callouses on his palm, not expecting him to have hands that did manual labor. Then his head swiveled back to look at me before he spoke.

"I wasn't looking for a relationship when I came back to school, Becca. You were a happy little surprise to me. If it works, it works." He reached around and grabbed my ass before continuing. "I will say, I do hope we can continue. But if not, I understand. It's what we agreed."

Our faces were mere centimeters apart, breaths mingling. Our eyes searched each other's—for what, I didn't know exactly.

"If I kiss you now, I have a feeling you won't make it back downstairs to your girls' night." He placed a chaste peck on my lips and pulled away immediately.

I wanted to whine.

"Will I see you tomorrow? Are you going to Mid Street?" I asked, genuinely interested.

He nodded. "I offered to drive the gang over in the pickup. I can bring you and your roommates if you need a ride." I wasn't sure what he meant by "the gang."

"I'll definitely take the offer of a ride. It's hard to get over there, living off campus." I started getting up from the bed, but he held me in place.

"Ty is part of the group I'm driving over." His voice was serious.

"Does Ty know that?" I asked incredulously, truly thinking Ty would accept nothing from Gage.

"He was right there when the plan was being made. He knows. I offered because I have to meet with a professor later tomorrow, so I can't drink."

Gage seemed as skeptical as I was. But Ty was not a malicious person; I wasn't going to jump to conclusions about him.

"Well, OK. It's OK; it will be OK. Ty's a good guy, Gage. You'll see."

I only hoped I was right.

And I wondered if Gage realized I never really answered his question about slowing things down.

CHAPTER 12
Becca

"Becca! Let's go! The truck is here!" Lanie yelled from downstairs. I was putting the finishing touches on my makeup because I had to look perfect. I was going to be with both the guys in my life today.

My life. How did it get so complicated? After Gage left last night, the girls were full of questions for me, and I had no answers. I had no idea where my relationship was at with either Ty or Gage.

Can a heartbroken person still in love with you walk away that easily? But as soon as he saw me at the start of the semester, it was as if the abandoned months of the summer hadn't existed. Sure, he had given me some answers, but was that enough?

And in walked Gage. The handsome stranger who offered me a long-term booty call with no strings attached. Yet there were strings attached. The fraternity they were both a part of was a huge rope tying us all together.

And here I was, on my way out to a truck that was holding both the guys I was involved with.

"Shit, Lanie, how am I going to do this?" I asked as we approached the truck. The bed was already full to the brim with guys and girls. Ty had to be somewhere back there, but I couldn't see him yet.

"You're going to hold your head up high and just do it." Lanie entwined her arm with mine, thank God. Because if she hadn't, I didn't think I could stand, I was shaking so bad.

When we walked up to the bed of the truck, we saw Ava and Macie squished on the floor. I looked around and found Ty, both of us making eye contact and smiling. My stomach still got butterflies when I caught sight of him. He seemed to try to make room for us, pushing the people near him over. It was too crowded, though. It wasn't happening.

"Doesn't seem like there's room, Lanie." I looked at her nervously, thinking we wouldn't have a ride to the tailgate.

"Lanie! Becca!" Macie called as she tried to make room for us as well. She was pushing the guys next to her, attempting to get them out of the bed of the truck, it appeared.

As we walked closer to the truck to talk to her, Macie leaned her head down a bit. "Thanks, Macie, but it doesn't look like it's going to work," I told her.

She looked around, and then her eyes lit up. "Up front, go sit up front!"

Lanie grabbed my hand and dragged me to the front of the truck where the window was open.

"Hey, Gage," Lanie said.

"Hi, girls. Looks like it's pretty full back there. Sorry 'bout that. But if I let you get back there, we might get pulled over. I can either come back for you or you can get in the cab with me." The twinkle in his eye and the smile on his face told me he was not upset with this option.

I looked at Lanie and shrugged my shoulders. "I don't want to wait for him to have to come back, so let's just get in," I said.

We nodded in agreement and she opened the door. I intentionally did not look at the back of the truck; I didn't need to see Ty and how he felt about this development. Lanie was standing there, holding the door for me to get in first, which made sense. I should be the one to sit closest to Gage.

Once I slid across the bench seat, I got a look at Gage. He was dressed in faded jeans that looked years old and a school T-shirt that looked equally aged. Just like the night before, he looked so much younger than when in his expensive dress clothes. A nice touch today was a pair of worn work boots and a backward cap on his head.

He looked hot.

"You're really working to fit in with the crowd today, huh?" I asked, the sarcasm dripping from my words.

"Have you been to Mid Street? No way I'm wearing anything nice to that place," he said as his eyes fixated on my outfit, or lack of one. "Fuck, Becca." His mouth came close to my ear, I assumed to prevent Lanie from hearing him. "You look amazing. What I'd really like to do is say, 'Fuck Mid Street,' and take you back to my place right now."

I peeked down at my self-created halter top, which was doing a pretty good job of holding the boobs in place, and my little white shorts. I knew when I stood they were short, like, really short. But like I'd always said, these were the years to flaunt what ya had. They wouldn't be around forever.

Gage's hand landed on my thigh after he put the truck in gear. He slid it up higher as the truck jerked forward, his fingertips between my two legs, working dangerously close to the hem of my shorts. With Lanie basically sitting on top of me, I knew I should stop him, but I didn't want to. I stole a glance at Gage as he turned to look at me. The heat in his gaze went straight to my core, forcing me to rub my thighs together. His grip tightened on my thigh, feeling the contraction of my muscles, knowing what I was doing. A low groan came from his side of the cab.

"All right you two, you know I'm here, right?" Lanie blurted out.

I turned to look at her at the same time I pushed Gage's hand from my leg.

Gage let out a cackle.

My face got hot.

Lanie leaned toward me, trying to whisper. "Didn't you just tell me last night he suggested you take things slower?" Her eyebrows lifted in question as I stared at her.

Gage was the one to answer. "Lanie's right. I did, but Becca never really gave me an answer." He was leaning against the door, further away from me now, with a sly smile on his face. The hand that was once about to be inside my shorts now firmly gripped the steering wheel. "But Lanie, you have to admit, she looks hot. What am I supposed to do when she's sitting this close to me?" His bright white smile shone at both of us as we looked his way.

"She is hot, Gage. And guess who else has taken notice?" Lanie said with some concern in her voice. She was sitting with her back against her door, sideways, facing me, because it was tight with the three of us. That afforded her a view of the bed of the truck—a view of the people in the bed of the truck.

And that was when I froze. Stock still in my seat, facing forward, arms crossed. The lump in my throat made it hard to swallow. I knew I was going to be with both of them today; I'd dressed for it.

But I also knew how seeing Ty with Kayla made me feel. This had to be so hard for him, seeing me up here, basically sitting on top of Gage.

"Is Ty watching us, Lane?" I asked, robotically. My mind felt that if I stopped moving altogether, he would lose interest and look away.

"He hasn't taken his eyes off of you, Becca," she said.

OK, that was OK. Because from where he was, there was no way he could see over my shoulders and what Gage's hand was doing moments ago.

But it also shouldn't matter, right? I was free to do what I wanted, yet I didn't feel free most of the time. The tether attaching me and Ty, it was frayed, but it was still attached; I knew that deep down.

I composed myself, my breaths returned to normal, and I chanced a look at Gage. He was facing forward, driving, wearing an unreadable look.

"Let's try to keep today uncomplicated, if we can," I said in his direction softly. "Let's all just have fun at the first tailgate and football game!" Hoping my enthusiastic attitude might improve my mood, I started hyping myself up.

"Hey, Becca," Gage started, "just remember, I'm not here for complicated. As soon as it gets to be too much for you, just say the word." He reached out and grabbed my hand, squeezing it. "I want to have fun with you, make your life better while we're together." He gave me a smile, but not his typical thousand-watt smile; this one was more con-trolled, as if forced, as he continued talking. "You're right. Let's have fun today. Get drunk!"

Hmm, mixing alcohol with me and these two. A bad recipe.

"Lanie! You barely cut any material off of your shirt! You need to show that killer body of yours!" Ava screamed over the music.

At least it wasn't me saying it to her. She heard it enough from me, the comments about the conservative way she dressed all the time. Her loose jeans and sweatshirts hid her curves. But I knew why.

"Xander knows what's under here; that's all that mat-ters," she replied. She motioned to the bit of belly that was showing from the midriff shirt she made.

"Ooh, is he the jealous type? Is that why?" Macie asked, genuinely curious. They didn't know Xander well, nor much about what the two of them went through last year with her ex, Max. Lanie was pretty close-lipped about it with them, so I hadn't talked about it much.

Right then, a thick set of muscular arms wrapped them-selves around Lanie's bare middle, pulling her against an even more muscular body. "Nah, I'm not the jealous type." He addressed the crowd but spoke the words into Lanie's neck. A wide grin spread across her face. "Lanie is free to dress how she wants, be who she wants, in any way she wants." She twisted around to face Xander, who now had her ass in his hands. "Every night she comes home with me, I count my blessings."

A hush had come over our tiny group as his declaration settled in their minds. And then there was a collective *"Aww!"*

"I'm stealing her for a bit, girls. Not for long, but I need her for a minute." And the two of them wandered off, as they usually did, to find some dark corner.

But now I didn't have my rock with me. Lanie always knew how to keep me from losing my shit when things got too crazy. And that was bound to happen today.

But then I turned and looked at my other roommates, realizing I had two good friends in them as well. We'd been getting closer, especially Ava and me.

"You guys ready?" I asked.

They nodded with enthusiastic smiles.

We were ready to mingle, drinks in hand. Most people who didn't attend BRU had no comprehension of what the tailgating event was truly like. Imagine around twenty run-down fraternity shacks (because these were not the actual frat houses, but annex buildings solely used for game days), ten on either side of a grassy lot that was their shared backyards. Each house had sectioned off "their property" or party area, because you had to be allowed into the party. As girls, we were lucky; we were let into any party. The guys, not so much. That was why pledging happened so quickly for the guys here at BRU. If you weren't in a frat, it restricted your social life to a sports team or an academic group.

In my attempt to avoid drama, I dragged the girls to a different frat party, leaving Ty and Gage behind. I knew a couple people at the one we were at from freshman year, and so did Ava and Macie. We were doing OK, dancing and drinking. That was until I looked across the grassy field and found his eyes trained on me.

He looked sad. A little like he wanted to come across the way and drag me back to his side, but mostly sad.

"Who are you having the staring contest with? He's a hottie. Christ, Becca, do you have all the hot ones claimed already?" Macie asked, sidling up next to me.

I turned to look at her, the comment taking me off guard. Macie was gorgeous, and I had no idea why she always came across so insecure. Her eyes remained glued across the way, a lofty look in them. I wanted to ask her, find out what was going on in her head to make her say such a thing.

But I didn't. Because at that moment, the nostalgia of mine and Ty's relationship hit me hard. It was in that exact house, last year, that he took care of me when I drank too much. He took me upstairs and found me a bed to rest in. He checked on me every half hour instead of partying with our friends. He cuddled with me when I drunkenly demanded he get in bed with me. And then, when I refused to stay in said bed any longer because I had hot guys waiting for me outside, he helped me outside. And stayed by my side, making sure I remained upright and safe.

And no, a boyfriend taking care of my drunk ass at a party was not the most romantic gesture. But it was who he was: always there for me, no matter what.

And I missed him.

"That's Ty," I replied to Macie. "He's my ex-boyfriend. Though he wants to change that status." I stared back at Ty.

Macie jabbed my side. "Ya know who he looks like, don't you?" she asked.

Her beauty struck me when I turned to look at her. The sun was hitting her eyes at an angle that made them sparkle. Her darker skin with the bluish-green eyes was a knockout combination. "Who?" I asked.

"A young, hot Jensen Ackles."

I turned to look back at Ty, who hadn't moved. And I saw it; she was right. Throw some golden eyes on Jensen and voila, you have Tyler Brennan.

"May I ask why he's your ex? I mean—" She faltered, her words stopping.

I looked at her again. "We went out all last year, but we hit a roadblock. He needs to figure out a way around that roadblock."

Macie nodded. "Well, it looks like he's more than willing to keep trying. I don't think I've seen anyone look at another person like that. Well, maybe Xander at Lanie, but, yeah. You're it for him, that's for sure." She shrugged her shoulders and walked back into the mass of people behind us. Turning my head back across the yard, I saw Ty was still there. He raised his red cup to me and took a chug of what I was sure was warm frat keg beer. His smile was wide, even from across the way. But though he had been standing there, watching, I felt no pressure from him. It was as if he was still just watching over me, making sure I was safe.

Always making sure I was safe.

I zigzagged around body after body, being pushed back and forth, looking for Macie and Ava in the crowd. Where had they gone? The sudden urge to head back to our party, to him, overcame me.

Finally, I found Ava doing a keg stand with Macie cheering her on. Making my way over to them, I got near Macie's ear. "You guys OK if I head back over there?"

Macie grabbed my arm and pulled me away from the larger crowd. "You heading over to see Ty?" she asked, concern in her voice.

I avoided making eye contact with her, looking into the crowd instead.

"Becca, listen, I've made my share of mistakes with guys. Don't be like me, learn from your mistakes." Then she snorted, I presumed laughing at herself.

I looked at her, seeing a different side of Macie for the first time. She looked . . . vulnerable.

"See, I never learn from my mistakes. You can ask Ava. I keep going back, even when I shouldn't. I haven't quite figured out why yet. But don't make my same mistake. Make sure he's the one. Or that he's going to be the right one, someday."

I felt as though I didn't have time to completely unpack what she was saying to me, but I knew I wanted to revisit that with her. "Thanks for that, Macie. That's good advice."

"Ava and I are good," she said. She smiled and disappeared back into the crowd.

I made my way through the barrier to Ty's frat house, the guys letting me stroll right in. It was equally crowded on this side, people shoulder to shoulder and rushing the DJ table. Many of the frats provided their own music, each competing with the next, making the entire area impossible to talk in, let alone hear much of anything in. Looking around, I felt his eyes on me but couldn't find him in the crowd. Turning my head slightly to the right, I found him, close to where he had been standing, watching me. His long strides brought him to me in three steps.

His mouth travelled to my ear, but he still had to talk loudly. "You came back over." He pulled back to look at me once he said that, searching for my reaction. And of course I smiled because, yeah, he knew I had come back over for him.

"I did," I said into his ear. I lingered against his chest, the familiar scent of him invading my thoughts, my memories.

But Macie's words were forefront in my brain. Shaking them away, I looked back at Ty.

"I remembered the last time we were at this house together." Letting out a laugh, I hoped he had kind thoughts about that day here last year.

His knowing smile, a smile I knew so well, spread across his face as he came near my ear again. "Oh, I remember. And I remember the next morning, too. You didn't feel so good. We both missed class so I could bring you Gatorade and soup, if I remember correctly."

I nodded, reminded of that terrible morning. It was a bad one.

A group of people bumped into me, almost sending me onto my ass, but Ty grabbed my arm and pulled me close, keeping me steady. Conveniently, we were then so surrounded by people, we couldn't pull apart if we wanted to. Chest to chest, he leaned down, and I stared at his lips. I didn't realize how much I'd been missing those lips until now.

"Do you want to . . .?" His words trailed off, lost in the surrounding noise.

Trying to push away to look up at him, I gestured to my ear, letting him know I couldn't hear him. He immediately grabbed my hand and led me to the deck stairs. Forging a path through the mass of people on the deck was no joke, but Ty got us to the door leading inside. It was better once there, but not much.

"Let's head upstairs and see if there's someplace we can talk!" he yelled.

I hesitated. This should not be what we were doing. But I was definitely the one giving mixed signals; I had come to him.

So I nodded, and he pulled me along. The feeling of my hand in his, following behind his powerful body as he took charge in the room—I liked it. I missed it.

We walked through the masses of people in what I would consider a living room when Gage caught my eye. He was standing in a corner talking with a group of people, watching me walk toward the stairs with Ty. His eyes lingered on our joined hands, but Gage's face stayed neutral.

I quickly pulled my eyes from his, but not before noticing who he was talking to. Surrounding him were three beautiful girls, each prettier than the next. But that wasn't allowed to bother me; Gage and I were not in a relationship, and I had no hold over him. And I was in the hands of my ex, heading up the stairs.

So why did my heart sink when my eyes met Gage's?

"C'mon, Bec. There's a room up here we can use to talk, get some quiet."

This felt reminiscent of our first day seeing each other only a few weeks ago, and that didn't go well. I was regretting my decision to do this. To be here, going upstairs with Ty. Was anything good going to come of this?

He opened the door to a room, and we both slid inside, glancing around and listening. No one was on the bed, and it was significantly quieter, so we both felt like we'd found an empty one. Ty pushed all the dirty clothes off the bed and grabbed a blanket from the closet, spreading it out across the mattress. One never knew the cleanliness of us college students.

"Wanna sit?" he asked as he gestured to the cleared surface of the bed.

"Sure," I said, moving to sit up against the wall for support. Ty joined me and we sat shoulder to shoulder, knee to knee, quiet for a while.

"You look beautiful today, Becca." Ty pulled his knees up and rested his hands atop them, his head turned toward me. I bent my knees to the side in order to twist my body in his direction. Our faces were closer when he continued. "But you always look beautiful, not just today. Every day."

His smile was a shy one. He was nervous. And I hated I'd done this to him. Ty had never been nervous around me, never. But I guess I didn't really do this to him; he did it to himself. But it was still hard. Hard to be this close to him and not want things to go back to the way they were.

It would be easy. We would just never go to his parents' house. That's the only place we ever had a problem. Here at school, we were in our own little cocoon—a blissful, ignorant cocoon. Things were perfect between us here at school.

But things weren't perfect.

I smiled back at him but said nothing. Which was unusual for me. And he took note.

"Are you OK?" he asked gently.

I shrugged, because I honestly didn't know. "Why are we up here, Ty?" I looked into his eyes when I asked that question, hoping to discern if he was going to be honest. I wasn't sure if he was going to want to talk about the ride over with Gage, or even what we saw on the way up. Or us. I really didn't want to talk about us. Today was supposed to be fun, and talking about us was heavy stuff. "What are we doing right now?"

He blew out a heavy sigh and looked away. "I just needed to feel like we were 'us' again for a minute." He gestured to the room, his hands splayed out. "Being here, at this house again, and seeing you. I miss us so fucking much. I couldn't take my eyes off of you, not since the moment you came out of your apartment." He laughed at himself. "Makes me sound like I'm stalking you a bit." His whiskey eyes found mine as his face turned, the long hair from the top partially covering that brown iris. There was a wetness building in his eyes, and that was breaking me.

"Ty," I said, my voice tremulous.

"Hey, I promised I wouldn't make today a drama-filled day for us." He cackled when he said that. "Shit, imagine me being the one causing more drama than you. I never thought the day would come." A warm smile spread across his face, the humor evident in his tone. "Today is going to be fun. The first football game this year, and we're sopho-mores. I guess I just needed a moment alone with you."

I leaned my chin on his shoulder, appreciating his words.

"Well, this moment alone was nice, thank you," I offered.

Ty remained quiet for a bit longer than I anticipated after my response. His throat clearing was my only alert that he was about to talk.

"So," he started, then paused again. "I don't know how you would feel about this, considering I said I would give you space and all..." He was fidgeting with his fingers, an imaginary hangnail possibly, as he avoided completing his thoughts.

But I knew where they were going.

And, crazily enough, I felt the same way he was feeling. Being back here, in this space where we had special memories last year, created the desire to try to make this work between us again. Well, maybe not go back to what we had, but to spend time with him.

"Ty," I said, and his head spun to look at me. The compassion in my voice seemed to give him hope.

"Bec, what would you do if I happened to show up at your place tomorrow morning, to pick you up, let's say to go grab breakfast?" The small smile on his face was full of optimism.

This was not supposed to be happening. He said he would give me space. The guy I'm spending my time with now is downstairs. The dark, hot new guy who gives me incredible orgasms.

So why, when Ty asked me that question, did my stomach do a flip? Why?

I returned the smile. "I'd say, I would walk out my door and get in your car."

His head bobbed up and down in gratitude while his mouth spread into a wide grin, his bright white teeth on show. I couldn't help but widen my smile as well.

What was I doing? I was complicating my life was what I was doing.

But it felt right. In that moment, it felt right. I needed to give us that chance. Didn't we deserve that?

His hand cradled my cheek. "I was going to ask you for a kiss, but I feel like I'd be pushing my luck," he said. "And I don't want to jeopardize our day tomorrow, so this little time with you will be all I ask of you today."

I nodded, appreciating his regard for my feelings. But his hand remained on my face.

"But I can't seem to let you go without asking for one. Can I get one before we go back downstairs? I just need to feel your lips against mine. My dreams aren't cutting it lately."

I stared at his lips. They were addictive: soft, and pillowy, the bottom one plumper than the top—lips any girl would give their left tit for. I wanted this kiss as well.

I pushed my chin along his shoulder to let him know my answer. The hand still cradling my face moved behind my neck, working its fingers into my hair, guiding my lips to his. His warm breath blew out against me as his lips pressed against mine. There was no collision of mouths, no battle of tongues.

Rather, there was tenderness and a beauty in our union. It radiated from our lips through to my heart. He ended it before I was ready, but came back to kiss each of my lips individually. The top got a peck, then the bottom, before he pulled away and searched my eyes.

"I love you, Becca Reynolds. And I will fight for you, for us. Please know that." His look lingered.

"Ty, I . . ."

"Don't say anything. I didn't say it to hear it back. I'll wait to hear it again when we're in a good place." He said it with such confidence, he even made me feel we would get there.

"It's not that I don't . . ." I started, but he stopped me.

"I know, and it's OK." And then suddenly he jumped off the end of the bed and extended his hand to me. "C'mon, let's get back downstairs. Lanie will have my ass if I keep you away from her and the party for too long."

And for a second, it felt like old times. I grabbed his hand, and we started for the door together. Bounding down the stairs, excited to get back to the crowd, I wasn't paying much attention to the surrounding people. As we tried to find Lanie and Xander, Ty held on to me because it was so crowded.

Why wasn't I prepared for it when Gage showed up, right in front of me?

"Hi, Becca," he said in his sultry voice. How was it that his voice carried over all the noise? "Everything OK over here?" He looked between me and Ty, his eyes staying passive.

Ty backed away, I knew suddenly more on edge than he'd been. I didn't want this to take an ugly turn between the two of them.

I didn't need to say anything, though. Ty spoke up before I could.

"Yep, all good, Gage. Bec, I'll see ya later. I'll tell Lanie to come look for you."

I looked at Ty to ascertain his mood before he walked away. But he wasn't looking at me. His eyes were on Gage. The testosterone was pungent between the two of them. Gage had flipped his cap forward, his eyes looking out from under the brim. It darkened his eyes, making his stare appear almost deathly. Ty gave him a small grin and moved along.

"Gage." I pulled him to look at me when I said his name. "What are you doing?" I was pissed. He was out of line.

"I was only making sure you were OK. Seemed like things were getting a bit heated over here," he responded. But I knew that wasn't it. He wanted to break up whatever it was he thought was going on between me and Ty.

"Or maybe you were a bit jealous watching me talk to him?"

Suddenly, Gage looked years younger than he was. The contrite look that overcame him, coupled with his clothes, suddenly made me realize maybe he wasn't this sophisticated, grown-up man I thought he was. Maybe he had insecurities like the rest of us.

"I thought we just had a talk about everything going slow, and I've been watching you have a serious conversation with him in front of me. What the fuck, Becca?" He was angry but trying to keep his cool, his biting words coming through tight lips. "That doesn't seem very slow to me."

Well, it was with *him* we talked about things going slow; it had nothing to do with Ty. But I didn't point that out to him.

"Oh, you mean when I walked right by you as you were being dry humped by three other girls? That time, is that the time you're talking about?" I countered. I was not going down without a fight. He didn't get to do this. "And not that it's any of your business, but Ty and I went upstairs to *talk*." My finger jabbed him in the chest for emphasis.

He grabbed a hold of my finger, working his hand into mine and bringing it to his side. I felt like my life was on repeat, because he dragged me to the stairs and up we went. He turned us into the first room we got to, the bathroom, and swung the door closed. Spinning me around and up against the door, his arms caged my head.

His eyes stared into mine as we both let out bated breaths. My pulse was rapid as his stare didn't waver; there was a combination of angst from the argument and a bit of something else. His nose came close to mine, and he rubbed it along my cheek.

Fuck! What the hell was I doing? How in God's name had I allowed myself to get into a situation where I was upstairs with two different guys within five minutes of each other?

"The wheels are turning in your head. Calm down," he said. "I'm sorry. I shouldn't be putting pressure like this on you." He dropped his forehead to mine, his breaths regulating. "I shouldn't have jumped to conclusions."

I wasn't about to tell him about the kiss with Ty at this point; it wasn't worth it. Nor was it his business. That was a truth I wasn't willing to tell. I'd just continue hearing his apology.

"And those girls, they were nothing. Nothing like you, anyway." His dark eyes were hooded when he pulled back. "I, uhm, don't know what came over me, Becca. I really am sorry." He had a sheepish look about him. "I feel like I stepped back in time, acting like I did when I was . . ."

"My age," I finished his sentence.

"I was nothing like you at your age. I was an immature asshole. Kind of how I acted today." His arms were still surrounding my head, our faces close.

"Gage, listen. It's OK; I get it. I was jealous when I saw you talking to those girls, so I can only imagine how you felt if you thought Ty and me were hooking up." I held his face, needing him to hear my next words. "But if you don't take me downstairs, like, now, everyone is going to think I not only hooked up with one but two guys!"

He had a silly grin on his face. "You're jealous?"

"Oh my God, that's all you got out of that? Please, let's go downstairs, Gage." I started pulling away and grabbed for the doorknob. He stilled my hand on the knob, and I turned to look at him, impatient. But he yanked me back and I fell into his arms.

"We can go downstairs if you promise me we're good, and that we can see each other one night this week." His boyish grin made me giggle as he bargained for my time.

"I think that can be arranged," I said breathlessly as he pulled the door open behind us.

"Let's get you back to your party," he said as he guided me out the door and down the stairs. As we descended, he leaned into my ear and whispered, "The hard work on your halter top needs to be seen, and I'm glad to see it stayed up." I turned to him on the last step to see his face. "I wasn't planning on sharing you, Becca, but I also didn't think it would bother me if I had to."

He gestured with a raised eyebrow across the room.

At Ty.

CHAPTER 13

"Dude, what are you doing up so early?" Jake whined as he lumbered into the kitchen. "Early" is a relative term to college students. Especially the day after a football game. It was already after eleven. He was scrounging through the cabinet looking for something. "And what smells so good? I'm fucking starving. We're already out of food and we're not even a month into school." He walked over to the island and inspected the bags of food I placed there moments before.

"Asshole, don't even think about it!" I warned. "Those are for me and Becca. I'm picking her up soon."

Once I talked to my parents about staying here at school for the first football game, I took full advantage of them giving me this opportunity. Knowing I had these extra two days I wasn't expecting, I came up with this idea to see Becca today last minute. I had no idea if she would go for it, but I was fucking ecstatic that she did.

Jake backed up, hands in the air. "Whoa, no problem, man. Up early to impress the missus—I get it." He went to the refrigerator next; I knew he hoped something of interest would materialize. But we had nothing, which was why I went out for food.

I chose not to drink too much yesterday, knowing today was important. I didn't want to be hungover. Looking at Jake and his current state, I was pleased with my actions.

"You look like shit," I told him. "What are you even doing up?" He had found a half-empty carton of OJ and was chugging it from the container. When he finished, he threw it across the room, attempting to make it in the trash can, but missed.

"I have a test I need to study for," he replied. "A test already. Can you believe it? And the professor is an ass, too. No study guide or anything. I'm meeting up with a study group soon." He continued searching for something he could put in his stomach. "I'm going to have to leave earlier than I thought to get something else to eat." He turned to look at me. "We need to come up with a food plan for this house, a better one. Who's in charge of food shopping?"

"Don't know, man. I think all four of us need to talk and figure that out." I didn't disagree with Jake about that. We needed a plan. Aaron and Ben, the other two guys we lived with, I was sure would be on board with doing something like that: a shopping and cooking schedule. "Maybe like a house meeting or something."

Jake nodded vigorously. "Yes," he agreed. "I'll see if the other guys are around tonight. You around? Nine work for you?"

I kind of hoped after my day with Becca I wouldn't be around tonight, but that was wishful thinking.

"Yeah, I'll probably be around," I told him.

"OK, good. Got any aspirin? My head is pounding," he said as he started back toward the stairs. "I really shouldn't have drunk as much, knowing I had a study group this morning."

"Up in the bathroom cabinet. Help yourself," I told him. He mumbled something on his way up the stairs that was probably a thank you, but I couldn't hear him. I was thankful we weren't holding any grudges from our tiff. I didn't need any more drama in my life.

I went back to gathering everything I needed for the day I had planned with Becca. I told her we were getting coffee and breakfast, and that was true. But I didn't tell her where we were taking it. And everything else I would have hiding in the trunk of my car.

I only hoped my little surprise for her would help me.

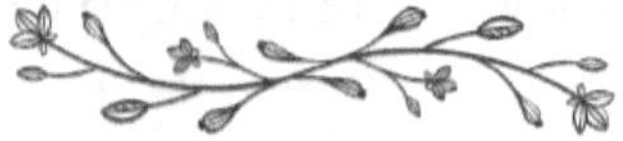

I took out my phone and shot Becca a text when I arrived at her apartment.

Me:

Hey Bec, I'm here when you're ready

Knowing her, she wouldn't be out for a while. But to my surprise, the door opened only two minutes after I hit send on the text and Becca strolled down the path to the parking lot where I was waiting. I jumped out of my car and hurried to open her door.

"Morning, Bec. You look beautiful." And she did. She was in a little dress that reminded me of the one she wore the first day back at school. This was one was a deep red, my favorite color on her. She wore a little white sweater over her shoulders, and there was a hint of fall in the air, considering it was still kind of early in the day. Her hair was a shiny black in the sunlight; the hint of red highlights seemed to have faded, which I missed. She wore it down her back, long and wavy. I hoped she wore it like that because she knew I loved it that way.

She stopped when she got near the car door and looked up at me. "Thanks," she said with a smile. As she slid into the seat and I closed the door, I realized I was nervous.

Was this going to do us any good today? Was she expecting me to tell her anything else? Because that was not in my plan. My plan was to woo her, treat her like a princess, and try to remind her of what we once had.

As I got in my seat, I noticed her eyes on me, watching my every move. "You don't seem hungover," she said, almost in disbelief.

"Well, that's because I'm not." I put the car in gear and began our drive to the coffee shop downtown, the cozy one I knew she liked. "I chose not to drink too much yesterday, knowing we were seeing each other today." She remained quiet after I said that. She propped her elbow on the car door as her hand held her head up and she continued to watch me.

"What?" I asked, genuinely bewildered by her stare.

The slow shake of her head as she turned to look out the front window made me think she wouldn't answer me. But a few moments later, she did.

"Thank you," she said. "That's all. Thank you."

Her tiny smile was only visible in profile since she kept her gaze out the front window as she spoke. But it did something to my heart; it squeezed it tight in my chest. Because if it weren't for me putting us in this position, this all wouldn't be necessary. I wouldn't have to be walking on eggshells around the girl I loved trying to win her back. Instead, we both would have enjoyed the party yesterday and stayed in bed all day today.

But I fucked up.

Few people were up and about the day after a home football game in this town, especially the first game. Downtown was quiet and I could park right in front of the shop. Becca got herself out of the car before I could get to her, but I grabbed her door to close it before she did.

Suddenly, I worried I was trying too hard. But these were things I would have done for her anyway, so I knocked that thought clear out of my head.

There were a few students and some older residents in line for coffee. The students looked to be getting ready for study sessions, similar to Jake.

"So, what will it be? Your typical pumpkin latte for the season?" I asked her. She was standing next to me, looking up at the menu.

"Yeah, but are you getting anything to eat?" she asked, turning to look at me. "I think I'll get one of those egg sandwiches. Can you order that for me? And I'll go grab a table."

"You don't need to order any food, and we don't need a table."

Her head snapped up. "Why not?" she asked.

"I've got the food thing covered," I responded, "and I have a plan for us that doesn't include eating here." I smiled down at her inquisitive eyes.

A wide, conspiratorial smile took over her face. "Well, aren't you full of surprises today, Mr. Brennan?"

She remained in line with me as I ordered our drinks. The urge to grab a hold of her hand consumed me. Such a strong desire for us to be the way we were was hitting me hard. Finally, we got our order and made it back to my car.

"Where are we going, Ty?" she asked through a slurp of her coffee. "Christ, that's hot!"

"Don't worry, it's not far."

We were going to a special place right on campus.

"The pond?" Becca's question held a note of something else to it, but I couldn't quite place exactly what it was. She seemed a bit off as we pulled into the lot closest to the pond on campus. It was a beautiful spot, and I knew it would be deserted on a Sunday morning.

"Yeah, is that OK?" I asked, nervous that she didn't want to be here. I put the car in park and looked at her, trying to figure out what was going on. She turned to me, and her face was more relaxed.

"It's perfect. Are there tables somewhere I don't know about? For us to eat on, I mean."

I reached into the back seat and pulled on the bag I had packed, which included the food. "No, not that I know of, but I brought a blanket. I thought we'd have a picnic." I slapped the bag on my lap to show her I'd thought of everything. "When I checked the weather and saw how perfect it would be today, I came up with the idea."

Her entire body relaxed. Her brilliant green eyes crinkled with a smile that displayed her white teeth. "That sounds amazing, Ty." We met at the front of the car and both searched the area.

"What looks good?" I asked. "Where do you want to go? There's a grassy area that way, toward the path." I reached for her hand and walked in that direction.

And she let me take it.

Her hand felt like warm satin in mine. I made a point of not taking for granted any moment of the day. I would mark every milestone in my mind, just in case. I gave her hand a gentle squeeze. "Want to go toward the path?"

She shook her head. "How about we go to the other side of the pond? There seems to be more sun over there, so it might stay warmer." She pointed to a patch of grass that led to the pond's edge that had no trees nearby.

"Perfect," I told her. With the bag on my shoulder, I pulled her along to the spot she pointed out.

She was right about picking a spot in the sun; the shade spots as we walked were cool. The area was pretty clear of rocks and lumps, so I took the blanket from the bag to spread it out.

"Here, let me help you," Becca said as she grabbed the other corners. We flapped it up in the breeze and watched it settle on the ground. She plopped in the middle as I took out the feast I brought along. "Oh, wow, this looks amazing, Ty!"

Strawberries with a cream cheese dip, veggie omelet bites, blueberry muffins, and mini bagels. My momma taught me right. Well, she taught me how to shop and order food. I could cook, but that wasn't happening quite this early, so I ordered it ahead. But I guess I got it right, because Becca seemed happy.

And that was all that mattered.

"Well, I'm glad it looks good. Here are some plates and napkins. I even remembered plastic utensils." The pride in my voice came through, and she chuckled.

"You did good."

We settled in, eating quietly. Both of us looked around at our surroundings while picking at the buffet of food. Low clouds hung over the mountain range in the distance, giving us a pretty cool backdrop. That was one reason this was such a popular spot with students, mainly couples.

"Have you seen the otter yet, in the pond?" she asked, breaking the silence. She looked over at me as she leaned back on her elbows. She appeared to be done eating.

"No. Have you?"

It was rumored that there was an otter that lived in this pond; some even called it 'Otter Pond' for that reason. But I hadn't been here enough to catch a glimpse of him.

"No, I've only been by the pond one other time, other than quickly walking by."

And then the silence returned.

"How are your brothers doing? Everything good at home?" I asked her. Becca always struggled being at her house with the chaos of her family. We haven't spoken about anything personal in quite a while, so I thought family stuff might break the ice.

"They're good. The twins are getting big, although Jonah isn't as tall as Sam and that's pissing him off a ton." She laughed to herself after saying that. She always complained, but when she spoke, you could tell how much love there truly was for them in her voice. They might drive her crazy, but she loved her brothers, all four of them. "And the other two, well, the teen years are tough with them, but they're still decent kids. My parents are still . . . working a lot, even though I'm here." She paused. Then seemed like she wanted to change the subject, shrugging her shoulders as if nothing was going to change her parents.

"How are your classes going?" she asked, diverting.

"They're fine," I said. "Lanie told me you got an officer's role in your business group—that's awesome. Phi Beta something?" I couldn't remember the other Greek letter.

"Phi Betta Lambda, and yes, I might actually become president of BRU's chapter this year," she said proudly.

"That's amazing, Bec. Congratulations."

"You should join it, Ty. All business majors should be in it," she scolded, somewhat jokingly.

"Yeah, well, I was busy with my own frat shit," I told her. But she was right. The group she was in was more likely to land her a job than my fraternity was.

Our conversation had hit a comfortable lull. We sat looking out over the pond again, the sun sparkling on the small ripples the breeze made on the water.

I wanted to talk about *us* today. Maybe talk about some of our memories from last year to remind her of what we had that was good. But suddenly, I was nervous that doing that might put everything in jeopardy. My promise to her to take things slow was already broken by simply being here with her.

"Becca—"

"Ty—"

"You first," I said to her.

She shyly looked away, out over the pond, looking as though she didn't want to continue. But then she turned back toward me. "Yesterday was harder than I expected."

Without making her say it, I knew she meant being at the tailgate with both me and Gage. And I wouldn't disagree that it sucked. I wanted to fucking punch the guy in the face when he walked in between Becca and me after we came downstairs. But in his defense, he felt he was the one in Becca's life and that I stepped in on them.

He just didn't know yet that she was mine and always would be.

"I'm sorry if I had anything to do with that." And I meant that. It took everything in me to leave her with that guy and walk away. Everything. But I knew if I didn't, I would destroy any chance I had with her. But I didn't know if there was something I could have done to make it easier on her. Or maybe not done, like not kiss her. But I wasn't sorry about kissing her; I would never be sorry about kissing her.

"It's not you, Ty, not you at all. It's me. I've put myself in this situation." Her contemplative look returned as she scanned the pond again, looking for what, I wasn't sure.

"See, that's where you're wrong, Becca. You need to stop taking any responsibility for the mess we're in. It's all on me. You asked me for something and I didn't give it to you. It's as simple as that." Her eyes stayed glued to mine as I talked, like she was wondering if I would be divulging any further truths to her. "Am I happy that you're hanging out with someone else? That's a big hell no. But I don't blame you, not one bit. I've put us in this spot. Me, only me." She turned to look out over the pond, deep in thought but oddly quiet. "My job now is to work as hard as I can to win you back. To show you that what we had is worth fighting for. That *we* are worth fighting for." My hand was gripping hers by the time I was done talking, an effort to drive home the intensity of my words.

She remained quiet for a few minutes, very different from the normal Becca. And I hated that this was what she'd become lately. Her feistiness seemed to be waning, her fire going out.

Because of me.

"Why don't we finish eating?" She nodded, and we set out to put our plates together and enjoy the food. We made some more small talk about classes and our roommates as we both enjoyed the meal.

"This was delicious, Ty. And really thoughtful of you. Thank you." She smiled as she started putting the garbage away in the bag.

I didn't want our time to come to an end. Thankfully, she sat back on her elbows and looked out to the pond, apparently not ready to leave yet either. Once I had the rest of the mess cleaned up, I cozied up a bit closer, leaning on an elbow.

"I appreciate you telling me about what you went through at home with your ex-girlfriend and your parents," she said, turning to look at me. "That must have been hard, and I understand, I do. Paying for college myself would not be an option for me either, at least not without a lot of difficulty."

I wasn't expecting us to have this talk today. But then she stopped talking, and that made me nervous. It seemed like she was on a roll of forgiveness, but then she came to an abrupt halt.

"Bec, listen, I know you're not completely satisfied with what I've told you about my parents. I get it," I said.

But she stopped me.

"Ty, no, listen to me. Lanie helped me understand why you probably didn't want to tell me last year. If anyone understands issues with parents and problems at home, it's that one. She helped me think more clearly about what you must have gone through." Becca moved herself closer to me, her hand on my arm, gripping it for emphasis. She shook her head slightly before talking again. "I'm sorry if I've been too hard on you. I only wish I knew back then what I know now."

The guilt, the fucking guilt, was eating away at me. I needed her to stop blaming herself.

I reached out and held her face, taking advantage of her being so close. Her skin was warm in my hands as her doe eyes looked up at me. Those brilliant green eyes that looked at me with a love and understanding I didn't deserve.

Right then, I decided as soon as I returned from fall break, I was telling Becca everything.

No more of this shit. She deserved better. She needed a better me. I would tell her everything, even if it meant her walking away, because she deserved the whole truth.

Just a couple more weeks. I needed Becca to give me a couple more weeks.

"Bec, I know I fucked up. I know I should have done everything differently. I'm going to fix everything, you'll see. I just need a little bit more time. If you're willing to give me that, I *will* fix us."

Her face remained settled in my palm, her head tilting as if she was basking in the feeling of my hand. She eventually opened her once closed eyes and looked up into mine, giving me a slow nod.

"I've waited this long, Ty. I'm still here, in the shadows, waiting for you to figure it out. I know it's gotten complicated, but I'm not going anywhere. Not yet."

I leaned toward her, and she didn't push back, her body willingly going to the ground under me. Balanced on one elbow, my hand cradling her face, I asked her the all-important question. "Becca, is this good?" I lowered my face to hers, waiting for her answer. "Can I kiss you?"

She wrapped her hands around the back of my head, pulling me toward her with intensity, my mouth crushing against hers. I nearly cried; feeling her lips melt against mine was something I continued to not take for granted.

Her hand went around my waist as my one leg slid between hers, my body angling over the top of her. The swell of her breasts pushed against my chest with each of her breaths. Her short little dress was riding up, giving me an eyeful of her long, full legs. I had a hard time keeping my hand from wandering under the hem, so I moved it to her stomach. But that did me no good, either, my fingers itching to grab a hold of the taut nipple pushing through the thin material.

Resting my head against hers, I slowed things down for a moment. I looked up, seeing how low the sun had already gotten in the sky; our talk lasted longer than I thought. My eyes scanned the area, and I realized we were still alone, no spectators for our escapades. But I wasn't sure I wanted to pursue this out in the open.

When I looked back into her eyes, I really needed to know moving forward was OK. "Bec, are you sure about this? I mean, this is the furthest thing from me giving you space."

"Ty," she said. A small moan escaped after she said my name. "I've missed you. I want nothing more than for you to keep going." She pulled me closer to her, our bodies grinding against each other.

"Becca, fuck, I want to do things to you right now so bad," I whispered in her ear. "I wish we weren't on this fucking blanket."

Her mouth went to my ear as she whispered in return, "Then take me back to your place."

My head snapped back, and I stared at her for further confirmation. The tiny smirk on her face told me everything I needed to know.

We laughed out loud as we threw everything in my bag and grabbed the rest by hand while running wildly for the car together. I don't think everything made it back in my car, but neither of us cared much.

The drive to my place was a blur; Becca's kisses on my neck, ears, and mouth were a dangerous distraction. Thankfully, it was less than a mile's drive to my apartment.

We hurried inside, and she followed me up the stairs to my room. She hadn't been to my place yet—a stark reminder that this year had been so different.

Once in the room, I closed the door and turned toward her. The laughter and giggles subsided. The room filled with an awkward quiet, our ragged breathing the only sounds.

"You're so beautiful, Becca. I miss you so much," I said, filling the silence. "You're sure this is what you want?"

"Yes, Ty. I want to be here with you." Her eyes held a confidence no one would deny. I saw the Becca I knew emerging right before my eyes.

"Will you take your dress off for me? I miss seeing your beautiful body." I sat on the bed as she sauntered toward me. She walked the few steps needed for her to be standing in between my legs, nudging them apart. My hands immediately went to the backs of her thighs, so tempted to reach under and grab her ass. But this was always my favorite part.

She started with the strap on the left, sliding it off her shoulder. The thin piece of material hung against her arm, teasing me. Her eyes never broke contact with mine. But I had to look away, because there was a show to watch: the show she was putting on for me. As her hand slid down her left shoulder, the fingertips crossed her chest, ever so lightly dipping into her cleavage, over to the strap on the other side. Once that strap was pushed down, she was holding her dress up with her hands over her breasts. Then, each arm worked its way out of the straps, the dress ready to fall to the ground. But she continued to hold it with one hand while the other lifted the hem. She dragged it up her leg, torturously slow. Once the dress was as high as her hip, she slid it over, giving me a glimpse of what was to come.

Today, it was a white lace thong. The contrast of the white against her still somewhat tan skin was fucking sexy as hell. The thin material curved around her hip. My hands trembled with the need to reach up and grab a hold of that round ass cheek she was teasing me with, but I knew she wouldn't let me.

"Bec . . ." I moaned her name.

"Not yet." She wagged her finger at me as she let the bottom of her dress fall back into place. Both of her hands went to the bodice of her dress, barely covering her ample tits spilling over the top of the cotton material. She slowly started sliding the material down her torso.

Fuck, my dick felt like it was about to bust out of my jeans. I needed to move it to the side to give it more room. Becca saw me do that and gave me a knowing smile as she released one large tit from the top of her dress. She gathered it in her hand, pushing it up the way she knew I liked as her fingers neared the hard tip.

I couldn't take it anymore. I gripped her firmly by the hips and she startled. Her hand dropped from her breast, allowing the dress to sink further down.

"Becca," I blurted as I abruptly stood. "I can't wait for this dance to be over. Sorry, baby, but I need you now." Reaching out, I took a hold of her dress, pushing the soft cotton down her body until it pooled at her feet. She looked up at me, surprised, but the look quickly turned to desire. Spinning her around, I tossed her on the bed with a bounce as she let out a stunned laugh.

Reaching down, I hooked my thumbs under the thin straps of her thong. Pulling on them slowly, she lifted her ass in the air to allow them to come off.

It brought a smile to her face; she was enjoying this already.

I stood over her, taking a moment to admire the perfection that was Becca Reynolds.

From the sultry look in those deep sea-green eyes looking up at me, to the dark pink circles on her tits begging for my tongue, to the tiny patch of light-brown hair just above the apex of her legs.

Absolute. Perfection.

"Ty," she almost moaned as she rubbed her thighs together.

That movement made my dick twitch. I reached for my fly, popping it open, needing to give myself some breathing room.

"Let me touch you," she whined, trying to sit up.

But I forced her back down with my hands on her belly, grazing up to those wonderful tits. "Not yet, babe. Let me take care of you first." I remained standing, needing to continue to soak in the beauty in front of me. She got shy and covered herself up. I reached down and pulled her hands back from her body. "Never cover up perfection, Becca. You see this right here?" I motioned to the side of her breast. "I love the natural look of you, how they fall a bit to the side when you're in bed but they're still fucking firm enough that they almost touch right here." I touched her right at her cleavage. Becca had perfect tits. Kind of big. Not so big that everyone stared, but definitely more than a handful. "And this up here." I touched her forehead, motioning to her head, her brain. "I love how you approach life. I love how you think, the snarky way you handle life." She rolled her eyes at me for that one, and we both laughed. "And this, right here. I love this part of you." I rubbed her belly. "I love how it's perfectly rounded and not flat."

"Ty!" she screamed, and her hands went straight to her stomach. I pulled her hands away and continued rubbing her belly.

"Babe, I mean it. The gentle curve of it is sexy. I'm not a flat, skeleton kind of guy. You're it for me." I rubbed along her sides, down her legs, then back up the side of her breast, landing on her chest, over her heart. "But most of all, I love what's in here." Her eyes softened when I said that. "I love who you are as a person. How you treat people, the respect you demand for yourself. Everything about you, I love."

I leaned down, hovering over her, nose to nose. Our mouths were close, as if we were about to kiss. My lips went in, both our mouths opened, but I stopped and pulled back a bit.

"But I also like to make you come. And that's what I'm going to do right now. Is that OK?" I asked, looking right into her eyes.

All she could do was nod.

"Good. I'm going to go down and taste you. I've missed that. And while I'm doing that, I need you to be thinking about how you want me to fuck you when I'm done."

CHAPTER 14
Becca

Holy shit. I'd forgotten how fucking amazing Ty was at everything. Absolutely everything with my body and sex. Fuck the whole idea of him giving me space.

"Are you thinking about how I'm going to fuck you, Becca?" he asked, pulling his mouth away from my clit.

I looked down at him, his hooded eyes returning the look.

"Ty," I said in between moans, "I can't think about anything at the moment."

"Good, baby doll."

His tongue dipped inside me as his finger found my clit, pulling on it and rubbing it. As my fingers twisted in the quilt on the bed to ground myself, my body lifted in mounting desire. My muscles were already tense, closing in on an orgasm quickly. My hips lifted and Ty used his hands to push me back to the bed, which meant his hands left my pussy.

I whined.

"Don't make me have to hold you down, baby. Then I can't keep my hands where they're needed." His words vibrated against my opening, the sensation coupled with his thumb returning to massaging my clit in torturous circles.

"Fuck, Ty, you're gonna get me!" I moaned.

"That's it, Bec," he whispered in between licks. "Come for me, baby. Come in my mouth. I want to taste you, all of you." His tongue pushed inside me, deeper, as his fingers pulled instead of rubbed.

You know when you're climbing that hill and you see the top? And you just need him to keep doing what he's doing, not change it at all, to get you to the top? That's where I was at. Usually Ty would take me to the edge, then back off, keep me from going over.

But today was different. He knew I needed this release. He forged ahead. He didn't stop. I ran to the top of the hill, and screamed once I got there.

"Fuck!" I yelled. "Oh my God, Ty! Yes!"

And what he was best at was not stopping just because he thought I fell over the top; he kept that orgasm rolling and rolling. He got every toe-curling drop out of it he could. My body contorted and begged him to stop, but his mouth held on.

Finally, his lips conceded and pulled away, kissing along the lips of my pussy. His hands reached up and tweaked my nipples and massaged my breasts as he lifted his head. Looking up at me, he smiled.

"That was better than I remembered," he said, his voice sounding like silk.

"You are so good at that," I told him as I sat up on my elbows, looking down at him. His hair was mussed up and his lips were puffy from his work on me; he looked damn sexy. "Come here, Ty."

He stood up, and that was when I realized he still had all his clothes on. He reached over his head and pulled his shirt off in that sexy way guys do. His stomach muscles were on full display as he did it, flexed and tight. Next, he undid his zipper, pushing boxers and jeans down at once. His full erection popped out, snapping against his thigh. It had been a while since I'd seen that cock, and I'd forgotten the absolute beauty of it. So thick my fingers barely could grasp it. The silk skin of the taut head. I loved licking that tight skin, especially when that bead of liquid was waiting for me. I peeked over to see if he was hard enough to show off the thick veins that protruded from his dick when he's fully erect. And he was, completely ready for me.

"How long do we have, Bec? Do you have homework to do?" he asked.

"Yeah," I said. Not wanting to be brought back to reality, but always thankful for his consideration.

"OK, so we don't have too much time left together. It's getting late already." He looked at the clock, and it was already 6 p.m. I couldn't believe so many hours had passed in our day. "So let's make this worth it, babe. Tell me, what have you decided?" His look went immediately back to full-blown sex god. "How am I fucking you right now?"

"You should know," I teased. "You know how I like it." His knowing eyes focused on mine; a sly smile took over his face.

He stalked toward me like a predatory lion and grabbed my ankles, which were still hanging off the edge of the bed. Lifting my legs up by my feet, his hands slid down the backs of them, to my ass, landing on my hips. Once he had a firm hold, he flipped me over to my belly, pulling me toward him with his hands firmly gripping my waist. My ass slapped against his body, the length of his dick pressing into me. His one hand slid under my belly, holding me close to him, while the other pushed the back of my head gently onto the bed. I turned my face to the side, enjoying the feel of him taking charge.

"You like when I force you into position, Becca?" he asked.

"You know I do, Ty."

"You want me to slide my dick into you from behind, don't you?" he whispered, his voice gravelly. His hand left the back of my head; I could tell he was stroking himself, readying his dick for me.

"Yes, Ty, you know I do." I missed this. I missed him. I hadn't realized how much until I saw the way he looked at me when I was on the bed. The look of adoration he always had for me was addictive. He was a fucking tiger in bed.

His body fell against mine as he reached under, desperate to grab my tits. He pawed at them, crazed, in a frenzy, a man starved for sexual release. His fingers found my nipple, pulling it between them. At the same time, he grasped his cock with his other hand and dragged it along the seam of my ass, teasing my entrances.

"You're so wet, Bec. I can't wait to slip my cock inside you." His words were against my back, a whisper as he kissed me between syllables, as if in worship.

He perched the tip at my opening, teasing me, rubbing its swollen head against me. He would pull back and cover up; he always did.

But so quickly he reared back, grabbing my hips, and rammed his dick inside me, filling me to the hilt with his full length.

"Fuck! Becca! You feel so good!"

And then he froze. Completely inside me, he froze.

We both did.

"Are you OK, babe? Did I hurt you?" he asked, barely a whisper.

I shook my head slightly, afraid to move. "No, it feels amazing," I answered. "But, Ty, you don't have on . . ."

"I know." That was all he said as he pulled out slightly.

And then he slammed back into me harder yet. Filling me once again, completely.

My eyes sealed shut; part ecstasy, part pain. That beautiful, searing pain as he slid in and out of me over and over again. His fingers dug into my hips, possibly drawing blood, he held on so tightly. I wrapped my arms around the pillow I held, my mouth shoved into the material to drown out my screams, my sounds of desire.

"Ty!" I grunted. "Oh, God."

I panted as he impaled me, the speed increasing. This was not a gentle reunion. This was carnal.

We were colliding.

There were no more words. The grunts and moans of our desire filled the air between us. The rhythm was steady but rough at the same time. He was hungry.

But then he stilled.

I wiggled my ass against him, teasing him to keep moving.

"Shit, Bec, cut me some slack. I don't want to come yet," he panted. "It's been so fuckin' long and you feel too good." He pushed in hard again but had to stop. He pulled out all the way and swiftly flipped me over onto my back.

I looked up into his eyes and saw the desire, but I saw so much more. It was as if his eyes caressed my body as he took me in. I watched him look at every part of me from top to bottom. He dropped his body on top of me, his face hovering, his eyes searching mine.

"Do you know how much I love you? That I haven't stopped loving you one bit during this? Becca, you will always be my perfect."

With his arms caging my head, his hands cradling my face, he slid himself inside of me. This time, he was more controlled. The slow torture as he pulled in and out was sexier than the manic fucking I was getting just moments before.

His love for me was sexy.

His golden-tipped locks from the summer sun were sexy.

His tight, ripped abs that flexed with each thrust above me were sexy.

His dirty mouth combined with words that sounded like original poetry was sexy.

His enormous cock was sexy.

Our past together, which felt like home, was sexy.

And then his rhythm increased. His movements were still fluid, but faster. He pushed himself onto one arm as he continued to rock inside of me, using the other to reach between us. His fingers deftly found my clit as his steady tempo brought us both closer to the top of our hill. My hands reached around to grab on to his ass, that fine tight ass of his. I dug my fingers in, pulling him into me even deeper.

"Fuck, Bec, that's gonna get me. Are you close, babe? Are you gonna come?" he said, winded, in my ear.

"Keep rubbing my clit, Ty. I'm so close," I told him.

His thumb and finger grabbed a hold of it and gave it a little tug, making me see stars. He held on as he pumped into me.

"Baby, you'll have to take over. Let me ride you and watch you touch yourself."

I moved my hand between us, finding my swollen clit with my fingertips. My hand circled and rubbed as he lifted his torso from me, up on his knees. Lifting my ass in his hands and holding me by my sides, he continued with rhythmic thrusts. His eyes drifted to my hand between us.

"Watching you do that, touch yourself, fuck, Becca." His words came out in uneven staccato breaths. "It's going to make me come, baby doll."

He was trying to stay in control, to keep his movements smooth.

But he couldn't. Not anymore.

He abandoned all control, and the divine assault began. As he pumped in and out of me with a vigor I'd never seen from him, I was struck by the beauty of his body. The strained muscles in his forearms as he pushed and pulled, the veins bulged through his skin. His broad shoulders flexed with every movement as they held his body over me. The planes of his abs tensed as he fucked me, emptying himself inside me.

That beautiful body of his collapsed onto mine, sweat mixing as our chests collided. We stayed like that for minutes, allowing our breathing to return to normal. Eventually, he lifted himself onto one arm and his mouth found mine for a simple, tender kiss before he pulled away.

Leaning down again, he put his mouth close to my ear.

"So, it's been a while since I've done this without protection," he said, sounding embarrassed. "Do you want me to get something to clean you?" He pulled away again, this time pulling himself out of me.

"That's OK; I can take care of it," I told him as I started getting up from the bed. However, his hand came down on my belly, holding me in place.

"No, I think I want to do this for you. Let me take care of you." His steps were quick as he retreated to his bathroom. The water turned on from the faucet and continued running as I heard cabinets banging open and closed. A hushed "dammit" emitted from the partially closed door before he hastily returned to me.

"So, apparently I need to do laundry," he said, the frustration clear. "I don't have a single clean towel or washcloth. But I have this." He stood over me at the side of the bed with what appeared to be a balled-up T-shirt in his hands, dripping on the floor. The small smile was endearing as he tried to hold the wet shirt out toward me. "This'll work, right?" he asked, then looked at the puddle forming on the floor. "Shit, wait, let me go wring it out more."

I jolted up in the bed as he ran back to the sink because he knew that the cleanup needed to happen soon.

Or there would be no need for the shirt.

It's such an awkward thing that no one ever talks about. It's definitely not in any romance book I'd ever read. And I always wondered, *Why not?* They make it seem like the after-sex mess just disappears somehow.

But it was most definitely not disappearing at the moment. Instead, it was now making a mess all over Ty's sheets. He came running out of the bathroom with the shirt folded up in his hands, ready to go.

"Hey, where ya going? Let me do this, Bec." His cool hands separated my knees to begin wiping me clean. As he bent down, our heads collided, his forehead to my crown.

"Shit!" I yelled while snapping my head away from his and rubbing the tender spot.

Ty slumped to the floor in defeat, dropping the shirt on the way.

"Well, this didn't end the way I envisioned it," he said as a hint of a laugh escaped his mouth.

"Well, it's the sentiment that counts. Isn't that what they always say?" I offered.

His eyes softened as he sat back on his knees. I plopped backward onto my elbows and spread my legs wide for him. "Have at it, babe. Use that damn shirt you worked so hard to find and clean your cum out of my body. And while you're at it, clean off your sheets a bit too!"

He stayed where he was, leaning against his dresser. I turned my head to find him when he hadn't gotten up from the floor. He was smiling at me. A curious smile that did funny things to my insides.

"I have an idea," he finally said as he rose from the ground, looking at the clock. He grabbed my spread legs with his hands, now empty of that wet T-shirt. He surprised me more when he yanked my legs up onto his shoulders. "How about I add to that cum inside your body and fuck you again before I let you leave?"

I had a feeling I was going to be up very late to get my homework done.

CHAPTER 15
Becca

This past weekend. Where do I start? Some would call it a success, others a disaster. I might go with a real fucking disaster. Game day was stressful, being at the tailgate with both Ty and Gage. I really thought they were going to wind up fighting. Thank God Ty was mature enough to walk away when he did. And I saw a new side of Gage, a jealous side. I admit, it made me feel good, but after thinking about it, I realized it was only going to complicate things.

Then there was my breakfast date with Ty.

First of all, the fact that he turned it into a picnic by the pond was amazing. The thought he put into it filled my heart. He was adorable with how prepared he was, and he even brought me flowers.

Our day was perfect. He was perfect. He showed me exactly why I fell in love with him last year. Why *I knew* I was still in love with him. He may not have been telling me everything I wanted to know, but he took a step in the right direction. He made a promise to fix it soon.

We had sex.

Like, incredible, mind-blowing sex.

Why was I not falling back into his arms? Why was I not going back to him?

But no, what did I do? I texted Gage that night. After I had amazing sex with Ty, I texted Gage!

Like I said, a fucking disaster.

And to make things worse, Lanie wasn't around to help me through this. She was at Xander's. I texted her asking when she would be around, and she said later today after class. I needed to bounce all of this off of her because she would have the answers. She would know why I texted Gage when I felt like I was still in love with Ty. Because none of it made sense to me. At all.

As I tried to fall asleep late Sunday night, my feelings for Ty got clouded by my thoughts of Gage. Whoever named it a "love triangle" never lived it. A triangle has straight lines. There were no straight lines happening in this triangle; every path wavered from side to side as I tried to navigate my way through.

While thinking of my lovely day with Ty by the pond, the images of what Gage and I had done by that very pond only a week prior took over my thoughts.

Invaded my thoughts.

And that was when I texted him.

Me:
Hey I can't stop thinking about our time
by the pond

Once I sent it, I wanted to unsend it. But he responded immediately.

Gage:
> You and me both, I wouldn't mind a re-peat, but how about in a bed this time

Fuck.
See. A fucking disaster.
But it didn't end there. I kept going.

Me:
> That sounds enticing

What was I doing?

Gage:
> What are you doing tomorrow night, Becca

I had just spent the day with Ty—a wonderful day with Ty. I had sex with Ty. I made him think we had a chance of getting back together. What was I doing?

Me:
> I think I'm seeing you tomorrow night Gage

And that was why my weekend was so fucked up.
And why I needed to talk to my therapist, otherwise known as Lanie. But she wasn't around. And I was going to

be seeing Gage in approximately four hours. There was no getting out of it.

But that was the thing; I didn't want to cancel.

I enjoyed the time I spent with both of them. Maybe I was just a confused girl with two fantastic guys in her life. That was when I heard the front door.

"Lanie?!" I screamed. "Is that you?" I went running down the stairs, hopeful she had come home early. Unfortunately, it was Ava getting back from class.

"Hey, Becca, what's up? Sorry, not Lanie." She looked at me with concern. "You OK, hon?"

She followed me to the kitchen. I wasn't sure I wanted to divulge any of my issues to another person. I was reaching for a soda in the fridge when she grabbed the door and held it open.

"Becca, what's wrong?" she asked. "You look like you're about to cry."

She let go of the fridge door, and I plodded to the couch.

"My life is in shambles at the moment. I needed to talk to Lanie." I curled up in the corner of the couch and pulled a blanket over me, wanting to disappear and make it all go away.

"Well, I may not be Lanie, but I'm a pretty good listener. Macie usually has some shit going on in her life, and I give her some sound advice at times. Why don't you lay it on me, girlie, and give me a try?" She settled herself on the opposite end of the couch, alert and ready for me to spill my guts to her.

The four of us had been spending more and more time together. And Macie started opening up to me a bit the other day. But I hadn't really done that with them yet.

"Listen, I know basically what's going on in your life already, Becca. Ty wants you back, you've taken up with the hottie, Gage, who looks like a broody, bearded Henry Cavill, and now you don't know what to do. Am I right?"

Well, fuck. How the hell did she do that?

"Do you do crystal ball readings on the side or some shit like that, Ava?" I asked as I buried myself deeper into the couch because I was hesitant to divulge my current dilemma. But I thought Lanie might not make it home before Gage was due to pick me up. And I needed someone's perspective on this. "It's a little more than that, but you mostly got it." I snuck a peek at her from my side of the couch and caught her staring right at me.

Waiting. Patiently.

"I'm not gonna force ya, Becca. I'm here if ya want to bounce it off me." She stood up and headed toward the stairs.

"Ava?" I called out.

She came running back, threw herself onto the arm of the couch, and sat with her knees pulled up under her chin. "I knew you'd change your mind. No one can resist talking to me." Her cute smile matched her equally cute face and hair. Her short black hair worked so well with her vibrant green eyes; it was mesmerizing. Maybe that was why people couldn't resist talking to her? Maybe she cast a spell or something on people. I loved her cut-up jeans, which she always paired with a flannel of some sort, and her Doc Martens. Very emo in a chic, sexy way. She was hot.

"Well, you're right about Ty wanting me back. He does. And, yeah, I'm kind of hanging out with Gage. We have an unconventional thing going on." I didn't know how to explain what we had.

"He's your long-term booty call, a boyfriend without the drama. It's perfect; I wish more guys were into that," she said matter-of-factly but with a tinge of jealousy. "So, what's the new development?" She slid off the arm of the couch onto the cushion and pulled my blanket over her as well, both of us getting cozy underneath it. I appreciated she was nonchalant at the same time she was trying to make me feel comfortable.

"Well, Ty actually gave me a little of what I needed, some part of his truth he'd been keeping from me. It was the reason I broke it off. I knew there was something he wasn't telling me." She didn't react, only kept listening. "I still don't think I have the whole truth, but he's trying. But the thing is," I said, but needed to sit up, feeling the story getting more complicated. And Ava leaned in, feeling the intensity change. "Once he told me, I wasn't feeling the pull to go back to him the way I was expecting. Not at first, anyway. But then yesterday, he put this whole great day together. And he made me remember what we had. He was sweet, and cute, and sexy, and . . ." I stopped talking, not sure if I wanted to divulge the details of my sex life. But what the hell? "And then we had sex. Like, our first time in months. And it was fucking hot!"

"Ooh, tell me more!" Ava said, liking the dirty details.

"Well, that's where it gets really fucked up, where I don't understand myself." It embarrassed me to tell her what I did. "Last night, after I got home from spending the day with Ty, I, um . . ."

"You reached out to Gage," she offered.

I stared at her. Lanie was in jeopardy of losing her status as my therapist. All I could do was nod.

"Well, I get it. Hottie Gage came into the picture and has you all upside down. I mean, it's understandable. The guy is sex on a fucking stick. But here's the thing," she said as she sat up, getting to the point of her words. "He's not making any commitments or promises to you, am I right?"

I shook my head.

"Well, then you have a decision to make. Which I'm pretty sure is what you already know, but maybe you need to talk it out. Are you willing to let go of what you and Ty had, and might have again, for some hot guy offering sex and only sex?" she asked.

"Plus, Gage is only here for a year. He goes back to New York in May," I offered softly.

"Well, that's even more of a reason to decide, probably sooner than later. I know Gage is the shiny new toy to play with, and that's exciting and all. And that's fine, if that's what you want. But when he's gone, or if what you two have ends, will you regret not making it work with Ty?"

Ava was putting into words all the thoughts that had been swimming around in my head. But there were still more thoughts that she hadn't even come close to touching.

"Gage and I haven't had sex. Not yet. I mean, Gage and I have done stuff, but we haven't had sex."

Her look softened a bit. "Do you have feelings for both of them?" she asked.

Damn, she was good.

And my silence was loud between us.

Eventually, I found my voice. "I still love Ty, no doubt there. That doesn't just disappear. And after yesterday..." My voice trailed off as the words I wanted to say seemed to get stuck in my throat. "My day with Ty yesterday seems to have confused me more instead of making things more clear. But Gage, I don't know what I feel about him. Not yet." I threw my head back against the couch in frustration.

"Is it really fucked up to be stringing along two guys? Or worse, hooking up with two different guys?" The tears were close, and I didn't want to cry in front of her. We didn't know each other that well yet.

"Hey," she said as she scrambled over to me on the couch, "you're not stringing anyone along. From the sounds of it, communication is not your problem. Sounds like you've been upfront and honest with both from the start." She pulled me against her side; I resisted at first, but she wouldn't let me for long. She was strong for a tiny thing. "If they both know about each other, and I don't mean the details, I think you're fine, Becca, so don't worry about that. Basically, it sounds like you need to nail down how you feel for Gage." My head was on her shoulder as she continued counseling me on my life. "If there are feelings there, then you need to tell him. Maybe that changes things for him. Ya never know."

She was one hundred percent correct. I thought the potential of something with Gage had been hanging over my head. Feelings for him had been creeping in over the past few days, and I wasn't expecting that. I probably needed to let him know that. But I was pretty sure I knew the answer I would get from him, and maybe that was why I felt the way I was. Maybe I wasn't cut out for the booty call thing, after all.

"What has made you so good at this, Ava? You seem to have all the right things to say. Why don't you have some hot sexy guy by your side?" I asked her.

Her head fell back against the couch in frustration before she spoke. "I don't need a steady guy. I have my share of hook ups, my share of sex. That's all I need. I'm not interested in anything long term. That's not for me. At. All." Her words were final. Her message definite. But there was something hidden underneath she wasn't ready to share, I could tell.

"Sounds like there's a story there we need to unpack," I said, hoping she would want to share more. But she clammed up and remained silent.

I snuggled in closer to her, thankful for her words of advice and her growing friendship.

"Well, you are the total package. Any guy would be lucky to have you," I told her. And I meant it.

She guffawed. She actually guffawed.

"What?" I asked incredulously. "You sound like you don't believe me."

She didn't answer but started sitting up, forcing me to pull away from her.

"Enough about me. Back to you. Ya know what you need to do, don't you?" Ava asked.

"About what?" I asked, looking at her, awaiting her words of wisdom.

"Gage," she said. "You need to fuck him."

CHAPTER 16

Becca

"Hi, beautiful." His voice always went straight to my nether regions. Like, straight between my legs. It never failed.

"Hi, Gage," I said into the open door. My stomach did tiny flips when I saw him standing there. He came to the door to get me. Most guys just beeped. "Do you want to come in?" I moved to the side to let him in. "I just need a minute to get my stuff upstairs. Be right back. Macie and Ava are in the living room if you want to wait with them."

He walked down the hall, and I took a second to watch him. This time, he had on a pair of gray sweatpants that clung tight to his ass. I hadn't taken the opportunity to see how they looked on the other side. Did these guys not know what gray sweatpants do to us? Scratch that. I think they knew exactly what they do to us. He wore his long-sleeve shirt pushed up on his forearms, accentuating the veined muscles as his arms swayed at his side. I ran up the stairs two at a time, knowing that leaving him alone with Ava after our talk would be dangerous. As I bounded down the stairs, I could hear Gage's deep rumble of a laugh. Rounding the corner of the hall, I found them all at the island. Gage looked up when I came in and gave me a wide smile.

"I got my wallet. Wasn't sure what we're doing tonight."

He got up from the stool and stalked toward me in that way he does. My breath hitched as he got closer. He bent his mouth close to my ear before talking.

"My plan was to take you back to my place," he whispered. "If that's OK with you?"

I literally had to swallow around a lump in my throat and I was nervous it had been audible. Stealing a look at my roommates to see if they'd heard Gage's plans for our night, I knew they had.

Macie's eyes were wide with excitement for me while she tried to act nonchalant as she stepped down from her stool.

And Ava. The conspiratorial smile that came across her face as she walked past us up to her room was almost embarrassing. "Well, whatever you guys do, have fun. I'm heading up to do homework. I'm sure you will find something more exciting than that to do." As she walked by, her finger jabbed me in the rib.

"I'm sure we will," Gage responded. "See ya girls later." But his eyes were on me. "Let's get going."

I wasn't sure why he insisted on picking me up. He literally lived about three blocks from us. But he did. He pushed the door to his place open once he'd unlocked it, and he held it for me to enter first.

"After you," he said.

I entered an alternate universe.

His townhouse appeared slightly different from the others in the neighborhood.

It didn't have backpacks all over the entranceway or red solo cups scattered on the floors. There weren't random bottles of half-drunk liquor left in various places around the room.

Rather, I felt as if I'd walked into a sleek NYC apartment. Somehow he made modern accessories work with the casual farmhouse furniture he picked out. The living room was a concoction of white and tan materials combined with silver metals in the lamps and chandeliers. It just . . . worked.

"Oh my God, Gage. This place is gorgeous. And your couch is here!" I exclaimed. "It looks amazing. Did you design all of this? I never would have chosen these unique elements, but they work." I meandered around the room, taking it all in, my hand dragging along shiny pieces on the sofa table.

He had a sofa table.

"Well, I helped pick out the stuff. I mean, you helped me, too. But my family sends in a company that puts it all together. It makes moving around as much as we do that much easier." He had moved to his bar to pour himself a drink. "Would you like a drink, Becca?"

"No, thanks. I'm good."

He stalked, in that sexy, predatory way he does, back toward the living room. That was when I got a glimpse of the front of him in his gray sweatpants.

And, yep, he knew exactly what he was doing. The soft material clung to the outline of him. I swear I could make out the veins in his dick through his pants. I knew he felt huge when I leaned up against him by the pond. But, fuck! He *was* huge! I mean, really fucking huge!

"Becca?" he asked, as if he was repeating himself.

"Yeah?"

"Want to come sit down?" He was gesturing to the couch with the hand that held his whiskey. The to-die-for couch we had picked out together.

"Oh, sure."

He definitely caught me staring at his dick. The wicked smile on his face was just short of a laugh. I was circling around the sectional, eyeing up that big seat in the middle where the sides meet, when his phone buzzed. We both stared at it on the glass-and-hammered-metal coffee table as it vibrated with the incoming call. His hand rushed to quiet the phone, and he noticeably turned it over once he did.

But not before I saw a heart next to whatever name was on the screen.

But what business was it of mine? Right? Without jumping to conclusions, I decided it could be a family member. Like maybe his mom.

Placing his drink on the table, he sat and patted the spot next to him.

"I want to sit over there," I told him as I crawled into the corner. "Ahh, it's still a really comfortable couch. We made the right decision." I sank into the cushions as I leaned my head back. It felt amazing compared to the plastic leather thing they tried to tell us was a couch in our place.

His phone buzzed again. He reached for it quickly, about to silence it, when I noticed his face transform into something I'd never seen on him before. The anger darkened his eyes as he peered at the screen.

"Becca, excuse me for a minute. I have to take this."
He got up and went into the kitchen before answering. His
hushed words were barely audible, but the tone was clear:
hatred.

I didn't want to eavesdrop, and I really wasn't. I couldn't
hear what he was saying. But I knew it was a call he wasn't
happy to be on. The only thing I could have done was go
outside to avoid hearing him. He'd never made it seem like
he had problems with his family. But we really didn't know
each other at all. I didn't even know what his family's business was.

I busied myself on my phone when it sounded like
the call was ending. He came stomping back into the living
room, reaching for his glass, which he downed in one gulp.

"Do you mind if I have another?" he asked, a slight
edge in his voice.

"Why would I mind? I'm not your mom or anything.
Have another drink, Gage. Sounds like you need it."

His pour was heavier this time, but he added a balled
ice cube to the glass as well. He returned to the couch and
fell against the back of it with an enormous sigh.

"Sorry about that. I didn't want to take it, but if I hadn't,
they wouldn't have stopped calling. Business." He gave me
a sideways glance before rubbing his face with both hands,
as if trying to rub away whatever he'd just dealt with.

"Do you want me to go, Gage? If you have work to do,
we can get together another night."

His head snapped in my direction. "No, please stay.
I've been looking forward to seeing you for days. I'm sorry."
He sat up and leaned against his knees before looking side-
ways at me again. "If you left, my day would be even worse.
Come here." He extended a hand for me to take.

I reached out and took it and he yanked me off the couch, right onto his lap, my legs straddling his. His hands moved to my hips, holding me in place as his back settled against the couch cushion. Looking up at me, he pulled aside my flannel shirt. And smiled.

"I was hoping there was going to be a tank top hiding under there," he said as he slid the flannel off my shoulder. "I've been dreaming about having you on this couch since that day in the store. It got delivered a couple days ago, and I haven't stopped thinking about you being on it with me. In a tank top."

I allowed the shirt to fall to the floor behind me. I pulled my hair back from my chest and shoulders, moving it to my back. Gage had the reaction I was hoping for.

"Are you not wearing a bra, Becca?" he asked.

I shook my head, feeling every bit the naughty girl that I was.

I had every intention of coming here to do exactly what he was thinking as well.

His one hand left my hip and migrated up my side. He stayed on top of my shirt, grazing the side of my breast before finding the small mound in its center. His thumb rubbed it, which encouraged my nipple to respond immediately. The other nipple grew in anticipation of it being touched, both of them hard peaks under the cotton of my tank.

"Fuck, you have no idea how hot you look right now." With both hands now, he pushed my tits together, thumbs flicking my nipples as he kneaded them. "The weight of them in my hands is enough to get my dick rock hard."

And I felt him underneath me. Rock hard.

"Take your shirt off, Gage. I haven't seen your body yet." I grabbed the hem of his T-shirt to help him lift it over his head, eager to see what was underneath.

Of course, I was neither shocked nor disappointed by the six-pack of abs that stared back at me. What did shock me was the tip of his dick sticking out the top of his pants. His cock was so fucking big, it stuck out of the waistband of his sweats!

I couldn't restrain myself; my fingers went to the almost purple head. The smooth skin was hot to the touch. I was tempted to pull it completely out and lean down to taste him. I looked at Gage to consider my options.

"You'll have time to get to know him soon."

"Oh, it's a *him?*" I asked, the smirk obvious.

"Yes, I like to refer to *it* as a *him* most times," he laughed. "*He* is attached to me."

"Yes, *he* is," I responded. "I would like to touch him, maybe taste him. He's a big *him,* isn't he?" I asked. I stared at him through what I knew were hooded eyes. He had me so turned on already.

"I've been told."

That was all he said. We looked at each other in silence for a few moments before he broke the spell.

"Stand up and take your pants off, but leave the tank on. Please." He finished the request with a smile.

Standing to take my shorts and thong off, I teased him even more by turning around. My ass was at his eye level as I bent to remove my clothes. He rewarded me with a swipe of his finger against my sex all the way to my clit.

"Ahh!" I cooed. I turned around, facing him.

He reached up and pulled me back onto him, my now bare bottom spread wide across his lap. He lined his dick up against me, pushing against my pussy, my opening, my clit. It was an amazing sensation.

"Becca, I'm going to make you come with my hands, and then I'm going to fuck you. Hard."

He pulled me down onto him harder, grinding against me as he held me in place with his hands on my hips. My hands fell to his shoulders for support. I got to know his body, running my hands along his chest, down to his abs. The muscles rippled in my hands as he moved below me. His hands had returned to my breasts.

"You like my tits, I take it."

"Can you tell? And I love them in this white tank top. I love how the material gets stretched, how the side of your tit is showing over here." He rubbed along the side of my breasts with both hands while slipping his thumbs under my shirt, searching for my nipples. "I love how your nipples look when they get hard. Becca, it's the hottest thing I've ever seen." He leaned forward and pulled a nipple into his mouth through my shirt, biting it between his teeth. He pinched the other one at the same time, the sensation almost too much to handle.

"Oh, Gage, fuck," I moaned.

"You like that?" he asked, his words garbled with my shirt and nipple still in his mouth.

All I could do was nod against the top of his head as he continued sucking on my breast. I cradled his head in my arms, keeping him in place. The bottom half of my body continued to gyrate against the hard length in his pants.

Suddenly, he lifted me from the couch and flipped me around, dropping me into my favorite corner spot. My legs fell open as I lay on my back, fully exposing my sex as he stared down while standing above me. Dropping to the floor, he gripped inside my knees, spreading my legs even farther apart. With seductive eyes still looking at me, his hands worked their way up the inside of my thighs.

"I've been dreaming of tasting you," he said as he brought his face between my legs.

In my next breath, his tongue was on me, lapping me from top to bottom. It probed deeply inside me as his fingers made quick work of finding my clit. Spreading me wide with his hands, his tongue and fingers worked as if I were an instrument, the rhythm creating sounds from me like music.

"You taste like a sweet wine, Becca," he said, his mouth pulling back for a moment. As he peered up at me, our eyes connected as his thumb still worked my clit. With that connection, he grasped my clit between his thumb and finger, twisting it.

My back arched off the couch, the pleasure so close to pain, I wasn't sure what to do. Staring at the ceiling, I heard Gage's directions.

"Breathe, Becca. Breathe through what you think is pain. It will cross over to the most amazing orgasm you've ever had."

I listened. I took deep, even breaths and calmed myself as his fingers continued their torture, twisting and pulling.

Suddenly, he pushed what felt like three fingers inside me. The combination of him filling me up and assaulting my clit had that familiar feeling building. But then suddenly his fingers abandoned their post as his mouth returned to my clit. As he sucked it between his lips, deep into his mouth, my back lifted off the couch. There were stars flashing behind my closed eyes as the climax built with intensity.

And then it didn't take long. The wave came crashing over me like a tsunami; every cell in my body thrummed with energy. I felt like I had lost control of my mind, my muscles, as I lay there. My body quivered with satisfaction as Gage's hands slowly withdrew from inside me. He rubbed my wetness along my sex, priming me for what was to come.

Suddenly, he pulled me up off the couch, spinning me around. Gage pulled me onto his lap in my favorite corner.

"I want you to ride me, Becca. I want you to slide that pussy onto my dick and ride me. Can you do that?" he said with his porn star voice. A condom had appeared out of nowhere, and he placed it in my hand. "Put this on me."

I tore the square packet open and positioned it atop his shaft. Rolling it down the length of him, I confirmed what I'd thought.

His dick was big.

I didn't think it would fit in me this way, with me on top. Once the condom was in place, I rose to my knees, and he saw my hesitation as I lined him up with my opening.

And fuck if that didn't scare the shit out of me.

"Hey, are you OK with this, Becca?" he asked.

I stopped and looked at him, hoping my actual fear wasn't all over my face.

"Of course," I said, but I knew I wasn't very convincing. He grabbed my hands and stopped me from putting him inside myself.

"What's wrong, Becca?" he asked.

My shoulders deflated in defeat, and I was mad at myself for ruining the mood.

"I'm such a buzzkill, I'm sorry, but I'm really afraid that you won't fit. I'm so scared that this is going to hurt."

His face softened, and his hand came to my cheek.

"Hey, I'm glad you said something. We can try it this way, slow. But if it doesn't work, we'll do it another way, OK?" he whispered, and I nodded.

Reaching down, he guided his massive length into me. Grabbing my hips, he literally held me above him, my entire weight in his hands.

"I've got you. I'll let you down slowly, and you tell me how it feels. You tell me when to let you down more, OK?"

He slid me onto his shaft with care, his eyes on mine the entire time.

The stretch as he entered me caused a burn beyond anything I'd ever felt, bringing tears to my eyes, and he immediately stopped and pulled out.

"Becca," he said low, "are you a virgin?"

My eyes went wide. "No!" I yelped.

His head fell back against the couch as his grip on me got tighter. "You're so fucking tight, Bec. So fucking tight. I don't want to hurt you, but you feel so fucking good."

"I can take you this way." I motioned with my fingers to show his width, making that circle to show him. "But I'm just not sure about this way." I held my hands apart like a fisherman would to show their latest catch.

Gage laughed out loud.

"Just keep going slow," I told him. "I'll tell you if I can't do anymore."

He nodded.

"I'm trying, but it's a slow torture," he confessed with hooded eyes as he returned his cock to my entrance, this time not as slow. "Breathe and relax—you're tense. That will make this hurt when it doesn't have to." He looked at me again. "Do you want to flip over? Try that way first?"

I didn't want to give up on the challenge I faced. For some reason, I felt like I would disappoint him if we went missionary. Gage seemed like more than missionary, like he needed more than that.

I shook my head.

"How about you support more of your weight on my shoulders?" he suggested.

This was turning into a project instead of being *sexy* sex.

I moved my hands up and held on, taking the weight off of him. Suddenly, a few fingers found my clit, rubbing and massaging. My head hit his shoulder with the intensity of the sensation that hit me. Gage obviously approved of the sounds coming from my mouth.

"Yeah, Bec, you like that?" he whispered. I nodded against his head as he slowly started pushing himself inside me, one inch at a time. If my body tensed, his fingers worked their magic on my clit to relax me again. Before I knew it, he was fully seated.

I looked at him, a bit astonished.

"Will you fuck me?" he asked.

I moved my hands behind me to his thighs and started rocking back and forth. The sensation of his full cock inside of me was intense. I knew it was hitting parts of me that had never been touched. Once the feeling of him inside me became comfortable, I knew I could start doing more. I moved my hands from his legs to his shoulders and pushed up a bit on my knees.

"Are you sure, Becca?" he asked.

I didn't answer him. I pushed up and came slamming back down on him.

And it took my breath away.

In the best possible way.

"Fuck!" I yelled. "Gage, you feel amazing!"

I found a rhythm that worked; it felt good.

"Jesus Christ, Becca, this is better than any fantasy I could have dreamt up." He reclined against the couch as

I rode him, bouncing atop him like some porn star on the internet. "The way your tits bounce in that tank when you're fucking me, I'm having trouble holding back." He moaned. He reached up and grabbed a hold of them, roughly pawing at them as I was close to catapulting from his body. "Slow down, Bec."

And I did. But I didn't want to.

His hand pulled down my tank, my tits barely contained by the straps now across my nipples.

"I wish you could see how fucking sexy you look."

His finger started at my chest, right under my neck, dragging between my breasts. He traced over one nipple and moved to the other, both hardening from his attention. Once he finished there, his finger moved down my stomach, over my shirt, and finally to where we were joined. His flat palm pushed against my lower abdomen, creating a pressure inside I'd never felt before.

I threw my head back in complete ecstasy, the moans continuous.

And that was when the shrill of his phone started.

My eyes darted to the device vibrating on the glass table.

"Ignore it," he commanded.

His tone startled me, but I did what he said.

He helped by latching on to my hips with a firm hold and encouraging me to move up and down again. My eyes landed on his torso as the muscles strained with his exertion. The ripples of his stomach glistened with sweat, tempting me to rub my hands along his skin. Moving my hands from his shoulders to his chest, I felt the tension in his muscles as he used them. The sparse, dark hair under my fingers was just the right amount. It disappeared as my hands roved over his taut stomach, the smooth skin pulled tight over rippled flesh.

But then my fingers hit that line of hair at the belly. The line that would usually disappear below the band of pants. But I had an up-close look at where the trail ended. I ran my fingers through the tight curls at the base of his cock, my nails grazing the skin of him as he pulled in and out.

"Oh, fuck, Becca, that feels amazing." He almost growled as he increased the speed at which he was rocking me back and forth on top of his dick.

As our rhythm built, that familiar crescendo neared. I reached down, between my legs, helping it along.

"Yeah, touch yourself, Becca. That's so fucking hot," Gage said breathlessly.

And then. The phone shrilled again.

"Jesus Christ!" Gage yelled as we both stilled.

I wanted to know why he didn't have it on silent.

And then suddenly, he flipped me over onto my back and hastily thrust inside of me.

And within a couple minutes, his heavy body collapsed on top of mine.

He finished.

His head hung next to mine as his breathing slowed against my cheek.

"This didn't go exactly as I'd planned," he said into my ear. He started pushing up on his elbow and against the side of the couch as he looked down at me. "I'm sorry; it must be work."

"It's OK," I said. But I was a bit confused, considering he told me he stopped working to come back to school. But I guess once you work in a family business, you can never leave it behind.

He continued to get off of the couch, the message that our time together was over coming through.

"My bathroom is in the same place as yours." His eyes gestured down the short hall toward the stairs. I got up and gathered my clothes, suddenly uncomfortable with the mood in the room and between us.

I closed the door just before the first tear fell. Sliding along the back of the door, I buried my face in my hands to hide my sobs. There was no way I could let Gage know I was upset. Caring was not part of our deal. Our deal was only sex.

So why did I care it seemed like this *was* only sex?

I finally got up and got my clothes on. After splashing some water on my face, I looked in the mirror. Swollen eyes stared back at me, but I felt I looked presentable enough to head back out. Walking into the living room, I found it empty. Then I heard hushed voices coming from the kitchen. I leaned against the back of the couch, not sure what my next move should be.

After a couple minutes of standing there, completely alone, I reached for my keys on the sofa table. Gage must have heard me, and he peeked his head around the kitchen doorway.

"Hey," he said, covering the phone with his hand. "Sorry, I've got to finish this. I'll talk to you tomorrow?"

There was a hint of an apology in his eyes. But nothing more.

"Yeah, sure."

And I left.

I left and walked home because he forgot he had picked me up.

It wasn't a far walk, but that wasn't the point. And the entire walk home, I kept thinking I'd hear the familiar roar of the Mustang engine slide up next to me.

But I didn't.

The sun had already set, twilight even close to over, as I pushed the door to my apartment open. The first floor was empty of noise and people, which made my heart feel even heavier. Though I knew if anyone had been around, I wouldn't have wanted to see them or talk. My emotions were all over the place. I didn't know what I was feeling as I stood frozen in the small foyer.

Finally, I decided being alone in my room was my best option. I made the hard right turn to head up the stairs when I heard footsteps come from above.

"Becca?" a voice called out. It sounded like Lanie.

"Yeah, it's me," I responded.

She came bounding down the stairs, excitement all over her face and in her movements. She grabbed a hold of my hand and dragged me toward the kitchen.

"Lane, I just want to head upstairs," I whined, pulling back on her arm to get out of her grasp.

"Uh-uh, not so fast. You, my dear, have to see what came for you," she said in a sing-songy voice. "You got a delivery." She pulled me along into the dark kitchen, then blinded me as she flipped the switch.

Once my eyes adjusted to the bright light, I focused on the bouquet of roses on the island.

A dozen roses, mixed pastel colors, in a vase. But they were also filled in with greenery and baby's breath to make an arrangement that took up half our counter. They were stunning. More than stunning.

"Who do you think they're from?" Lanie asked. "Do you think you know?"

She had no idea I was just with Gage. I'm sure she probably thought they were from him. And I would have as well, under different circumstances.

"Yeah, I know."

My melancholy demeanor came through in my voice, I guess.

"OK, Bec. Well, I'll leave you to it. There's a note with them. Love ya, hon." And she left me alone.

Alone with the roses from the man I should probably be with.

The man I knew loved me but who was holding something back—a secret.

I reached into the stems and pulled out the tiny notecard. But it wasn't a tiny notecard; rather, folded up inside the small envelope, was a piece of paper with a handwritten note.

> To my beautiful Becca — You are like the butter in my popcorn, and the bubbles in my soda, you are the best of all the good in my life. The sun shines brighter with you by my side. I hope these flowers made you as happy as you make me. Yesterday goes down as one of my best days.
>
> Ever.
>
> I only hope you will let me continue to give you more best days ever.
>
> You are my perfect.
>
> Love — Ty

I admired the flowers; they were beautiful. Each color more vibrant than the next.

Yellow, red, pink, coral. They looked so pretty together.

I folded the note back up, returned it to the envelope, and tucked it prettily in the bouquet.

And then I burst into tears.

Chapter 17

Ty

"Hey, man, are you around tomorrow to help with the fundraiser?" Xander asked. I'd stopped at his place for a fraternity meeting. Apparently on the last Tuesday of each month, we needed to meet to organize the philanthropy events that were expected of us. But we didn't mind, because it was just another excuse to get together and have a drink. I was playing a game of pool when Xander approached me.

"Sure, I can help out tomorrow. My classes are done by one. I'm open after that. Is it in the student union?" I took my shot as I was talking and really fucked up my game, the eight ball curving into a pocket. "Shit," I mumbled.

Xander chuckled beside me and took the stick out of my hand. "You have no right to be playing this game, dude, not with a shot like that," he scoffed at me. "And yeah, but it's outside the union as long as the weather's good. Miller and Evans should have a table set up long before that, so get there when you can to take over." He pushed me out of the way and moved in on the table. "Now get out of here and let a real man take over."

I didn't mind. I was playing as a distraction, but it wasn't working well. Working my way over to the couch, I squeezed between some guys playing video games. Maybe watching them play would take my mind to a better place. I reached out for one of the unopened beers on the table, twisting the cap, knowing I shouldn't be drinking much more to drown out my sorrows.

It had been three days since I sent Becca the roses, and all I got in return was a thank-you text with a heart face.

Three days.

And I hadn't even seen her on campus. I had hoped we would run into each other, giving me an excuse to talk to her, maybe ask to see her again. But no such luck. I didn't want to seem desperate. I sent her the flowers. I kind of felt like the ball was in her court at the moment. But waiting for her to make the next move was driving me fucking insane.

Making the commitment to give her space after the day we spent together was hard to stick to. I mean, staying away from her after the mind-blowing sex we had was fucking impossible, especially knowing she was spending time with that asshole. We never discussed that night if we were even still doing the whole "space" thing anymore. I would think having sex would make that moot.

I jumped to my feet, too antsy to sit any longer. Heading back to the pool table, I waited out Xander's game. He and an older guy, Nate, were in a duel at the moment, a fight to the end. A much better game than I had given my opponent.

Jake sidled up next to me without me hearing him. "You OK, dude? You seem out of it tonight."

As we stood there together, we both watched Xander knock three balls in a row in their intended pockets, one ball away from winning.

"Eh, I'm OK, just got some shit on my mind." I didn't know if I wanted to talk girl crap with him. I wasn't sure if our friendship was at that stage yet. Jake had driven me and our other roommate, Ben, here in his car. Seeing the beer in Jake's hand told me we were going to have to find a different ride home later.

He threw a heavy arm around my shoulder and wrapped it around my neck. With his head so close, I caught the drift of his booze breath, a further sign of his level of intoxication. "Well, we've got some Sigma girls coming soon. I'm sure one of them can help get that shit off your mind, am I right?"

This was Jake's favorite kind of night: drinks, buddies, and a plethora of girls to fawn over him. Because they always did. He was *that* guy. The one at the party who every girl had their eye on, trying to get upstairs. Well, it would have been Xander, had he not already committed himself to Lanie. But Jake was right up there with him. Not being one of those girls, I couldn't exactly pinpoint what it was about guys like them that did it to the girls. But I was not in their league.

I pulled myself from Jake's hold, shaking my head. "Yeah, I don't think so, man."

He shook his head as he pushed a pointed finger into my chest. Hard.

"Ty, you're not into it because you only have eyes for Becca. But if she's cutting you out, man, it's time to move on." Although it was obvious he was frustrated with me as his finger continued to jab me in the chest, he seemed concerned for me as well.

I didn't know what to do with that. It wasn't often that guys expressed themselves in a way that showed they cared.

My spit became hard to swallow as I searched for something to say in response to Jake. We continued to stare at each other as the silence remained. Finally, I found my balls and my voice.

"Yeah, well, about that. She hasn't cut me out, at least I don't think so," I said. "We spent the whole day together last Sunday." I didn't even believe what I was saying, my words sounding baseless when I knew she hadn't reached out since. Jake saw my face.

"So you two are back together?" he prodded, sounding as if he already knew the answer.

"Well, not exactly," I said. "But we had a good day. We hung out." He didn't need to know our personal details.

"Yeah, well, maybe it's time to move on, Ty. I know Kayla really likes you," he said. And that just didn't sit well with me, thinking that meant she would show up any minute. I also didn't appreciate the way he just kept pushing me. He quickly went from being a concerned friend to acting like a dick.

"I have no interest in Kayla, Jake. I actually thought she was into you by now."

He shook his head as he lifted his beer to his lips. "No, I think it's still you she wants. Why don't you want to fuck her, man? She's hot as hell. But if she's not your type, I'm sure we can find someone else for ya, dude," he said. "But, c'mon, stop waiting on this one chick. I mean, Becca is hot and all, but is she that good a fuck?"

I lost track of exactly how things happened next.

The anger clouding my vision and my judgment were exactly why I reacted the way I did. The bone cracked satisfyingly under my hand as my fist connected with his face. Jake flew to the ground, his beer bottle crashing against the wall near us. All eyes were on us in a matter of seconds, most guys rushing to Jake as he lay bloodied on the floor.

"What the fuck?" one brother yelled in my direction. My adrenaline was still rushing too hard for me to notice who it was.

Then a set of powerful hands got a hold of my shoulders and pulled me back. I was swinging around, ready to fight whomever was pulling me from my opponent, when I saw Xander staring me down.

"Ty, settle the fuck down." His voice held an authority that brought me back to my senses. He pushed me away from where the other guys were pulling Jake from the ground. "Whatever he said, it's not worth it. He's your brother and your roommate. Calm the fuck down."

Shit.

I fucked up.

All this shit going on with Becca was destroying me, and I was allowing it to destroy the rest of my life as well. This was my new family here at school, and I should have been working hard to make these bonds strong, not destroying them.

I nodded toward Xander as he kept his hold on me with his hand on my chest. Pushing his hand from me, I walked away and headed upstairs, desperate to distance myself from the situation. Opening the slider, I found myself outside, searching for some fresh air. I heard Xander's steps follow me outside.

The only people I'd ever cried in front of so far in my life were my mom and Becca; I didn't want that to change. But it felt like it was going to. The knot welled up in my throat, preventing me from talking. I walked into the yard, hoping the wetness forming in my eyes would dry up before Xander noticed. I ran my fingers through my hair, across my face, as the first tear came out. I stifled the sob, completely embarrassed I was going to lose my shit in front of my friend.

"Ty."

That was all it took.

"Fuck!" Fumbling to the wall of the house, I punched it multiple times as my knuckles split apart and were bloodied by the shingles. I was like a crazed animal that was finally let loose. "Fuck!" I yelled again. But then I almost couldn't find my voice for my next words for him. "I don't know what the fuck to do, Xander. She's already seeing someone else. She fuckin' kissed someone else." The defeat was just as much physical as it was emotional as I leaned against the wall for support. I stared at my hand for a moment, unclear why I didn't feel any pain from the shredded skin. "I'm going fucking crazy. It's fucking up my whole life, everything! She won't even give us a chance, nothing, because I won't, I can't . . ." I had to bend over to catch my breath. The entire time, Xander remained standing at a distance, watching, allowing me to let it all out.

I felt his hands on my shoulders as he pulled me toward some chairs that were set up in the yard. "C'mon, man, take a seat." He pushed me down but went in the house, returning with two bottles of water for us. "Here, drink." He downed his in one gulp, but all I could do was take stupid pansy-ass baby sips because I couldn't catch my breath. We sat there for a couple minutes, neither saying a word. I wasn't sure he was going to talk, but suddenly he cleared his throat.

"I completely understand the despair you're feeling, Ty," Xander said. "It may not be exact circumstances, but when Lanie and I were forced apart last year, every breath I took, I felt like I had to force my body to take it."

Looking up, I realized I was sitting with someone that may have been through something even worse than what I was going through. He wasn't looking my way, but off in the distance, as if thinking back to the horrors they went through. If he and Lanie could get through their ordeal, Becca and I had a chance. Even coming to that realization, though, I didn't see a way out of what I'd done tonight.

"I assume Jake isn't messing around with Becca as well? That was not the cause for what happened, right?" he asked with a smirk.

That got a chuckle out of me. "No," I offered. "He was just trying to get me to move on, hook up. He really didn't do much of anything wrong; it was all me. And I probably fucked up my friendship with my roommate now, too."

Xander shook his head. "Nah, let him cool down. Once you both sober up, things will be like it never happened. Trust me."

The sweat on my face, down my back, helped me cool off as we sat in the night air. The defeat I felt about my entire life exhausted me. Xander seemed to notice.

"You ready to head out? I can give you a ride home, or wherever you're headed," Xander said. Neither of us was interested in staying for the rest of this stint of the party. Hooking up was not on either of our agendas for the night.

"Yeah, I'll take a ride," I said. "I think you'll have to take me home, if that's OK. I haven't heard from Becca in a few days. I don't want to just show up."

We climbed into his Jeep and started the drive to my complex. He conveniently drove by Lanie and Becca's place on the way out, giving me a chance to see that she was home, her light on in her room. I continued to stare through her window as we drove by, hoping to catch a glimpse of her, but had no luck.

Xander was rounding the corner to exit the complex when a familiar convertible Mustang pulled into a spot. I knew Gage lived nearby, but didn't know he was this close to Becca. The doors of the car opened on both sides, and my heart sank. I prayed it wasn't Becca I was going to see exiting the passenger side of the car. Instead, I saw a tall, slim blonde get out and wait for the driver to come around to the front of the car.

Xander slowed, knowing this was something we needed to see.

She had a small bag over her shoulder, which Gage took from her as they walked side by side to his door. They may not have been all over each other on the short walk up the path, but it was obvious they knew each other. I didn't know how I knew; it was just in the way they looked at each other as they walked side by side. There was a level of familiarity between them, as if each knew what the other would do next.

Kind of how Becca and I would look.

And I was back to seeing red.

The rage was consuming me.

Because I was sure Becca had no idea that this was going on.

"So, you've already busted one person's nose tonight. I'm going to keep driving, and you're going to stay in the car. OK?" Xander's voice held a hint of warning. He waited for Gage and the woman to close the door to his apartment before driving on.

My mind couldn't process what it had just seen. I didn't want to jump to conclusions. But I also wanted to jump to the conclusion that he was an asshole who was fucking another girl while seeing Becca.

I wanted to shout it from the rooftop.

At the very least, I wanted to tell Becca.

"You know you can't tell Becca, right, Ty?" Xander asked.

"Why the fuck not?" I yelled back. "He's a fucking cocky bastard taking advantage of a girl almost six years younger than he is. All while he has another one on the side. Fuck no. I'm not letting him get away with that!" I was furious.

"You're not telling Becca because if *you're* the one to tell her, she will hate *you*. And you don't need that," Xander said. "Let me talk to Lanie. We'll figure out what's best. Will you wait for us to do that?"

I wasn't normally an angry person. But the fury raging inside of me was hard to contain. If Xander hadn't driven away, I knew I would have torn out of the Jeep straight for him. Forcing myself to take measured breaths helped me calm down enough to answer him.

"Fine, but she's gotta know, Xander. Someone has to tell her, and soon."

CHAPTER 18
Becca

It's funny how a mind works. I was so angry at Gage when I left his house Monday night. Angry enough that I was content to not call him for a ride to class on Tuesday morning. Or Wednesday.

But when he hadn't called to offer a ride . . . it hurt.

Even if he had called, I wouldn't have taken him up on the offer. I would have come up with some excuse. But I still wanted him to fucking ask.

My mind and my heart wanted him to ask, and it hurt that he didn't.

And on top of that, the guilt I felt for only sending that one text to Ty ate me up inside. When I got home that night from Gage's and saw the flowers, I wasn't in the right headspace to accept them the way I should have.

And then the rest of the week had just been one big fuckup.

When I didn't get the call Tuesday morning for a ride to class from Gage, I was late and missed the bus. That in turn made me late to class. My entire day went downhill from there. I didn't even want to revisit that day in my mind; I'd rather forget it completely.

Seeing the flowers when I got home only reminded me I hadn't talked to Ty since I'd last seen him on Sunday. But other than the flowers, he hadn't reached out either. But he was giving me *space*, right? Were the flowers my volley? Was it my turn? Ugh.

Escaping to my room, I locked myself inside and stayed there the rest of the night. I think I was in and out of sleep, probably because I got little the night before. I did anything and everything to keep my mind off of my current life status. I even did homework willingly. Like, ahead of time. It wasn't even due for days.

And as the anger wore off, it was replaced by self-doubt and worthlessness.

And this was so unlike me; allowing men to literally change my persona was pissing me off. Why was I letting this happen?

I continually stared at my phone, willing it to light up with a message or a call from either of them.

How was I involved with two guys at the same time, yet pushing them both away? I decided it was an art. Only someone like me could be capable of something like that.

And that got me crying again.

And that was the cycle for a couple days. I finally made it to Wednesday, hump day. And it was October already. Six weeks of this madness and I was in no better a position with either of them. Actually worse.

I only had one afternoon class on Wednesdays, which allowed me to sleep in. While I was making coffee, I spun around, unaware I wasn't alone in the room.

"Oh my God, Lanie, I had no idea you were here!" I cried out in surprise with my hand over my heart.

"Sorry, I just got home. I was at Xander's last night."

Instead of joining me in the kitchen, she went directly to the couch in the living room, almost as if she were avoiding me. I watched her as she sat, her eyes avoiding me the entire time. I didn't know if I was making it up because of my state of mind, but this was not like her.

"Do you want a tea?" I asked as I reached into the cabinet to get her a mug. I wanted some "Lanie time" before I had to go to class. It had been a few days since we'd seen more than a glimpse of each other running in or out of the apartment. And I blamed myself for that. I wanted nothing to do with anyone lately.

"Sure," she responded, but she still hadn't looked my way.

At that moment, Ava and Macie came racing into the kitchen with their bags over their shoulders, obviously in a hurry.

"Shit! We are so late for a study session. Are there granola bars anywhere we can steal?" Macie asked.

I went to the pantry and grabbed a few. She stuffed them in her pocket as Ava grabbed their full water flasks.

"Thanks, Bec. We owe ya. I'll replace them when I go shopping next."

"Bye!" Ava yelled as she waved.

They both ran down the hall and out the front door, slamming it behind them.

"We lucked out with them as our roommates this year, ya know? We have two great new friends," I said to Lanie. I watched her nod, but she was still acting strange. I put her tea on the island, waiting to see if she would join me in the kitchen. Eventually, she stood from the couch and traipsed to the stool in front of her mug, plopping down. I leaned against the granite, my chin in my hand, keeping my mouth shut to see if she needed to talk about something more than I did.

She was acting a bit like she did last year. When things were terrible in her world and she just wanted to curl up and disappear.

Yeah, exactly what I'd been doing.

"They are good roommates," Lanie finally offered. When she finally looked up at me, I could tell something was off.

Keeping my eyes on her, I moved on with the conversation.

"I have a meeting later today with the business frat. Remember I told you about this? I think I might get the nod to be the president after all." My good news didn't quite get the reaction I was expecting.

"That's great, Bec." Her distant, monotone response was very unlike her.

"What's wrong?" I asked. "Are you and Xander OK? Is it Max? Did something happen with him?"

That was always what the problem was last year.

Max. Her ex. The mafia son.

But he was supposedly in jail for everything he and his father had done. I only hoped nothing had changed.

"No, nothing like that, Bec. Nothing with Max or Xander. All good," she said. But then she sat there, silent for a few minutes as she sipped on her tea.

I drank my coffee, waiting for her to direct the conversation. Even though I had plenty I could have talked to her about, it was obvious there was something on her mind. Lanie was the type of person who needed time and space to talk. I'd learned that about her from our year together last year. And just like I thought, she started talking.

"So, Bec, there is something I need to talk to you about," she started.

"OK, lay it on me, kid. What's going on? I've had a shitty week, so you can't have much worse going on in your life right now." Walking around the island, I sat on the stool next to her, grabbing her hand. She clenched it.

"It's not about me, Bec."

My puzzled look must have convinced her I was still not catching on.

"Becca, Xander saw something that he feels I should tell you. And I'm not exactly sure how to. But, I don't know, it may not be that big a deal," she said.

Stalling.

"Lanie, what are you talking about? *Who* are you talking about?" I asked. At that moment, I knew it had to be about one of the two of them.

But which one?

Ty or Gage?

"Bec, Xander saw Gage with another woman, or another girl. I'm sorry," she said. "It was last night, as he was driving Ty home from his place. They had a frat meeting and Ty had been drinking, so Xander drove him home. When they were going by Gage's place, Gage and a blonde were going into his apartment. She had an overnight bag."

Lanie was talking so fast, she sounded a lot like me. I understood how it felt to be subjected to listening to me ramble all the time. But she was nervous about how I would react. I got it. I would be, too.

Funny thing was, it didn't surprise me. Did I *know* he was fucking someone else? No. But did it surprise me? Also no. We had a very non-committed thing going on. And guess what? I fucked someone else, too.

To be honest, it made me feel slightly better about how our night ended on Monday. I would have preferred that he separate the two of us. Finished with me before he dealt with whoever she was. Because that's obviously who he had on the phone while I was there.

And that was what pissed me off. Not that he was sleeping with someone else, but that he couldn't give me the time I deserved while I was with him.

"Becca, did you hear me?" Lanie asked.

I stood from the stool to refill my mug with more coffee. "Yeah, I heard you." This time, I felt like making it a pumpkin-spice-flavored coffee, so I went to the fridge and took out the special creamer I hid in the back from everyone else. As I slowly stirred my coffee, I heard Lanie getting restless.

"Becca!" she yelled.

I was in no hurry to answer her as I leaned against the counter with my coffee in my hands. I took a big sniff, relishing the aroma, before lifting it to my lips for a sip.

"Lane, don't you remember we aren't in a committed relationship?" I finally asked her.

She stared at me in disbelief before answering. "Well, yeah, but still, that doesn't bother you? I mean, I didn't think he would take that seriously, did you? You don't consider this him lying to you?"

Her annoyance with him came through. Let's face it, she wasn't his biggest fan in the beginning. This sure as hell wasn't going to help.

"Well, yeah, it bothers me. But I guess I feel like it shouldn't because of the agreement it all started with." I shook my head as I stared up at the ceiling, as if the answers to my problems were in the cracks above. "I don't know. I'm so confused. He didn't come out and tell me he was seeing someone else, if that's what you mean. But it was always, from the start, supposed to be casual. You knew that, I knew that. And I don't know if I consider it lying or not. We are not exclusive. We were always just, I guess, a long-term booty call. He knew I was still talking to Ty." I moved from the counter and started toward the couch in the living room, motioning with my head for her to follow me. "There's something I need to tell you, anyway."

We both settled in as I took stock of the dismayed look on her face.

"He's not the only one sleeping with someone else, if that's indeed what he's doing." Blurting it out was the best way. I just needed to tell her. There wasn't as much shock on her face as I had expected.

"When?" she whispered.

"This past Sunday, the day before he sent the flowers. We spent the day together, remember?" I told her. She nodded, looking over my shoulder at the bouquet that still sat on the island in all its glory.

"Why didn't you tell me?"

I needed to think about that one myself. Normally, I would have run to her with that news, but she wasn't home the night I came home from Ty's. And then when I came home from Gage's, I was in no mood to talk, even to her. But I needed to understand why. Last year, I would have spilled everything to her no matter the mood I was in.

I didn't like change, and things seemed to be changing already.

"Well, you weren't here Sunday night. You stayed at Xander's. And then Monday night, when I came home from Gage's, I, um, wasn't really in the mood to talk."

She nodded before speaking again. "OK." There was a thoughtful pause. "But I'm here now. Do you want to talk about anything?"

I sank into the couch and pulled the blanket over both of us.

"How much time do you have?"

Lanie agreed with me about the other girl probably being the one who kept interrupting Gage and me the other night, the one he was then talking to instead of taking me home. Yeah, he was a dick that night. He didn't handle that well at all.

And I guess I was hurt.

And I was pissed.

But more by how he treated me during *our* time together.

I was also confused whether I actually had a right to be.

I'd never done a "long-term booty call" before. This was not something we had planned for or discussed.

But I knew that if my phone started ringing right in the middle of Gage and me fucking, even if it was Ty, *especially if it was Ty,* I would not have stopped. And I wouldn't have answered it while Gage was with me.

And I had kept Gage in the loop about everything going on between Ty and me—well, almost everything. I didn't feel the need to update him on my sex life. But he should have at least told me there was someone else in his life. Even if it was casual.

Lanie was also thrilled to hear how Ty had planned an entire special day for us. I didn't give the details, only that we wound up in bed together. She thought I owed him more than the one text I sent him, and I agreed. The only problem was, it was now three days later, and I wasn't exactly sure how to go about doing that.

"Xander and I are heading to his mom's house for fall break this weekend. Are you going home?" she asked.

"I wasn't planning on it. You know I try to stay away from my crazy house and my brothers as much as possible."

"Do you want to come with me to Xander's?" she asked.

I stared at her.

"OK, well, we need to make some time for us, either before or after fall break," she said.

I continued to stare at her.

"OK, I have to make time for you. You're right, I'm spending a lot of time with Xander. I'm sorry." She hugged me before heading up to her room. "I have to get ready for class. You too, right?"

"Yeah, I need to head to campus. Is Xander picking you up by chance?" I asked, trying to score a ride. I still hated trying to catch a bus. Getting a parking pass for my car was next on my to-do list. Why had everyone thought of that but me? Ava and Macie both had parking stickers for their cars. Lanie didn't have a car, but I was sure she'd have a sticker on it if she did.

"He is, and he'll be here in ten minutes. Does that work?" she asked.

"Perfectly."

Thankfully, Lanie and Xander didn't force the topic during the ride. I sat in the back of the Jeep with my earbuds in, so that may have hinted I didn't want to talk. The looks I got from Xander in the rearview mirror told me he had things he wanted to say, but I kept avoiding direct eye contact until we arrived on campus.

"Thanks for the ride, Xander," I said while hopping out of the back seat. "Lanie, I'll see you back at the apartment later."

"See ya later," she said.

Both her and Xander's wary eyes were on me like hawks as I exited the Jeep. Before I could get an earful, I took off to my class. I saw it in both their faces, the pity and concern. Now I completely understood why Lanie acted the way she did most of last year. I had no desire to talk to anyone, to see anyone. I only wanted to curl up in my bed and make it all go away.

Of course, I knew that Gage and I were in a casual relationship. But I guessed it hurt more than I realized that he was actually hooking up with someone else.

But that made me a hypocrite.

Because I had Ty.

My ex, who I had sex with the day before hooking up with Gage. Exactly what I was upset with Gage about. And I didn't tell him about that, did I?

If I'd done the same thing to him as he'd done to me, why in the hell was it hurting so much?

I couldn't think about this anymore. I sank into the hard wooden seat in the cavernous lecture hall my class was in. Pulling my hood over my head, I hoped the monotone voice of my professor droning on about statistics would help drown out the noise in my brain. But as class progressed, I realized I wasn't focusing on the material at all. Before long, it ended, and I had less than half a page of notes written. I would need to get the notes I missed from someone.

Not really feeling the desire to head back to the apartment yet, I took my time packing my things. Our place would be empty. I hadn't realized everyone was leaving for the three-day weekend. I mean, I could go home, but being surrounded by all my younger brothers wasn't high on my list of things to do at the moment.

The sun was bright when I made it out of the building, blinding me the moment I opened the door. Finding a ledge nearby, I balanced my bag in search of my sunglasses, needing to dig deep to the bottom.

I was completely distracted.

"Hey, Bec," the familiar voice said behind me. I froze with my hand still buried in my bag. I knew I had to turn and see him, talk to him. But I had no idea what I wanted to say. Even three days later. I gathered my strength, knowing once I turned around, my resolve might crumble.

Twisting my body slowly to face him, I caught his handsome face smiling down upon me. Not prepared for the onslaught of butterflies that took flight in my stomach, my voice wavered when I spoke. "Hi, Ty," I said. "How are you?"

Searching his face, I knew he had no idea how nervous I was. Instead, his somber, bloodshot eyes told a story of how his past few days had been spent.

He was devastated.

More than devastated.

Destroyed.

And I did that to him.

But he put on a brave mask quickly. "I'm good. You?"

I had no good reason for not texting or calling him; at least, not one I was willing to tell him. And as each day passed, it became more uncomfortable to reach out to him. But it was shitty of me to only have sent a text after he sent me flowers. And after we spent that day together. A day that might have been better than any day we had together up to this point.

We talked, we connected, we laughed, we had sex.

We had fantastic sex. Like, it was as if it was make-up sex and we really weren't even making up. Or were we? I didn't even know. If I had reached out to him, maybe I would know.

So it appeared it was now me screwing things up.

Because when he said he was "good," it was obvious to both of us he was full of crap.

His smile wavered as he looked around, avoiding looking at me.

And Christ, that hurt.

"Ty—"

"Bec—"

We both laughed nervously.

"Let me go first, Ty," I insisted. "I'm sorry. I'm sorry I never called you. It was shitty of me. I only wish I had a good reason for not calling, but I don't. It was just a terrible week so far."

Ty's face morphed from hurt to fury as I spoke. And that was when I remembered he was with Xander and saw Gage, too. He thought that was the reason for my week being shitty. Little did he know, that was only part of it. He would never know what happened between Gage and me the other night. Ever.

But the fact that my ex was standing in front of me, aware that I was in a bad mood because another man had betrayed me, well, that was weird.

No, it was so fucked up.

"You deserved a call after the wonderful day we had Sunday, you did. But I didn't want to make it seem like us spending one day together made all the other issues just disappear." When I said this, I noticed the hard swallow in his throat. He looked nervous suddenly, as if he didn't want the conversation to continue, afraid to see how it would end. "I wish it could, but it doesn't."

His look had softened, and a warm smile formed as he hiked his backpack higher on his shoulder. "Bec, I know one day isn't enough to fix us. I only hoped that might be the start to getting the chance to fix us." He sighed before he continued. "I have to get to class. I wish I didn't have to leave you right now, but this professor is being a dick about taking attendance lately." He started backing away.

"It's OK, Ty. It was good to see you."

His white teeth reflected the sun shining on him as he smiled wide in his retreat. His summer blond highlights, I noticed, were fading a bit. He was back to his darker-blond hair, which went so well with his whiskey-colored eyes.

Ugh, whiskey. Why did Ty's eyes have to remind me of the man who was pissing me off at the moment?

My small wave to Ty as he walked away made his smile grow. I put my sunglasses on and continued on my way home, happy my glasses were hiding the sadness.

CHAPTER 19

y entire life seemed to be crumbling around me. I fucked up my relationship with Becca, and now I had fucked up my friendship with my roommate as well. I made it home before Jake last night and didn't come out of my room when I heard him stomping around in the kitchen. Every decision I made lately was either the wrong one or backfired on me.

It was time to make some changes.

For starters, I needed to make amends with Jake. There was no way I was going to allow what I did to linger and affect what was showing signs of being a true brotherhood between us.

But as I made my way to my bedroom door to head downstairs to him, my phone pinged. My heart always rose a little with the hope it would be Becca, but when I checked, I saw Lanie's name on my screen.

Lanie:

> Want to go bowling tonight Thought
> you could use some time with friends
> before fall break Xander and me and
> some of his brothers are going

Putting my phone back in my pocket, I decided to wait until after talking to Jake to respond to her.

My feet felt heavier with every step I took down the stairs; I was tired of dealing with *issues* I'd created in my life. Hopefully, this one would be easier to handle than Becca. As I rounded the corner to the kitchen, I found Jake sitting at the island with a bag of ice held up against his face. He heard me, evident as his head slowly turned in my direction.

"Hey," I said, the apology already starting in my voice. "How ya feeling?"

His eyebrow notched up a bit at my question, maybe wondering if it should be a rhetorical one as we both looked at the ice he put on the marble counter in front of him. Moving closer with slow steps, I motioned to his swollen nose and split lip.

"I thought I broke your nose—glad to see I didn't," I told him, a little laugh escaping my mouth, trying to lighten the mood. His nose was puffy, but not broken.

Jake laughed with me. "Yeah, your hook is harder than I expected, man."

"Jake, man, I'm sorry," I started, but he held his hand up, stopping me.

He stood from the stool and grabbed the bag of ice as he walked toward the sink. When he threw it in the sink, it crashed against some of the dishes that were awaiting the dishwasher. Turning around to face me, he leaned against the counter, his arms now folded across his chest.

"I deserved it, Ty. I was an ass, and what I said about Becca was wrong. You deserve the apology," he said as his eyes lowered to the ground, his voice fading as well. "I'm sorry."

"No one deserves to be hit, Jake. I shouldn't have done that." I moved to take a seat on a stool, wanting to make sure that this conversation wasn't going to end, that he was going to stick around for a bit. "I appreciate you saying that, but I'm still sorry I hit you."

He nodded, his head still bobbing as his face transformed with a wider grin. "I'm serious, Brennan; you have a serious hook. Have you ever considered underground boxing or anything? We could make some cash off of you." He laughed out loud now. "Besides, after you left, I got so much attention from the Beta girls, I should be thanking you."

I joined in his laughter, picturing the sight of him being fawned over by the sorority girls due to his injury. I'm sure he milked it for all it was worth.

"Glad I could help," I joked. "So, are we, uh, good?"

He tried to smile, but stopped, his hand rushing to his split lip, which seemed to hurt as he tried. "Yeah, man, we're good." As soon as he said that, he stood and went straight for the fridge. "I need to drink my food for a few days. We got any beer?"

"I think it's a bit early for that, but any interest in coming bowling tonight? Lanie, Xander, and some of the guys are going. Thought I'd see if you'd like to come."

He swung around, the fridge door still open in his hand. "Today's Wednesday, right?"

"Yep," I answered, knowing exactly where this was going.

"It's sorority night at the lanes, isn't it?"

"Pretty sure," I said.

"I'm in," he said.

And just like that, we were OK.

The bowling alley was packed by the time Jake and I got there; I had to work, and my last delivery was pretty far away. But it was fine because Lanie was organized enough to have reserved two lanes for all of us. She was like having a mom for our frat.

Me:

Hey just got here what lane are you in

Lanie:

Let me come find you stay by the entrance

That was weird. Why would Lanie need to meet me by the entrance? Jake already took off toward the lanes filled with sorority girls, and I wasn't sure I would see him again until closing. But I knew he was going to take off; he said he was going to look for Kayla. Apparently, she was one of the girls helping make him feel better last night, which didn't surprise me.

The speakers were blasting songs of the 90s, which was cool. My parents brought me up on that music, and I actually loved it. I decided to go switch out for my bowling shoes while I waited for Lanie to find me.

"There you are," her winded voice sounded behind me at the shoe counter. "Listen, I need to tell you something." Her face fell when I turned to look at her, her eyes definitely telling me that she had news I wouldn't like. "Becca's here."

My immediate response was a faster heart rate as I looked around, trying to catch a glimpse of her. But then I allowed reality to settle in. Though we had what seemed to be a nice conversation this morning, this may not go well with us being at the same place right now.

"Do you think I should head out?"

"No!" Lanie yelled. "I invited you, I don't want you to leave. Ty, you're my friend. Regardless of what's going on between you and Becca, you will always be my friend." She grabbed my arm once I had my bowling shoes and dragged me from the counter. "Becca wasn't supposed to be here tonight. She told me she wasn't in the mood to come out; that was why I asked you. No offense, I don't mean you were second fiddle or anything . . ." Lanie looked so nervous; she was struggling to navigate this breakup between her two friends.

"Hey, no worries, I appreciate the invite, and I don't want to make this stressful, for you or her. I can go, it's no big deal." As I started heading back to return my shoes, Lanie grabbed my arm with more force.

"Absolutely not!" she yelled. "That was not why I told you." She pulled me in the direction of the bowling lanes. "I only wanted you to be prepared before you made it over to us. Becca knows you're here; I told her when she showed up. Unannounced, I might add." She scrunched her face up in obvious annoyance, but I didn't want her to be mad at her best friend. "There are two lanes; if it really is that big a problem, the two of you can bowl in different lanes. But I don't want this to be an issue, Ty." She stopped and stared at me, looking more stern than I'd ever seen her. "Are *you* going to make it an issue?"

When I put my hands up to my chest in mock offense, Lanie softened and smiled back at me. "Lanie, I will not be the cause of any issues tonight, I promise. I just cleared the air with Jake, so I'm in no mood to start something with anyone, especially Becca."

She continued pulling me by the hand. "I know, Ty, I'm sorry. I'm just so upset about the two of you. I only wish that you guys could fix whatever is going on between you both."

And that hit me straight in the heart.

Because that was all on me.

But I had no more time to wallow in my self-loathing because we walked up on our group, the lanes full of my frat brothers, including Xander. I wanted to look around, find Becca, make eye contact with her, but Xander's large frame filled my vision as he stood in front of me, a silly grin across his face.

"Are you a glutton for punishment, man?" he asked, followed by a laugh as he sidled up next to me. "You just can't stay away, can you?"

I knew it was most likely a rhetorical question, but I chose to answer it as my eyes tried to scan the crowd nonchalantly.

"Would you stay away from Lanie?" My voice was low; I didn't want anyone else to hear. But I also didn't want it to come across as confrontational. It wasn't meant to be, and

I didn't think Xander took it that way as he made a hmph sound under his breath.

"Touché," was his response.

As I looked at Xander, his facial expression softened. "And I haven't talked to Becca tonight either, so I have no idea what kind of mood she's in. So, I'm no help," Xander said as he shrugged his shoulders.

"This is hard on Lanie, making this work between the two of us. I hope she's doing OK," I said to him. Catching a glimpse of Becca talking to a girl I didn't recognize, I worked my way to the opposite lane to find a ball. Xander followed close behind me.

"She's fine with it. I mean, yeah, she'd be happier if you guys were together, but we both want to still be friends with each of you." He pulled on my shoulder, turning me around to face him. "You were there for both of us last year when things got tough. We wouldn't take off on you guys when you need us most."

I nodded, hoping he understood how much I appreciated him and Lanie at a time like this.

"That being said, I'm steering clear of Becca tonight, no offense," he said, then chuckled as he tried to hold back a smile. He walked away, I was sure to find Lanie.

My hand went down to the ball return to find a bowling ball that would fit it, and I landed on fingers that made my skin tingle. The feeling went from my fingers straight to my dick, which twitched in my pants. Looking up, my eyes met with a pair of sparkling green eyes I knew so well.

Her small smile told me she might be feeling something similar to what I was. And that made my heart swell, among the other body parts. She pulled her hand away, though, pushing both into the pockets of her jeans. Jeans that I knew, if she turned around, would be hugging every curve of that round ass of hers. Her hands pushed the waistband of the jeans down even lower, exposing a stretch of skin on her stomach underneath the tiny thing she called a shirt she was wearing. It drew my attention to her tiny belly button, and the urge to lick around it on my way lower became all encompassing.

She was intoxicating.

"Hey," she said in a quiet voice. It was nothing I was used to hearing from Becca Reynolds.

"Hey yourself."

Her eyes moved to the ground, avoiding me now at all costs. It was unusual, this feeling between us that reeked of uncomfortableness. I wish I knew where it was coming from, considering I was knee deep inside her only five days ago. Pushing those thoughts aside was what I needed to do at the moment, though.

"Have fun tonight, Bec," I said. Reaching down to grab the ball I needed, I felt her eyes on me but resisted looking up. I turned around and walked toward the opposite lane, heading toward my brothers already involved in a rowdy game. They welcomed me with hugs and high fives, a welcomed distraction. The urge to turn and find Becca was pulling on me like she was a magnet. She had to still be there; I felt her. But I knew this is what we need.

Space.

At least tonight.

"Hey, Ty, good to see you," Nate said as he slapped me on the back.

Being an upperclassman, a senior, to be exact, Nate wasn't around for the fraternity events quite as much as others. Even though we were in the same "family," we didn't see each other very often, so it was cool to be out with him.

"Hey, man, good to see you, too." We both walked over to the bank of seats near the back of the lane we were playing, and I took a seat. "How's your semester going?"

Nate fell into the seat next to me and let out a loud sigh. "Ahh, it's going. Can't believe it's my senior year and this is it for me." He cracked open a can of beer and took a long chug, almost draining it at once. "Christ, this time next year I'll be sitting at a fucking desk while you're still here getting your dick wet." Leaning back, he looked around, scanning the crowd. "You have an admirer. Who's the hot chick in the pink tank over there?" He gestured with his can of beer toward the lane across from us.

My eyes followed his line of vision, seeing Becca's striking green eyes peering at me from under her dark lashes. "That's Becca, my, I guess, ex-girlfriend. It's a bit complicated at the moment." She *was* looking at me, but her eyes shifted away as soon as Nate and I both noticed.

"Well, I have an ex-girlfriend, and she doesn't look at me like that. Nothing at all like that. You better stay on top of that, dude, in more ways than one, if you catch my drift," he said, his sarcastic laugh making my stomach churn. "If you don't, someone else will."

He had no idea how right he was.

"C'mon, we're both up next," he said.

The rest of the night went by in a blur, mainly because Becca continued to send those seductive mixed messages with her eyes. Every time I looked over, I caught her looking at me. And not just looking at me. She was *looking at me.* Like, literally eye fucking me. It did wonders for a guy's ego, and don't get me wrong, I wasn't complaining. And maybe I would've thought I was making it up if Nate hadn't seen it, too. But it was happening.

And I fucking loved every minute of it.

"So, Becca wasn't the tyrant tonight that I expected," Xander said as he came up behind me. We were getting ready to get out of here since the lanes were closing soon.

"Uh, no, not at all."

His confusion seemed to match my own.

Becca was a puzzle, that was for sure. Trying to figure her out made my brain hurt, and I didn't think it would ever be possible. Instead, I decided going along with her current mood was the smartest move.

"How'd you get here?" Xander asked.

"I drove, but I brought Jake and I still need to find him. Well, I need to make sure he doesn't need a ride. He very possibly got a ride to someone else's place tonight." Xander and I laughed about that as we started walking to the shoe return together. "How are things? With Lanie, I mean. I don't like to ask about Max and all that shit."

Xander nodded, completely understanding. "OK, I guess. It's been quiet since him and his dad have been in jail. Karl was put in the witness protection program since he fessed up all the shit he could to rat them out." Xander shook his head, seemingly upset about that. "I don't agree with that one. I think he should be in jail, too."

He caught my raised eyebrows at his last comment.

"I don't give a shit that he saved Lanie's life. That was at the last minute; he had plenty of other opportunities he could have helped her and didn't."

Karl was Max's "best friend" back in Texas, and part of the mafia ring. He was also the one that pulled her from Max's grip in the showdown last year, taking a bullet from Max's gun to save Lanie's life. Karl had come to take Lanie away, Max thought, for him. But Karl was going to let Lanie escape somehow from Max. Yet, Xander didn't seem to care, and I guess I understood.

"Well, she seems to be doing so much better this year. It's been great to see this side of her, ya know?" I told him. "You've made her...happy."

A huge smile took over Xander's face at that notion. He remained quiet as we were handed our own shoes and took a seat to put them on. As I came up from tying my laces, I saw him staring at me.

"What?" I asked.

"She wasn't very discreet tonight. If she was trying to be, she wasn't," Xander said.

Confused as to who "she" was, I shook my head at his comment.

"Becca."

"Hmph, you noticed, too, huh?" I asked. "Yeah, I don't know what to make of it. I seem to be getting some mixed messages from her. She says she wants space, but then she's basically fucking me with her eyes all night." I ran a frustrated hand through my hair.

Xander stopped walking, and I turned to look his way. "I will never claim to understand women, not a single one of them. But I now have to get in the car with yours. I'm bringing her and Lanie home. I'll see ya."

I didn't need to understand Becca. She could continue to be a mystery.

I just needed to make sure she was my mystery.

CHAPTER 20
Becca

"Let's go grab a bite to eat before we head to campus," I said to Macie as we walked out the front door. We were in a rush; we needed to get to the library to meet with our study group in thirty minutes but we were both in need of food.

"Oh shit," Macie said. "I left my bag inside."

I nodded as I reached in my pocket for my keys to let her back inside.

But they weren't there.

And I panicked.

I hadn't been thinking straight lately. After seeing Ty at the bowling alley, I'd been even more confused than ever. My emotions were all over the place. I decided last minute to go, knowing he would be there. But I figured we could be out together and hang out like friends. But as soon as I saw him, fuck, it was like a bolt of lightning hit me. This intense urge to be near him, for us to go back to the way we were last year, consumed me. I didn't know if it was because we were at the bowling alley, which we had done last year, or if it was because we were there with all our friends. But it was overwhelming, and it took me off guard.

"Fuck!" The sweat was immediately dripping down my temples as my stress level went sky high. I dropped my backpack to the ground and tore it open, praying I'd thrown my keys in there without realizing.

"Macie, please tell me you grabbed your apartment keys." My hopeful voice alerted her to the problem at hand. As I ripped every piece of paper from my bag, a futile attempt at finding keys that weren't in there, I lifted my head to find Macie staring down at me. Her wide eyes and tight-lipped mouth told me everything I needed to know.

"Becca, they're in my bag." Her statement wasn't accusatory. She was just as panicked as I was.

We knew Ava was in class, so she wasn't an option.

"I'll call Lanie," Macie said, pulling her phone from her pocket and dialing.

I sat on the front step, feeling the defeat creep into all of my bones. I kicked my feet out straight in front of me as I leaned back on my hands, and my eyes caught sight of what was above us. Macie plopped down next to me, startling me out of my thoughts.

"I left a message, she didn't answer," Macie said, coming up next to me. She was looking up at our balcony with me. "What were you looking at?"

"Might be our only option if we can't get in touch with anyone," I told her. My eyes gravitated to our balcony one floor above.

Macie's eyes followed, and her eyes widened right before she scoffed with a loud bellow. "What! You're crazy,

Becca. That's too high. And how do you even know the balcony door will be open?" Macie stood to get a better look, shielding against the sun with her hand over her eyes.

"Ava keeps it unlocked all the time, I know that for a fact," I told Macie. "Let's wait it out a bit, see if we hear from anyone."

We sat in the shade of the stoop, both completely discouraged by the position we had gotten ourselves in. It wasn't worth trying to catch a bus at this point to make it to the study group; there wasn't even time for that.

"I texted Mara, one of the other girls in the group. Told her what's going on and that we won't make it today," Macie said.

"Thanks, Macie," I said. "I'm sorry about this. I'm sorry I forgot my keys." I was so confused with everything in my life at the moment, this was about to put me over the edge.

"It's OK, Becca. I forgot my keys, too." Her shoulders lifted as she smiled, trying to make us both feel better about being airheads.

"So what's your story, Macie? Why no boyfriend for you?" I asked. We had some time to kill, so I figured getting some dirt on her would take my mind off of my own.

"Ugh, I don't know. I always seem to make such shitty decisions about guys." She picked at a dandelion growing between the cracks of the sidewalk at our feet. As she aimlessly peeled away the tiny petals, she went on. "I always get caught up in those amazing feelings you get at the beginning of a relationship. You know the ones, when you get the butterflies in your belly and you can't stop thinking about him."

Yeah, I knew those feelings well. Was having them for two guys at the moment, and one of them has been in my life for over a year already.

"I know exactly what you're talking about," I told her.

She mewled a soft sound of agreement as she stared off in the distance. "Well, I get too caught up in that. I guess I'm too much of a romantic?" She threw the dandelion, now petal free and a bent, limp green stem, onto the small patch of dead grass that was supposed to be our front lawn. Taking the hair tie from her wrist, she wound her long hair into a low bun and wrapped the tie around it.

Not sure if she was done talking, I was about to keep the conversation going. But she cleared her throat, so I glanced her way.

"I stay in things a lot longer than I should. I don't read the signs. Does that make sense?" she asked, looking back at me. Her eyes were expectant, as if I could help answer the world's problems.

"I don't think you're much different from most of the population, Macie. People want to see the good in others; they want to hope that it will work out. Turn a blind eye." God knew I was guilty of doing almost exactly that with Ty most of last year.

Macie made that deep scoffing noise in her throat again. "Nah, not you, Becca. All I've seen you do since I've known you is stand up for yourself. I wish I could be more like you."

And now it was my turn to scoff. "Ha! If you only knew the half of it! Come on, I'm done sitting here wasting our time. Let's try to get me up on that balcony."

We both stood up and stared at the looming structure about nine feet above the ground. Macie was taller, so it made sense for her to lift me, and I would try to scale the railing and make it over.

She stood with her hands on her hips, resisting. But eventually she relented, knowing we had no other choice. "Fine," she said, begrudgingly.

Stepping forward, she put her hands on her thigh. Pushing against her leg, she launched me into the air a bit and I grabbed for the lower railing of the balcony. Luckily, I got a hold of it with both hands.

"Christ, Becca, this is crazy!" Macie screamed up at me.

As I swung my legs to get some momentum, one of them finally caught on the railing as well. I dug my foot between the rails and tried to pull myself up. But that was when I realized my mistake.

"Shit," I mumbled.

"What's wrong?" Macie yelled up to me.

I didn't want to worry her, but I knew I was now stuck. Basically upside down on the underside of our balcony. This wasn't going to end well if we didn't get help.

"Macie, take my phone out of my bag now. Call someone, anyone. Call Gage. Call Ty. For fuck's sake, call Xander if you have to, but I need a big guy here fast to get me down! My foot is stuck." My arms were already starting to shake from trying to keep my body in this position. If my arms gave out, I would be hanging upside down by my foot, and that would be bad. Really, really bad.

"Oh shit, Becca," Macie cried as she fumbled with my phone. "What's your password?" She got the phone open and decided Ty would be the best first call, even though Gage lived so much closer. "Ty, oh thank God, you have to come over. It's Becca—she needs you!"

I didn't think Macie even needed to finish her sentence, as I could hear Ty screaming through the line that he was coming. My hands were getting sweaty, and my biceps were hurting. I was not going to be able to hold on until Ty got here. He lived over a mile away. With one final burst of energy, I reached up and wrapped my arm around the railing, my elbow now hooked around the metal. Feeling more secure, my breaths slowed.

Then I heard the best sound my ears could hear: the 'Stang.

"Macie, I hear Gage's car. Go stop him!"

Macie ran to the street, but Gage had already stopped, obviously seeing what had been going on.

"What the fuck are you doing up there, Becca?" Gage yelled as he ran up the walkway to my apartment.

"Well, you know, thought the view might be better from up here," I mused.

"We locked ourselves out," Macie offered.

Gage was busy looking for something. What, I didn't know. "Christ, was there no one you could call with a key? What about the front office?"

Macie's head snapped up and her wide, rounded eyes mirrored mine. We were so stupid. In our crazed stupor, we really hadn't thought this through. And then I heard the screech of another car pulling up.

Ty.

"Becca!" he yelled. "What happened?" But then he slowed his approach when he saw Gage was already there, seeming to help.

"Hey, Ty," Gage said. "We should probably lift Macie together and have her loosen Becca's foot; that might be the best way to do this. I already looked for something to stand on, but there's nothing."

Ty and Gage lifted Macie onto their shoulders with ease. Her hands deftly loosened my foot, and they quickly put her down.

"Just let go, Bec. We'll catch you," Ty said with such confidence.

I didn't think I had much of a choice—my arms were like jelly and ready to give out. My hands slipped away from the railing and I closed my eyes, praying the two men in my life would catch me as I crashed to the ground.

They did. Ty had me under the arms and Gage by the legs. Gage gently put my feet on the ground, allowing me to stand, though Ty hadn't let go of me, making sure I was steady.

"How do you feel?" Ty asked.

He turned me toward him, my face in his hands, inspecting me, top to bottom. The worry etched into the lines around his eyes made my heart ache that I had done this to him.

"I'm fine, Ty, really."

He pulled me into his arms, holding me tight, and that was when I realized he was shaking. "You scared the shit out of me, Bec. When I pulled up and saw you hanging from there, Christ, my heart dropped." He pulled back and showed me the inside of my one arm. "You're going to have a terrible bruise here, look."

As I looked down at my arm that had been clinging to the railing, my attention was drawn to a retreating form walking away. Gage was heading to his car. He got in and closed his door, our eyes connecting for a brief moment. He gave me a nod and what seemed like his version of permission to be with Ty. I think he realized Ty needed this.

My attention was brought back to my arm as Ty rubbed it and I jerked it out of his reach.

"Sorry, I didn't mean to hurt you," he said.

"It's fine. I'm just mad at myself for being stupid," I told him.

He scoffed at my insolence. "I would expect nothing less of you, Becca Reynolds."

Macie came to our side, checking out my arm as well. "Oh Becca, we need to get you some ice. That's getting swollen." Her lips were drawn together as she stared closer at my wound. She furrowed her brows as she pulled out her phone, hoping someone would be home soon. Her face lit up once she checked her messages. "Lanie'll be here in five minutes!"

Ty guided me to the front step, forcing me to sit. His hand was on my back, rubbing in small circles. I realized that since I came down, he hadn't let go, touching me in some way at all times.

"Thanks for coming to help me, Ty." Suddenly all the emotions I'd been feeling over the past few days came bubbling to the surface of my heart, my head. I felt as though I was either going to blurt out something I would regret or burst into tears.

That was when I saw Lanie walking up. Macie ran down the parking lot to meet her, I assumed to bring her up to speed with what transpired. Lanie picked up her pace, both of them standing in front of Ty and me.

"Are you OK?" she asked.

"Yep," I said. "Just need to get inside, if you don't mind."

Lanie walked around us and opened the door. Macie and I almost raced one another through the door, as if we thought we'd never see the inside of our apartment ever again. When in reality, it had only been about thirty minutes since we had left it.

Ty and Lanie followed us into the kitchen, both watching as I made an ice bag for my arm. "I'm fine, guys, really."

Ty came around, helping me tie the bag off and taking it from my hands. Turning around, I noticed that we were now alone, which kind of surprised me. He guided me to the couch, and as we sat, he wrapped the bag in a dish towel. "Here ya go."

Even though I expected it to be cold, the ice startled me as I applied it to my arm. I flung myself against the back of the couch, the adrenaline catching up to me, exhausting me. The exaggerated sigh that came from my mouth made Ty chuckle.

"You good now, Bec?"

One of my eyes peeked open to look his way; I was too tired to open both eyes fully. "Mm hmm," I told him.

He pulled my legs onto the couch while taking my shoes off. I nestled my head into the pillow as he covered me with a blanket, tucking it in around my body. He hovered over me for a moment, and I could feel him. "Are you going home for fall break this weekend?" he asked.

I opened my eyes to see his tall, muscular form, and it took my breath away. God, he was fucking hot. "Uhm, no, I'm not. I'm staying here."

"Okay." And he continued to stand above me, looking down at me. His whiskey eyes stared into mine, making it obvious he had something else to say. "So, I was wondering if we could maybe meet up, just to talk, nothing else, after break, when I get back."

The tremulous tone in his voice made me take notice of how nervous he actually was. Sitting up a bit on the couch, I saw his trembling hands as they moved to grip the back of his neck.

"Sure, Ty. We can talk next week," I said. "Does Monday work? I don't have anything Monday night."

He let out an audible sigh. "That's perfect, Becca. That's great. Thanks. Are you sure you're OK?"

I leaned back against the pillow again. "Yeah, I'm fine. Let me wallow in my embarrassment alone for a while." While I was chuckling at myself, I felt his lips on my forehead, a warm kiss left behind.

"I'm glad you're OK."

And then he was gone.

CHAPTER 21

The fact that all I could think about was getting back to school to see Becca wasn't good. I had a lot to focus on this long weekend while I was home. Seeing her hurt and how she looked made me want to tell her everything right then and there. But I couldn't; I needed to make certain everything was in place the way we'd been planning for. Once it was, I could win Becca back.

But she would have to give me the chance to explain it all first.

And that wasn't a guarantee.

Fall break allowed me to head home on Friday. But as I pulled into my driveway, both my parent's cars were in it, so I knew they were home from work. That was a good sign; things were in place and happening.

"Mom? Dad? Where are you?" I yelled as I dropped my things in the entryway. It was odd to be home and not have to head right to my job. This year had been such a challenge between classes, pledging, and driving home most weekends to work. It was not how I envisioned my college years to be, but life isn't always how we envision it.

"We're in the den!" my dad yelled back. I walked through the kitchen and noticed my favorite meal, chicken parmigiana, was in progress on the stove. That put a smile on my face. Upon entering the den, I came across a typical scene to come home to. My dad was in his recliner, his usual spot after a long day at work. My mom was at her desk on her computer. She never stopped working, since she worked from home some days as a freelance writer for a magazine. "Hey, Ty. Glad to see you home, son," my dad said.

"Hey, Dad. Kelly's not here yet?" My hope was all parties involved in our planned meeting would be present already, but no such luck.

"She called. She and her parents should be here soon," my mom explained. She was up from her chair and coming in for a hug. "Oh," she said, squeezing me, "I know you don't like coming home so much, but I love it." I hugged her back, knowing she was really trying to just make me feel better.

At that moment, car doors slammed out front. The three of us walked out the door to meet our visitors. My mom was the first to Kelly's car, as always.

"Where is she?" she squealed as she rounded to the passenger side. "Let me have her!"

Kelly popped out from the side of the car and handed her to my mom.

My daughter. Savannah.

"There she is, the little beauty queen. Oh my, Kelly, look at this adorable dress you have her in," my mom exclaimed.

Kelly was a pretty girl with her short blonde hair and hazel eyes. Her smile was wide for Savannah as she watched my mom, her grandmother, hold her. Apparently, I had much blonder hair as a young child, similar to that of my mom's. The three of them huddled together looked very much like family with my daughter's light fuzz starting to get a bit longer on her head.

Kelly's parents were slower to emerge from their car. They joined us in the driveway, ogling over the little bundle in my mom's arms. Everyone was all abuzz about the baby and how she'd grown.

The four women gathered together, mother, child, and the two grandmothers, and walked into the house together, followed by us men.

"How are you, Mr. Roberts?" I asked Kelly's dad. It had taken some time, but he and I were on good terms now.

"I'm well, Ty, and you? How's school going?" he asked.

I hesitated before answering. "Classes are going well, sir. Everything is, um, just great. My grades are all A's and B's so far, just like last semester."

He nodded as he and my dad moved into the den and sat down.

All six adults crowded into what was not a small room, but it suddenly felt void of air. I loved this room on any other day. It was the room, when growing up, where we would gather for movie nights and spend Christmases by the tree in front of the picture window. It was the quintessential family room with one of those lived-in comfy couches that everyone fought for because it was their favorite seat. Well, everyone, that was, except my dad, who had his own chair that no one was ever allowed to sit in.

And even though I had been looking forward to this meeting, it was still not a walk in the park having our parents together, considering the circumstances.

My mom still had Savannah in her arms, likely not about to give her up for quite a while. As I walked toward her, the chubby-faced baby caught sight of me and broke out into a wide grin.

"Oh, Ty, she knows who you are," my mom said gently as she sat with the baby on her lap.

Kelly came to sit near me on a chair, her on the cushion, me on the arm.

"So," Mel, Kelly's mom, started, "I know it's been tough on Ty, being in school, and Kelly's been working. They take care of the baby when they can. But I do feel that the four grandparents have chipped in more than most would. So, there's that." Her eyes landed on Kelly and me.

Her disapproval always came through eventually. She was the one of the four who struggled the most with all of this. I always wondered if it was because Kelly didn't go to school, but that was Kelly's choice. And she made that choice long before she got pregnant. Her parents wanted her to go; Kelly chose to delay that for now and opted to work instead. However, I got the feeling, mainly from her mom, that they weren't on board with that decision and potentially blamed me for it. Or at the very least were angry that I was away at school getting my education while Kelly was not.

"But Savannah is finally old enough to enter the baby care program at Kelly's job, so we thought that might be the best decision," Kelly's mom continued. "I think that eases your responsibility during the week the three days you've been watching her, Colleen. And it helps us all out, allowing us to watch her more on the weekends."

Everyone digested the plan Mel, Kelly, and I had come up with. The hope was Kelly and I would get some relief on the weekends and not work constantly in between child-care. All four grandparents started buzzing with conversation about the new plan.

"I want to say something," I started, getting their attention. "I need all of you to realize that Kelly and I know how lucky we are to have the four of you in our lives helping take care of Savannah. We know this was not an ideal situation, and we appreciate all you do to help her, and us, so I can continue with school and Kelly with work." I moved from my seat to take Savannah from my mom, needing to hold my daughter. She snuggled into my chest as I held her head against me, my lips atop the fine hair on her head.

They all smiled and nodded, even Mel. My mom came to me once I had Savannah settled in my arms and kissed my cheek as she headed to the kitchen.

"Can we talk?" Kelly asked. The last time she said those words to me, she told me she was pregnant. At least I knew that was not the case at the moment.

The three of us went into the yard and found a seat at the table on the patio. I turned Savannah around on my lap so she could see the nearby bushes, a bird sitting on a branch. "We won't have much time before she's going to get fussy for a bottle. But I need to tell you something."

"OK, what's up?"

"So, I wanted to let you know I met someone." Her eyes wouldn't meet mine as she spoke. "I kind of figured you'd want to know, since he'll be spending time with Peanut."

And here I was, concerned for the past year about moving on. Well, showing anyone that I had moved on.

"That's great, Kelly. I'm happy for you."

And right then, Savannah let out a big laugh. As I picked her up off my lap and faced her toward me, her smile remained but no more sounds emanated from her. Her big saucer blue eyes were looking back at us.

"Oh my God, Ty, did you hear that?" Kelly said as we both leaned in to stare at her as if that would induce another laugh. When our stares didn't do a thing, I stuck my tongue out at her, but still nothing.

"She's never done that before?" I asked.

"No, that's the first!" she exclaimed. "That has to be the cutest sound I've ever heard." Savannah started reaching for her momma, so I handed her over. "I met him at work," she continued, not giving up on the topic, it seemed. "And he's stopping by here to meet everyone."

Oh.

"So, I'm assuming he knows about Savannah and this whole situation?" I asked.

"Of course he does, Ty. I wouldn't go into something with someone without them knowing all about this," she said. "I would hope you wouldn't either."

Well, fuck.

Like, seriously. Shit.

I felt as if I was going to vomit. I mean, I didn't care one fucking bit that Kelly was with someone else. Actually made my life easier. But I made my life a living hell for the past year, I guess, for no reason.

Because she was right. One hundred percent right. And I had royally fucked myself in every way possible. But I'd already decided to tell Becca everything once I returned after this weekend. I didn't know why these new arrangements made me feel better about telling her. My mom wasn't working as much as she liked, since she was watching Savannah during the week, so I took a job here on the weekends to take up some of the slack. She told me I could give that up now and that they would even help with the daycare costs until I finished college.

I knew I was one of the lucky ones. Few young adults in our situation had parents who helped to the level that ours were. Kelly put off school, but that was her choice. Her parents were willing to help her with that as well. And Kelly and I had worked on keeping our relationship amicable.

"Ty," she said, watching me over the top of Savannah's head. "Are you OK with this?"

"Yeah, of course I am. I mean, as long as you trust him. And you trust him, right? Around Peanut?" I leaned in and tickled Savannah on the belly to get her to laugh again, but all she did was give me a huge toothless grin and reach out and pull my hair.

But then, like clockwork, the beast emerged. It started with tiny little whines and built to a loud wail within seconds.

"Can you warm the bottle for me, Ty? It's in the bag right there." I grabbed it and went inside. My mom was in the kitchen making coffee for everyone while I popped the open bottle in the microwave.

"I hate that you kids warm it up like that. Don't overheat it. It will burn her." She shook her head at me as she put mugs and creamer on a platter, and I turned and wrapped my arms around her. "What's this for?" she asked as she gripped my arm.

"Just a thank-you hug. I don't think I say thank you to you guys enough for all you do for me, for us." I kissed the top of her head before letting go.

Her eyes were on me as she started making her way back toward to the den. "Ty, you guys made a mistake. But that mistake gave us that beautiful baby. Whatever decision you would have made, I would have supported, but I do love her." She smiled before continuing. "You're a good boy, Ty. I want you to succeed and be happy."

"There's something that would make me really happy."

She stopped her advance to the den and looked my way. "What's that?"

And then the microwave beeped at the same time Savannah let out a scream.

"Can we talk?" I asked.

She nodded, but concern was in her eyes—I could see it. I had opened the door for the talk; I would have to have it now.

Suddenly, Kelly popped into the kitchen and quickly grabbed the bottle from my hand. "She needs this now," she said with a smile.

"OK, sorry. I'll be a sec. I need to talk to my mom," I told her.

"Of course," Kelly said. "Take your time, I've got Peanut." She nodded on her way back to the banshee crying in the other room.

I turned my attention to my mom, who decided to stay in the kitchen and work on dinner, but also to hear out what I had to say. As I approached her at the island, her eyes followed me while I took a seat on a stool. She kept peering up from the cucumbers she was butchering with a knife as if they had hurt her best friend or something. Her nerves were rattled by my need to talk.

"Don't worry, Mom. I haven't gotten someone else pregnant."

Her sharp cackle lightened the mood.

"Well, that's good to know," she said. "What is it, Ty? You seem really upset about something." She put the knife and vegetables down, giving me her undivided attention.

"Let me help with that," I told her, getting up to take the knife from her hand. As I went to grab it, she stilled my hand on the cutting board.

"Put it down, Ty. Let's talk." She motioned for me to sit as she sat as well.

I took a moment to gather my thoughts. Even though I wanted to have this conversation, I didn't necessarily have the words prepared in my head for it.

"So, I know how me doing well in college is important to you and Dad. It's important to me as well. And I think I've proven I'm capable of it, at least much better than I did in high school."

Her smile of approval was a good sign.

"I know you think I have a lot on my plate between Savannah, work, school, and travelling back and forth." I paused. I really didn't think my parents were going to have a problem with me being with someone; they'd probably be happy for me, for all I knew. "But last year, before I even knew Kelly was pregnant, I met someone. Someone very special." It's kind of awkward telling your mom about the person you're in love with.

She reached out and grabbed my hands. Her eyes stayed glued to mine and were hard to read; she only continued to look at me, waiting for me to continue.

"Do you remember Becca? She was the girl who came home with me when we brought Logan home last year," I said.

"I do—the pretty brunette with the green eyes," she responded.

"Yeah, that's her. Well, we were in a relationship all year last year. I kept everything going on here at home from her, everything. And the two times we came here, she could pick up on how I treated her differently." I pulled my hands from hers and started wringing them together against the granite counter; I was embarrassed of my own actions. "And then she broke up with me right before Savannah was born. I figured it was for the best, ya know."

My mom's sad smile told me she understood my melancholy demeanor.

"But it wasn't. I never stopped thinking about her all summer. Probably because I'm in love with her, Mom. She's the best thing that's ever happened to me." My voice cracked. "But I really fucked everything up, and now I don't know how to fix it. And I don't even know if you and Dad would be OK with meeting her, or with me being with someone else going through all of this, and . . ."

"Ty," my mom interrupted me. "Honey, calm down and take a breath. You've been through a lot this past year and I'm sorry if you feel we wouldn't support you being in a relationship." She came around and pulled me to standing, wrapping her arms around me. With her head still against my chest, she continued talking. "Your father and I are very proud of you and how you've handled everything that's come your way. Most young men wouldn't do it with as much grace as you have." She pulled back to look up at me. "We probably should make sure to tell you that more often." Her warm smile spread across her face, some un-shed tears twinkling in her eyes. "Your life can't come to a screeching halt simply because you have a baby; it doesn't work that way. Do I want you to be involved with someone so soon, with everything you have going on? Probably not, but love doesn't work on a schedule."

I pushed out of her arms, even more frustrated with myself. Why had I waited so long to come to her with this?

"I really messed up, Mom. What am I going to do? How do I get her back? All I've done is feed her a bunch of lies."

"Well, why don't you tell me what's been going on?" she said as we sat back down at the island.

"It was nice to meet you, Tim. Take care," I said. Shaking hands with me, he left the yard where the three of us had spent the past hour talking and getting to know one another. Kelly was right—he was a good guy, and they seemed good for one another. And he loved to be around Savannah.

Kelly was gathering up all of Savannah's toys, which meant she was planning on heading out as well. This was the hard part about our situation. I only had Savannah for oc-casional overnights when I made it home on the weekends; her leaving was always difficult.

"Ty, you will always be her dad." Kelly's hand was on mine as we packed up the baby bag. I looked at Savannah, who had fallen asleep on a pallet of blankets we made on the grass next to us. "You don't have to worry about that. We will always make it work out somehow. OK?"

I nodded. But I wasn't sure it would be as easy as she made it sound. Savannah was only five months old, and it already was getting complicated. If I was able to add Becca into the mix, who knew how things would work? But the advice given by my mom gave me hope I may be able to rectify the situation when I got back to school.

"I appreciate that, Kelly. Let's get you two into your car. Can I carry her?" I asked.

"Of course."

We walked around the side of the house. Her parents had left hours ago, giving us more time together. Savannah stirred awake on my shoulder in time for me to give her a proper goodbye. Lifting her in the air, I suspended her above me, smiling at her chubby cheeks as she stared down at me. And then she let out a big, from-the-gut laugh once again.

"Did you laugh at Daddy?" Kelly squealed.

"*Daddy?*" a voice in the distance said in horror.

Both mine and Kelly's heads snapped to the sidewalk at the end of my driveway.

"Becca?" I whispered, almost to myself. But then louder, I said, "Becca! Wait!"

She was already running back to her car, which was parked down the road. I handed Savannah off to Kelly to reach Becca in time.

But it was no use.

Her car peeled out of its spot before I could even make it to the end of my driveway.

CHAPTER 22
Becca

What in the actual fuck? *Daddy?* Ty had a *baby?* A fucking *baby?*

Once I got down the street from Ty's house, I drove in the opposite direction to what I should've, heading away from school. The need to *not* see him was so strong that I had to make sure he couldn't find me. Plus, I was in no condition to drive. Pulling over in a nearby fast food parking lot gave me the time to calm down.

And to call Lanie.

"Hey, Bec, are you doing anything fun?" Lanie asked when she picked up the call.

I couldn't even talk. The sobs streamed through the line.

"Becca, what's wrong?" she asked with fear in her voice. "Honey, where are you? Are you safe?"

"Mmmhmm," was all I could get out.

"OK, honey. Just breathe and let it out. I'm here." She knew not to tell me to stop crying or calm down. She knew those words weren't helpful at the lowest of lows. "When you're ready, you tell me what you need to tell me. I'll be here." She just kept repeating that to me through the phone line, over and over. Her calm voice eventually helped me find my breaths. They evened out.

I felt as though I could form words, but I didn't want to. If I put it into words, it would make it real.

"Bec, you still there?" Lanie asked.

"Yeah," I whispered, "I'm still here."

She waited a couple more minutes to see if I was going to offer anything else, but when I didn't, she pushed for more.

"So, are you at the apartment? Are you alone?" she prodded.

"No, I, um, decided last minute that I wanted to surprise Ty at his house for the long weekend." I let out a tremendous sigh as emotional exhaustion set in.

Once I went back to my empty apartment, my mind got the better of me. I decided I would be brave and meet our issues head on by going straight to the heart of it. I felt going to Ty's house might show him I was willing to put aside how being there made me feel.

That I was ready to move on with making it work with him.

Because that was what I had decided.

I wanted to make it work with Ty.

"Oh," she said. "So you're not far from me. Ty is only like an hour from Xander's house. Do you want me to come to you?"

Of course she would offer that. And for a second, I contemplated saying yes. But then what? We would sit in this parking lot and talk just like we are now on the phone?

And I had no intention of going to Xander's house with her.

Instead, I cut to the chase.

"Lane, I've figured out his secret."

Silence. From both of us.

"Okaaay," she finally said. "Are you ready to share it with me?"

My mouth was dry and my eyes were wet, the tears still trickling out. I searched my car for something to drink, anything, even a days-old bottle of water or soda, but there was nothing. I got in the drive-through line of the restaurant attached to the lot I was in. I pulled up to the window and was about to order . . .

"Bec, are you there?" Lanie asked through the Bluetooth in the car.

"One sec," I told her.

"Welcome to Cook Out. What can I get you?" the server asked.

"Can I have a large Diet Coke, please?" I drove through the line and got my soda, knowing Lanie was waiting the whole time to hear from me. I knew I was stalling. But once I said the words and they were out to the world, they were real, and I wouldn't be able to take them back. I pulled my car into a spot along the side of the lot and took a long sip of my soda. I stared out at the cars driving by while trying to gather my courage for my next words.

"Lanie," I started, "Ty has a baby. He's a father."

Dead silence on the line. I pulled the phone away from my ear to make sure the call was still live, and it was.

She was as dumbfounded as I was.

"OK," she finally said. "How did you find this out, Bec? And are you OK?"

"As I walked up to his house, he came around from the back with another girl and a baby in his arms. I didn't think much of it at first, thought maybe it was a cousin or something." I had to pause because my words got caught over the lump in my throat. "But, uh, the girl called Ty 'Daddy' when she took the baby back in her arms."

There, I said it. And the heavy feeling of bricks on my chest lifted a bit. I still felt like throwing up, but I could breathe better.

"Where are you, Becca?" Lanie asked, her voice tinged with concern. I could hear Xander asking her questions in the background, their voices muffled as she covered up the phone.

"I drove a little ways from his house so he couldn't find me and pulled into a parking lot," I told her. "I didn't know if he would follow me, so I didn't want to head right back to school. He's been calling and texting me since I left his house." Ty ran after me. I saw him in my rearview mirror as I drove away. But I had no idea what he did once I turned the corner. I hoped he decided not to follow me.

"Xander and I want to come and get you. Drop me a pin."

"Not a good idea, Lanes. I'm in no mood to be around the two of you, no offense. But seeing how perfect the two of you are will put me in a worse mood, trust me. I think I'm going to stop home while I'm in the area, then head back to school, our apartment. Or better yet, maybe I'll hit Gage up," I said as I thought out loud. Lanie groaned as I continued. "Whatever. I know what you think about him, but I'm doing the same thing he is. Or I was, anyway. What's the difference? If he's alone now, maybe he can take my mind off of this shit going on. Lord knows that's what I need at the moment. Definitely not watching the two of you going gaga over one another." I took a sip of my soda when I finished.

"Are you done?" she asked. She always said that to me when I rambled, which I did a lot. But who wouldn't after finding out what I just did?

"Yes, I'm done."

"OK, good," she said. "Go home. I would prefer you actually stayed there overnight. Maybe wait until tomorrow to head back to school. But if not, I understand about wanting to see Gage. I'm sure he'll do the job of taking your mind off of things. But do me a favor—text or call me when you get to your house. I'm gonna be a wreck with you driving upset. Promise me."

"I promise," I told her.

"And I am going to head home early to be with you," Lanie continued.

"You don't need to do that," I said, but inside I was happy. "Let me go. I want to get out of here so Ty doesn't find me."

We hung up.

And I drove home.

To my parents' house.

I didn't know what to expect when I got there since my family had no idea I was headed home. Forty-five minutes later, I pulled into my driveway, which, per usual, was littered with bikes and scooters. My mom's car was there, but not my dad's. Since it was a weekend, it would be hard to know if they would be working or not.

My dad was a high-profile executive at a financial firm. He worked long hours that required him to work on the weekends most times. My mom did HR for her company. She'd been able to do more remote work in the past few years. One would think that would give her more time to be a "mom," but it didn't seem to. Once I went off to school, they needed to hire a babysitter for the after-school hours.

My parents relied heavily on me to help with my brothers. And the house. On top of doing my homework while I was still in high school.

I couldn't wait to go away to college.

And every time I visited, the responsibilities and expectations remained the same. It was assumed that I was the "second mom" in the household. Honestly, Jonah and Sam came to me more than Mom when I was home. They knew I would take care of things quicker than she would.

It wasn't that my parents didn't care. They did. But their jobs were important to them, for several reasons. First, they both enjoyed their work. More importantly, though, they needed to keep their jobs to pay for all the kids they had. And now that I was in college, the expenses had grown. But they committed themselves to paying my way. So, I felt as though I should put my time in with the boys when I was here, to do my share. But I was more than happy to be out of the house as much as possible.

As I reached for the handle on the door, I remembered my promise to Lanie.

Me:
Made it home

I saw the heart appear over my message as I pushed the door open.

As I walked up the path, I moved the bikes and other riding toys out of the way, knowing I would need to put them all in the garage before I left later. Opening the front door, I prepared myself for the onslaught of loud, raucous noises coming from all parts of the house.

But it was quiet.

I made my way to the back of the house toward the kitchen. It was the heart of our home, with a huge island that could seat all seven of us for dinner. It connected to a big family room with comfy furniture and a big TV for movie nights when we were able to get all of us in the same room at the same time. Those nights were rare.

But again, empty.

I decided to check my mom's office. And that was where I had luck. I heard her typing away on her keyboard. I tapped on the door gently. "Mom?"

I heard her desk chair swivel at the sound of my voice.

"Becca, is that you?" Her voice was full of surprise.

I opened the door as she was standing from her chair.

"Hi, Mom. Where *is* everyone?" The raise in my voice asked so many more questions than just that one.

"What are you doing here, honey? I thought you said you weren't coming home this weekend?" My mom was up and wrapping me in a hug before I could answer her. Even though this house was chaotic, and I enjoyed my time out of it, I did miss the smell of my mom's hugs. She smelled like home.

"Yeah, I wasn't planning on it . . ." My voice trailed off as I heard the front door slam and voices echoing in the halls.

It was Dad with the older two. I could hear Mason and Nate fighting over something as they progressed closer to the back of the house.

"He had them at the driving range," my mom explained.

I nodded as we both moved to leave her office and meet them in the kitchen. But she stopped me by the door, her hand holding me back. "Are you OK, Becca? You seem off?"

Shaking my head, I pulled from her grip. "I'm fine, Mom. I think I was just missing home, ya know?" We continued toward the others. "Where are the twins?"

"Oh, they made some new friends at school," my mom said. "They have playdates at their house every so often."

Literally as she finished her last word, the two monsters came blasting through the front door.

"Becca!"

"Bec!"

They both came tearing around the corner of the hall from the foyer, their sneakers skidding on the wood floor as they crashed into my legs.

"I told you that was her car," Jonah said, trying to push Sam off of me. The two little monsters looked like they had grown even more in the few weeks since I'd seen them last.

"Alright you two, upstairs and in the tub," my mom ordered. And to my surprise, they listened. "I'll be up in a minute."

And that surprised me even more. I would have expected her to ask me to bathe them. And I think she saw my face, my astonishment hard to hide. But she chose to not make a big deal over it.

"Are you staying for dinner, honey?" she asked. "We're eating early tonight."

I really hadn't thought this visit through. My original plan was to just stop in, throw Ty off my tail, then head back to school. But being back here made me want to stay a bit, which I wasn't expecting.

Without warning, tears sprung to my eyes.

The thickness in my voice was hard to hide when I answered her. "Yeah, Mom, I think I will."

She came to me, hugging me. "I miss you, too, honey." Kissing the top of my head, she went up the stairs to take care of the twins. And I turned toward the voices in the family room, finding my dad and the other boys watching a game.

Waiting for me.

I decided to spend the night with my family. It surprised me as much as them. A movie with popcorn and all of us crammed in the family room normally would have had me scampering to my room with an excuse of some sort. But this time I relished in the pandemonium and actually enjoyed it. And a night in my own room, in my bed with the use of my bathroom, was much more inviting than being alone back at school.

My parents seemed to have turned a corner with the handling of their family unit. Maybe it took me leaving for them to realize they needed to step up and do more. I didn't care what it was; I liked it. And the boys liked it, too. Don't get me wrong, there was still chaos in the house. There was no way there couldn't be with four boys running around. But the chaos was a bit more under control.

Around midday my social battery expired though, and my need to head out grew strong.

"Mom," I said as I walked into her office. "I'm gonna get going."

She turned in her chair to face me with a huge smile on her face.

"Loved this impromptu visit, sweetie. Will they keep happening?" she asked as she stood and came to hug me.

I nodded against her. "Yeah, I'll make sure to be home more."

But as I walked to my car, the reality of the other shit going on in my life hit me hard. Other shit in my life I wanted to forget.

But there was someone I hoped could help me do that.

Turning my phone on, I was inundated with missed calls and messages I'd received in the past twenty-four hours from *him*. It didn't surprise me; but it still pissed me off. It made me want to call Gage even more.

I dialed his number once I got in my car.

"Becca."

His sultry voice still did things to me.

"Hi, Gage. Are you home? Or will you be home in a couple hours?" I asked quickly.

"Yeah, listen. I'm sorry I haven't reached out this week, it's . . ."

"Gage, I don't want to talk about anything that's happened in our lives this week, I really don't. I'd just like to see you. And I'd like to forget everything else."

I knew I sounded desperate, but I really didn't care.

"OK, Becca. I'll be waiting for you."

As I approached Gage's door, my heart palpitated and my palms were sweaty. I wasn't sure if it was from what happened the day before or that we hadn't really spent time together since our somewhat failed attempt at sex.

I kinda thought it was both. My hand moved up to knock but hit air as the door swung open before I could.

"Hey," he said in a low, seductive timbre.

I guess I'd forgotten how fucking gorgeous he was. Because when he opened that door and I saw him for the first time in days, he took my breath away. My state of mind, I'm sure, had something to do with it.

"Hi," I returned, trying to be equally seductive, but feared I failed. Regardless, he gathered me in his arms and pulled me close, which was the reaction I was aiming for. I fell into his embrace, and we stood like that for a few minutes.

"You OK, Becca?" he whispered at the top of my head. He pulled away slightly and looked down at me, those dark-chocolate eyes inquisitive.

"I'll be fine. Even better if we don't talk about it. Can we just go inside?"

He grabbed me by the hand and pulled me through the open door. It was quite dark in his apartment but smelled amazing. When we reached the living area, I realized why. He had the lights down low and several candles lit around the room.

It was positively enchanting. And sexy.

The glimmer of the candles reflected off the metal tables they rested on. Eventually, my eyes landed on Gage.

"You look beautiful in this light," he said. "And listen, this was not with any intention of, well, anything. I heard something in your voice, and I just thought this might be kind of nice, that's all."

Well, fuck. He was being thoughtful. That was not expected. And not what I really wanted at the moment. What I wanted to do was rip his clothes off and fuck him.

"We can pop a movie on if that would help. Whatever you want, Becca. You tell me."

So accommodating. Possibly feeling guilty? But I didn't care at the moment. I just needed to forget everything that had happened to me earlier.

"Anything, Gage. Anything to keep my mind off of my weekend so far, please." I whispered the cracked words through the tears I held back. My phone continued to ping in my pocket, adding to my addled mental state.

"OK, Becca, come sit down," he said as he led me to the couch. He sat me in my favorite spot in the corner of the sectional. As I curled up against the cushion, he covered me with a blanket. "I'll be right back."

While I waited for him to return, I shot a text to Lanie.

Me:

Made it to school now I'm at Gage's

Lanie:

Perfect I should be back in a couple
hours

Gage came back in with a big bowl of popcorn and two cans of soda. "So, action movie or chick flick?" he asked.

"Action all the way. The louder and noisier, the better, and you pick. My brain is shot." I reached for the bowl, suddenly starving. "But I need something stronger than soda tonight. That will not cut it." I motioned to the cans.

"Well, OK," he responded as he sauntered to his bar. "What will it be? Wine? Beer?"

I felt like that wasn't even enough to drown out the chatter in my head.

"How 'bout some of that brown shit you always drink?" I offered as I watched him over the back of the couch.

He turned slowly toward me, his eyebrows raised high. "You want a bourbon?" he asked incredulously.

"Sure, why not?" I retorted. "Are you insinuating I can't handle it?"

"No, not at all. It's just that bourbon is an acquired taste." He stood at the counter, mixing something up in a glass. When he finally made his way back to the couch, the drink in his hand was covered in fruit. "This will be a way to ease in. It's an old-fashioned. I think you'll like it."

The dark cherry at the bottom of the glass combined with the slice of orange made it look appealing. "Where do you get these huge ice balls? They are so cool." The first sip was a shock as the brown liquid bit at the back of my throat. But the fruitiness of the additives tempered the aftertaste. I took a bigger sip.

"I assume that means you like it," Gage said approvingly. "And, by the way, they are a sipping drink." He watched with horror as I downed the entire drink in my next swallow, the fruit and ice clanking to the bottom of the glass as I slammed it to the table.

The burn was rough; as it brought tears to my eyes, I held out my empty glass to Gage.

"I'll have another, please."

Taking the glass, he walked back to the bar and started preparing another drink. "I think this should be the last one, Becca. You don't know how this *brown shit* will affect you." This time he came back with two glasses in his hand, one for each of us.

"Cheers." It was a simple clink of our glasses, because we both knew there was nothing I was cheery about at the moment. He took a small sip of his, so I followed his lead and did the same. After putting our glasses on the table, we found a position that was comfortable for both of us on the couch. That entailed me cozying up into the crook of his arm, my head on his shoulder. I felt enveloped by him, by his arms and his heat. I didn't know if it was the alcohol hitting me or not, but I relaxed against him. I did more than relax; I snuggled in close.

And I thought I let out a sigh.

"This is exactly what I needed," I said. "Want to pick a movie?" I asked as I tilted my head to look at him. His eyes were on me, and I could tell a movie was not what was on his mind.

"Listen," Gage said. "I know you don't want to talk about anything. But I feel as though I have something to make up to you. I can do that without talking."

That made me sit up a bit. My rounded eyes must have showed my astonishment at his words.

"I'm pretty sure I can help you relax even more than the bourbon can," he said with a sly smile. "And my phone is silenced." We both let out a low chuckle. Then his one hand came to the side of my face, fingertips grazing from my cheek to my jaw. My eyes fluttered closed as that hand trailed down the side of my neck, down the center of my chest, between my breasts.

"Gage, that wasn't the reason I came over," I whispered. Or was it?

"I know, but that doesn't mean I can't make you feel good," he offered. "Do you think it will take your mind off of what's bothering you?" His hands lowered to the bottom of my sweater and lifted it over my head. "Black lace," he said with approval as he pushed me away to get a better look. "Take your pants off, Becca."

Lying back on the couch, I peeled my leggings off. I was about to take my thong off as well, but he stopped me.

"Leave the bra and panties." He pushed me onto my back on the couch and laid next to me. "I love how your nipples come through the lace of your bra." His mouth was on my breast, over the lace, sucking. His hand squeezed the other breast, pinching the tight bud almost to the point of pain.

"Gage," I said, stopping him by pulling his mouth from me. "Take your shirt off, please. I need to see you, some of you, feel your skin against me. The warmth of it—please."

His dark eyes zeroed in on mine as I spoke, as I almost begged for him to do this. He reached above his head and pulled his shirt over and off. Supporting his weight above me with one arm, he used the hand of the other to touch my face. The trail of heat he left behind as his fingers traced a line from my jaw to my chest was enough to leave me breathless. His finger looped under the strap of my bra, playing with it.

"I'm torn between ripping this off of you and keeping it on. You look so damn sexy in black lace." His warm breath as he spoke against my cheek made the hairs lift on the back of my neck.

The bra stayed on as his mouth moved to explore the tender skin between my breasts. My hands gripped his back, the tense muscles taut under my fingers as he suspended himself above me. Digging my nails into his skin elicited a growl that vibrated against me. He shifted himself against my lower half, his fully hard erection pushing against my leg.

His hand slowly wandered lower, grazing my stomach, reaching the band of my thong. He easily pushed his fingers under the thin material as he used a knee to separate my legs. His slow, torturous descent through my folds had me squirming underneath him.

"Someone is anxious," he whispered against my ear.

But he obliged.

Two fingers drove inside of me hard and fast. The moan was involuntary, and he swallowed it with a deep kiss as his tongue invaded my mouth. He pushed his fingers in even deeper, thrusting with a rhythm that started the crescendo.

I suddenly realized I couldn't get my mind off of what I had seen in Ty's driveway.

The baby, in his arms.

Daddy.

I tried to force my mind to forget all of that, to focus on what was happening in the present.

"Becca, you are so fucking hot," he mouthed against me as he pulled up for air. "Can I taste you?" He started maneuvering his way down my body, taking my panties with him as he went. I tried to get back into what we were doing. I mean, fuck, this hot guy was asking to go down on me. I would be a fucking idiot to say no to that. Right? I relaxed against the couch and worked real hard to get out of my head, to focus on this beautiful specimen of a man who was shirtless and between my legs.

But then there was a knock at the door.

Not just any knock—a hard, let-me-in kind of pounding on the door.

"You've got to be fucking kidding me!" Gage growled as he pulled his mouth away from me. First, he looked up at me, then toward the door.

"Are you expecting anyone?" I asked, though not entirely upset by the interruption. My mind wasn't allowing me to connect with him the way I wanted to.

"*No!*" he yelled, obviously frustrated. "Stay here and don't move." His heavy steps as he stormed to the entry way made me shudder, afraid for whomever was on the other side of the door.

I heard him throw the door open and yell, "What?"

I heard the response to Gage's question.

And I couldn't believe what I was hearing.

He wouldn't have.

Chapter 23

"Hey, Gage. Sorry to bother you. I was wondering if Becca's here? I see her car here, and I'm really worried about her and can't find her anywhere. We, uh, she . . ." I didn't really know what else to say to the guy I knew was fucking the girl I loved. But as he stood there, shirtless in his entryway, his hand turning white where it held the door, rage poured from him. "She was really upset when she left my house and drove off. I just want to find her and make sure she's safe, that's all."

Gage's demeanor calmed a fraction once I finished. His hand slid from the door and he flexed it repeatedly, as if to release the tension in his muscles.

"Ty," he said, firmly but calmly, "I don't really think it's a good idea that you're here right now."

As soon as he finished saying that, a sound caught his attention behind him. He turned to look down his hall, and I caught sight of something that will forever haunt me.

My words caught in my throat. I could no longer speak. But that was not Becca's problem at all. As she stood there, obviously mostly naked under a blanket she had wrapped around herself, her words came flying out of her mouth.

"Ty! What the fuck are you doing here? You have some fucking nerve coming here looking for me. Jesus Christ! What the fuck? After what I saw yesterday? You're coming looking for me? Who the fuck do you think you are?"

She started storming toward me, out the door. Gage grabbed a hold of her by the waist, pulling her back into his apartment.

"Bec, I only wanted to know you were safe. That's . . ." I tried to get some type of explanation out, but she cut me off.

"I don't give a flying fuck what you want. You have no right to know anything about me anymore. We are over. Do you hear me? O-V-E-R! Over! There is no coming back from this, Ty. Ever!" She started for the door again. "I want to go home. I can't do this anymore. I'm done with this shit!"

"Becca," Gage said as he pulled her back inside once again. "You can't go out like this; plus, you've been drinking. You can't drive." Gage gave me a pleading look at that point. However, if I stepped in, I would only make things worse. "Come on—let's get you dressed and I'll drive you home, if that's what you want."

At that, the two of them went back inside, and Gage closed the door.

The thought of him in there, with her, without her clothes on, nauseated me. I wanted to break the door down and drag her out of there. I didn't want him seeing her, touching her, doing any of those things with me right on the other side of the wall.

It destroyed me, being a spectator to a scene ruining my life.

But I took care of ruining my own life long before Gage came into the picture.

I decided to sit on the stoop and wait until I knew she was safely in his car and on her way home. I'd spent the past twenty-four hours looking for her, I wasn't going to let her out of my sight now. Though I knew a big part of it was that I wanted to make sure she actually was getting dressed and leaving his apartment.

"What the fuck are you still doing here?" she yelled as she threw the door open. I didn't have time to get off the step before she came stumbling out. My hands instinctively went to help steady her. "Get your hands off of me," she seethed.

Gage came out right behind her.

"Why the hell did you let her get so drunk?" I asked.

His head snapped in my direction at my words. "Ty, I think the better question is, what did you do that made her want to get so drunk?"

"That drunk girl you're referring to," Becca said as she pointed at the both of us, "is right fucking here. And I'm not that bad." She stumbled again as she attempted to descend the two steps to the parking lot. Gage got a hold of her and placed her in his car. Neither of them said another word to me as they drove off.

But I couldn't leave.

There were still things that had to be said. So I resumed sitting on his stoop.

And I waited.

At first, I was nervous that Gage was going to stay at Becca's place. About twenty minutes had already passed and he still hadn't returned. But then I heard the rumble of his engine and saw the headlights of his Mustang come around the corner. I steeled myself for a conversation I really didn't want to have, but knew I had to.

He shook his head at me as he walked toward his door, his disbelief obvious.

"Is this where you beg and plead for me to help you get your girl back?" he asked.

I stood from the brick step and went chest to chest with him. "No. That'll be on me. But I do need to talk to you. Can we go inside?"

He didn't answer me right away. And I didn't blame him. He had no real reason to allow me the opportunity to talk to him about anything. The only thing we had in common was our mutual interest in Becca.

And I guess he felt that was enough.

"Sure." He held the door open and followed behind me.

His place was different from what I was used to seeing around these parts. I knew he had worked for some years, but this looked like he had to come from money. This was not the apartment of a guy in his mid-twenties coming back to school.

"Want a drink?" Gage asked.

"No, I'm good." I needed to get right to the point. This was not a social call. This could turn ugly between us. "Listen, um, this isn't an easy thing for me to do. Talking to you about Becca, well, it's probably the last thing I'd like to do, ever."

He had walked into the kitchen area, taking a seat at the island, so I joined him.

"Well, you're the one who asked to do this, man. No one is forcing you."

"I'm not doing it for me; I'm doing it for Becca. It's always for Becca." I paused to gather my thoughts. I needed to say this right the first time. "I saw the girl who was here with you last week. She looked like more than just a casual hookup." I studied him for his reaction, but he was stoic. "One thing you need to know about Becca is she hates lies."

I refused to lose it in front of this guy. The lump in my throat was getting harder and harder to swallow over as the tears welled up in my eyes.

"Can I have that glass of water now?" I asked.

"Sure," he said. He got a bottle from the fridge and placed it in front of me on the island. I drained the entire thing in one gulp.

"Even if what you two are doing is 'casual,' she won't forgive you if you're lying to her. It's where she draws the line. I'm pretty sure Lanie told her about whoever was here, so she already knows. But what she doesn't know is *who* she is." And now I really studied him. The fidget as he adjusted his watch, the rubbing of his eyes, the folded hand now under his chin. "I think she'd be pretty devastated by that information, wouldn't she?"

He stood up from his stool and stared down at me. "I think you've done a pretty good job already of devastating her, Ty, don't ya think?" he asked.

"Yeah, I know I have. That's why I'm telling you this. She can't handle any more. Don't hurt her. And if you are lying to her, fix it. Fix it, unlike I did."

CHAPTER 24
Becca

Jesus fucking Christ. I couldn't believe Ty showed up at Gage's place. He actually showed up at the house of the other guy I was sleeping with.

The car ride home was really uncomfortable. I wasn't sure what made Gage more angry: that Ty was there or that we, once again, had our sex interrupted. But he was quiet on the ride. Thankfully it was short, only a block to my place. We said a simple goodbye and I hightailed it out of his car.

And I wasn't sure what I was most mad about. Having Ty show up there was . . . embarrassing? Maybe that wasn't what I was feeling. My emotions were so jumbled up in my head and heart. I couldn't make sense of them.

When I barreled into the apartment, I heard voices. Lots of voices. And I couldn't be happier. I thought I was going to be coming home to an empty apartment, and I had no interest in being alone after what just happened. Rounding the corner from the hall to the kitchen, I caught sight of the three of them unpacking bags of food into the fridge and freezer. They hadn't noticed me as they continued with their conversation.

"Ava, do you have a boyfriend?" Lanie asked.

Ava was bent over, putting food into the fridge. I could only imagine Ava's eyeroll at Lanie's question. "No, I'm not the relationship kinda person," she responded as she closed the refrigerator.

"She used to be," Macie offered.

And Ava shot her a look.

I decided now might be a good time to let them know I was here, considering they were still oblivious.

"Guys?" I said, timidly.

"Becca?" Lanie said, spinning toward my voice. "You're here!" Her arms were around me before I could move completely into the kitchen. "I'm so glad to see you in the flesh, Bec. How are you?"

And then I burst into tears. I was so happy she came home early for me.

They were all here.

Ava and Macie stopped what they were doing, the food they were putting away still gripped in their hands as their concerned stares landed on me.

"I'm so glad you guys are back. I thought I was going to be alone all night, and after the couple days I've had, well, I just don't think I could've done it." My words came out between a few broken cries as I struggled to keep it together. The three of them stood there, waiting to see if I would say anything else, but I had nothing. "Wait, what are you two doing back already?" I asked Ava and Macie.

They both looked at each other before Macie answered for them.

"Lanie called and said you needed us, so here we are."

My tears immediately became more abundant. "Are you guys for real? You all came back early for me?" The snot was coming now, too, as I wiped it all away with the back of my sleeve. All three of them surrounded me in a big group hug.

"I think we could all use a girls' night," Lanie added, pulling out of the huddle. "And me and Xander stopped at the store on our way home, thinking this might be needed. See what I brought?" She opened the freezer and fridge to show us what they picked out.

Chocolate ice cream. Vanilla ice cream. Chocolate peanut butter ice cream—my favorite. Chocolate sauce. Whipped cream. All the makings of a night in to rag on guys.

"I could kiss you," I told Lanie, not exaggerating. I made a beeline for the cabinet, pulling four bowls out. "Everyone having some?" I yelled over my shoulder. When my head turned that way, they were all there, in the kitchen with me, helping get out the spoons and prepare the ice cream.

Lanie was right there, her arm going around me. I dropped my head to her shoulder, thankful as fuck I had her at my side. The tears welled in my eyes again, threatening to spill over, and I rushed to wipe them away. But she caught me.

"Hey, we're here for you," she whispered.

I nodded against her. "I know," I said. "I think that's why I'm crying." I stayed where I was, positioned away from the other girls, not wanting to continue to show my vulnerable side.

Becca Reynolds was a hard-ass bitch. But I didn't feel like such a hard-ass at the moment. I finally turned toward Ava and Macie to find them not even paying attention to me. They were busy getting their dessert bowls readied.

"Which ice cream do you want, Becca?" Ava asked.

I looked around at the three women surrounding me and realized how lucky I was. Lanie came back to my side. "Do you want your chocolate peanut butter? Xander remembered that was your favorite, too."

And that made me burst into tears yet again.

"Christ, why is it that your boyfriend remembers my favorite ice cream flavor and the guys in my life are doing everything possible to make me miserable? I mean, for fuck's sake, is it so hard to love me? To be a good guy for me? What the hell did I do to deserve this shit?" I ripped off some paper towels and blew the snot coming from my nose into them. "And yes, thank you, I'll have chocolate peanut butter!"

I was yelling.

I was abrupt.

I was borderline manic.

But they were good; they all got it.

"How about we head into the living room, get cozy on the couch or the floor? I'll get some wine to have with our ice cream, and we can either pick a movie or just talk." Lanie shooed us out of the kitchen as she handed me my overflowing bowl topped with a cherry. Ava and I huddled on the couch while Macie grabbed some blankets to make a pile on the floor for her and Lanie.

"I could use a bitch session myself tonight," Macie said. "This guy I've been hooking up with completely ghosted me a few days ago. What the hell is wrong with these guys?

They get what they want, then walk?" She was talking over mouthfuls of vanilla ice cream.

We were all shoveling spoonfuls of the cold deliciousness into our mouths.

"Wait," Ava said. "I thought you gave up on Jace already?"

I realized we hadn't done this enough. I was completely unaware of much going on in their personal lives. We spoke about general things like our classes and shit around the apartment. But we hadn't all sat around and gotten to know each other like this. Last year, living in the same dorm room with Lanie seemed to force us to talk more. Well, let me rephrase that. I forced her to talk more in the beginning. It took her some time to warm up to me, to us, but she did. And living in the small confines of a dorm, there was little room for secrets. We knew what was going on with each other most of the time, even though Lanie kept her fair share of stuff from home secret. But in this four-bedroom townhouse, there was privacy.

"Well, I did, for a like a day," Macie started, "but he came groveling back to me, so I gave in. But the shithead stopped texting two days later!"

We all scoffed at that. That was just downright wrong.

"That's a dick move, even for him," Ava said. "You're so outta his league, he should bow at your feet for even giving him the time of day."

Macie gave Ava the sweetest smile after that compliment. "Thanks, hon, but I only bring it up as a point." Macie stopped talking and looked around at all of us, making sure she had our attention. "All men are assholes."

The two of them continued their banter, complaining about the various guys in their lives. Lanie remained quiet.

I knew she was not about to contribute to the conversation about "asshole guys." Her ex took the cake. And she also never talked about him anymore unless she had to.

And mine. Well, right now he was in contention to be second on the podium for the biggest asshole in the group.

Lanie looked my way, a small smile touching her lips, and her eyebrow lifted toward Macie as she blabbered on and on. This was exactly what I needed, and maybe Ava and Macie knew that.

Eventually, they quieted, and we all resorted to eating from our bowls. Once our metal spoons scraped the bottoms of our bowls, all eyes fell on me. I fidgeted, not liking the scrutiny for once.

I wasn't sure I could tell the other two my news. I wasn't sure I could get the words to come out of my mouth.

"Bec, you obviously need to talk about something. Do you want to? Or are we just putting a movie on?" Ava asked. Her pierced brow lifted with her question.

I wavered, not sure what to do. I knew I needed to; I just didn't know if I could.

"Bec, do you want me to tell them?" Lanie asked, looking up at me from the floor. She leaned up against the couch with her hand resting on my leg, the small touch offering solace.

All I could do was nod.

I turned my head toward the back of the couch as though if I didn't hear her say the words, words I already knew to be true, they somehow wouldn't be.

"You guys know she's been struggling a bit with Ty, but they've been talking a little," she started. "She, um, drove to his house to, I guess, surprise him for the weekend?" The question in her voice came through. And the groans from the other two told me they knew I had made a poor choice. "Listen, I'm just gonna say it." But she still paused, and I held my breath, knowing what was coming. "Ty has a baby. He's a dad."

I still had my head turned away, but I heard a tiny gasp come from Macie.

Ava remained quiet.

And that was it; no more words were said. I slowly swiveled my neck, my eyes peering under my arm, to see anyone's expression. Lanie and Macie's eyes held sadness for me.

But Ava was waiting for me to look at her. As soon as I did, she sat up straighter, leaning closer to me on the couch. "You know all of you are just making assumptions, right?" she started. "You are all assuming the worst. I'm not saying the worst isn't what's going on with him, but you can't do that with people."

"But he has an infant, Ava," I said, incredulously.

"How old?" she asked. "These conclusions you're jumping to may not be what's really going on. That's all I'm saying. Fact find, my friends. Facts are your friends." She fell back against the couch.

"Ya know, she's right, Bec. You need to talk to him," Lanie said.

"No!" I yelled. "I can't. There's no way I can. Not after seeing him with her and his . . . his daughter. Fuck!" I screamed. "They looked like a perfect little family getting into the car." I jumped from the couch, needing space from them, needing to move, to pace. "You didn't see them. They were *smiling*—they were happy. Like, what the fuck? It's like he has this whole other life that he never told me about." I wrapped my hair around my fingers as my nails dug into my scalp, the pain grounding me in the moment. "Holy shit." I froze and turned my gaze on the three of them as they stared at me. "I've been the other woman the entire fucking time!" My sudden realization not only angered me but brought a new veil of sadness over my heart. "He's been cheating on her . . . with me."

I barely got those last words out. I couldn't believe what Ty had done to me, to her.

Lanie's arms were around me in seconds as she brought me back to the couch, sitting with me. "Hey, Bec, relax," she murmured. "And Ava's right. You're jumping to conclusions before getting any of the actual story."

"I don't know, I'm with Becca. This shit is fucked up," Macie chimed in. "I mean, is there really an explanation that can make this OK?" The laser eyes that landed on her from Ava and Lanie made her scoff. "What? I'm just saying what you're thinking, that's all."

"Macie doesn't know Ty the way we know him." Lanie grabbed my face and made me look at her. "Right? Tell me you're going to talk to him about this, Bec. You can't jump to conclusions, just like Ava said. There has to be more to this story." Her eyes didn't waver from mine, even as a scoff came from Macie's side of the couch.

"I guess I don't know him as well as you guys do, but guys are assholes," Macie muttered, almost to herself, as she stood up and walked toward the kitchen.

Ava stood to follow Macie, suddenly seeming concerned for her friend as she walked away with her shoulders slumped.

"Need some more ice cream, kiddo," Ava said to Macie's back. Then she turned toward Lanie and me. "I think we have two girls tonight that need some cheering up about their love life," she proclaimed. She went to Macie, her arm going around her body and pulling her in close for a hug. Macie resisted at first, but eventually gave in.

"I really liked him," Macie whispered into Ava's shoulder.

After a brief moment, Ava brought the two of them back to the living room, and they were ready to join us.

"I'm sorry he did that to you," I said to her. "Guys *can* be assholes, and he has no idea what a great thing he's fucking up by ghosting you. You will find someone who deserves you, Macie. Don't worry about that." Not that I was the one that should be giving advice on guys at the moment, but she looked so sad, I needed to say something.

And she smiled when I was done.

"And like they're saying, I don't really know Ty. I think you need to give him the chance he deserves. He's sticking around and working hard for you, unlike Jace. So maybe he is worth giving another chance to," she said, her small smile a bit of an apology.

Ava crawled closer to me, her tiny frame squeezing next to me on the couch. "I say you listen to Lanie—consider talking to him when you're ready. And in the meantime, we put on the movie and get back to our girls' night." She pulled the blanket over us and grabbed the remote from the table.

I had a lot to think about. They had given me a lot to think about.

As Ava started scrolling through the channels, Lanie's phone lit up with a message that grabbed her attention. As she looked at her phone, her eyes found mine.

"Is it Ty?" I asked.

Lanie nodded as she resumed reading from her phone. "He wants to meet tomorrow, to talk. To me." She sounded unsure and nervous. "What should I say?"

At first I was pissed; he reached out to her and not me. The little fucker! But he knew as well as I did I wouldn't talk to him right now, let alone read a message from him. It made me think back to last year, when Xander faced having to leave school, and Lanie, and couldn't tell her about it. He spoke to me and not her, and it devastated Lanie. But now I understood.

"Do it," I told her. Even though I was in no mood to see or talk to him, I wanted information. This was the best of both worlds. "Do it for me, and him, please."

Lanie nodded and typed a response to Ty. Once she'd put her phone down, we resumed our spots, and the room lit up with blue light as the movie began. Ava chose a sappy love story, which was fine. More crying was bound to happen for me tonight, anyway. Might as well be about a movie.

But as the first scene started, Lanie's phone lit up again.

"Is that Ty again?" I asked.

"No, it's not . . ." Lanie responded.

Her answer seemed distant.

"Well, just tell lover boy you're all ours tonight. I'm not giving you up," I told her. She laughed as she looked at her phone.

But then she stopped laughing.

And by the light of the TV, and the look on her face, I knew who the message was about.

I jumped off the couch and was immediately by her side.

"Who is it, Lanie?" I asked her. Her hands were shaky as she held her phone.

"It's Bryce," she said.

Bryce was Xander's brother, but he was also a detective that had been involved with her case last year.

"What does it say, Lanie?" I asked.

She handed me her phone.

Hey Lanie just wanted to give you a head's up that Max and his dad were let out of jail last night, they're both on house arrest until the trial but the charges they put them in for couldn't keep them in any longer. THEY ARE NOT IN JAIL ANY MORE

Well, fuck.

CHAPTER 25

I sat there for a very long time. Just sitting in my car, staring at her apartment. The lights were on, so I knew someone was in there, though since she wouldn't answer me, I didn't know if it was her. My fucking tears of rage had long since dried up. Now I only felt sorry for myself. Regretting every wrong move I'd made over the past year as I went over them all in my head repeatedly.

The talk with my mom had put me in such a good mood. She understood. She was even happy to hear that I had someone who made me happy all while I had all this other shit going on. She didn't agree with how I handled things and wished I had told Becca about Savannah last year.

Yeah, that hindsight thing. I knew that now too.

But this really fucked everything up. Maybe even ruined my chances of us *ever* getting back together. Every call I made to her went straight to voicemail. Every text went unanswered. When I got to her place, I saw her car was parked nearby, but there was still a nagging at my heart.

What if she went back to him?

What if she ran right over to his place to cry on his shoulder? It wouldn't surprise me if she had. She did it last time. But I was too chickenshit to go knock on her door to see if she was home. Too chickenshit, knowing she would probably refuse to see me or talk to me.

Did I blame her? Did I fucking blame her? No. The answer was a resounding no. And that was what scared me most, because I had no idea if there was any way to come back from this.

I was thankful Lanie responded to my text. Knowing I would at least see her tomorrow and be able to tell her the entire story made me feel a little better. But it was Becca I really wanted to be telling.

I felt like I wanted to sit in front of her place all night. Maybe to catch sight of her, or maybe to make sure she wasn't running back to him; I wasn't sure which.

I had finally decided heading home was my best bet when I heard a car speeding into the parking lot. A Jeep screeched into a spot near their place, and I realized it was Xander storming out of the door. His head turned immediately toward my headlights, and he began stalking toward my car. I was turning my car off to get out and see what was going on when he yanked my door open.

"What the hell are—" Xander yelled.

"Xander, man, what's going on?" I asked, leaning away from him as he lunged for me through the door. He got a hold of my shirt and started pulling me from the car. I heard female voices screaming in the distance, and I knew immediately one of them was Becca. My head swiveled in search of her, even as I knew my life was likely in danger from Xander's rampage.

"Xander, stop!" a voice screamed, which I think was Lanie. She ran toward us and grabbed a hold of Xander once she got to the car. "Xander, it's Ty. Leave him alone!"

Xander's grip on me loosened and his glazed eyes seemed to focus on my face, the recognition coming slowly. "Fuck," he whispered as he let go of me and backed away from the car. He bent over at the waist and leaned against my car while Lanie talked to him quietly.

I sat back against the headrest, trying to catch my breath, and looked out my windshield.

Across the sidewalk, our eyes met.

And hers held tears.

She stared for a moment, shook her head slightly, then walked back inside with one of her roommates—the one with the short black hair and the piercings. I didn't even know which one it was. I was that removed from her life. Macie? Ava?

My heart should have been in my throat from almost being on the ground with Xander's fist in my face, but it was the look on Becca's face that was doing it to me.

"Ty." I startled when Lanie came to me at my open door. "Ty," she said again. "Are you OK?" She pulled on me out of the car. Xander was still leaning against the side, breathing heavily with what seemed to be pent-up anger or frustration. Confused about the situation, I exited the car.

"I'm sorry," Xander said quietly from a few feet away. He straightened to his full height, the tension still evident in his stance as he moved to hold on to Lanie. The moment I saw how he was acting with her, I knew.

"Is Max here?" I asked them both, my anxiety rising as I watched them closely. The monster from Lanie's past could be the only reason for Xander's actions.

"No," Lanie answered. "At least we don't think so. But we think he's been released from jail. I just found out, and Xander was coming to get me." She looked at him with compassion in her eyes, knowing he felt bad for what he did.

"Ty, man, I saw someone sitting in a car across from her place, and I flipped out," Xander explained. "I jumped to conclusions. My mind just snapped. I thought it was him. I'm sorry, man. Really, I'm sorry." He advanced toward me with his hands running through his hair, nervous about his actions. But I was sure more nervous about now keeping Lanie safe.

"Dude, no worries, man. I would have done the same thing," I told him. "You have to do whatever it takes to keep him away from her. We all do." I looked at Lanie and offered her a small smile. Right at that moment, Xander's phone rang.

"It's Bryce," he said to us as he motioned to his phone, walking away to take the call. I assumed Bryce was calling to tell Xander anything else he might know.

"I'm so sorry, Ty," Lanie said as she came to my side, her hands gripping my arms. I put my arm around her shoulder, pulling her in close, knowing she must be an emotional wreck.

"How are you doing, Lane? This must be a terrible shock, hearing this. Are you OK?"

She leaned into my side as she looked over toward Xander. "I'm not as much of a mess as I thought I would be. I'm in a different place than I was last year. He's helped put me there. I just hope I can stay there, ya know?" Her voice held something that told me she didn't trust herself to stay strong. But I did. She had come such a long way; she would not let herself go back to the way she was when she came to school. Neither would Becca nor Xander. Especially Xander. It was his life's mission to keep her safe and make her world a perfect place for them to live in.

I aspired to be like him. I wanted to make a world that was perfect for Becca and me. Where she could once again trust me. Love me.

I only hoped she'd give me the chance to try.

"I have faith in you, Lanie. In you, and him, to keep you both exactly where you need to be. Xander won't let anything happen to you." She nodded into my chest as Xander came walking back toward us.

"The only thing Bryce could tell me is that he is out and wearing a house arrest anklet, so they're able to monitor him," Xander said as he enveloped Lanie with his arms. He extended one hand over her head to me and I gripped it, shaking it hard. "I'm sorry again, Ty. Really am."

"It's fine, man. I would have done the same thing." I started walking away, toward my car, to make my exit. "I'm going to leave you guys to it. I'm assuming you have a lot to talk about. Keep me informed, and let me know what's going on if I can do anything, OK?"

And that was when Lanie looked at me with *that* look. The look that told me we were about to change the subject. I figured with the recent events, there would be no *talk* with us, which I was OK with, to be honest.

But Lanie's hand landed on my arm as I was stepping away from them.

"Hey, Ty," she said. "We can still talk tomorrow." Her blue eyes were soft and sincere as she looked right into mine. "If I've learned anything from my past, it's that my life has to go on. I can't let Max stop me from living." She looked over at Xander. I wasn't so sure he agreed with her, but she kept talking. "Come to Xander's tomorrow. That's where I'll be staying for a while. We can talk there. I still want to help you. Help you and Becca." I nodded. Me agreeing to see her sent a wave of nausea through me.

I would have to tell her everything tomorrow.

The nausea hadn't passed as I knocked on Xander's front door. I barely slept, tossing and turning as I thought about the best way to explain the past year and a half of my life. My only consolation was that Lanie and Xander were two very level-headed people. Telling them first would hopefully give me some guidance on how to approach Becca.

"Hey, Ty," Xander said as he opened the door. He stood in front of me in a pair of shorts and nothing else. He was an intimidating figure with his wing-tattooed chest as he loomed over me. I was tall, but he had me by about two inches and twenty pounds. And a shit ton more muscle.

Yeah, I'd be scared of him in a dark alley.

"Hey, Xander." I followed behind him into a, thankfully, quiet apartment. And considering he lived with three other of our frat brothers, the place was surprisingly clean. It was pretty plain, only some beer posters on the wall. But the place wasn't littered with empty bottles and dirty dishes everywhere, like mine was.

The drink caddy shook in my hands as we walked toward the living room, evidence I was more nervous than I'd realized. The creamer pods and sugar packets stuffed in next to the hot drinks were at risk of toppling over as we walked. I needed to hold it against my body to steady it all as we found Lanie on the couch, watching a show on TV with the volume down low. She muted it as we approached and sat up with a smile for me.

"I brought you a tea, Lane," I said, handing her the cup. I put the holder on the table in front of the couch, which held the two remaining coffees. "Didn't know how you took your coffee, Xander. I have everything there to make it up the way you need."

"Thanks, Ty," Lanie said as she blew into the opened container to cool off the hot liquid. "That was so nice of you."

Xander was making up a cup of coffee as I stood wringing my hands, too nervous to drink mine. Once he was finished, he started making his way out of the room.

"I'll leave you guys to it. I'll be upstairs," Xander said.

"Hey, I was kind of hoping to talk to both of you, if you don't mind," I said.

He looked surprised but pleased when I said that. He backpedaled into the room and took a seat next to Lanie, pulling her onto his lap. "Of course, but I don't know what's going on. Lanie was a good friend and kept it to herself."

I smiled at Lanie in appreciation but wasn't the least bit surprised. That was just who Lanie was. I sat in a chair across from them and tried to prepare myself for what I was about to do. Sweat built up on my brow and my hands. I wiped them across my thighs, hoping my jeans wouldn't discolor much.

I knew I needed to just blurt it out.

"I have a kid. I have a baby."

Lanie remained calm with no reaction. But Xander flinched under her, and his surprise was obvious.

"I know. Becca told me," Lanie said.

I guess that shouldn't have surprised me. They would have talked once Becca got back yesterday. She would have been nonstop about what she saw all night long, I'm sure.

"How did you not tell me that?" Xander asked her incredulously. She pushed his hand off of hers and turned her attention back to me.

"Ty, I think there's a bit more that needs to be said, though, right? I mean, I have to believe that you weren't cheating on Becca. I need to believe you weren't cheating on Becca. Please tell me you weren't cheating on Becca." Lanie sat forward, removing herself from Xander's arms, her brow furrowed as she stared back at me.

"I never cheated on Becca, Lanie. Never. I never would have. She's my one," I said. "She's how you are to Xander. She's everything to me. There's no one else for me."

The power of those words had my face in my hands to cover up the emotion. And at that exact moment, I heard movement on the couch from both of them. Lanie was by my side, on the floor by my feet, her arms around me. And Xander stood above, looming. I peeked up and saw an unexpected but sincere look on his face.

"Hey, man," he said. "That's good to hear." His smile was genuine. "If that's true, I have to believe this can work out." His eyes bounced from me to Lanie, looking for the answer.

"You do know this is Becca Reynolds we're talking about, right?" I offered, my frustration with myself coming through. "She won't even answer a call or a text. There's no way she'll consider seeing me to hear me out." I abruptly stood and started pacing around the room. "What the fuck am I gonna do?"

"Tell me the whole story, Ty. Who's the mother? When did this happen?" Lanie asked.

So I told them.

"Ty," Lanie said as I walked toward the front door, "I'll talk to her. I'm confident I can get her to talk to you. The rest will be up to you. But I think if we can get her to hear you out, you guys will have a chance. She might need some time, though."

Xander walked beside her, both of them being more than supportive about everything. I wasn't expecting any of this. I was walking away with a positive outlook and a smile on my face after talking to them both.

"Yeah, if she gives you the time to tell her what you told us, she might come around. And hey, congratulations on being a dad, man. You sound like you're a good one, too. Good job. It's not easy being a good father."

I stopped at the front door and turned to both of them. Two people whose fathers had failed them. His father: a low-life, abusive man now in jail for his wrongdoings. Her father: a coward who allowed horrible things to happen to his daughter. Yet Xander and Lanie were two of the strongest, most giving people I knew. It was a testament to their character. I also thought they were examples of people who were determined to not be like their fathers.

Lanie reached up and hugged me, my hug back tight because I was so thankful for how they'd helped me. When she finally let go, Xander's hand gripped mine and the bro hug followed. He held on for a second longer than I expected, which felt nice.

"Thanks. I wasn't sure about coming over today, but I'm glad I did." I started down the path to my car as I continued talking to Lanie. "You'll let me know once you've talked to her?"

"I will," she said.

Nodding, I got in my car.

Driving away, I felt better than I had in months. I put the music on loud. I rolled the window down. And I felt like life just might be on the right track once again.

CHAPTER 26
Becca

Jesus Christ. I couldn't believe that sick motherfuck-er got out of jail. Last year, Max ruined his fair share of nights for Lanie and I. Last night, he did it again. She and Xander freaked out, and Xander raced to our apartment to scoop her away. She was going to be living with him now. I mean, I get it, Xander's a bit paranoid when it comes to Max. But Max is under house arrest. The guy is wearing an ankle monitor, so he won't be able to get anywhere near Lanie. I was feeling like the moving out into Xander's room was a bit overkill.

I lost my roommate.

And during all of that, Mr. Shithead was fucking out-side stalking me. He had the audacity to be sitting in his car, just watching my apartment. Did he really think I would talk to him if I saw him?

But of course, my heart fucking betrayed me when I did see him. It hurt. Bad. Like, ached for him. I wanted to run to him in his car when I saw Xander about to punch him in the face. I wanted to make sure he was OK. Then I wanted to yell and scream at him. And punch him myself. When our eyes connected, I still felt our connection. I felt the pull between us, begging me to go to him, to fall back into his arms. To forgive and forget so we could go back to the way things were.

But things will never be the same, ever again.

He has a child with another woman.

That he never told me about.

How does one get over that?

Ava and Macie were gone by the time I woke up. And with Lanie now living at Xander's, there was no one to help keep me from going crazy.

Of course, I did what any insane young college girl would do at a time like this.

I texted the long-term booty call guy who's also been a douche lately. But he was good for one thing: mindless sex to distract me.

Me:

Hey can we get together today

The three dots popped up immediately.

Gage:

Yeah, I've been hoping to hear from you to see how you are, want to come over later

Me:

can I come over now

Gage:

sure

Grabbing my sweatshirt, I made the ten-minute walk to his place. I thought walking would allow me to clear my head. Unfortunately, it didn't. My mind was still consumed with the vision of Ty holding that baby and that beautiful young woman calling him "Daddy."

I was even more angry by the time I rang his bell.

When Gage opened his door, I stomped past him and down his hall.

"Well, hello to you too," he said as he followed me down the hall. When I got into the living room, I felt his body pressed against mine as I leaned up against the back of the couch. His mouth came down to my ear. "How are ya doing, Becca? Things any better?" he asked.

"Not really, and that's why I'm here," I said as I swung around, our bodies now flush against one another. "I want you to help me forget. Make me forget, Gage. Everything." I leaned up and grabbed the back of his neck, pulling his head toward mine. My mouth was on his before he could answer. Our tongues collided, fighting each other as his hands slid down my sides. The butterflies started flapping in my core, exactly what I was hoping for. He lifted me up, his hand under my ass, resting me against the back of the couch. Separating my legs with his own, he pushed himself against my core, his length already hard as it lined up with me.

"I need you to fuck me, Gage. Hard and now," I breathed into his mouth.

"If that's what you need, Becca," he responded. His hands went under my ass and he lifted me up, wrapping my legs around his waist. He carried me effortlessly to the other side of the couch, all while still kissing me. Dropping me onto the cushions, he stood above me and stared. "Look at you—you're a goddess. Who wouldn't want to fuck this?" He started undoing his button.

"Make me forget, Gage," I said, looking up at him. I started taking off my pants, sliding them over my knees. "Make me forget all the lies I've been told. I can't take it."

I started lifting my shirt and noticed that Gage was standing still with his pants undone, but no longer moving.

Just staring down at me.

"Do you want me to undress you?" I said as seductively as I could muster.

But he just shook his head and stepped back out of my reach.

My puzzled look caused an almost wince to appear on his face as he put his hands on his hips and then refused to keep eye contact with me.

"What the fuck is going on, Gage?" I asked, not hiding my sudden anger. "You told me to come over. You said you wanted to fuck me. Now you're acting like a cold fucking bastard." Reaching down for my pants, I completely dressed and sat up on the couch. He continued to stand, stock still, in the same position. "Why are you doing this?"

This time, my voice cracked. I was cracking. There was only so much one person could take, and I had reached my limit. If I didn't get out of here, I feared I was going to be a blubbery mess in front of him.

And he heard it. Because he finally looked at me. And the look on his face told me I was right; I was going to break.

"What's wrong? What did I do, Gage?" I cried, the tears sliding down my cheeks.

He came to me and pulled me to standing by my shoulders. Cradling my face in his hands, he forced me to look at him. His eyes held unshed tears as we stared at one another.

"You've done nothing wrong. Nothing. To anyone, Becca. You're perfect, in every sense of the word."

But as he said these beautiful words, I knew he was going to destroy me.

I wiggled my face from his hands, not wanting to hear his next words. Whatever they were going to be.

"Then don't say whatever you're going to say next. Can we just go back to what we were going to do? Let's just go back to kissing, to enjoying each other's bodies. We're casual fuck buddies, right? Isn't that what we are? So the other shit doesn't matter. Please, Gage." I was begging; I knew I was. But I didn't care.

Gage pulled me into his arms, a hard embrace. As he held me tight, his mouth came close to my ear.

"Becca," he started.

"*Stop!*" I screamed against his chest. "I can't take any more, Gage. This wasn't supposed to happen with us. We weren't supposed to care. Why do you care?"

He pulled me even closer, if that were possible.

"I shouldn't have cared, Becca, I know," he said. "But you're hard to not care about, hard to not fall in love with."

I heard the tears in his voice, in his declaration. "But I can't love you. You're not mine to love, and I'm not yours to love."

His hand threaded through my hair, and I felt his desperation. A racing heartbeat thumped against my temple as he held me against him, not letting go.

"Becca," he whispered into my hair. "I'm married."

CHAPTER 27
Becca

"Becca, honey, eat something," Lanie said to me through my closed door. I'd been holed up in my room for over twenty-four hours. At first, when I got home, the emotions exhausted me and I slept. For about ten hours. Then, when I awoke at midnight, I spent the next six or seven hours trying to distract myself with whatever I could within the four walls of my room.

I took a shower.

I watched Netflix.

I read a book.

I took a bath.

I even did homework.

By then, it was approximately 3 a.m. Then I paced, stared out the window, and cried.

I did a lot of crying. I couldn't understand what I'd done to deserve two assholes in my life. My thought process went spinning round and round, and I'd decided that I must be a bad person. I must have done something to someone in my past that was so terrible, and I now had karma knocking on my door.

But it was actually Lanie knocking on my door. I walked over, unlocked it, and held the door open an inch while peeking out.

"Oh, Bec, want some company? I can come in and hang for a while," she said. She had a bag of food in her hand, and it actually made my stomach rumble. Opening the door wider, she walked in behind me as I climbed back on my bed.

"How did you even know I was up here? You don't live here anymore," I scoffed. Probably bitchier than I needed to be; she had her own shit she was dealing with.

"I stopped by last night to see you, but you didn't answer your door. Ava told me you've been up here since early yesterday." She climbed on the bed with me and held out the bag like a peace offering. "It's a Fabulous Fred's sandwich, two of them. Thought we could eat together."

I grabbed the bag and tore into it, suddenly famished. The girl even thought to bring me a Diet Coke and some BBQ chips, both my favorites.

"Thank you," I said meekly, afraid my earlier comment may have angered her. But she snuggled closer to me, taking her sandwich from the bag, and began eating in silence.

She was good like that. Knowing at that moment talking was not high on my list of priorities. We ate. Then we talked a little about her moving some of her stuff over to Xander's and how I would help her later that day with some of it. We chit chatted about our classes and how much homework we were getting.

And we ignored the devastation and drama in both our lives.

But then we really had nothing left to say.

And the silence in the room became deafeningly loud.

I felt her eyes on me.

"Bec," she said. "I talked to Ty."

"Fuck, I forgot you were doing that," I told her. I dropped my face into my hands, not wanting to face anymore of my life.

"Isn't that what this is all about? Why you've been up here in your room?" she asked.

I turned my head to look at her. "He's only half of what's known as the ruin of my life, Lane. A lot happened since I saw you last." Turning myself to face her completely, deciding I was ready to tell her, I took a deep breath. "Gage's been lying to me, too. More than we originally thought."

Her eyes widened before the sadness set in. She reached out and clenched my arm, holding me, trying to steady my nerves with her grip. "Becca," she whispered.

"He's married."

"What!" she yelled. "What the fuck? Are you kidding me?"

Her reaction mirrored mine, which I knew it would. That was why I loved her.

"Completely not kidding. He told me himself, yesterday. I went over there to, um, take my mind off things. And instead had that shit land in my lap. I should have known he was too good to be true. You knew he was trouble right from the start. You tried to warn me." We were both finished with our sandwiches, so I gathered the paper wrap and stuffed it all in the bag it came in. Leaning against my pillows, I found her still staring at me.

"You don't seem as frantically 'Becca' as I would expect," she said.

"I've been in this room since twelve noon yesterday processing the shit both of them put me through. I've had plenty of time to wallow; now I'm just pissed."

Lanie crawled up the length of the bed, lying down on a pillow. I put my head on the same pillow, and we were almost nose to nose, our assumed position when we needed to get to business.

"How did he tell you something like that?" she asked tentatively.

I chuckled before starting. "Well, I went to him, basically begging for sex, to help me forget the lies Ty had been telling me. I guess his conscience won out." I sat up, uncomfortable with my own story. "It was humiliating. I mean, you guys told me about the other woman, but I never saw this coming. I hightailed it out of there, was practically still half naked when I ran out of his apartment. I needed to dress myself as I ran out the door."

Thinking back to the prior night, I was getting myself all worked up and mad about what happened all over again.

"Well, you're doing great, all things considered." She smiled, and her sparkling blue eyes lit up. She was so gorgeous. I hoped she felt that way—she never did last year. Xander did a great job of always telling her; it had to sink in eventually.

"Thanks, babe," I told her. "But I'm actually a mess on the inside." I let out an enormous sigh and rolled onto my back, staring at the ceiling. The eye contact was too much for the next question; I was nervous to hear how things went with her and Ty.

"I wasn't expecting to be so upset about Gage. I don't think it's so much that he was with someone else; I was OK with that. And not even that it was someone that important to him. It was the gravity of the lie." Turning back toward her, I continued. "Married? I mean, for fuck's sake, he's only twenty-five. Why the hell is he already married, and cheating on her?" I suddenly bolted upright with a realization. "Fuck! I've been the other woman with both of them!"

Lanie sat up with me and grabbed my hands. "No! Relax, Becca. You were not the other woman with Ty. Don't worry," she said. She pulled me back to the pillow, us both getting comfortable again.

"What did Ty say?" I asked her.

"Well," she started, then paused. That made me turn to look, but her face was neutral, and even a small smile appeared. "I think you need to talk to him yourself. He needs to be the one to tell you this story, but just know this one thing: he was not cheating on you."

Hmm. I digested that bit of news.

He didn't cheat on me.

But he had a baby with another woman.

And never told me.

I found out myself.

After over a year.

Not sure that absolved him of his sins.

"So?" I countered.

Lanie scoffed with all of her face, all of her being. She sat up on the bed as her mouth fell open and her eyes were wide with disbelief, staring back at me.

She was on Ty's side.

"So?" Lanie said back. "That doesn't mean anything to you? That none of this happened while you and him were together?" Her voice got louder and louder with each question.

"But it *was* happening while we were together, Lanie. If what you're saying is true, the only thing that didn't happen while we were together was them fucking. Everything else did. You didn't see them. I did. They have a relationship still. Even if it's only for the kid, they still do. And it was happening without me knowing." I sat up with her, eye to eye. "I don't know if he and I will survive this, I really don't."

She looked sad. I mean, nowhere near as sad as I was, but still sad.

It was sad. Because Ty and I were good together. No, were more than good. We were perfect together.

But he fucked it up with his lies. I really didn't know if I could come back from this, regardless of how incredible our time was together.

Lanie's nod was slow to come, but it came.

"I get it, Bec, especially when you put it that way. I do. But maybe, one day, you'll let him tell his story," she said. "He loves you still."

We both lay back down, arms around each other. The recent events in both our lives were enough to send us both packing. But we were strong women, and we had each other to fall on.

And as we cuddled in bed together and I pulled out my laptop to put on a show, I felt like we were going to fall on each other.

Hard.

A couple weeks had passed; I was trying to create a new normal. But this new normal was kinda boring. It involved going to class, doing homework, watching TV, cooking dinner. All alone.

Well, without a man in my life, alone.

I hadn't really been *alone* alone since before coming to college. Ty and I met the second week of our freshman year. We didn't start talking immediately, but our attraction was strong. So the flirting was always happening between us right from the start. By the second month, we were hooking up, and eventually we had to tell Lanie and Logan. The four of us hung out all the time, and it was too hard to keep it from them.

Starting this year without Ty was hard—harder than I thought. But I came to school thinking I would win him back.

That didn't happen.

Instead, I got myself mixed up with someone else. Who has also now left me alone.

And it didn't help that Lanie had moved out and I wasn't seeing her as much as I was used to. Ava and Macie did their best to keep me company. They tried, they really did. But I wasn't reciprocating their efforts very well lately.

As I hopped off the bus, I pulled my bag onto my shoulder and put my sunglasses on. They didn't disguise me so much as cover up the dark circles that were perpetually living under my eyes lately. The need to not see Gage on campus overwhelmed me. My eyes darted back and forth from behind the glasses with every step I took. Thankfully, I'd gotten to know his schedule pretty well and was able to avoid bumping into him so far.

My first stop was the Phi Betta Lambda office in the upstairs of the student union. I won the presidential position in the group and needed to pick up some important papers to work on a project. As I started down the path toward the union, however, I saw familiar golden locks up ahead. He was talking to what appeared to be some of his frat brothers. I quickly spun on my heels and went in the opposite direction. I'd been successful in avoiding him as well up to this point, and I didn't need today to be the day I failed.

Maybe I'd head to the pond and sit there for a while until my class began. I could pick up the papers later.

I only got about five steps before I heard it.

"Becca!"

I didn't know what to do. If I stopped, we would make a scene. If I didn't stop, he would chase me down, and we would make a scene.

He hadn't stopped trying to contact me. Every morning I got a "good morning" text from him. And every night I got a "good night, I love you" text from him. And then occasionally, in between, I'd get the request for us to talk. The begging request for me to listen to him and his reasons for not telling me sooner.

But I continued to ignore him.

I had to.

But it didn't seem like I would be able to much longer.

"Becca, wait up!" he said as he got closer.

I felt cornered, even though I was out in the wide open.

Ty came up next to me, but I couldn't bring myself to look at him; I didn't trust myself.

"How are you, Bec?" he asked.

I looked out at the oval and watched the passing people.

I counted the buildings in my field of vision.

I was doing everything in my power to ignore and avoid.

And I was being a bitch.

Taking a chance, I glanced his way. Standing in front of me was the guy I fell in love with a year ago. His tall frame was still fit, though maybe thinner than when I saw him last. The long-sleeve tee he wore hugged the lean muscles in his arms, showcasing them. His jeans hung low on his hips but formed around his thick thighs. I always loved his body. And his hair was growing out, definitely in need of a cut. It looked shaggy.

And then I found those whiskey eyes. They were staring right through me by the time I made it up there. His eyes . . . were sad.

"I'm good, Ty." I lied. I had to. What was I going to say? I still cried myself to sleep every night.

"Do you have a minute?" he asked.

He didn't know that I did. I could lie again. But I was sick of lies. Utterly sick to my stomach of lies. I nodded, and he led me to a bench close by. We sat, but not extremely close to one another. I could see his nervousness as he twisted his hands between his legs and moved them to his head, running his fingers through his hair. It made the longer strands stick up, adding to the crazed look. A light sheen of sweat appeared on his brow as I watched him fidget, seemingly as uncomfortable as I was. He finally turned to look right at me.

"It's good to see you, Bec. I've missed you," he said, calmer than I expected. He pivoted his body to face me head on before his next words. "I don't want to do this here, but can we please do this sometime, somewhere? I'd really like you to hear me out, please."

I had to look away; the wetness was already forming in my eyes. There was a good reason I had kept my distance.

I think I knew I'd have a hard time resisting him in person. I always did. History had proven that.

"Please don't cry, Bec. I didn't want to make you cry. I'm sorry."

"What do you expect, Ty?" I asked quietly, a lone tear rolling down my cheek. "Did you think I'd be able to get beyond this and forget all the shit that's happened? Or better yet, forget you?"

He flinched when I said that.

"What could you possibly have to say that would make any of this OK? You have a child with another woman and you didn't tell me about it for over a year. That's not OK in any way, shape, or form. I mean, fuck, when *were* you going to tell me?" The tears were more prolific now as my voice escalated with anger. "Christ, you were probably going to try to get away with this as long as you could, just keep getting a good fuck out of me on the side!" I jumped to my feet, done with this conversation. Once I did, I looked his way. But then a sound coming from him forced me to look back.

The Ty in front of me was one I'd never seen before.

The tears flowing down his face almost matched mine. I hadn't noticed he was crying because of my outburst; he was even struggling to breathe. He stood and took a step toward me, but I put my hand up to keep him back. I couldn't have him come closer, touch me.

"Becca." His cracked whisper hit my ears. I could tell he was trying to stifle his cries, not make a scene, but it was futile. "Baby, give me just one chance to explain. I can make it make sense." He was struggling to talk, to keep it together. He looked around, noticing that no one was paying us much attention, at least not outwardly. "I know I was wrong," he continued. "I'm a bastard. If I could take it all back, I would. But please, let me tell you why. Please!" He was begging, just short of going to his knees.

And it was breaking me.

I needed to get out of there. I looked around as if someone who could save me would appear. My desperate eyes searched but found no one. "Ty, I have to go," I said as I picked up my bag. He moved to stop me but thought better of it when he saw the look on my face. "I can't do this. Not here. I'm going to be late to class, if I can even sit in class like this."

He stepped back. But his heartbroken eyes grabbed my heart and wouldn't let go. "Becca, do you remember the weekend we took Logan home last year? The weekend Lanie had all those problems with Max?"

"Ty, I don't want to do this!" I warned with a hiss.

"Just answer this one question for me, please."

"Of course I do. It was the start of our demise. You treated me like shit at your house. I should have gotten out then when I could have," I told him. He acted like we were only friends around his parents—wouldn't even hold my hand, let alone engage in any PDA. It hurt so much. It was as if I embarrassed him.

"Do you remember what I said to you when we got back?" he asked.

I thought for a moment, but I couldn't. Thinking back, all I could remember was how angry I was at him and how I moped around for days. My complaints to Lanie seemed silly compared to what she was going through, but she always listened and made me feel better. But it never lasted.

I only shook my head at him, getting impatient.

"I told you I knew things didn't go as you wanted, but that I would make it right. To give me some time, and I would make it right. That even though we had only been together for a couple months, I knew I'd met my perfect. You're my perfect, Becca. I knew it then, and I know it now." He inched closer to me, and I let him.

My whole body shook. I wasn't sure if it was from his words or the crying. But as he got closer, I felt the gravitational pull to him growing, and my resolve lessening. My arms went around my torso, an act of protection, it felt like. As he stepped up to me, his fingers lifted my chin, our eyes connecting. Those golden eyes, wet with tears still, bore into my soul and tried to steal it back.

"I'm only asking for you to give me one chance to explain everything. Give me one chance to make things right. And if you still want to walk away . . ." He swallowed hard, his Adam's apple bobbing in his throat before he could finish his sentence. "I won't stop you."

My eyes closed of their own volition. I couldn't take the intensity of his stare any longer. I tried to move my face from his grip, but he held tight. His thumb came up and rubbed my lower lip. And my fucking body betrayed me as my mouth opened slightly, the reaction instinct with him.

My eyes popped open as I pushed myself away, my hands lingering a moment too long on his chest. "I have to get to class, Ty." As I stepped back, our eyes stayed on one another. After a few more steps, his pleading eyes forced an answer from me.

"I've given you lots of chances already, Ty. Why should I give you any more?" My biting words stung, and he flinched. But I couldn't leave well enough alone. "I'll think about it."

I spun around and ran to my building.

And kept my sunglasses on during the entire class.

CHAPTER 28

Why was I surprised that Becca hadn't contacted me yet? A couple weeks had passed and I hadn't even gotten a text from her. But that was the new typical Becca Reynolds; she always needed to exert her control in the situation. But this time, it was with avoidance, the newest tactic of hers. I wasn't sure which I liked better: being yelled at or ignored. At least if she was yelling at me, we were in the same room and talking.

Lanie assured me she'd been discussing it with her, and Becca was still considering seeing me. So there was still hope.

It was approaching the end of October, and the frat always had a huge Halloween party every year. My pledge class, being the newest guys, was responsible for running it. It was something to keep my mind occupied in addition to my classes and homework. And thankfully we were having the party this Friday, so I would actually be able to go to it before heading home the next morning. I hadn't been home in a couple weeks and wanted to see my daughter.

But until then, I had a lot to do.

"Jake, can you come with me to the party store?" I asked as I grabbed my keys from the counter. "I need to pick up a bunch of decorations for Friday." He was on the couch, controller in his hand. But I didn't know when his next class was.

"How long will it take? I have class at two," he said.

"C'mon, get your ass up. It will only take like an hour—you'll be fine."

The store was a short car ride into the next town. Jake fiddled with the radio and found some music we both agreed upon.

"So, I've been meaning to talk to you about something," he said as he settled back into the passenger seat. "Me and Kayla, we've kind of been hooking up a few times. Like, I guess we're seeing each other."

That shocked me. Jake prided himself on the notches in his belt each weekend. But I'm assuming that got old after a while.

"OK, man, that's cool. If you like her, that's cool." I kept my eyes on the road, waiting for him to say more on the topic.

"Well, I know she was all into you for a while, so I wanted to make sure you were OK with it," he continued.

My laugh came out before I could stop it. "Jake, I never had any interest in Kayla. Don't get me wrong, she's hot. And if I never met Becca, maybe there would have been something there. But go for it, man. I wish you luck. I'm happy for ya, if that's what you want." I wasn't convinced she was a one-man kind of girl, so I hoped Jake wasn't going to get hurt. But he didn't seem the type to want a long-term commitment, either.

"She's cool. We talk and shit after. I've never done that with anyone else. It's kind of nice." His smile was big. "Did you and Becca used to do that?"

I knew he didn't mean to slice my heart open with that question. But it was splayed open and bleeding at the moment. "Yeah, Jake, we would talk after sex. And lots of other times, too."

"Well, yeah, I get that. Kayla and I talk, but I've never had someone who wanted to stick around after and hang out. It's really nice. That's all."

He actually sounded like he liked her. A lot. Maybe this would turn into something for the two of them.

"I know things aren't great with you and Becca right now. Sorry, man. Do you think she'll be at the party?" Jake asked.

I didn't have an answer for him. I could only assume she would be, since Lanie would be there with Xander. But for all I knew, she would stay away because of me. Thankfully, we arrived at the store and I was able to avoid talking about the topic altogether.

"Let's get going. I don't want you to miss your class," I said as we got out of the car.

"Dude, you look amazing!" I told Jake. He was dressed as Danny from *Grease*, so I had to imagine Kayla would be dressing as Sandy.

"Thanks, so do you. Love the hat," he said, flipping it off my head. Lanie told me that Becca decided to come to the party and was dressing as a pirate. I took a risk and decided to dress as one, too. There was a couples costume contest, and I thought maybe, just maybe, we could enter if she decided to talk to me.

Xander came walking in the door next, all bloodied in ripped-up clothes. Wasn't quite sure what he was supposed to be, and it appeared no one else was either. We all stared, trying to figure it out.

"What?" he asked, putting his hands up.

"Just trying to figure it out, man," Jake said.

Xander laughed. "I'm a patient, and Lanie is my doctor. I guess without her here, it doesn't make sense."

"You look more like *Fight Club*. Maybe you should add some gauze or something," one of the other guys suggested.

"Hey, that's a great idea," he said, heading back upstairs.

The rest of us continued getting the house ready. It looked amazing with a smoke machine set up by the front door, glow-in-the-dark decorations, and a black light lighting up the entire floor. It looked quite professional, if you asked me. We were expecting over two hundred people tonight; it was our biggest event of the year at the house.

But all I could think about was seeing her.

My nerves were shot at the thought of seeing her after weeks of silence. I was giving her the space she'd asked for, but I didn't want to ruin any potential chance I had. Was she sitting at home wondering why I wasn't pushing harder to talk to her? I was still texting her consistently, letting her know I was thinking of her. Just not asking anything of her.

Xander came back downstairs with gauze wrapped around his head, and the gauze was covered with red sharpie marks. It looked like a five-year-old had put it together, but no one would ever say that to him.

"Ty, come help me with the keg," he said as he crossed the room to the kitchen. "You know Becca's coming tonight, right?" We emptied bags of ice into the keg bucket.

"Yeah, I talked to Lanie. Why else do you think I'm in this pirate suit?" I said, pointing to my outfit. He looked at my costume and nodded.

"I think you look better than I do. Lanie might be pissed at me." He laughed. "Anyway, do you think there will be some drama with her tonight?" He stood against the counter, looking at me seriously at this point, studying me.

"Well, I'm really not sure. All I know is I'm excited to see her, considering it's been weeks since I have. If I have to stare at her from across the room, then that's what I'll do. But I won't be the one starting any drama if that's what you're getting at."

"You rarely are, Ty," Xander chuckled. "Lanie just texted me that they were running a bit late because Becca was taking so long to get ready. Sound familiar?"

Very familiar. Last year, she would be late to every party she went to because it took her so long to get ready. I wasn't sure if it was a good or bad sign that she was putting in some extra effort to get pretty for tonight. It could go both ways, and by Xander's look, he knew it too.

"Yeah, well, I'll make sure to keep things under control. Don't worry."

He shook his head, and we both got back to getting the place ready for the horde of people arriving soon.

"Oh my God, this place looks amazing!" Lanie screamed in my ear as she hugged me. She'd come over to me once they arrived, leaving Becca with the rest of her roommates on the other side of the room.

"Thanks, we worked hard on it," I told her. "You look great in your scrubs, Dr. Montgomery. One day we'll be calling you that for real, too." She smiled wide at that. "How is she? I haven't talked to her at all. She's been ignoring me completely."

Lanie shrugged her shoulders a bit as she looked around the room, I think to make sure Becca wasn't watching us. "I don't know, Ty. She says she's fine, and she seems to be acting OK, but I know her pretty well, and I don't think she's OK. I think it's all a cover-up, but I don't know for sure." She looked straight at me before saying her next words. "One thing I will tell you is, be careful tonight. Be careful how you approach her if you plan on talking to her. She's definitely back to being snarky, even more than normal."

I nodded. "Thanks for the warning."

Xander came up behind her and pulled her into his arms. "Doc, I think I need you to take me to bed and check me out. Something seems to be wrong with me."

Lanie swung around to inspect her patient, eyes wide when she did. "Xander, you look adorable. Does my patient need some tending to?"

"I'm stealing the doctor from you, Ty. Any issues with that?" Xander asked.

But it was a rhetorical question, since they were walking away from me already.

And the two of them were off into their own little world. It kind of made me jealous. But I was also happy to see that they weren't sitting around worried about the shit with Max. They were living their lives.

"It's enough to make someone vomit, isn't it?" a voice said from behind me.

I turned to see a tiny-framed girl dressed as a grungy fairy, nowhere close to looking anything like Tinker Bell. Her short black hair was purple tipped for her costume—at least, I thought it was for her costume. Her black boots looked well worn. Something about her confidence told me not much about her was not a costume.

Then I saw her eyes.

They reminded me so much of Becca's.

The green was startling. And they seemed to see right into me, like she knew what I was thinking and feeling. Like she knew me. I recognized her as one of Becca's roommates, but we had never formally met.

"But it's also refreshing to see two people so much in love, right?" she added.

I still only stared at her, not sure if she was looking for answers from me or not.

"I find it interesting that you're dressed as a pirate tonight, Ty," the pixie said, gesturing to my costume. "It's a good pirate costume. Not just some cheap store-bought one either. You put some time into it. You look good."

By then, I was invested in the time she was giving me. I leaned one shoulder against the wall we were close to and took a long drink of the beer from my cup. She followed suit, lining her body up with mine, but about a foot below, meaning she needed to crane her neck, she was so tiny.

"Do you know who I am?" she asked.

"Well, I have a fifty-fifty shot at getting it right," I answered her.

She seemed amused by that.

"Well, take your shot, big guy."

I could very easily see this one being friends with Becca. They had to have become besties almost immediately; they were cut from the same cloth.

"Ava!"

Another girl yelled from across the room. The petite pixie tried not to respond, but the twitch of her head was just noticeable enough for me to see.

Then the other roommate joined us.

She was beautiful. The combination of her light-brown skin and light-blue eyes was stunning. It was her costume that was hard to decipher. She was dressed as a guy, I thought, wearing a blazer and a weird red hat with flaps on the side.

"Ava, I couldn't find you," she said. "Who is this you're talking to?" The flirtation came through in her voice as she turned to look at me. "Hi, I'm Macie." As we shook hands, a look of recognition overtook her face. "Oh, wait, you're Ty! OMG, hi! I didn't recognize you at first," she squealed.

"Hi," I said in return. "Macie, you said, right? So, you're Ava. Correct?" My voice held a bit of cockiness in it, knowing Ava was bitter at not coming out on top of this one. I held my hand out to the tiny vixen, and she grabbed it fiercely and shook it while I laughed.

"Always with the perfect timing, Macie," Ava grumbled.

"What did I do?" she questioned. "It's not like you can flirt with him. He's taken."

Both mine and Ava's heads turned toward Macie when she said that, but she had already gotten lost in the growing crowd.

"What is she dressed as?" I asked Ava.

"We don't really know. She's quite the book nerd, and she usually dresses as one of the characters from a book she loves."

I nodded, and silence settled between us. At least as much silence as one could find in the crowded basement of a college party. I wasn't sure what the purpose of her approaching me was.

"Well, it was nice to finally meet you. Thanks for coming over," I finally said. As I was about to walk away though, Ava grabbed my arm.

"Ty," she said seriously.

I looked down, suddenly curious about what she might have to say.

"Listen, I don't know you at all, and I know I've only known Becca for a few months. But I feel like she and I have bonded pretty well." Her eyes scanned the room, and I joined her. We both knew who we were looking for. "We talked before coming tonight. She's on fire, wants nothing to do with you tonight. She's on some roll about being independent, wants to start fresh, some shit like that."

My heart sank.

And I believed every word Ava was saying, because that sounded just like Becca.

"But Ty," Ava continued, "I don't buy it. She's full of shit. You shouldn't buy it either. I don't know if you should do anything tonight, but she's not over you. I just wanted to let you know." Her look lingered for an exaggerated moment to drive her point home before she started walking away.

"Ava, wait," I called out to her, and she stopped. "How do you know that? How do you know she's not over me?" I hoped my pleading eyes were enough for her to give me something.

"Let's just say the walls are very thin at our place."

I wasn't exactly sure what I wanted to do with the information Ava gave me. Becca was a tricky one when it came to figuring out how to handle her. Sometimes when she acted like she wanted you to leave her alone, it really meant she wanted you to fawn all over her. I was going to have to watch from afar tonight and try to gauge where her mind was really at.

I had stolen peeks of her here and there, but she had done a stellar job of avoiding me thus far. Not even once had she looked at me. Lanie and Ava weren't kidding; she was out for blood.

But I was ready for the challenge. And to pay my dues.

She looked amazing. Her pirate costume was seductive enough to make her look sexy as hell but not so much that I felt I was going to get into any fights tonight. She had one of those white tops that was off the shoulder with a wide, tight belt that cinched her waist. Her pants were tight, showing off her amazing ass, but she was covered all the way to her shins. She completed it with an eye patch, big black boots, tons of jewelry, a sword, and her long signature waves that hung down her back.

Amazing.

I was lucky enough to have borrowed my costume from my dad. It was quite authentic, with a long, sweeping, maroon velvet coat that had brasslike buttons on it. It came with a matching hat, and I paired it with tight jeans and black boots. I thought I looked pretty damn good.

But Becca wouldn't know, since she hadn't glanced my way once yet. I decided to see if any of the brothers needed help in order to keep myself busy. The room was hard to maneuver in because of the dark and the added smoke.

"Hey, Jake," I said, finding him behind the makeshift bar.

"Hey, crazy here already, isn't it?" he said as he worked the tap. "I saw Becca. You guys planning on entering the contest?"

That was my original plan, the whole point in dragging this costume all the way from home.

"Not looking like it. She hasn't even looked my way yet tonight," I told him. "I haven't seen Kayla yet. Is she here?" I was curious to see them in action as a couple, wondering if she was going to settle down and stop being the flirt she was known to be. I didn't want Jake getting fucked over by her.

"Not yet, but she should be here soon. Can't wait to see her in tight leather pants," he said with a shit-eating grin on his face as he wandered away from the table, but then he turned back around. "Oh, hey, by the way, I think Becca came to the party drunk already. I saw her hitting on Ben just before. Ben pushed her away, but she seems like she's going to be in need of some assistance soon."

Shit. Not what I needed for this night to go the way I'd wanted.

I felt the need to look around for her and make sure she was OK. As I was wading through the throngs of people, I realized the smoke was going to make this a more difficult job. Maybe if I found Ava and Macie, they could help me look for Becca as well.

So that was what I set out to do.

Instead, I ran into a body covered in black leather pants.

"Hi, Ty!" Kayla said enthusiastically. But for the first time, she wasn't trying to flirt with me. It was refreshing.

"Hey, Kayla." I had to lean in to talk to her due to the noise, and I found myself looking around, out of habit. "I hear you and Jake are giving it a go."

She put a huge smile on her face. Her costume was good, with her already blonde hair teased up high on her head and bright red lipstick. Her tight, all-black clothes were spot on for the look.

"We are—I like him a lot," she said with a smile, leaning into me as well when she spoke.

"I'm happy for the two of you."

But then I saw Kayla's eyes go wide as she looked over my shoulder. She shifted her eyes to mine, the uncertainty in them making me nervous.

I turned to see Becca's sad, bloodshot eyes staring holes through my head.

"Is she who you're with now, Ty? Have you moved on with Kayla? I always thought there might be something between the two of you, and I guess I was right."

Her slurred words told me how drunk she was. Turning toward Kayla, I shrugged my shoulders as a form of apology, and she understood immediately. She moved on, I was sure to find Jake. I turned back toward Becca.

"Becca, I was looking for you. That's all I was doing. I was trying to find your roommates to help me find you. Kayla was only saying hello." I reached out to help her stop swaying, but she pushed my hand away.

"Why are you dressed like a pirate, Ty?" she asked, anger coming through in her words this time.

I didn't think she was in the right state of mind for me to talk to her about that, so I avoided the topic. "Bec, why don't we find Lanie? It's getting late. She probably wants to get going soon, don't ya think?" I reached for her arm, but she pulled herself out of my reach, stumbling back. I grabbed her, steadying her with both my hands, pulling her close. She looked up at me with dagger eyes.

"I'm over you, ya know," she spat at me while I still held on to her. The redness of her eyes made the green seem more vibrant. We were close enough that she couldn't hide the wetness that was starting to gather in those green eyes. "I'm completely over you. All guys, to be exact. I don't want to be in any relationships. I just want casual sex, a new guy every week—literally just sex."

Some doubt crossed my mind. Maybe she was telling the truth. Maybe she'd been hurt enough recently that she didn't want to deal with relationships for quite a while.

"I get it, Bec, I know. It's OK. Let's go find Lanie. I'll hand you over to Lanie, and you never have to see me again, if that's what you want." I kept her walking ahead of me while I talked in her ear, hoping to calm her.

Her head snapped toward me. "I didn't fucking say I never wanted to see you again! Don't put words in my mouth, Ty Brennan!"

She was a walking, drunken contradiction at the moment. And she needed to get home and into her bed. If I couldn't find Lanie, I would get her into an Uber myself. But suddenly, two large hands were dragging both Becca and I to the back of the basement.

"Hey, you two, where are the pirates going? The contest is starting now. You can't leave," Nate said as he pulled us both by the shoulder. "You both look too good to not enter. We need you to do it. Not enough people are joining."

I tried stopping the progress as he pulled us along, my resistance not doing much since I was working to keep Becca upright.

"Becca, you look amazing. Everyone here should have the chance to see how good you look," Nate told her. "We made a stage over here, and I want you on it."

He knew exactly what he was doing, and I was not going to win this one.

"Why, thank you, Nate. I'm glad someone noticed how hot I look tonight," she said. Her eyebrows lifted at me as she turned around to make sure I heard her comment. "I'm not sure Ty is all that interested in being in the contest, though."

"Well, it's a couples contest, so it's both of you or nothing," Nate responded.

Becca deflated. Her eyes found the stage, and we both noticed a few couples starting to gather on it. Lanie and Xander were among them, as well as Jake and Kayla. As she turned toward me, I became hopeful that her desire to be up on that stage had trumped her anger with me.

"Can you let Ben borrow your costume?" she asked me.

I was stunned.

And speechless. For a moment.

"Are you kidding me?" I asked her.

"No."

"You're serious? The guy you were hitting on? My fucking roommate. You want me to give him my costume so you can do this with him instead of me? You're out of your mind, Becca!" I yelled and stormed off.

And for once in my life, I didn't stick around to make sure Becca got home safe.

CHAPTER 29

Ty

"Hey, man, want to hang out?" Jake asked. "Haven't seen you all weekend since the party." He had come into the kitchen while I was getting something together for dinner. "That looks good. What are you making?"

I headed home after the Halloween party to see Savannah, and it was already Tuesday. Already November. It seemed like the semester was flying by.

I didn't mind getting out of there after the party. It didn't go the way I'd hoped.

At all.

"Steak tacos," I told him. I actually loved to cook. It was a favorite pastime of mine, and I had a lot of time to kill lately. "I've got plenty, if you want some. Is anyone else home?" It was rare that all four of us were here at the same time.

"Aaron might be upstairs. I can check," he said. "But I know Ben is in class. His loss." He ran upstairs to check while I took out a couple more plates. It would be nice to have unexpected company to eat with to help distract me.

Both the guys came strutting into the kitchen, and the three of us began devouring all the food I made. It was a good thing Ben wasn't here.

"Ty, man, that was fucking amazing," Jake said. "Who taught you how to do that? The most I can do is make toast." He laughed at himself.

"My dad is a good cook, so I grew up learning from him. Mom cooks, but only because she had to. It's my dad who loves to cook." They were a good team; Mom would cook during the week, since she worked from home and had a more flexible schedule. She called it "sustainable cooking." But then on the weekends, we got Dad's gourmet meals.

"Well, he taught you well," Aaron said.

"Thanks," I told them. I cracked open another beer as they put the dishes in the sink. That was their idea of cleaning up. Those dishes would still be there until I put them in the dishwasher later.

They had already moved onto the couch, the game controllers in their hands. I joined them as they chose the game we would play.

"*Mario Kart* or *Call of Duty*. Whatcha in the mood for?" Jake asked us both. I didn't really care, but I knew Aaron would want to shoot 'em up in COD.

"Let's play COD," I said, and that seemed to make everyone happy. We settled into the couch, the three of us crammed in together, elbow to elbow. It felt good to be hanging with them, and to have my mind off of Becca.

My phone buzzed, but I wanted to get the last kill. Jake would be pissed if I got up before covering him in the corner he was trapped in. But then my phone pinged again. I threw my controller down in search of it; I left it somewhere in the kitchen.

Hoping it wasn't Kelly and something about the baby, I opened my messages.

It was Becca.

Becca:
Can we talk tonight?

My heart skipped a beat. I wasn't expecting this after the way things went on Friday. I wasn't expecting her to want to talk. At least not anytime soon.

Me:
Yeah sure my place or yours

Becca:
yours 9pm

Me:
I'll see you then

Holy shit.

She was giving me a chance.

Becca hadn't acted herself at the party due to how drunk she was. It didn't excuse her behavior, or how she treated me, but it was the reason. And it may have been a shitty reason, but we were in a shitty situation. To be honest, I was thrilled she reached out to me. Some might think that's a bit pathetic, but there's give and take in relationships. I was willing to talk to her if she was reaching out to me.

I looked at the time; it was already after seven. Running up the stairs, I realized I needed to clean up my room. And I wished she'd given me more of a heads up; I would have gotten a haircut. But at that moment, I wouldn't be picky.

"Dude, where ya going?" Jake yelled at me.

"Becca's coming over soon!" I yelled down to them. They didn't question it; they knew things had been rocky, and if she was coming over, it was a big deal. I hoped they would give us some well-needed space in the apartment, but if not, my room would have to suffice.

As I entered my room, I realized I had more work to do than I first thought. I jumped in the shower first; then I would get to work on the mess.

Should I change the sheets on the bed?

I decided making the bed would have to be good enough. I barely had time to put away all the clothes that covered my floor before the clock hit nine. I ran downstairs so that the moment she arrived, I could open the door. I was literally by the side window, waiting to see her walk up the path.

A few minutes passed before I got my wish. She dressed for the weather in jeans and a cozy sweater; the temperatures dropped significantly in Virginia by November. Her hair was straight and long down her back, shining in the street lamps of the parking lot. I pulled the door open before she even got to the top step.

"Hi!" I exclaimed, probably a bit too excited for what we were about to endure. But I was so damned happy to see her. It took all my restraint to not pull her into my arms and connect my lips to hers.

"Hi," she responded with a small smile and a wave. She was definitely hesitant as she walked in next to me, but she made sure to not touch me as she did.

"So, my roommates left and gave us some privacy, but it might still be better if we go up to my room. One of them doesn't know that this is happening. He might come home, and, well . . ." I didn't know how to complete my thought.

"Sure, that's probably best," she said.

She was quiet, which was unfortunately the new norm for Becca. But I understood. She was about to hear some shit she'd been dreading for a long time.

She waited in the entrance hall for me to start the trek upstairs, and she followed. I realized she'd only been here one other time, and that was heartbreaking. It was not how this year was supposed to be.

Becca didn't know where to go or where to sit, looking very uncomfortable as she searched my room.

"You can sit on the bed or the chair, wherever you're comfortable, Bec," I told her.

She sat on the edge of the bed, as if she would get up and run away at any minute. Knotting her hands together, she occasionally wiped sweat off them on her jeans.

"Lanie tried to use her 'therapist' stuff on me before coming. I mean, she *will* make a good therapist one day. She, um, was trying to make sure I came in with an open mind, ready to listen." As she spoke, she refused to make eye contact with me, so I wasn't sure how successful Lanie's talk was. "I know I said and did some really shitty things at the party that probably hurt you, and I'm sorry about that. I was upset and drank too much and . . ." And then she stopped talking. Her eyes flitted around the room, focusing on anything but me.

I needed to take over the apologies. Because regardless of what she did to me at the party, and it was shitty, it didn't take away all the things I needed to apologize to her for from the past year.

"I'm sorry," I blurted out to her. "A million times over, I'm sorry."

She looked at me, her eyes, her face, neutral.

"Bec, it's me who owes you all the apologies. Remember that weekend we took Logan home last year? I know it was hard for you. But that weekend wound up being hard for me as well." I started the story as I paced the room.

"I wasn't looking for a girlfriend when I came to BRU. I don't know of many freshmen who are, actually. But when I met you, I just knew." I paused and looked at her for a reaction, and there was a small one on her lips. "You were *it* for me the moment I met you. The way an entire room has to turn and look at you when you walk in, the way you command attention without being arrogant. It just happens. I love that about you," I told her. "But then there's the side of you many don't see. Like what a good friend you are, especially to Lanie. How hard you worked to make her feel comfortable last year when she had no one, making sure she always felt safe. You're special, Bec, a one of a kind." I came close to her on the bed and knelt on the floor in front of her, forcing the connection. "That's why, when I got the call the day before we brought Logan home, my life got turned upside down. I had already moved on, with you. I had already fallen in love, with you." I reached out for her hands, and she let me take them.

"Kelly called and told me she was pregnant. She assured me she hadn't been with anyone else yet."

Becca's eyes rolled a little, her disbelief expected. But there was no denying that Savannah was my daughter.

"We went out in high school, and we broke up when I left for college. But I don't think we were really into each other that much toward the end. I think we stayed together in high school because, well, everyone kinda expected us to be together. We were 'that' couple. The one that was supposed to make it. So, we forged on. But when it came time for me to leave, hours away from home, we both knew we didn't have it in us to make it work any longer. It was a mutual decision to break it off. I came here without a girlfriend, Becca. You have to believe me."

"Ty, that's not the problem. I do believe you about that," Becca said. "My issue is why you didn't tell me all last year that you had a child on the way. I mean, fuck, Ty, I had to find out by seeing it with my own eyes!"

Her calm demeanor was already cracking.

And, for the moment, I would let the "it" thing slide.

"Bec, when we went home that weekend, Kelly had already told her parents, who told mine. My parents knew." I flung my hands up in the air, my frustration with the situation last year finally coming out. "I didn't want to bring a new girl into the mix the very weekend we all found out I was having a baby, and that wouldn't have been fair to you, either. I felt sick that whole weekend. I didn't know what to do, how to handle it. On top of dealing with Logan, I prayed that Kelly wasn't going to stop by. Thank God she didn't. I don't know how I pulled that one off, but now that I look back, that would have prevented all of this."

Becca was just staring at me, wheels turning in her head.

"And why did you tell me your parents wouldn't let you have a girlfriend in college?" she asked, the sorrow evident in her eyes.

I paused, knowing I would have to take responsibility for yet another lie.

"Becca," I started, standing up, needing to pace as I came to terms with all I had done to her. I leaned against my dresser, needing something to help keep me steady. "I'm so sorry. I shouldn't have told you that. I was such a coward. When I told you that, it was only because I wanted to have something to tell you, to give you the idea that I was giving you some sort of a truth. But that was not what was going on at all. My parents are two of the best people in the world." My heart hurt so much at the fact that I used my parents in this whole charade, considering how much they had done for me. "I told my mom about you over fall break."

Becca peeked up at me, her interest piqued, but it faded as the reality of what I'd done came over her like a veil.

"Becca, think about it. Let's say Kelly showed up that weekend we were home together. And you found out that I was going to be a father, with my ex from high school. That early in our relationship. Would you have stuck around?" I asked her.

"I don't know, Ty. How can I answer that? You never gave me the opportunity to make that decision, did you?" she spat back at me.

We were both quiet after that, both thoughtful.

"What was going on recently that made you think you could finally reveal your big secret? You said you were going to tell me, so why now?" she asked me.

I fell onto my desk chair, the emotion of this taking its toll.

"Savannah was born a week after I got home from school in the spring," I said, and my smile couldn't be contained when I said my daughter's name. "You broke up with me a few days later."

Becca's eyes widened when she realized the timeline.

"I didn't blame you; I thought it was for the best at the time as well. I spent my entire summer learning how to be a dad at nineteen years old, all while working two jobs so that I could still come back to school. I wanted to come back to school for me, to get my degree. But the longer I was away from you, and missed you, the more I realized that not being with you was not the answer. I needed to try to make things right with us. I knew I wasn't giving up. Not yet."

She sat quietly for a moment.

"Savannah," she whispered. "That's a pretty name."

My heart stopped at her words. And then I noticed the tears streaming down her face. I moved, wanting to hold her, needing to hold her. But she held her hand up to stop me.

"Not yet," she said. "Keep talking. I need you to finish."

"OK. Well, I've been going home almost every weekend this semester to help take care of her, and to work some hours at a job up north." As I continued, Becca's tears continued to stream down her face. But I knew if I stopped, I would lose her, in every sense of the word. "It's been a lot, especially with classes, and pledging, and the delivery job I'm trying to do here, too. But, I mean, it's called sacrifice."

Becca continued to just look at me as I spoke. My hands itched and shook with the need to comfort her. I knew if I pulled her into my arms, I'd be better, we'd be better. But I continued on.

"Kelly had decided to take a gap year even before she knew she was pregnant, so she was home already and went to work. And our parents help by watching Savannah during the week while I'm at school and Kelly's at work. But now she's old enough to go to the daycare at Kelly's work, so that helps everyone out. My parents told me they will take two of my weekends, allowing me to stay here at school more often."

Becca nodded while she continued to cry, as if she understood. I took that as a good sign, like she was getting what I'd been going through. But then she stood up and darted for the door. I grabbed her by the arm and spun her around.

"Where are you going?" I yelled.

"I can't do this anymore!" she cried out as she attempted to push me off of her. "This won't work, Ty." She yanked her arm out of my grasp and made it all the way down the stairs.

Following her down to the front door, I held it closed, not wanting her to leave.

"Please, don't go. We've only scratched the surface of what we need to talk about, Bec. There's so much more. This was only the start. I need to remind you about us, and how I feel about you never changed during any of this."

But she shook her head, resolute. "You don't need to say any more. I know exactly how you feel about me, Ty. That's never been the question, never been the problem."

I didn't understand. She was talking in riddles.

"I've now realized the—" she said through broken cries, as her breathing became ragged. "You're not the problem. I. Am."

She tried to push me out of the way to get to the door, but I wouldn't let her. There was no way that after a comment like that, I was letting her walk out of here. I got a hold of one of her wrists and pulled her against me, my arms wrapping around her middle. She continued to fight, so I pushed her up against the back of the door. Our bodies now flush against one another's, our heartbeats fighting to make a rhythm together.

"What are you taking about, Bec?" I whispered in her ear, trying to keep the moment calm.

"Ty, let me go, please. I have to go. I have to get out of here."

At that exact moment, there was movement on the other side of the door. Both Becca and I retreated immediately, just in time before it flew open and Ben came rushing in.

"Oh, hey guys," he said. "You scared the shit out of me!"

"Yeah, don't worry," Becca said. "I was just leaving."

And she slid out the door and was gone.

CHAPTER 30
Becca

$\mathcal{D}$riving home when you're crying isn't the smartest thing to do, but I didn't have much of a choice. I had to get out of there. And I thought about not going home, but where would I go? A month ago, Gage would have been an option, but that was out the door. I could have gone to see Lanie, but I didn't feel like seeing Xander and his roommates in my wrecked emotional state. And I didn't think anyone was home at our place, so at least I'd be alone.

I was even struggling to get the key in the door, my hands shook so badly. Running up the stairs to my room, I slammed my door and flopped on the bed. The tears just wouldn't stop. Why was I such a bitch all the time?

Fuck!

I started storming around my room, throwing the clothes that were on my floor all over the place, looking for my journal. It was a journal I'd kept last year about all the things Ty and I did together and some of the sweet things he said to me. But I couldn't find it anywhere. Why was I such a fucking slob?

Fuck!

"Becca?" I heard a voice outside my door. "Are you OK?"

It was Macie. Shit, I didn't think anyone was here. I went to my door, opening it only a crack. "Hi," I whispered.

"Do you need anything?" she asked.

"No, I'm OK. Nothing a shower and some TV won't help. Thanks, though."

"OK, let me know if you want to hang out. I'll be here for a little while," she said as she headed down the stairs.

I needed to calm down.

So I did get in the shower, hoping that would help. I had actually never felt this way before. My breathing was quick, and my breaths were hard to catch. And now being alone seemed like a bad idea. I ripped my clothes off while I put the water on and stepped into the shower, all at the same time. The water was still frigid; I hadn't even gotten my underwear off yet.

Sliding down the wall, I fell to the floor while letting the water hit my face, and the stream mixed with my tears.

Fuck! I ruined us. It was me who ruined us. How could I do this?

The sobs wracked my body, my soul. I felt as though I would never recover.

"Becca?"

But this time, the voice was not Macie's.

My head turned to the voice. I should have figured he would follow me. And the traitor Macie let him in.

He was always making sure I was safe. I should get off my ass and lock the bathroom door.

But I didn't have the energy to move.

Defeat.

That was what I felt through my entire being.

"Becca," Ty said as he approached the shower. "Baby."

And that made me cry harder.

I didn't deserve him; I didn't deserve his love or his care. None of it. I was a piece of shit.

He walked right into the shower and picked me up off the floor, taking me in his arms. And I let him. Collapsing into his embrace, my howls got louder and louder.

"Hey, babe, it's OK. Whatever is making you feel this way, we can work it out," he said. "Talk to me, Bec. Tell me what I can do."

"Nothing!" I yelled against his chest. "This is my fault, Ty! I'm a bitch. I'm a selfish brat who never gave you a minute to even tell me anything going on in your life. What good girlfriend does that? What girlfriend breaks up without even allowing a conversation about it?" I howled into his shoulder.

Ty pulled away from me and grabbed my face with his hands. I tried to fight out of his grip, but he held on tight, forcing me to look at him.

"Becca Reynolds, you are at no fault at all. This is all on me. I walked away from you and didn't look back this summer. What kind of boyfriend does that?" He cradled my cheeks in his hands.

But I pushed at his chest, and his hold on me broke away. But he was blocking my escape from the shower, and I was stuck in here with him. I just shook my head at him, not sure I could keep going on.

"Ty . . ." I whispered.

"What?" he countered. "Tell me one good reason we can't try to make this work."

"Ty," I started again, but still not sure I could say it.

He stood a mere twelve inches from me, fully clothed, soaked to the bone, shoes and all. And I was going to break his heart, again.

"I don't know if I want to be a mother yet."

He stepped back, maybe only an inch, but I noticed. I hiccuped, trying to hold in the sob that wanted to escape, and brought my hands up to my face to wipe the snot running down from my nose.

Ty lowered his head to be more eye level with me before talking.

"Babe, I would never expect you to be a mother. That's not your job. Bec, baby, if that's what's holding you back, what you're worried about . . ." Slowly, his hands came back up to my face as he closed the distance between us. He pulled me against him, keeping my eyes locked on his. "I love you, Becca Reynolds. If you still love me, we can make this work. I want to make this work with us."

This was crazy. Could two twenty-year-olds make it work with a baby in their lives that was his—and not mine? Going to college, taking care of an infant, studying, partying, football, jobs, friends, family. That seemed like a lot. And I wasn't sure I had an answer as to whether we could do it or not, but I did know I didn't want the alternative.

I lived that for the past six months and was miserable.

I looked him square in the eye and nodded.

"Yeah?" he asked with enthusiasm.

"Yeah," I confirmed.

He tilted my face up a bit more and crashed his lips into mine. His hands trailed down my back, under my ass as he lifted me up. I wrapped my legs around him as he pushed me up against the tile wall. His mouth moved from mine and licked a trail to my ear, down my neck, and over to my shoulder. His one hand held me up while his other came around and grabbed a hold of my breast.

"Ty," I breathed out as he caressed me. "You still have your clothes on. Take them off, please."

"I will, but I want to take care of you first. Let me do this," he said against the skin of my neck, lapping up the rivulets of water running down my cheek into his mouth. "I need to do this."

His thumb began flicking the hard bud at the tip of my breast as his mouth sought mine again. Our tongues lashed against each other, so desperate to solidify our-selves as *us.*

His body pushed up against mine, grinding his hard length along me.

"I think we need to get those wet panties off of you, though," he said huskily in my ear as he put me down.

Getting on his knees, he looped his fingers in the strings of my thong and guided them to the floor of the shower. As I stepped out of them, I put my hands on his shoulders to steady my shaky legs. His arms went around my waist as his mouth landed on my belly, his tongue licking circles around my belly button. The sensation caused bumps to rise all over my skin regardless of the stream of hot water hitting us both. Slowly, his mouth moved lower. His hand reached the apex between my legs before his mouth did, spreading me apart oh so gently.

"Brace yourself, Becca," he warned.

He lifted my leg up and over his shoulder, forcing my hands to use the walls for support. My lower half was fully exposed to his adoration. His gaze wandered up the length of my body, our eyes connecting.

"You are perfection. Absolute perfection." As he said this, he caressed my thigh, which was wrapped around his neck. The fingers of his other hand were splayed across my belly, inching closer and closer to where I needed them to be. "Will you let me worship you, Becca? Can I touch and make you come all over my hand, my mouth?"

His words alone almost got me.

"Yes," I begged, my words echoing off the glass and tile. My head fell against the slippery wall as his fingers opened me up, spreading my pussy lips apart.

"Fuck, Bec," he said as he swiped a finger along my slit. "Even in the shower, I can feel how wet you are."

My body shook with anticipation. His finger circled and circled, my hips jutting forward, hoping he would take the plunge.

"Is your leg good up there, babe? Can I let go?" he asked.

"Mmhmm," was all I could get out as I hooked my knee tighter around his neck. Suddenly, one hand was pulling the hood of my clit back and his lips surrounded it, sucking it hard into his mouth.

"Oh fuck, Ty!" I screamed out as his tongue swirled around the bundle of nerves. Seconds later, he thrust a finger inside me, so deep I felt it in my core. His hand began rhythmically pumping when I felt a second finger join in.

And a third.

"Does that feel good, baby girl?" he asked, pulling away from my clit.

My hands still braced me on the wall, trying to find something to grip on the smooth surface. Instead, I pulled a hand away and pushed his head back to my body, keeping it there for support. "Yes!" I cried out. "But don't stop!"

He smiled against my skin before getting back to work. His mouth and fingers working in tandem, a steady tempo bringing me up that hill. Ty always knew the best way around my body.

Slow and steady, no interruption.

Keep going 'till I reach that summit.

I was climbing; the top was in view.

My body shook, the tremors starting deep within me.

"That's it, baby," he murmured, his tongue never stopping its assault. "I can feel it, babe. Come for me, Bec. Come all over me."

His words . . . Oh my God, his words.

They had me running to the summit and jumping off the edge.

My orgasm ripped through my body. I tried to push him off of me, the feeling too intense. But he forced my hands away as his mouth continued its brutal torment of sucking and licking my tortured clit. My body shook and quivered so much, Ty had to use a hand to hold me up, his other still pumping in and out of me.

One last jolt, and I landed at the bottom. My body settled and relaxed.

Ty's hand slowed inside me and started a slow retreat. His fingers caressed every inch of me as he removed them. His mouth released from me and his thumb took over rubbing my clit, making sure my orgasm had reached its peak.

"I can't, Ty. No more," I said, the spot now too sensitive. I slowly lowered my leg from his shoulder, straightening my body.

"Just making sure, babe." He looked up at me with a smile. But then the smile disappeared.

He pushed his forehead against me and froze suddenly, holding me by the hips.

"Becca," he murmured against my skin, the vibration making the butterflies take flight inside me. "I thought this day might never happen again. I will not take another moment with you for granted." His eyes turned up toward mine as my fingers gripped his hair, holding him against me. "Every day will be a gift, and each day we have together, I will spend earning back your trust, your love, your heart."

The tiny droplets of water that clung to his eyelashes from the shower accentuated the tears forming in those whiskey eyes. I wiped away as much as I could.

Looking down at him, I knew we were where we were supposed to be. There may have been a long and twisty road to get here, but nothing worth keeping in this lifetime was easy to achieve. We still had many obstacles to clear together, but I knew now that we could do that together.

As long as I allowed myself to trust him.

To trust in us.

"You never lost my heart, Ty. It was always yours. And you're already mending the cracks it got." I fell to my knees with him, and our mouths collided. But I pulled back. "My love for you is endless," I breathed against his mouth. "It was there, hiding under the cover of our illusion. We . . ." I hesitated while looking at him, the love for me evident in his eyes. His hand reached out, cradling my face, and my cheek fell into his palm, relishing its warmth. "We will be OK. We will come back from this. These lies, they will not destroy us."

CHAPTER 31

<those were words that I never thought I would hear
her say, ever. And here she was, saying them. Saying she loved me. That we were going to be OK. That we
were OK.

I held no illusions. I knew there were still road bumps
ahead for us. I think she knew that, too. But I was so appre-
ciative that she was willing to give this a go.

"Can we get these wet clothes off you now?" she said.

We both stood up in the shower stall, the hot water
still hitting us. I turned it off while she grabbed a towel for
herself. First, I pulled the shirt over my head and tossed it
on the shower floor. Next, the shoes and socks joined the
shirt. Then I began peeling off my soaking-wet jeans, which
was not an easy feat.

"Need some help there, big guy?" she said, laughing. I
still hadn't gotten them down over my thighs.

"Yeah, I actually do," I said, laughing as well.

She came behind me and tried pulling them off with me.

"Shit, what the fuck?" she said. "Why is this so hard to do?"

The puddle that was forming was immense and only made the conditions around us even slipperier.

"I have an idea, Ty. You'll have to lie on the floor and I'll pull them off. I think that's the only way. They won't come over these massive, sexy thighs of yours," she said as she came up and began stroking me in places that were not my thighs. "At least your dick is already out of them, because it's growing, and that would make it harder yet to get these off of you," she whispered in my ear.

Fuck, she was right. My dick was rock solid for her already, had been since my mouth first touched her.

"Get your ass on the floor. We need your pants off, pronto!" she laughed.

I positioned myself in the tiny bathroom the best I could so she could grab the bottoms and pull. But I was nervous she was going to slip on the floor and get hurt.

"Ty, are you wearing skinny jeans now? What the fuck?"

"No! Christ, they're just fucking soaking wet. They weigh, like, ten pounds. Here, let me help." We were both trying to shimmy them off of me and actually got them down to my knees when, as I expected, her footing started going on the wet tile. I saw it happening and grabbed her arm to pull her forward instead of onto her back. Her full, naked body landed on top of mine.

"Oomph!" she cried out.

"Are you OK?" I asked, truly concerned by how hard she landed.

"Yeah," she started, "my boobs acted as airbags on impact." She started laughing, and it was an amazing sound.

Her hair fell in a curtain to the floor next to my face as she held herself up over me, but I stopped her from getting up more. My hands held her in place on her ass, grabbing it without shame. "Hm, you like this, huh? Did you plan on this happening, Mr. Brennan?"

"No, I would never intentionally try to hurt you, but now that you're here . . ."

Her lips lowered onto mine, and the kiss was soft and sensual. And it went right to my dick as it pulsated between us. Her tongue darted between our lips, teasing me.

"I think we really need to get those jeans off of you, Ty," she said.

I gently moved her aside, knowing they would slide off my legs from where they now were. Once I added them to the pile of wet clothes, I stood and pulled her up with me. Heading toward the bed, I saw her glance at my wallet on her dresser. And I knew exactly where her mind went as she reached for it.

"Come here for a sec, Bec," I said as I pulled her to the bed and we both sat. "About the condom thing. I want to explain."

She started waving her hands at me to stop me from talking.

"No, no, you don't have to say another word. I get it now. I can only assume she was on the pill, too, but you guys still got pregnant. Am I right?" She sat staring at me, the wallet in her hands.

All I did was nod. And my guilt consumed me again. "Every time you yelled at me for wearing one, it was the perfect opportunity to tell you. But I was scared, so fucking scared you would walk away from me. I'm so sorry, Becca. I really am."

She crawled over me and straddled my lap, which was fucking sexy. "Ty," she said as she opened my wallet and removed the square foil packet. "It's all making so much sense now. No more apologies, at least not today." She tore the packet open with her teeth and removed the condom. She grabbed a hold of my stiff dick, which was standing up between us, and began rolling the condom from its tip down the shaft. "I think we need to get back to making up. What do you think?" she asked as she gripped the base of me and pumped me in her hands.

Still gripping her ass, I pulled her even closer yet and reached my mouth up to taste her. The dark tip of her breast met my lips, and I sucked her deep into my mouth. Her hands dropped a hold of my dick and reached for my head, holding me close to her chest as she ran her fingers through my hair. Small moans vibrated against the top of my head as she started grinding herself against my lap.

"Fuck me, Ty. I want you to fuck me," she moaned.

"You're on top, baby girl. Tell me what you want," I said.

She sat back and looked at me, the twinkle in her eye immediate.

She lifted on her knees and grabbed a hold of my dick. Rubbing it along her seam, she lined it up, teasing her hole, and me, by pushing me into her about an inch. Then lifting again.

"Oh, Bec, baby, you're killin' me," I told her.

"This is the best form of punishment, though, isn't it?" she asked with a smirk.

Before I could even answer her, she threw herself onto me, driving my dick inside her pussy.

"Ohhh," she purred.

"Fuck!" I yelled.

"Lay back, Ty," she said. Quite controlling, I might add.

I obliged. Willingly.

Looking up at her, the beauty of her sitting atop me, I was amazed that she chose me to be hers.

I was one lucky bastard.

And then she started rocking back and forth.

And I felt as though I would lose consciousness. Watching her fuck me was the single most sexy fucking thing I'd ever seen in my life. Her hands fell to my torso, digging in as she got into it. She flung her head back, her raven hair flying high behind her, framing her face as if she were an angel.

Then she reached back and put her hands behind her, on my thighs, leaning back.

And she rode me.

Like a fucking rodeo star.

"Jesus, Becca," I whispered through gritted teeth. "Slow down, baby. I don't want to come yet."

She did, and she sat forward, looking down at me, her hair draping around the sides of her breasts. I reached up and cupped them in both my hands, loving the weight of them. My fingertips swirled around the peaked tips and her head fell back in ecstasy, a moan escaping her lips.

I quickly sat up, needing to feel more of her, to be closer to her. My arm went around her back, pulling her against me as my mouth landed on the mound of her breast, my hand kneading it.

"Ty," she whined.

And I knew. I knew she needed more. Moving my hands under her ass, I lifted us to standing, spun around, and laid us on the bed, staying inside her. Her knees fell wide as I mounted her, preparing my onslaught.

And she knew it was coming. She grabbed the bar of her headboard just as I pulled out slightly. My hips pummeled toward her, her body lifting to meet mine.

"Harder, Ty. I want you to fuck me harder," she said as our foreheads came to meet between thrusts.

All of our pain, regret, and sorrow from the past six months was being released. We threw it all away as we hammered into one another.

Exchanging agony for ecstasy.

"I love you, Ty,"

I thrust even harder into her.

"Babe, I'm so sorry I hurt you. I love you so much," I told her. My words were staccato, but she heard me as we continued, our lovemaking our apology to each other.

"I'm sorry, so sorry I didn't trust in you," she cried, the tears falling as we fucked.

I leaned down, kissing and licking her tears away with every push inside of her.

"I know," I said as I pulled out and pounded her so hard the bed hit the wall. "I know we can make this work, Bec."

And then the momentum took over and the words quieted. The rhythm of our sex was building for me and her—I could see it on her face. Hear it in her moans.

The relentless motion, I couldn't stop.

I never wanted to stop.

I never wanted it to stop.

Her muscles quivered around my dick, pulling me back inside her, holding on to me, keeping me in her.

It was pure heaven.

I reached down and found the spot I knew she needed me to find to reach her climax. As I rubbed that hard nub, her moans increased in my ear.

"I want you to come, babe. Tell me you're coming on my dick."

"I'm coming, Ty. Fuck, I'm coming!" she screamed, and I swear the walls shook.

Bearing down, I pushed in and out of her at a pace that pushed me to the edge, finally getting there and exploding inside. My body twitched in her arms as her hands rubbed my back, my thrusts slowing down until I came to a stop. I lowered myself gently on top of her, trying to catch my breath. My sweaty brow matched hers, and I noticed her hair matted to the sides of her head.

Becca chuckled lightly under me.

"What are you laughing at?" I asked.

"Well," she said, "you've always been fucking amazing in bed. But this was a whole 'nother level. I just don't want us to have to have makeup sex all the time to do that again."

I laughed along with her, enjoying that we had gotten back some of our normal already.

"I'm sure we'll figure it out. No more fights—at least not like what we just went through," I told her. I moved off her and made her turn toward me, belly to belly. "I can't go through that again, Bec. Never."

"I know." She reached out and moved the long pieces of my hair out of my face. "I won't jump to conclusions anymore without talking to you first," she said. The contrite look on her face made me feel bad, but she had some culpability in this.

"And I will keep nothing from you again, even if it might make you upset."

She nodded, seemingly thankful for that.

"How about we pretend to be in a fight and get mad at each other and yell and shit so we can have makeup sex like this?" she asked.

"Or," I said, "and I'm going out on a limb, but what if we just up our game and do this next time anyway, without the fight? And maybe, if you're interested, and it sounds like you are, we can start spicing things up even more." I waited a second to gauge her response.

Her finger went to my torso, the nail scratching a line down my abs. "Tyler Brennan, what dirty things have you been hiding from me?" Her hand trailed down to the tip of my dick, the old condom still in place. She slid it off and wrapped it in a tissue. Her hand came back, cupping my balls, and that got an immediate rise from my dick. "Why don't we keep going right now? Who says we have to wait for *next time?*" Her sultry look had me ready to go.

Swinging her on top of me, I grabbed her ass and pulled her against me, my erection pressing into her belly. "Did I ever say we were done right now?"

She smiled down at me.

"I'm not letting you go all night, Bec. I'm going to fuck you until you beg me to stop, and then I might have to fuck you one last time, if you agree, of course."

She rolled us over again, with me on top of her this time. With her arms wrapped around my neck, she brushed her lips along mine. "I will never tire of you fucking me. Well, I might get tired, but as soon as I wake up, you will fuck me again and again. We have a lot of lost time to make up for."

She reached for my wallet.

"Bec, we don't have to wear those." And I meant it. "I'm in a relationship where, if it happens, I'd be happy."

Through a soft smile, she responded to me. "Ty, that means a lot to me, thank you. But one baby is enough for right now, don't ya think? Let's be kids with each other while we're here, together. And we will be adults when we go home on the weekends."

And right then I knew, one day, she would be my wife.

CHAPTER 32
Becca

"*L*anie, get your ass in this car!" I screamed at her. I hadn't seen her since Ty and I made up, and I needed to tell her everything. She took her time walking out of Xander's apartment, and he was walking her all the way to my car. Maybe this situation with Max was a bit more serious than they first let on.

"Hey, Bec," Xander said as he approached my side of the car. "Good to see you smiling." *His* thousand-watt smile was always good to see. He leaned in the car before talking. "Just keep an eye out for anything out of the ordinary while you guys are out, OK? Call me if you see anything weird."

I nodded, not liking how this was sounding.

"Xander, we'll be fine. Don't be so dramatic," Lanie said. "There's really no cause for concern. They are under house arrest and have guards in front of their homes."

"Yeah, and they're considering guards here soon, too, so it is a big deal, Lanes," Xander said, almost reprimanding her.

Lanie gave him a meek smile before kissing him goodbye.

Fuck. This was some big-time shit they had going on again.

"I'm on Lanie duty. Got it, Xander?" I said his way. "We're picking up Ava and Macie, too. They weren't ready yet. It will be the four of us going to brunch, so we should be good."

He nodded as he started back toward his apartment. "Have fun," he said as he waved.

I pulled away, headed back to my, or what used to be our, apartment to pick up the other two. I was quiet in the car, not sure if Lanie wanted to talk about anything. Last year, when she had her shit going on, she never wanted to talk. So I sat there and planned on taking her lead.

"Becca!" she yelled. "Why are you not saying anything?"

I looked over at her as I pulled into a spot in front of my place, ready to honk the horn.

"Don't honk yet!" she screamed at me. "You can't do this to me. Are you and Ty back together or not? I've been desperate to hear from you and you've been radio silent for two days."

Ty and I went back to his apartment, knowing Macie was home, and spent the first twenty-four hours "making up" at his place. But then his roommates made it very obvious they could . . . hear us.

So then we moved it over to my place for the next twenty-four hours. It wasn't spent *entirely* having sex. We ate, we slept, we watched some TV. Maybe a show or two.

But yeah, we made up.

Suddenly, the back doors of my car flew open and Ava and Macie piled into the car.

"I don't care that he has washboard abs, Mace. He is a manwhore, and you really should reconsider seeing him," Ava was saying as she got in.

"Hi, guys," Macie said sheepishly. "Sorry, it always seems like I'm hooking up with douchebags. Why do I always find the losers?" She folded her arms in disgust as I looked back at her in the rearview mirror and gave her the best sympathetic look I could muster up. "I did it again, Bec. I don't know what's wrong with me."

"Standards," Ava added. "Raise your standards. That's all you need to do. Let's take our friends Lanie and Becca, here." She gestured toward the front seat. I wasn't sure if I should start driving or not—had no idea where this was going. "These two both have fine young men that they are fucking. Loudly, I might add."

Shit.

"Becca!" Lanie yelled again while slapping me on the arm.

"What? That's what today was for. I was going to tell all of you the complete story," I said. I gave Ava a dirty look as I spun around in my seat. "I did not tell them."

"She didn't have to," Macie said. "We heard it all." She giggled.

Ava laughed out loud. "Damn right, we did. I think I came right along with you a few times. Christ, those walls are thin."

Oh my God, I was mortified. We had upped our spice game a bit once we got to my apartment. It may have involved some apparatus that used batteries.

"Shit, I had no idea you guys were home for most of that or could even hear us," I whispered. "Well," I said with more conviction, "that's OK. Better to hear us fucking than fighting, right?"

All I could do was drive. So I did; I put the car in drive and drove.

"Bec, all good, kid," Ava said. "Knowing you, you would *not* have taken his ass back if he wasn't worth it. I'm looking forward to hearing the story."

All the while, Lanie sat in the passenger seat, quietly watching me. With a smile on her face. She reached out and gripped my hand, which was on the shifter.

"I'm happy for you, Bec. Happy for both of you."

I nodded, a bit choked up and not wanting to cry.

"Me too. Thanks, Lane."

"I don't know anyone with a baby," Macie said. "Well, I didn't, but now I do. We don't even have any young cousins in our family or anything." She was thoughtful for a moment. "Have you met her, Becca?"

It was such an innocent question asked in an innocent way. But it hit me hard.

"Um, no, not yet."

And that was all I could give them.

"Mace, they literally just made up. When would she have met her?" Ava asked.

Macie shrugged her shoulders as her response.

"I think that's enough baby talk for today. I'm sure Becca could use a break from telling us all about the ins and outs of her life right about now," Lanie said, trying to change the subject, which I appreciated. "Besides, there's one more thing we want to talk to you two about." Lanie gave me a sideways glance as she said this. I knew she was wondering how this would go.

Ava and Macie gave both of us curious looks when Lanie said that. My hopes were high that Ava continued to be the sensible one in the group.

"Remember our friend Logan?" Lanie asked.

We thought having Lanie do the talking would make this go better, considering their past.

Both Ava and Macie nodded. Their interest was piqued as their eyes shifted back and forth between Lanie and me.

"Well, he obviously wasn't here this semester, but he's doing so well he's coming in the spring!" she announced excitedly. And she was; I could tell it was real. There was nothing fake about Lanie. "The only problem so far is that he hasn't been able to find a place to live. And since we have an open room at our place with me now living with Xander, Becca and I were hoping you two would be OK with him . . ."

Her voice faded out as she gauged the crowd. As we both scanned the others' faces, I noticed nothing that surprised me. Macie seemed unbothered by any of it. Ava was thoughtful and processing.

"Is he that hot blond in those pics I've seen with Ty? That tall one, the big guy?" Macie asked. Her eyes lit up a bit when she realized who we were asking to have live with her.

"Yeah, Mace, that's him," Ava responded. "Lanie, he's also the same guy you had a problem with last year, isn't he?"

Lanie and I exchanged glances, nervous things might take this turn.

"So listen," Lanie answered. "I know there's stories about what happened between me and Logan last year, and I will never diminish what he did to me. But my response was *my* response, due to my past. I think anyone else would have responded in a very different way to Logan's actions that night. He and I got past what happened, and I would never want you to judge him based on what happened between us."

Wow, even I wasn't expecting that. As I watched Lanie's expression for any sign of distress as she sat there, awaiting our roommates' reaction, I saw nothing. She was being honest.

Everyone was quiet for a few minutes. Ava was the next to speak again.

"And you would be comfortable with him living with us, your friends. Living with Becca, your best friend?" Ava asked, almost accusatory.

Without hesitating, Lanie responded, "Yes." She sat stoic for a moment, then continued. "If Logan needed a place to live, and I was the one still living there, I would be comfortable living with him. That's how much I trust him now. He made a mistake. One mistake. Once you meet him, you can decide for yourselves, but I would never ask you to do this if I didn't trust him."

Ava continued to look thoughtful, but not for long.

"I trust your judgment, Lanie. If you trust him, then I trust him," Ava said with a warm smile. "Macie, what do you say?"

"I say make sure he wears gray sweatpants, a lot!" she replied.

Ty and I were leaving the cafeteria after meeting up with Xander and Lanie for lunch. It felt pretty good to be getting back to normal. Walking to class, we hurried across the oval as a gusty wind picked up. The weather on campus was very unpredictable, but the closer we got to December, the worse it got. And I wasn't prepared for it, only dressed in a long sleeve shirt. We came to the fork in the path where we went our separate ways for our classes.

"Here, take my hoodie?" Ty said, stopping to take it off.

"I'm almost to the building. I'll be OK once I'm inside."

"Bec, please, take it. It will make me feel better." He held it out and I relented, wrapping myself in its warmth, which smelled of his scent: oak and patchouli. "I'll see you after class, OK? And listen, he's, um, waiting for you over by your building."

My head snapped up to Ty's face when he said those words.

"Who?" I asked, but from Ty's tone, I think I already knew who he meant.

"Gage." His voice was solemn but strong.

I looked toward my building and saw him watching us both. It was obvious he was waiting for me. "Do you want to come with me?" I asked Ty.

"Um, no. I'll be fine never talking to him again. Listen, he's not necessarily a bad guy." His eyes left mine and focused on something in the distance. He seemed uncomfortable with the conversation. "I just don't need to exchange any more words with the guy who almost stole you from me and was, well, sleeping with you. And, well, lied to you as well." His sheepish look told me he was still apologetic about his own lies.

And when he put it that way, I completely understood.

"Love you, Bec. I'll see you after class." He leaned down and placed a simple kiss on my cheek and walked in the opposite direction.

I stood watching him go for a moment longer than was necessary, then turned around. Gage was still standing at the top of the stairs to my building, leaning against the ledge near the door. As I walked up, I realized I was no longer cold, but now sweating in the sweatshirt Ty left me with. But there was no way I was taking it off. It made me feel like he was with me.

"Hi, Becca," Gage said, his voice still as sultry as ever. He dressed rather casually for him in black sweats and a long-sleeve tee. His beard was longer than his typical five o'clock shadow, but still attractive.

Still fucking hot.

"Hi, Gage." I tried to keep my voice neutral, no emotion. But I fear I failed.

He hurt me.

And even though I was fine with us no longer hanging out and "doing" what we were doing, he still lied and hurt me.

"I see you and Ty are back together." He gestured toward the oval, where he had seen us, and our kiss.

And I heard something in his voice when he spoke. I didn't think it was jealousy, but maybe a bit of longing. Longing for what Ty and I have, and what he wanted for himself, maybe.

"We are," I said simply.

"I'm happy for you. I really am."

And he sounded genuine. He stepped closer but kept a respectable distance between us. "I'm going inside. Let's head in—it's getting cold." He walked to the door and held it for me, assuming I would follow him.

But I didn't have a choice; my class started in five minutes. And he knew that. I walked through the open door, and he came in behind me. As we started down the hall, our steps fell in line, but we remained quiet.

Finally, he broke the silence.

"Becca," he said, stopping and reaching out for my arm so I would stop as well. "I know you don't have much time, but this won't take long. I wanted to tell you I'm sorry and that I'm . . ."

"Gage, it's OK," I said. "We were never supposed to be anything more than casual. We never talked about your life, and I never asked about it. It really is OK. I think we just both, well, it became something more than we thought it would at a time that didn't work for either of us, right?"

He stared at me. Those dark, sultry eyes making me think back to the first moment I saw them when he pushed me up against the wall of Xander's house that day back in August.

The day Ty crushed my heart.

And it needed someone to bandage it.

Gage did that.

He was my bandage.

But I needed to rip that bandage off and get rid of it. For good.

"He's a good guy, Becca. I'm happy for you." His somber tone struck me, spurring me to look at him after his kind words. He looked away when I did, his sad gaze focusing on something in the distance.

Well wishes. I would accept well wishes from him at this point.

"Thanks, Gage. I hope things work out for you in your life, I really do."

I gave him one more moment of my time, our eyes finally connecting as he looked down at me. A small smile touched the corner of his mouth, and I turned and walked away.

Chapter 33
Becca

It was nice settling into our new normal. We were going to class. We were hanging out with friends. We were hanging out together. The only difference was every other weekend, Ty headed home to see Savannah. Ty and I made the decision that I would not go home with him just yet. We would decide together when I would be ready for that.

And I wasn't entirely sure when that would be.

But for now, I was completely content with our "new normal."

"Hey babe, do you have your clothes ready for your ceremony tonight?" Ty asked. He had come over after his classes were done for dinner, a common occurrence for our "new normal."

Ava came waltzing into the kitchen, checking out what I had in the pots on the stove. She loved that I enjoyed cooking for Ty because she and Macie reaped the benefits of my dinners as well.

"Ya know, we're coming tonight, too, Bec," she announced.

"You are?" I was stunned. I had no idea Ava and Macie even knew about the award I was receiving from my business organization. "Why does everyone feel the need to be there tonight? Christ on a cracker, I don't need this much attention, guys."

Ava gave me a side hug as I stirred the sauce. "I like this feisty Becca,. Where has she been hiding?"

"I've been here all along, girl. Just needed to find my way out of the fog," I said as I leaned my head down onto her shoulder, and she squeezed me tighter. I smiled at Ty, letting him know I was in a good place.

I loved that we were getting closer. Each night that I wasn't with Ty, she and I would fall asleep together watching TV or talking.

She took the spoon out of my hand and tasted the sauce. "Oh my God, this is amazing. Where did you learn to cook, Bec?" Throwing the spoon in the sink, she grabbed another from the drawer for me.

"She grew up in a large family," Ty offered. "She cooked for her brothers a lot." He looked over at me with affection and understanding, knowing that I had come to actually miss my family, at times, recently.

"I know all about her crazy younger brothers. I have younger brothers too. Didn't make me a chef." She pulled open a cabinet and started taking bowls out to set the table for dinner. "Will Macie be eating?"

"I don't know. Why don't you text her?" I said. "And yes, Ty, to answer your question, my clothes are all pressed and ready to go upstairs. I'm wearing that red suit you like on me so much. After we eat, we should probably head up so I can get ready."

Macie came strolling down the stairs, and the four of us ate a meal together.

A new normal.

The auditorium was buzzing with people by the time we arrived, making me more nervous than I already was. Ty already had a hold of my hand, and he squeezed it tighter, knowing I was anxious about what I needed to do tonight. But I was ready; I had practiced a ton in front of the mirror.

"Good luck with your speech, babe," he whispered into my ear as he pulled me close. "I'm so proud of you, Ms. President."

His tender kiss on my temple sent shivers through my whole body. He wrapped an arm around my waist, holding me close to his body, so I know he felt it.

"Thank you," I whispered back. I was thrilled to have him here by my side and hated that I was going to have to leave him to go backstage. My eyes darted around, scanning the crowd for my advisor, hoping to find her so I wouldn't be alone once I got back there. Ty picked up on my nerves.

"You OK?"

"Yeah, just, um, what if I mess up?" I asked. As I looked up at him, his tender eyes came to down to my level. He was about to speak when we were interrupted by a boisterous crowd.

"Becca!"

"Bec!"

It was Lanie, Xander, Ava, Macie, Jake, and Kayla.

They had all come to see me.

I couldn't believe the amount of support I was receiving from my friends. It could have made me more nervous, afraid to make a mistake in front of all of them. Instead, it made me feel . . . loved. Even with Kayla here.

Then my phone pinged.

Mom:

> Hey Becca, sorry we couldn't make it tonight, the twins have a basketball game otherwise we would have made the trek. Good luck babe, we are so proud of you! Dad sends a kiss.

"What is it, babe?" Ty asked.

I didn't answer right away, my throat clogged with emotion. Lanie had come to me, her arms around me in a tight squeeze. My arms went around her as my eyes remained on Ty, his knowing smile moving from me to the crowd of our friends surrounding us. As Lanie retreated into the group, Ty asked me again about my text.

"Everything OK on the phone?"

"Yeah, it was my mom, wishing me luck."

A loud voice boomed over the loudspeaker:

-WOULD ALL THE ATTENDEES PLEASE RE-PORT BACKSTAGE PLEASE-

"C'mon, I'll walk you back there until you find your advisor; then I'll meet up with these guys," Ty said. As he turned to talk to Xander, his phone pinged in his hand.

Ava and Macie were wishing me well when I noticed Ty spending a bit more time tending to his text than I thought he should be at the moment. Everyone other than his actual family was kind of here with him.

Then I saw his face.

"What's wrong Ty?"

His face was white as a ghost.

"Uh, it's Savannah," he said, his voice wavering as he was still looking at his phone.

"What's wrong with Savannah?" I implored, my heart dropping due to the grave tone of his voice.

"Kelly took her to the hospital."

"What!" I came running to his side as he continued texting. "What is she saying?"

"It's my mom I'm texting; she's headed there to meet her." He hesitated, his voice fading as he seemed to be lost in thought. "My mom told me she doesn't think I need to come," he said as he looked up from his phone. His mother knew where we were; she had called me earlier to wish me luck, which was the sweetest, since we hadn't even met yet.

But that was ridiculous.

"Ty, you absolutely need to meet them at the hospital," I told him. "Did your mom say what's wrong with her?" But I didn't wait for him to answer me; I sprung into action, finding Lanie and asking her to make the necessary arrangements for me. Once she understood what was happening, she took off for backstage. Making my way back to Ty's side, I grabbed his hand and started leading him to the rear exit.

"What are you doing, Bec?" he asked, trying to pull his hand out of mine. "You need to go. You need to get backstage, babe." The worry on his face broke my heart. He was torn: he needed to be with his daughter but wanted to be here for me. I took away the need for him to choose.

"I'm coming with you to the hospital, Ty. No argument—let's go."

"Becca." My name barely came out of his mouth; it couldn't even be called a whisper. "Baby, you can't leave. This night, it means so much to you. It's too important." He stood his ground, grabbing a hold of my hands and looking me square in the face. "I don't want to be the reason you miss it."

My heart was breaking for him; I needed to make this right somehow. I could only hope he would believe me.

"Ty, I *want* to go with you. The second you told me about your daughter being in the hospital, there was no question that was where *we* needed to be. I can't explain it. A feeling came over me. It was if . . ." I tried to find the right words to convey what was in my heart at the moment. "It was as if I knew I needed to be there with that baby, your baby, and you," I told him.

He reached out and cradled my cheek with his hand as his adoring gaze lingered.

"Becca, you are my perfect. I love you."

"I love you, too, Ty. Let's get going." I started pulling him out, but he stopped me again.

"Seriously, though, what about tonight? What about your speech?" He truly looked concerned for me.

"I sent Lanie to find my advisor. Our friends are taking care of us, Ty. We're good. It's all good."

Savannah's fever had finally come down to 101 degrees. It had been at 106 when she was brought in. Kelly said she had tried to bring it down with medication and cool baths for most of the day but to no avail. She called her mom, and they both decided a trip to the ER was in order. Good thing, because she apparently had some type of infection and needed antibiotics.

"How are you holding up, sweetheart?" Colleen asked as she sat in one of the hard chairs next to me in the family waiting area they provided in the pediatric suite of the emergency room. "I'm sure this wasn't how you expected your formal introduction to the family and the baby to go."

I sat up a bit straighter when she joined me, still not comfortable around her yet. Although, she had been nothing but nice to me since the moment we arrived at the hospital the night before. Ty came to give me updates when he could, and sent texts every so often, but he was with his daughter.

As he should be.

"I'm OK, thanks, Colleen." Of course, this wasn't how I wanted it to go for my first time officially meeting everyone as Ty's girlfriend. But that would sound selfish if I fessed up to that, so I let it go. "It's good news to hear that her fever broke. I guess the antibiotics are doing their thing."

Colleen nodded, her smile cautious; she was a nervous grandmother, I got that. "The doctor said they'll be sending her home in about an hour, I think. I wish they would have admitted her, though. I know fevers don't scare doctors, but they sure scare me."

She fell back against her chair, obviously exhausted. She looked years younger than I believed her to be. Her light brown wavy hair fell below her shoulders, and her make-up-free face showed no sign of wrinkles. She was beautiful.

"Well, I wanted to come check on you, sweetie. Make sure you knew we didn't forget about you. Ty hasn't forgotten about you. He'll be out soon." She looked toward me, her smile warming her face. "He speaks very highly of you, and I look forward to when you can visit again under better circumstances." She reached out and grabbed my hand, giving it a squeeze.

I squeezed it back.

When we arrived last night, it was chaotic. Ty was frantic by the time we got here. I drove his car for the three-plus hours it took to get here so that he could communicate with Kelly and his mom on the ride. Running into the hospital, him yelling at the staff and asking where his baby was, made it feel like a movie scene. When we finally found everyone, it didn't get much better. There were so many people in a tiny space. Her parents, his parents, him, Kelly, her boyfriend Tim, and me. Eventually, they made all of us but Ty and Kelly leave and go to the waiting room, and I'd been in here ever since.

It wouldn't be so bad if I wasn't in the clothes for my presentation. I was in a business suit and heels. To say I was uncomfortable was a gross understatement. Dreaming of sweatpants, or better yet, my pj's, as I sat there with my eyes closed, a body plopped down next to me.

"Hey, babe," a tired voice said as his head leaned on my shoulder.

My hand immediately went to hold his face, needing to touch him. Missing him.

"Hi," I said quietly. "How are you doing?"

He looked exhausted, with dark circles under his bloodshot eyes. The pallor of his skin almost made him look as though he could use a doctor himself.

"I'm better now." He reached up, placing a kiss on my lips, and lingered there; we savored the moment of quiet togetherness. "She's doing better, too. Kelly's changing her diaper. It's finally wet enough to need changing."

I remember that happening to Jonah once when he was a newborn and wasn't eating enough; we always needed to check the urine output to see if enough fluids were going in. There's so much to think about as a new parent. And Ty had so much else on his plate as well as being a college student.

"I'm glad you were here to help her through this, Ty," I told him.

He sat up and squared himself to sit facing me, turning in his chair. "Becca, you'll never know how much it meant to me that you came with me." The tenderness in his words almost meant more than the words themselves as his hands came up to cradle my face. "Thank you. From the bottom of my heart, thank you." He leaned in and his soft, pillowy lips connected with mine again, our eyes not breaking their connection. The soft kiss was quick but he stayed close, our mouths almost touching, our breaths mingling, when he spoke again. "I love you so much."

"Ty," a loud booming voice said as the door opened with a bang. His father stood in the frame of the door, a sheepish look taking over as his color changed to an embarrassed shade of pink. "Uh, sorry. Um, I was sent in by your mother to get you two." He was looking everywhere but at the two of us.

We had separated by the time he found us, but were still sitting close enough that it was obvious we were sharing a moment. Standing, we both laughed at his dad and started for the door. "Thanks, Dad," Ty said, the humor still in his voice. Ty took a hold of my hand as we walked past his father, who was still holding the door open for us. We strolled down the long hallway, a lightness in our step from being on the other side of this ordeal. As I exited the double doors, the gray clouds that hung in the sky surprised me; it was a contrast from the warmth of the night before. November weather in Virginia could vary from feeling as though it was still summer to having a snowstorm. This day had the feeling of snow in the air, and I didn't even have a coat.

"Let's get you in the car," Ty said. "Are you OK following my parents home to my house? I'm going to go home with Kelly and get Savannah settled; then I'll meet you at my house."

It was interesting how if he had asked me that same question yesterday, the jealous side of me would have raged and I'd be overreacting right now. But meeting Kelly, seeing the dynamic between them, and seeing her with her current boyfriend, Tim, changed my opinion on everything going on with Ty when he comes home.

"Of course, Ty. Go take care of your daughter."

He reached in through the window, kissing me full on the mouth for a good, long time. "I love you, Becca. So much."

CHAPTER 34

I thought she would have been sleeping, but as soon as I opened my bedroom door, her head turned my way. Seeing her lying in my bed was such a beautiful sight. Her smile warmed me as she pulled back the covers and patted the bed by her side. Noticing what she was wearing made me take pause: she had on a pair of my sweats and one of my old T-shirts. She looked amazing. Shucking my sneakers to the floor, I climbed in beside her. My arm instinctively went under her as her head rested on my shoulder, and she was immediately enveloped in my hold. I loved how her arm wrapped around my torso, holding so tight, as if I might think of leaving. Her one leg entwined with both of mine like we were a puzzle.

"Why aren't you sleeping?" I asked her.

"I couldn't sleep without you here," she said as a jaw-breaking yawn escaped her.

Kissing her hands, I already heard her breathing leveling off. It was still only midday; most of the excitement happened in the middle of the night into the early morning hours. It wouldn't be smart to drive back to school without getting some sleep first. So we settled in and took a nap.

"Your parents are super nice, Ty. I absolutely loved meeting them. Well, officially meeting them. Even under these circumstances, they were amazing! I can't wait to come back and spend more time with them. And Kelly, too. I mean, it's kinda weird that I like her, ya know, the fact that she's the mother of your child and shit, but she's really cool. If her and I met a different way, we would totally be friends."

She was rambling as we drove, but I didn't mind. I let her go on and on because she was so damn happy. When we had finally woken from our sleep it was around 3 p.m. and we sat with my parents for a bit before heading out. This wasn't a planned trip home, and we had shit going on at school we needed to get back for. Becca and I had missed some classes today. Looking over at her as I drove, admiring how cute she looked still dressed in my clothes as she blathered on, I realized how damn lucky I was.

She caught me looking. "What?" she asked, with some accusation in her voice.

"Nothing," I said. But my smile told her otherwise. Not only did I know she wouldn't let it go, I didn't want her to. "You're just fucking adorable." My hand reached out and grabbed her thigh. "And you look hot in my clothes."

She looked down at what she was wearing, an incredulous look coming across her face as her mouth fell open. She pulled at the T-shirt and the pants. "This? This is sexy?"

"You make anything sexy, Bec," I told her. And I wasn't lying. My blood rushed to my loins when she was in a simple sleep shirt. It helped that her sleep shirts usually clung to her tits and showed the outline of her nipples. Shit, I was horny.

She smirked, but then turned a bit in her seat to face me. The mischievous glint in her eyes intrigued me, making me turn down the music on the radio.

"I have a secret, Ty."

The sultriness in her voice made my dick jerk in my pants. I pulled my eyes from the road once again to see a seductive smile on her face.

"What might that be?"

She tugged on the neckline of the T-shirt, pulling it low enough to expose her breast, most of it anyway, and my eyes widened at the sight.

"I'm going commando," she teased. "Everywhere."

Fuck. I was immediately squirming in my seat, and she took notice. Her tiny squeal of approval didn't go unnoticed. "You're my little temptress, aren't you, Becca?" I reached over and pulled the band of her sweatpants away, attempting to confirm there was nothing underneath.

And there wasn't.

"Want me to take them down for you?" she asked. Her hands were already on the elastic waistband before I answered.

"Yes!"

Shit, this was every guy's fucking dream. She shimmied them down under her ass, keeping the safety belt across her lap. Soon enough, her bare ass and pussy were on full display. Thankfully it was already dark out, but I still decided moving over to the right lane of the highway was a shrewd decision.

"Becca . . ." My desire, my wonder, my hope, all came through in the drawl of her name.

She opened her legs wider, an offering that was near impossible for me to enjoy fully while keeping my eyes on the road. "I don't want to crash, Bec."

"Then keep your eyes on the road. I only need your hand," she cooed.

As I slowed the car down even more, my hand made its way across the console. She grabbed it and placed it exactly where it needed to be.

"Bec, where's all the hair?" My fingers rubbed against her pubic region, the area smooth and clean shaven. My eyes darted from the road to hers, a sly smile forming on her mouth.

"I may have gotten a Brazilian this week," she said breathily. "I was thinking we would be celebrating after my speech."

Well, fuck.

She was soaking wet as my fingers pressed into her folds, a moan escaping her lips. "Make me come, Ty. I'm so fucking horny," she said as her head fell against her headrest. "Make me come all over your hand."

Her words had my dick growing in my pants, and it was torture, not being able to touch it. With one hand on the wheel, I plunged the other inside her tight hole. First two fingers, then three. The walls of her pussy squeezed around me as her moans filled the inside of the car.

"Ty, fuck, that feels so good!"

Her hand moved to her breast, pawing at it through the oversized T-shirt. My eyes were bouncing from her to the road and I was having a hard time concentrating on my driving. I knew I should probably pull over, finish this on the side of the road, but there wasn't even a safe spot to do that on this highway.

"Pull your shirt up, Bec. Let me see your tits."

She did what I asked as my hand continued its welcomed invasion between her legs. Her hands pushed her tits together, and I ached to taste them.

Frustrated and concerned for our safety, I scanned the landscape of the highway surrounding us as I drove. Up ahead, I saw a pullout, just small enough for my car to fit safely, away from the eighteen wheelers flying by.

As my hand retreated, Becca whined. "What are you doing?" Though, as she looked out the window, she immediately figured it out.

"Hold on, baby doll," I told her. Pulling off the highway, I put my hazards on. Then, I turned and gave my full attention to the goddess in the seat next to me.

"Where was I?"

Undoing her belt, I grabbed her by the hips and shifted her body to face me better in her seat. Her pussy glistened with wetness in the light streaming from above. My hands spread her pussy wide, opening it like a pink flower. With one featherlight finger, I found her clit. A sharp intake of her breath alerted me I had hit it just right. I rubbed in light circles, and her hips began bucking against my arms as I held her in place. "Is this good, baby doll?"

"Mhmm." She hummed with satisfaction as her head fell against the window.

Although I didn't want to rush her orgasm, I knew our time here was limited. At any moment, a highway patrolman could pull up. Turning to look out the back window, I confirmed there were no approaching flashing lights yet.

My one hand remained attentive to her clit as the other trailed down, finding her entrance and slightly pushing inside. Her ass came off the seat to meet my hand as I pushed my finger in further, the walls of her pussy pulsating with each of her moans.

"Ahh, yes!" she yelled. "More, Ty. I need more." Her eyes opened and connected with mine, her plea matching the begging in her piercing stare.

As I pushed more of me inside of her, I saw the shake begin in her thighs. They convulsed slightly as she tried to hold her body still. My hand continued slamming into her, skin smacking against skin. Then, as her eyes squeezed shut and her chin tucked in toward her chest, I knew the sensations were getting too strong for her. But I didn't relent; the circles I was making around her clit intensified, as did the quaking of the muscles in her legs. She was holding back, not wanting to give in.

"Ride the wave, baby. Let it take you," I told her.

Leaning over her, I pulled a nipple into my mouth, between my teeth. That sent her over the edge. She was writhing beneath me now, the orgasm flowing through her body. Pulling away, watching her from above as my hand worked inside of her, I admired the beauty of it as rolled through every muscle in her body. Her mouth was open but void of sound as her head fell back.

The final ripples swept through her body as I held her, and then she stilled. She lay there, motionless and quiet, for long moments. As my hand carefully retreated from the soft walls of her sex, her eyes lazily opened and landed on mine.

"Holy fuck," she said. "What kind of magic did you just perform on me?"

I smiled. She had no idea how easy she made it for me to want to do that to her, over and over, for the rest of eternity. My eyes scanned the sculpted body in front of me, and I almost stopped breathing. "No magic needed when it comes to you, Becca." I reached to the floorboards at her feet, pulling the pants up from her ankles. "C'mon, let's get you covered up before anyone sees us. I don't need a truck, or worse, a cop, stopping thinking we need help."

She pulled her pants up and got herself situated in her seat. "What about you, Ty?" she asked, the mischief still evident in her voice. "I can see your dick from here. You're telling me you're going to be able to concentrate on driving right now?"

And it was true; my hard-on was uncomfortable in my jeans. But I would live. I'd survived for six long months without her; I could make it a couple more hours. "I'll be fine, but you better be ready when we get back."

Becca fell sound asleep during the rest of the drive home. The slight snore combined with what I swear was drool coming from her slack mouth still hadn't taken away from her beauty. She held my hand even as she slumbered. The past twenty-four hours had been exhausting, and I couldn't be more grateful that she was there, by my side, while I went through it.

When she grabbed my hand in that auditorium, clearly deciding she was coming with me, my heart swelled. I wasn't expecting her to welcome my life into hers anytime soon. Accepting that it would be a process, and one that would take time, I was OK with that. More than OK, I was willing to do whatever it took to make our life together work for her. Thinking it would be months before she would even meet my parents, let alone my daughter, yesterday was a surprise.

But here we were, thrust into it. And we were doing OK so far. I wasn't naïve; I knew there would be ups and downs, and I was prepared for them. But I really did feel as though we'd be able to weather them.

Pulling into town, I made the decision to go to my place. As I parked and the car stopped, Becca stirred from her sleep.

"Hey, baby," I whispered. "Let's get you inside. We'll go right back to bed." It was evening. But considering the day's events, I thought we deserved an early night. Going around to her door, I reached in and helped her out. We walked in, arm in arm.

And it felt . . . right.

Once upstairs, she immediately plopped on my bed. As I changed out of my jeans into sleep pants, I watched her long, dark eyelashes slowly cover her emerald eyes. I climbed in behind her, and she moved a bit, making room, knowing this was the way we needed to be in order for me to sleep. My arm went under her head, enveloping her, as the other came over top of her, resting on her breast, over her shirt. It wasn't sexual; it was just the closest I could get to her heart, to feel the beat against my palm.

"Sorry I didn't bring you home, Bec, but you had a change of clothes on already. You OK with sleeping here tonight?"

She jutted her ass into me, I assumed her form of acceptance. But then she turned her face toward mine, her eyes surprisingly bright.

"Wherever you are *is* home, Ty."

Bringing my hand up to her face, I held it in adoration and lowered my lips to hers. A soft, gentle kiss as I grasped her face.

She was right. As I watched her settle back in, I knew we were "home" for each other. She had come back to me in more ways than one. She was back to being Becca. The snarky, confident, loud, rambling woman I fell in love with.

She was perfect.

She was my perfect.

Chapter 35

Gage

I had no interest in being back in New York, but the meeting with the lawyer had to be in person. Walking into my family's building made my skin crawl. There was a reason I decided to go back to Virginia for a while. I needed a well-deserved break from everyone here in the Big Apple.

I was early for the meeting, so I decided to stop in my office. Pressing the button for the top floor, I leaned back against the wall for the ride up. The view of the city on the ride was a sight to see; a glass elevator was one of the modern enhancements of the Parker Building. As I stepped off onto the executive floor, my breath hitched a bit. I would have liked to get to my office unnoticed, but no such luck.

"Mr. Parker, how nice to see you," Maryellen said. "I didn't know you would be stopping by. I would have tidied things up for you. Your brother has kept me quite busy during your absence." She stood from her desk in a form of greeting, her manicured brow rising with her comment about my brother.

"No worries, Maryellen, I'm sure everything is in fine order. I just need to pick up a file before my meeting on floor thirty. Good to see you." I rushed into my office and shut the door, not wanting anyone else to know I was here. And, as expected, my office was in pristine condition. Not a thing out of place. The only thing she would have done if she knew I was coming was put some fresh flowers on the coffee table.

And then there was a small knock on the door. "Mr. Parker?" Maryellen asked, timidly. She peeked her head in and found me sitting in my desk chair, staring at nothing. "Do you want Chase to know you're here, sir?"

"Not really. Why?" He was exactly who I didn't want to know I was here. My brother would make a huge deal of me being in town. He would make me go out to some ridiculously notorious nightclub or something, and I had no interest.

"Well, he just arrived, sir," she said. "I'll make sure he doesn't find out. He doesn't come in here, so that's not a problem. When is your meeting, sir?"

I looked at my watch and realized I didn't have as much time as I thought. "I have to be downstairs in fifteen minutes. Shit."

"Don't worry, sir. I've got this," Maryellen said as she closed the door with a quiet click.

I hated that she called me sir. I thought she was only about ten years older than me. We could be friends outside of the walls of this place. But in here, I was the end all, be all for someone like her. But damn, she was good at her job. I would do anything to keep her around.

And just like that, she buzzed me on my phone.

"Sir, Chase was sent to floor fifteen for an emergency. He should be there for the next twenty minutes."

I jumped out of my seat and took off for the elevator, making sure to get to my floor unnoticed.

"Thanks, Maryellen!" I yelled as I passed her desk.

"For what, sir?" she answered discreetly with a wicked smile. She was worth her weight in gold, and I needed to make sure she got a raise.

Hopping out on the thirtieth floor, I made my way to Jared's office, hoping I had arrived first. His secretary stopped me at the door.

"Mr. Parker, Jared is expecting you. I'll let him know you're here."

"Don't bother—I like surprising him," I said as I continued to his office door. Jared and I were buddies in college, down at BRU. I brought him up here with me after we both graduated. It'd been helpful having him here as a cohort and a friend.

I just barged in.

"Hey, asshole, how are you?" I walked into his office like I owned the place.

Well, I did.

"Fuck you, Gage," Jared replied. He was pouring himself a drink at his sideboard. "Want one?" He gestured to the bottle of Blanton's in his hand.

"Yes, please."

We both sat at the small conference table he had in his office. It was prepared with the files necessary for the meeting, all set out in front of us, pens ready. The empty third chair was waiting for our final guest to arrive.

And right on cue, the buzzer sounded.

"Mr. Foster, your expected guest has arrived."

"Send her in," Jared said.

I wasn't quite sure I was ready for this to happen. For the past two years, it was all I wanted. It was all I could think about. It was all I needed. But when it came time to sign the deed, there was always some ambiguity.

It was the visit three weeks ago that made it seem like it was the wrong decision. But that was probably her intention.

We both stood as the door opened and she walked in. She went to Jared first and kissed him on the cheek; they'd known each other just as long as he and I had.

She didn't come to me, only smiled across the table as she took her seat.

"Hi, Gage," she said.

"Hi, Rebecca," I replied.

"Shall we get started?" Jared asked.

Jared, our divorce attorney.

EPILOGUE

One month later...

Waking up with her in my arms would never be something I took for granted. Ever again. Each morning it happened, I tried to wake before she did so I could watch her sleep, which sounded stalkery. But she was the most beautiful creature I'd ever seen and, well, Becca didn't sit still much.

She added the red highlights to her hair again, and I was thrilled. At the beginning of the semester, when she had them the first time, we were not in a position for me to tell her to keep them. But she looked so fucking hot with those colored streaks. It was my favorite color for her to wear as well. *Red.* The suit she wore the night of her ceremony...needless to say, if we hadn't wound up at the hospital for Savannah, I don't think that suit would still be in one piece.

Moving a strand of the reddish hair from her cheek caused her to stir against my chest as a small burst of warm air escaped her parted lips. Lips that were red as cherries. I was torn. If she stayed asleep, I could continue to admire her beauty in the solitude of my bed. But if she woke, I might be able to admire the nakedness of her body before we needed to pack up.

Today was the last day of the fall semester, and we were heading home for winter break. Exams finished up for me yesterday, and Becca finished the day before that.

"I feel you staring a hole through my head," she mumbled. Her eyes hadn't opened, but her mouth turned up into a small grin.

"It's one of my favorite pastimes, you know that."

She snuggled into my chest, pulling me closer. The scent of vanilla with a hint of something else, something nutty, consumed me as I breathed her in. It might have been from her hair or skin, but I could never quite figure out where the divine fragrance came from. And it was always subtle, never overpowering.

Then there was how she felt in my arms.

There was really no way to describe it. It was something a person had to experience. From the firmness of her breasts pushed against my chest to the suppleness of her ass in my hands. And her skin...it was always so fucking soft and smooth.

"I love the feel of you in my arms, Bec. There's something so comforting about it, even when you're dressed in your flannel pajamas."

Her deep laugh reverberated against my chest and made me laugh with her.

"Well, maybe if you put some heat on in this place, I wouldn't have to wear anything in bed with you."

But we both knew she really had clothes on because my roommates sucked and invaded my room at all hours of the night. Even if the door was locked, they seemed to make their way in; one problem with this older apartment. But it was fine because they'd come to love Becca and her them. As I pulled away from her, the tiny whine that emanated from her throat was sexy as hell and tempted me to abandon all responsibilities ahead of us.

"Bec, if you make one more sound like that, we won't make it back to your place on time," I warned.

She jolted up in bed, searching for her phone. "What time is it?" she shrieked.

"Don't worry, we still have twenty minutes before we're supposed to be there."

Becca and her roommates had planned a sendoff brunch before we all went our separate ways for the holidays. She'd gotten close with Ava and Macie. And even though Lanie wasn't living there anymore, she and Xander were coming by as well. The plan had been for Logan to stop by today, to meet his soon-to-be roommates before next semester, but something came up with his counseling session, and he wouldn't be able to make it.

My eyes took in the sight of her as she sat up in bed. And I couldn't help but smile.

"What?" she asked.

"I don't know, you might need that twenty minutes to tame that head of hair of yours."

It was wild, no doubt from the animalistic sex we had the night before. But the next thing I knew, she took a thin elastic from her wrist, did some twisty thing with her hair and hands, and bam! Her hair was in this adorable, messy bun-type thing on top of her head.

"How did you do that?"

"It's magic," she said as she slid out of bed. She rummaged through the bag she had packed for the month-long break. "Let me get dressed so we can get going."

After throwing on a pair of jeans and a sweatshirt, I checked my bag once more and zipped it up. I wasn't sure how our time at home was going to work out. It would be our first time away from each other since things had finally gotten back to our normal. Even though we both lived in northern Virginia, we were an hour apart, so it would be a commitment to see each other over the next month. And between trying to spend time with Savannah, time with our respective families, and work, it would be challenging.

"Ready?" she said, popping out of the bathroom. She had on a pair of those skin-tight leggings that drove me fucking crazy because her ass looked amazing in them. And I knew she had to be wearing thong underwear since there were no lines visible on her cheeks.

I know because I looked.

"Yeah, let's get out of here, now!" I said.

She knew exactly why I was frustrated, and her sly grin grew.

We grabbed our bags and headed downstairs.

If you'd like to read the rest of Ty's Epilogue, please follow the link provided to my website. Once you do, the rest of this chapter will be waiting for you...

Acknowledgments

It has become hard to thank all the people that help with this process, but I will try...

My Street Team—I've got a Street Team now! It is full of wonderful women who, of all things, want to rally around me and my books. It is truly amazing to be a part of this group of humans. They inspire me to be a better writer all while taking time out of their lives to promote me and my work. So, thank you, ladies. From the bottom of my heart, thank you for all you do for my books and me. I look forward to a long and fun journey ahead with you.

My Alpha readers—yes, I used actual alpha readers this time. I'm not sure I actually knew what I was doing...but it was amazing to receive the early feedback from them. Meg, Maria, Amy, Amanda and Marci, thank you for taking the time out of your busy lives to read the early version of Surviving Lies. She may not be the same now, but you helped create what she became.

My Beta readers—Jen, Wasy, and Morgan—what can I say? The work you put into this book for me was invaluable. Thank you, thank you, thank you. Thanks for your honest feedback that forced me to take a close look at the story and give everyone the best version of SL I could. Your critical eyes caught things I didn't, the exact purpose of a great Beta team!

Jen—my marketing guru! I love being one of your buttercups gf! You are always there with the best advice, an ear to listen, and a crap ton of laughs along the way. I'm so glad I found you, and now that I have, I never want to lose you. You are so much more than a professional relationship and I can't wait to read your book.

Emily M.—my proofreader. I failed miserably my first go round by leaving out thanking you. Neither All My Firsts nor Surviving Lies would be what they are without your keen eye for my oversights and errors. When I receive my manuscript from you my excitement level is at its highest because I am so close to publication. But when I go through and see all the silly mistakes I've made that you've caught for me, I thank my lucky stars for having you! Thank you, Emily!

Niki—my cover designer. We continued making magic together! I've been blessed so early in my career to have people like you in my corner. You are the sweetest, easiest person to work with, and you continue to deal with my indecisiveness, though I'm getting better. Can't wait to see what we come up with for the next two in the series.

Chloe—my editor. My rock. Kind of my everything. I hit the jackpot when we found each other. And if you will have me, I won't be letting go of you for a very long time. You put up with my constant emails, my imposter syndrome, my silly ridiculous questions, all from half-way across the world. Chloe, here's to you continuing to 'chuckle' at the scenes that are only getting hotter with each new book.

My sidekick in life is still my biggest supporter. I couldn't be doing this without you, nor would I want to be. Scott, your support is so instrumental in my success thus far,

I hope you know that. Many people ask if you are the inspiration for 'Xander' in AMF. (Well, he also goes around claiming to be Xander, let's be clear about it.) There is not a straightforward answer to whether he is or isn't because I am not Lanie. But are there elements of my life partner that found their way into my first MMC? Of course there are. Which ones? I'll never tell...

My readers—I actually have readers! Wow, thank you so much for believing in me enough to pick up a book by some indie author putting herself out there with a story itching to get out of her head. It's surreal to think that you want to read what I've written. But I hope you never stop, because I've got so much more to come...

Author Bio

Krista Swanson lives in New Jersey with her husband of 28 years. They have three children but are now empty nesters. Travelling across the US and Europe is in their plans. She loves the beach, mainly the Jersey beaches, which she feels don't get the love they deserve.

When she's not writing, she is most definitely reading. Her lifelong love of reading romances gave her all the ideas busting to get out of her brain. While doing either, though, the mug in hand will not have coffee in it. The blasphemy—it will be tea!

So far, her books are full of angsty characters forced to navigate the issues they face. The scenes are hot and the friendships are strong all while your emotions are sent on a wild roller coaster ride.

She's newish at the social media thing but working hard at it. You can find her on TikTok and Instagram at kristareadsandwrites. Also hop on over and join her Facebook reader's group, Krista Swanson's Booklover's Besties. Make sure to sign up for her monthly newsletter on any of those platforms for the most recent news, freebies and giveaways.

Newsletter Sign-Up

Would you like to receive monthly updates? Would you like sneak peeks on the next book on the series? For that and more, sign up for my monthly newsletter at:

kristaswansonauthor.com

Stay Tuned...

Book 3 (Logan's story) & Book 4

(another Lanie and Xander story) in

the Blue Ridge University Series:

To be Released by the end of 2024